HARBOR'S EDGE

FROM AUTHOR SANNE ROTHMAN

©SUZANNE ROTHMAN

SPECIAL THANKS TO:

RETIRED SPECIAL AGENT LARAE QUY FOR HER ARTICLE "9 TIPS ON HOW TO READ PEOPLE"

ILLUSTRATORS KRISTIJANP AND IMAM MAHADI FOR BRINGING MY DESIGNS TO LIFE

RIVER ROTHMAN FOR HIS RESEARCH, KEYNE'S SPEAR AND PROOFING MY NOVEL

DEDICATED TO THE WILD THINGS

I never saw a wild thing sorry for itself
A small bird will drop frozen dead from a bough
without ever having felt sorry for itself
D.H. Lawrence

BE THAT TO CATCH THE MONSTERS,
BE THAT AND THEY WILL NEVER CATCH YOU

 *the Author*

ALL I WANTED WAS FOR THE NIGHTMARES TO STOP. I DISTRACTED MYSELF BY WORKING LONG HOURS, BUT I SOON LEARNED THAT NIGHTMARES ARE CHAMELEONS

&

THEY WILL CHASE YOU WHETHER YOUR EYES ARE OPENED OR CLOSED.

My name is Harbor

& WHAT I SAW WHEN I LOOKED OVER THE EDGE, LOOKED RIGHT BACK WITH DEATH IN ITS EYES, DESPERATE FOR LIFE ~ ESPECIALLY IF IT'S YOURS.

Today, this is our story.
Not where it begins, not where it ends –
just where we are right now

CHAPTER 1

Their bodies glided up and down through the rough waters. Together they could be mistaken for a mammoth, slow moving wave.

The one whose size stood out from the rest led the pack. His existence so enormous, he alone could crack through the tons of pounding water to clear the passageway for the others. Older and the most ferocious, all thirty feet of its oddly oblong slick, hairless, scaled skin had recently carved its way up from the trenches, forging the path necessary to hunt. They rarely entered the surface these days, but when they did, it was always at night. For darkness was all they knew, and darkness camouflaged the monsters' every intent.

Their short necks impaled the water, in and out, scouting and preparing for the day they would strike. Their powerful tails were sharp; used to crawl up mountains or to dig into the sand and enter the shore. Massive barrel eyes provided acute vision. They could navigate the depths of the ocean with one eye while their second eye peered above. The sea creatures possessed the power to see into both worlds at the same time.

All of them grizzled and hungry, each varied in size. All of them were tinted a deep, pitch black, for they had been dispelled to a place where light does not reach. They stretched in lengths of 12 feet, 16 feet, 20 feet, with torsos like that of scaled casks that curled into one soaring arch across the ocean in a dead heat to rush the shore, doggedly alongside the leader. All of them reflected the moonlight in the tough, rigid gloss of their skin.

They were survivors of primeval seas, centuries old waters born in a time when the Earth was an unbroken, endless playground. They knew every drop that filled the 60 million miles of ocean, every fissure on its floor, and every trench. The monsters once inhabited ancient seamounts that legend says reveals the source of all evil. It was their duty to guard this power. And like heinous hounds, they did so until they themselves became angry. The large sea monsters became resentful as humankind evolved, casting out the beast. They hid in the crevices beneath the seamounts outlasting the Cretaceous Period. So when the Pacific became their refuge, it would never be their source of nourishment. They preferred to hunt on land and did not limit their indulgences.

They knew that the night sea provided camouflage and so they kept close watch until a visit was necessary to quench their appetite. Who was it that they were watching? The only rival they had: humankind. The only other animal who adapted and had the urge to conquer both the mighty sea and its land.

Some say the monsters crept onto the mainland because they were bloodthirsty. But unlike the vampire, it had never been blood that they craved. Some say the monsters can only be seen by the light of a full moon. But unlike the werewolf, they were quiet in their attacks and did not howl. Prehistoric depictions paint them as giant water lizards, but cold-blooded in this nature - they are not. The elders still whisper today what the ancient caves narrate.

Those who watched from the dark, murky waters were the Mo'o, villainous, mystical water creatures who could transform into warriors resembling humankind. Nevertheless, the sea vipers did share a trait with all other monsters. They too breathed and exhaled malevolence.

The lore of our lush volcanic islands and the haunting of the Mo'o has not changed with time. The grave warning has been echoed through the generations. The Mo'o are shape-shifters who are able to fool us because *they are a part of us*. With origins in an ancient bloodline, the Mo'o were the embodiment of evil from an old land that even early humans wanted to be delivered from.

Stories tell of how the hungry Mo'o slithered onto the island, eager to sip on sin and feast on lost souls. Our ancestors learned that people don't actually go to hell. Instead, they open the door and welcome it right in. They understood that hell has never been one place. It isn't stationary. It wriggles its way in. It finds refuge in the weak soul. Hell is the real shape shifter. The Mo'o are simply its reflection.

According to legend, the Mo'o still watch from the shadowy mist and wait for an opportunity to pierce the surface, to stare us in the eyes and dive right into our souls.

What the wild creatures don't realize is that *they are being watched as well.*

CHAPTER 2

As I sit on the high cliff and stare across the waters, I realize no one can be 100% certain of what kind of world is truly deep under this vast expanse. The depths are filled with the rarest of secrets because there are parts of the ocean, humankind cannot reach. So whatever is down there sure doesn't care to share with humans.

Rocks and crags are positioned in a serrated labyrinth that only sea creatures can navigate. I reflect on the stories of my island and how far apart we are today from the beliefs of our ancestors. When I stare into the dark waters, it doesn't seem to matter how many generations divide today from my ancestors because the heartbeat of the Mo'o will always have a place in our culture.

I can't say I believe in the evil, giant water lizard. I often think that what our native ancestors actually saw were the island monk seals. Monk seals are humongous, and long ago, before the islands became densely populated, they had to be bigger. They may have even been sea giants. Plus, islanders know how to spin a good tale. Maybe our ancestors used the seals as a way to scare islanders into behaving. I imagine what it might have been like on the island centuries ago. Was there anyone like me? Watching the sea, feeling like they were on their own and wishing the sound of rushing water could make them feel whole again? Someone so tired of pain, they'd take the risk to stare right back into the eyes of the Mo'o.

I love this spot just off the bend. The clearing. It's secluded and peaceful. Even as much as the island has grown over the years, I don't know anyone else who visits the bend. My place. To figure out my story.

To get here, a person would have to choose to go off the beaten path, and in today's fast paced world, people usually opt for the quick and easy. The ride here is an experience every time. My breath races the wind, and my heart keeps count as I round the curves of the bend, breathing life right back into myself.

The stretch of road to get to the bend seems long forgotten. Along the curves and crashing waves is the only place I can be completely alone. We call it Ha'alele. It means abandoned. Crossing the bend and outrunning my own heart, I feel like I've been this way forever. Trying to defeat Ha'alele.

I've heard somewhere that the mind of a teenager is the only weapon anyone ever really needs because even if we can't conquer the world alone, we think we can. Even if I thought that way, I don't want to conquer the world.

As responsible as I am, I can barely manage my own life. I began working at an early age, and life for me has been anything but normal. If the life of a teenager doesn't already have enough to deal with, I got the added bonus of having mine completely turned upside down then stomped on by the person I once loved most. Ha'alele.

It's early morning, my favorite time to be alone on the open road. A road that turns into a curve that is hidden amongst the trees. I ride the bend into a vista few will ever see. A bend that leads to a cliff that overlooks the island. I try to stop in every day, to sit and clear my head. Looking across the ocean, listening to the waves helps to calm the sea creature. The one that, I sometimes feel, lives in me.

I'm lucky that the bend is a shortcut on my way to work. I don't have the kind of job where I'm saving up for college or a new phone or the latest shoes I've been dying to get my hands on. It's more the kind of job to help Tutu for all she's done for me. I try to make her life a little easier.

Tutu is my grandmother. She has been my caretaker for almost 3 years, and she loves me even more than her crazy recipes. Tutu owns a restaurant named The Shore and makes the most mouthwatering Hawaiian cheeseburgers and irresistible papaya shakes you will ever find. And that's where I work. Actually, it's practically where I live. And I love the ride in.

Waves are just waking up on the island, and little splashes of water are carried on the wind, cleansing the air around me. Sometimes I feel like they cleanse more than just the air. It's like they make life feel pure again, peaceful for a moment, cleaning up the mess that was left of my life. Washing the burn away.

Every so often, my eyes still sting, rage on as if there is a fire in them. I've tried racing to the mirror to catch the reason why, to see if the whites of my eyes turned red, because it feels like a little bit of hell is trapped in there. I hurry to remove my contacts, but nothing. Each time, nothing. Nothing but my natural eye color and pure pain. Ha'alele.

Full light hasn't fed through the trees yet, but the red and black Honeycreepers have already begun making their rare appearances, rushing alongside me. I would bet money it's the same family of birds each morning I ride out to the surf. I am not riding to the surf to surf though. The Shore is a burger joint on a little patch of beach, elevated along the sand with gorgeous views of the surf. The entire name is fixed above the rectangular, bright teal planks of the restaurant in a large, neon sign that reads *The Shore, Burgers and More*. And my Tutu is the owner. Purchasing her own excessively showy sign was her way to make sure tourists, travelers and planes would never miss us and a great way to compete with the big resort hotel restaurants. I never understood why Tutu insisted on adding the word "More" to the name. "More" could be anything, yet for us, it's a variety of shakes and fries. Either way, the letter "S" in Burgers went on the fritz and blinks constantly. Add to that the letter "R" in "More" which came loose months ago and needs to be hammered back up. Aside from that, the sign glows a pretty coral color, and its beams stretch out to the main highway. Whoever follows them will find a cool little hang out for delicious, local grindz and the best cheeseburger around. Tutu's life savings opened what the tourists fondly refer to as *a shore good burger*. Yay, me. Don't get me wrong, I love a juicy cheeseburger just as much as the next person. But sometimes, I wish I could be the teenager that society wants me to be. Eat, sleep, homework and think about me. Easy fix for society. Easy for me. But life isn't always easy.

CHAPTER 3

In between the day to day normal stuff, I work the drive-thru window at The Shore and use it to search the faces of every customer. What am I searching for? *Not* the faces of my missing parents. I'm using profiling tips and rules to find clues in the faces of parents *who do stick around*. Maybe that will help me understand why mine didn't.

I'm discreet about looking into the cars. I'm careful when analyzing the faces of hungry customers rushing through the drive-thru. It's not like I hand them a burger and shake while sketching their face for a photo lineup. I am, however, sincerely curious how a normal family works. I feel guilty admitting it, but the people I love could be in the same room with me, and I'd still feel lost. I hear them, eat with them, talk to them, but I still feel apart.

The Samoan crab is also native to our island. It's easy to pass up if you're not looking for it. It dwells in the mud, which doesn't make it very appealing and gives it the nickname mud crab. Whether you're looking for one or not, its muddy camouflage makes it even more dangerous if you accidentally surprise one, and God forbid if you try to corner one. Its claws are said to be some of the strongest and can easily snap a large branch in half. I can relate. Maybe some of us share a percentage of DNA with the Samoan crab. Our claws reaching out, but no one really sees or hears, because like the mud crab, they can't see past the camouflage. That's me in the drive-thru. Camouflaged by the novelties in the window. Maybe I should practice snapping branches in half. But as therapeutic as that sounds, I'm cured each time I hop on my ATV. Each time I'm away from the window, out of the eyesight of customers, Tutu or Fig or anyone else who's eyes may stumble upon me. My ATV takes me to a place where I'm finally free. Free to feel alone.

Tutu would throw a fit if she knew I took off my helmet along the curve. Fig would snitch in a heartbeat if she found out. Poor kid loves her big sis too much. It's like living with a short stalker. And I wouldn't do anything dumb to hurt either of them. They're my world. I understand tragedy, and things can get ugly in an accident. So, I do wear my helmet...until it's just me and a little piece of the passageway I call the bend. Inside the bend, I'm transformed into the closest version of the real me. So, yeah, I know if I wanna keep being me, I'm gonna need a working skull. The helmet always goes back on.

There are the pros and cons of working at The Shore.

Pros: Free Hawaiian cheeseburgers and fries every day of the week and free access to profile carloads of interesting people.

Cons: Working the window in the hot sun. My left arm is so much darker than my right arm because of the extra sun exposure from the drive-thru window. I recently started wearing my long sleeve Shore shirt thinking I could even out my tan before school starts.

Even though analyzing faces is my own personal hobby, there is a drawback to the car loads of families that seem to squeeze every member and their pets into the car. Their super-duper long orders! Does any car really have enough elbow space for everyone to lift the burgers, dip the fries and slurp the shakes?

Oh, that is another pro. The shakes. One of Tutu's secret recipes equals the best papaya shake on the island.

Working the drive-thru is not the hardest job. Rarely does anyone pay with actual cash money anymore. So, I mainly take the order, swipe the card and hand them both over. I rarely see hard cash. We are living in the swiping world. Swipe your phone, send an order. Swipe your card, get your order. Swipe your phone to take a message or get a picture. I call it the virtual slap. Maybe it's what really irritates me about the car loads of families. It's not just the hems and haws as they ponder the entire menu before they order. What bothers me is I see a family I will never have. They all sound alike; they act alike, and they are alike, because they are together. They're not just a picture. And that reality makes them a virtual slap that leaves a concrete sting.

So, when I'm riding the bend, I am truly alone. And when I'm not, I just feel like it. Ha'alele.

Chapter 4

When I am not serving burgers at The Shore or riding the bend, I'm at school or at home taking care of my little sister. And when she's not spying on my every move, I'm engrossed in my dad's old FBI manuals.

I say old, but his books are in great condition, and considering he was in the prime of his career, they are updated with the most current FBI training information. I have his old notebooks too. Although, they are mostly filled with scribble of jargon that I don't understand. Still, trying to follow his train of thought or how he proceeded in an investigation intrigues me. Reading his old notes and books are my second favorite pastime. The first? Sneaking off to ride the bend.

I don't sneak out in the sense that I don't have permission. I'm pretty responsible, and Tutu trusts me, but she does worry. Because in all the natural beauty of the island, there are hidden dangers. Not like the Samoan Crab but concealed by the lush landscape are outliers, including large, homeless make-shift camps. Many started as temporary shelters but are now permanent staples of the island. Local islanders are not happy about the increase in crime and disease flowing out of the camps. Tutu says too many people have become unaccustomed to the norms of society, or they simply outright refuse to be a part of them. She says it's a hard problem to tackle because bona fide criminals take advantage; steal from hurt people and hide among the sympathy of good people.

I'm young, but I see it too. As free spirited or imaginative as living outdoors sounds, the fact of the matter is that the camps create a lot of trash, debris and sadness. No one can truly live free in those circumstances. Unfortunately, the unsheltered eventually become trapped; their pain, illness or dependency on drugs grows. And guess who pays for it? Anyone who works. So I learned about taxes early. Money is deducted from each paycheck I earn. All that cash from working people helps society and funds programs to help the homeless, but what good is it if they don't know about or get the help?

Tutu and some neighboring businesses use to hand out blankets on the rare cold nights we have on the island. They would give leftover trays of food. As much as it made us feel good to help, we learned quickly that the only thing we were helping was bad habits stay in place. We stopped giving away to the camps and started giving to the organizations set up to help the people get some medical care, a decent place to sleep and skills for a job of their own.

News stations recently started reporting on the crime being traced back to the camps. It seems like the news, like everyone ignored the problem for a long time, but this past summer alarmed islanders. Especially parents. There have been a couple of child abductions in the last half year and it's frightening to think how close crime will get to your own street if you let it.

On top of that, we also have an insane amount of tourists every year. Most appreciate the history and natural beauty of the island, but still all the comings and goings have made Tutu even more protective of my little sister, Fig, and I. So, I usually send Tutu a quick text letting her know when I'm going to take the bend to work - which is always.

Truth be told, I am protective of what I love and that includes the bend. I don't think anyone else would understand why. And I don't want the bend ruined by anyone trying to understand. It's my place.

And how do I get to the bend every morning? I drive a rusty red '95 ATV. Its official name is the Argo Kohler 8x8. My dad left it for me, and Aadya saved it for me. She taught me how to drive it the year before she went missing. We fondly nicknamed it the Argo. Some people have pets; we had the Argo.

Driving up the bend in the Argo, pulling into the wooded hideaway, shutting off the motor and releasing myself from the helmet is an almost daily activity for me. The bend provides the most panoramic views of the ocean and a glimpse of an inlet that many won't experience in their lifetime. The bend is off a high cliff. It's not a wide cliff, nor is it narrow. It's as big as our kitchen. I'm elevated and can see for miles. The Pacific blues of the sea washing over the rocks is captivating. The sound of crashing waves travels upward, providing a surge of immediate relief for my soul.

Mother nature is sacred to Hawaiians. For instance, rocks are not to be damaged or relocated. However, it has been known to happen. A simple act where a rock or two walks off is seen as taboo. I don't know what it's called when those same rocks turn up along the curve, off the bend, and right in the center of the clearing. Mysteries.

I can't imagine how heavy the shoreline boulders weigh. Tons, I'm sure. And in this curve of the bend where I sit, I've collected my own miniature stockpile. Smooth rocks, a manifold of colors and none much bigger than the palm of my hand. I try to stack the rocks to simulate the larger ones on the beach. I've seen rock-stacking online, but my rocks aren't arranged for others to see. They are here for me and better than any friend I've ever had. Assuming I had real friends. The past isn't very easy for me to remember, and that's why the pebbles on steroids help me feel grounded. They are sacred to me. They are mine to gloat over, and they are always waiting when I return to the clearing. Deep down, I know I could search the world and never find a place like this. So, I appreciate it and ride the bend whenever I want a break. Sometimes, I add a rock or rearrange the ones I've already collected. Sometimes, I watch the shore for hours, and other times, I try to remember what my life was like before the bend, before I landed on the clearing. No matter how hard I try, I can only remember very little. Ha'alele. Even the memories left me.

A brand new school year opens in a week, and I am hustling in as many passes through the bend as possible. My place. My time. My freedom to be alone.

Chapter 5

When I am home, I can usually be found hanging out with my kid sister, Fig, or reading dad's old FBI books in secrecy.

Fig is an adorable little kid, but she can be quite a handful. I can't blame her though. She lost her mom, our mom, at such a young age. My presence, the affirmation that I am here for her, is how she copes.

And for a little squirt, Fig is very independent. Her real name is Makani, not Fig. Makani means wind, but Tutu dubbed her Fig because of the soft amber color that smoothes over my little sister's tan Hawaiian skin, hair and eyes, all of which hold subtle and delicate amounts of golden highlights. All her features match, and that means we couldn't look more unalike.

Fig has a different dad. Rob is very involved in her life, but he asked Tutu to help raise Fig when our mom dropped out of the picture. So, Rob was never officially my step-dad, and Fig only knew our mom for a couple years. It's a long story, but we were almost all a happy blended family until Aadya, a.k.a. mom, went MIA approximately 3 years ago. Fig was nearly 3 and swears she remembers Aadya. I let Fig have that dream; it helps her sleep when I can't.

Rob didn't raise me, but he did try. To this day when Rob picks up Fig, he always tries to include me. I can't think of a time that I've been left out, but I guess neither of them realize that even when I'm included, I feel left out.

Rob calls Fig by her given name. Fig leaves every month or so to visit him for a few days, and since we are pretty close, yeah, I miss the kid when she's gone. Each time Rob carries her off, he always stops to make one last request for me to join them. Even when her canopy of fluffy hair conceals their faces, it's clear that Fig whispers, if not begs, Rob to make me go, make me spend time with them. I smile, wave, and politely decline. All my extra time is dedicated to dad's training books or riding the bend. Well, that's only if Tutu doesn't have too many shifts for me to work at The Shore.

My Tutu, Bridie Kapule, migrated to the island with her family when she was a little girl. Her Irish dialect had already been sealed, but living on the island her entire adult life has created a unique accent. The mesh of words she speaks stick in your head whether you want them to or not. "Harbor, naming a child is like a prayer over one's life…" I've heard her recite this over the years, and maybe I shouldn't turn away, but I do. My mother named me, and my mother isn't around.

20

Mom's name was Aadya Kapule Ludovic. Ludovic is my family name. My dad's.

From what I remember and what Tutu tells, Aadya took the death of my father pretty hard. I have the pictures, but the truth is I don't remember him very well. I should. I know I was loved, but, somehow, I can't summon up the feeling when I need it. I envy Fig, who insists she remembers every last detail about our mom. Sure, I remember our mom, but I don't always want to.

Both my dad and mom served their country. Aadya was a state police officer, and Alexander, my father, was an FBI agent stationed out of the island's FBI office. Dad was killed in the line of duty near my 6th birthday. So, that makes the struggle of remembering details about him even worse. I was old enough to know them by heart.

Tutu won't discuss the specifics of what happened the night he was shot. She is vague about the subject altogether. She says that life is short and that my dad worked a lot. "Putting a nation's duty first was his passion, but you and your mother were his love, Harbor."

As if I'm not confused enough about the circumstances of the past few years, I try to figure out what my grandmother means. When I ask, all she says is both dad and my mom would be here if his passion and his love were the same. As I've grown older, I don't know if those two things can ever be the same.

I love my Tutu. I love Fig, but I am passionate, I am drawn to riding the bend. I'm drawn to my dad's old FBI books. Tutu loves us, yet she is passionate about The Shore and is constantly daring the big hotels to try to buy her out. She wouldn't trade me, Fig or Rob for anyone in the world, and she won't trade The Shore for money. So, as much as I'm told my dad loved me, I don't blame him for being committed to his passion. Even if he knew it would be his death. It helped him live to the fullest while he was here. When I scroll through the old pictures on my phone or pull out the wrinkled photo I keep in my belt, I see it. In that captured past, I see love. So, why can't I feel it? Why won't it punch back at Ha'alele?

I remember Mom crying when dad didn't come home, but she didn't abandon me *then*. I was young, but even I saw it in her face. Ha'alele. However, she never burdened me with what she was missing. She tried to make up for his loss by always being there for me - until she wasn't anymore.

I've never met my dad's family. They weren't in attendance after his death. Tutu says mom handled it on her own. When Aadya eventually returned to work, the department didn't immediately allow her to go back to patrolling the streets. She had to do a stint working the desk at the police station. Rob was, still is, a tourist and fishing helicopter pilot who used the helicopter landing pads at local police stations. He had to check in and out with the desk officer each time he needed a landing or take off. That was Aadya.

Tutu says the first time Rob saw my mom, he fell in love. But Aadya went there hurting and could only see what she lost. I remember the stories Mom told me. She said it took a year of friendship with Rob before she realized it was important to love again. I was just a kid, but I knew they were in love. My mom had many conversations with me. She would hug me and say she understood that I missed my dad. When she'd brush my hair and wrap the rubber band around my ponytail, she assured me that I could talk to her anytime I wanted. She told me that Rob would never replace my father.

When mom and Rob decided on a family, I was just a little older than Fig is now. Rob's job took him away for days at a time, so they thought it was best that we live with Tutu. The more family support, the better. The reality of my father's murder was still a fresh wound. Aadya and Rob refused to rush as they planned a new life and the wedding of their dreams.

The way Tutu tells it, "After so many years of protecting you, Harbor, Aadya was ready to heal. She was finally ready to add to your family and wanted to replace heartache with new love. She wanted the wedding to be a grand celebration to renew your lives."

Then Mom found out she was going to add to the family sooner than she thought. She glowed with excitement. Mom and Rob asked me to go with them to the ultrasound where they would find out the gender of the new baby. I saw Fig on the monitor in the doctor's office, and for the first time in a long time, my heart felt happy again. Before she was even born, I knew in my heart she was my sister.

With the news of a new baby, Mom decided to postpone the wedding. I remember like it was yesterday how she knelt in front of me, her big Figgy belly touching mine, smiling while she laid out the plan. She and Rob would wait until both daughters could walk down the aisle comfortably as flower girls, hand in hand. Rob had to fly out a lot. He was building his private tourist business, and Mom explained that by the time of the wedding, his business would be set. Fig would be walking, and we would have a huge wedding in our new house. It was to be a new beginning for us all.

So mom never actually remarried. She went missing before her wedding to Rob. Sometimes a sick feeling overcomes me, and I hate that some little part of me believes a new beginning was never meant to happen.

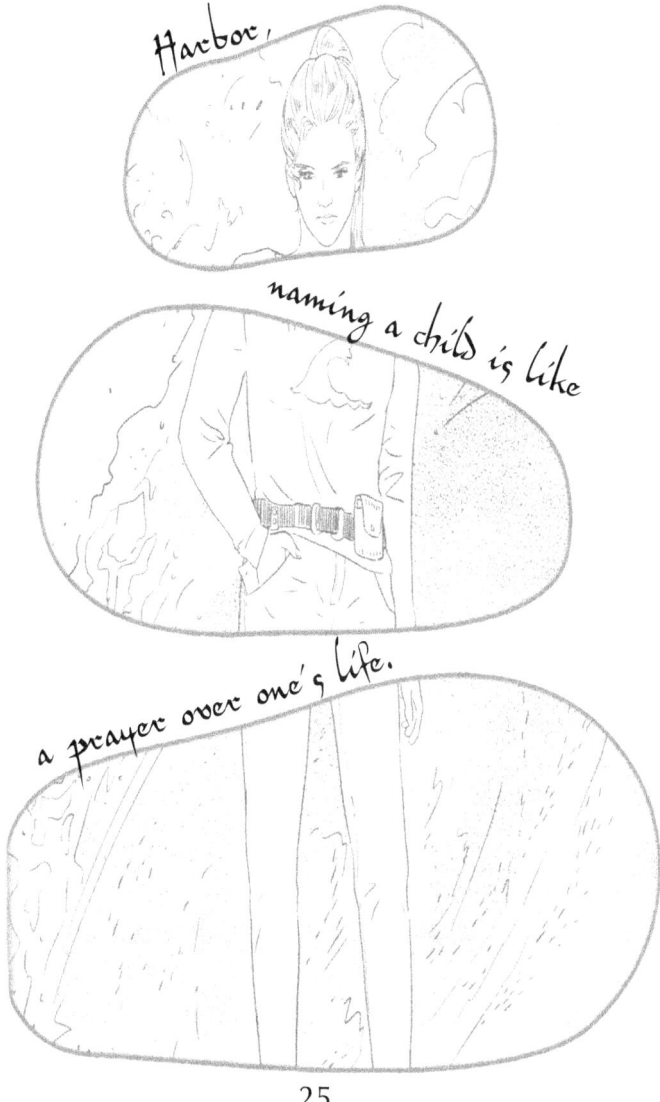

Harbor,

naming a child is like

a prayer over one's life.

CHAPTER 65

Mom disappeared without a trace before Fig had a chance to blow out the 3 twirly candles on her birthday cake, a few months before the anticipated wedding. Tutu baked a lovely strawberry tea cake that year. But not one slice was eaten. We were too full chasing every lead. The police department scrutinized all of Aadya's prior cases, looking for any indication of revenge. We checked the big hotels and the homeless camps. We inquired with neighbors and local businesses in a one hundred mile radius. Not many places on the island have security cameras, so we spent a lot of time on foot imploring islanders for any bit of information that might offer a tip. Everyone we came across seemed to sympathize, but no one held a clue as to what happened to Aadya. Soon, there wasn't anywhere left to check. The police ended their investigation because new leads were void.

It became apparent that whatever happened, I would only find the woman who was my mom in old pictures. Sometimes, I hold the pictures and think that she just couldn't do it anymore. She couldn't carry all our feelings and love Rob and my dad at the same time. Maybe she didn't postpone the wedding because she was waiting for Fig to skip down the aisle. Maybe Aadya was vulnerable, and this made her an easy victim.

After I vent to myself, I shake those suspicions. Aadya was the opposite of weak. She would never be an easy target. She would have fought. I know that. She went back to work when Fig turned 2 months old. She and Rob planned a wedding and were in love. Fig and I were supposed to walk down the aisle hand in hand. Life was supposed to be happy.

Rob didn't leave. He searched for Mom. We all did. The missing persons reports stayed idle. Neighbors, teachers, old friends, and people on the island began to see us through only one lens. Sympathy. I hated it. I still do. When Aadya went missing, living stopped and pushing ourselves through life began.

I was young, but I eavesdropped every chance I could. I heard Tutu and Rob in countless conversations, both frustrated that there were no signs of abduction. No clues. When Rob finally came to terms with this fact, I saw that familiar heartache all over again, but this time it was in Rob's face. Ha'alele.

Yet he still didn't turn away from us. Maybe it came across as uncaring, but I did. I turned away every chance I had. I set the Argo on the open road and escaped to the bend. Until I found the books.

Tutu returned to work, and I had the house to myself one day. I went into Aadya's room thinking that maybe I could find a clue. Instead, I found a cardboard packing box tucked in the back of her closet. Along with a jacket that still had the faint smell of him and his old flashlight, the box contained my dad's FBI profile training books. Buried beneath those were his little spiral notebooks. I vaguely remember him holding them up once, his hands seemed larger than life back then. He told me that each notebook represented a different case, and sometimes, some cases require more than one notebook. He said the notebooks helped him catch the bad guys. Reoccurring memories of him and mom make guest appearances sparingly, and I can't help but think that the box of his belongings keeps me close to the stars of the show.

When I scan the pages though, his writing appears erratic. None of it made sense to me, but it still didn't take a minute before I became enthralled in FBI training. I wanted to learn every tip and trick about profiling. I wanted to know if it was true that there was a way to figure out what people are thinking without ever having heard them say a word.

I never told Tutu that I dragged the box to my room, and I doubt she even knew that Aadya had it in her old room. We recently remodeled, and now it is Fig's new room. I sift through my dad's FBI books every chance I can, and even though it's only been a couple of years since I've claimed them, I like to think I've become pretty good at reading people.

Single parenting in your almost mother-in-law's house wasn't Rob's life plan, and since his job took him away so much, he asked Tutu to help raise Fig.

"If Makani can't have the love of her mother, she will know it and be stronger with the love of her sister."

Every night, I let Fig chant the flashbacks she remembers about Mom, and I hold her hand until she dozes off, and my eyes stop burning. I don't want her to see the emptiness of Ha'alele. I let her have her dreams.

CHAPTER 7

Fig is excited to start school this year. Little kids these days are programmed so differently. Fig is bordering on 6 but thinks she's my age. She loves learning and always has a ton of questions. I'm happy she enjoys learning. It keeps her focused on more than our nowhere to be found mom. In that way, we are a lot alike. I just prefer the kind of learning that requires studying people.

Yep, people watching is kind of a hobby for me. I'm not creepy about it. I try to take what I learn from dad's old FBI books and compare it in real life. There is probably no better place than the drive-thru window at The Shore to practice.

Everyone at some point, uses an App or word of mouth to find good local grindz, which leads them to The Shore and my window. Although, this year adds a cherry on top. I move up to a new school, and that will bring a new grade and new faces. Profiling candy.

The island attracts a flood of new people every autumn. Some are residual tourists or families looking for a slower pace of life. Others are adventure seekers or new business owners. And of course, we get a lost soul here and there.

I will recognize many faces like customers and islanders I grew up around. But, the halls are often filled with the latest batch of brand new citizens of the island. Newbies looking for a new life, a fresh start or just a break, make it easy to get lost in the year to year migration. Most newbies don't stay longer than a year once they realize that island life has its limitations. So the migration patterns out here give me tons of profiling material.

One of dad's old books is dedicated completely to the study of body language. I was a twerp kid when I started teaching myself. I was fascinated with how much information you can gather from a person's behaviors. According to the FBI, there are 9 rules to reading body language. My goal this summer is to recognize all 9.

I practiced every chance I got, applying the 9 rules when I handed someone their order in the window. At first, I was a bit clumsy; maybe staring into the cars in the drive-thru a little too long. I found out quickly that customers didn't appreciate their character profile handed over with their burger and fries, so I learned to be more discreet.

FBI Profiling Rule #1 says that each individual has a base, patterns that are fundamental to all humans. Usually, the signals are right in front of us, however, most people don't give these basic behaviors a second thought. Very few people look at the undercurrent.

For example, when we see someone or something we like, our eyebrows arch. Since this is true for most humans, it comes in handy. If we don't like someone, we can change the subject before they ask for our phone number as soon as we see the arch. But at the same time, eyebrows also arch when we see something we might *not* like. If a friend walks in the room with a new haircut that looks like it was cut with the blade of a lawnmower, we are usually thinking about what we'd rather *not* say. So, reading body language takes practice, and there are always exceptions to the rules. With each year I grow older though, I'm starting to believe the only pattern we can truly count on is our own gut instincts.

One area I am having trouble with are dad's old notes. When I first stumbled across the box, I wasn't interested in what my father wrote. All I cared about was missing him. I was young. Nowadays, I find myself trying to remember anything he said and trying to read everything he wrote. These notes are as close as I'm going to get now that Aadya is also out of the picture. But, his notebooks are filled with so much FBI jargon that I find them hard to follow. Still, I'm not giving up. I'm currently on the notebook dated last. It was written not long before his murder. A part of me thinks that if I analyze it enough - maybe I will find the clues. The clues that led to his murder.

Abbreviations, numbers and a few scattered sketches fill the small, thin pages of his notebooks. If I didn't know better, I'd say they appear to have been scribbled out of boredom. One of the first pages is inscribed with:

IO FI

So, I looked it up. Now I know that my dad was the I.O. or Investigating Officer, and he was conducting a F.I. or a Field Interview.

Beyond that, his notes get a bit more extensive, initials embedded in outlines, directions, and maps. The second page has a little star next to a string light of letters and numbers:

CI CA S HF DOB

The numbers have faded, smeared under the pressure of time and my tears.

I learn a lot each time I examine my dad's old pages. It surprises me how much a person can hear from a person who doesn't say a word. So, I don't mind one bit getting lost in the halls of a new school, examining all the new faces, figuring out what their personality might be before they show their true colors. I look at faces a lot. I look back at Aadya a lot. Scrolling through my camera roll on my phone is an addiction. When I can't find answers in my camera roll, I analyze the wrinkled photo I keep in my belt. I try to remember what I saw and compare it to what I missed. Was there a way to see the clues to warn us? Yet these search and rescue missions make my eyes burn, and it's not the expressions in the photo anymore I see, it's the voices from the past. I remember the tears, so many tears and the laughter. Tears and laughter are fraternal twins. Both conceal a lot. What didn't I catch that could have helped me spot the truth? Even if I had, could I have stopped the truth?

This school year, we finally learn about the Holocaust in history. My great-great grandmother on Tutu's side escaped Nazi Germany. And just like searching my old photos for clues, I'm drawn to finding out the truth. Was there a way to have avoided the mass devastation? As I slip my belt back on, I can't help but wonder if pain is unavoidable? How could humankind let one man influence and cause so much pain? Did anyone try to stop Hitler? Maybe there were clues that will give us the knowledge to never let tragedy like that repeat itself. But even the belt around me repeats a tragedy. One I choose to keep close.

The belt belonged to Aadya. It was part of her uniform. In old pictures, it was much shinier and not dappled with the fray and grey that has taken over on one side. I wear it to feel closer to my own history. A tarnished reminder around my waist of the battles past. A daily memo to be on the lookout for what I can't see. Ha'alele.

First day of school vibes charge the air as I help Fig with her outfit. Fig's teachers will know her by her given name, Makani. Tutu and Rob visited her class last week on Meet The Teacher Day. I am the one who will walk her to class on her first day of school. Tutu had to prepare for the day at The Shore, and Rob was delayed on a tourist excursion, so the honor fell to me.

As we approach the wide walkway of the one story schoolhouse, our small talk dances with the surrounding hub-bub. Kids and excited families are everywhere giving last minute pep talks. Fig is holding my hand pretty tight, almost as though she doesn't want to let go. Normally, Fig talks non-stop, but this morning, she is as quiet as a cellphone without a charge.

"Everything is going to be great, kid. You'll see."

She responds with a sweet pancake syrup smile. Oh, Lord, I hope she brushed her teeth.

"Did you brush your teeth?"

Fig places her free hand on her hip, "Of course I did, Harbor. I'm not a little kid anymore."

"Uh, yes, you are. Trust me, enjoy it while you can." Before I know it, we are outside her classroom, and she is squeezing my hand tighter than ever.

"Slight case of the First-Day-of-School Blues?"

Her skinny shoulders form an exaggerated shrug. For a fearless little walking Wikipedia, she can become a bit anxious every now and then. Kneeling to make eye contact with her, I brush back her soft, Figgy waves that seem to escape no matter how tightly I braid her hair. I give her hand a squeeze. Fig really is my strength, and I know I have to be hers.

"We will be chomping on a cheeseburger at The Shore for dinner before you know it. How about I let you choose all the toppings for my burger today? Only for today," I make pretend a worried face about the burger toppings, and Fig slowly forms a maniacal smile. Aadya is missing out.

As we walk into the classroom, I hand her backpack over and hear, "Makani Malie? Makani?" The teacher has already begun calling attendance.

36

"Here!" I perk up and call out to the teacher, who doesn't look like she can be much older than me.

"I pick your toppings," Fig smiles and lets go of my hand, waving good-bye. My empty hand waves back, and in a split second, she's gone.

I head out to the Argo, which is parked amid mini vans, trucks and fuel efficient family cars, many of which I recognize from The Shore drive-thru. Ala Elementary is adjacent to the newish high school, so my commute isn't long.

The familiar zing of energy ranges from the parking lot to the entrance and fills my new stomping grounds. However, unlike Fig's school, this hub-bub isn't from nervous kids and their parents. These are my peers, out in full force, and ready to conquer the world.

I pull up my schedule on my phone as if I don't know that my first class is Physical Education, a.k.a. P.E., a.k.a. yuck. I enjoy working out, but I don't enjoy sweating up a storm first thing in the morning. Then there is usually the rush to change into and out of our gym uniforms in the whole minute the coaches give us. I don't think even Spidy Man can change that fast, and he's fiction! He should be able to do anything.

Well, I have no intention of competing with a superhero, so maybe I won't rush to change.

The first period bell rings, and the Coaches have us pile into the gymnasium. They waste no time going over their rules; everyone must walk a mile a day; everyone must participate, and everyone must dress out starting next week, or points will be deducted from our grade, yada, yada. The coaches then detour into a statement that I interpret as *use your freedom wisely*. They make remarks about our age and how being older comes with responsibilities and that we need to learn how to manage our time. I guess that can be seen as a compliment. Besides, I hate wasting time. The coaches assign us a stretching routine and tell us once we are done, we can look over our schedules and relax. I'm cool with that. I figure I might as well take them up on their offer. A self-guided tour of my new school sounds like a responsible use of my time and the perfect way to relax.

I've lived here my entire life, and this old building is the one I've been most excited to get into. Kau High is one of the few buildings people aren't allowed to enter unless they have a reason. Last year, a new wing was added, so there is lots to explore. During my days in the lower and middle grades, I became very familiar with the outside of Kau High, examining it daily. A few years ago, the outside perspective of Kau High could have easily been mistaken for a haunted house. All that was missing was a sign hanging from the roof that read House of Terror. The school was so dilapidated that I'm sure the old, rusty planks were held up by the leeward wind itself. Many repairs have been done on this old building, and an expansive renovation was completed this summer. The gymnasium is in the original building, and it is not very impressive. It's altogether much darker inside than even I expected.

The new section of Kau, at least from the outside looking in, appears to be modern and sleek. It complements the beautiful natural back drop. No more twiddling my thumbs. It's time to tour.

Even though the coaches are clearly occupied, catching up and laughing with one another about their summer fun, I don't want to parade out. As I leisurely make my way to the gym door exit, I keep one eye on my escape route and one on the coaches. One of the coaches stands out. I see most islanders at least once a year around town or The Shore, but this guy is unfamiliar to me. I would remember golden hair. It reminds me of a wig on a mannequin. It's so blonde that the glare of the fluorescent lights actually bounces right off. Profiling him will have to wait because I make it to the gym door. Careful to be as quiet as a mouse, I begin to casually push open the shopworn door, but sure as heck it squeaks! No one seems to have heard. I lighten the pressure I am applying on the cold, silver rectangular handle, but trying to open a door slowly, ever so slowly, naturally creates an unnatural physical reaction in the face.

I can feel the frozen expression that has been sculpted into my face as though it will mute the sound of this old door. My *don't-make-a-sound, be sneaky* face is perfected, but the door swings wide open, ousting me into the dark hallway on the other side of the gymnasium doors. What the hell! Before I can blink, I face plant on what feels like kitten's fur, and the weight of my backpack is pinning me in place.

"I'm sorry. Are you all right?" an unfamiliar, quasi-gentle voice asks. Whoever it is smells of clean, fresh earth, and their steely chest is actually balancing me so I won't slide off and hit the floor.

I am pretty tall for my age. I took after my dad in that way, and I've always been considered above average height. That characterization kind of irks my nerves. I'm proud of how tall I am. I just get tired of hearing how tall I am all the time, especially from people who exclaim it as though they are filling me in on a secret. But whoever I've nosedived into has to be taller than

5'7", and they have an exceptionally strong grip on both my elbows. My sneaky face has half transitioned into shock face. My eyes are half squinted from practically flying at light speed into the dark, and I can feel that my smile is plastered in the shape of the Cheshire Cat's. Still, I try to respond.

I regain my balance and adjust my backpack. As much as I want to run off, I don't want to be rude, "Yes, thanks. Thanks for breaking my fall."

The corridor is dark, and as I try to return my mangled face to normal, separating my cockeye, I look up. Above my forehead are the brightest, mirror-like, green eyes I've ever seen. Even in the otherwise blacked out hall, they seem to glow. Maybe I have a concussion.

They belong to a guy I don't recognize. He is wearing a light jacket that broke my fall, and I am certain that the buttons from it are imprinted on my forehead. I feel a bit dizzy, but I was just ripped through the door. I realize he is still holding my elbows. *Who are you?* I think as I wobble one step back.

"Is your name Harbor?" he asks while he peers at me, probably noticing that my ponytail got shifted to one side of my head when my face slammed against his chest.

"Yes. Hi. I'm sorry, do I know you?"

I think he is smiling, but I am a bit disoriented. "From The Shore?" I ask.

He laughs, "Hey, Harbor. It's been a long time. We were in 1st grade together."

I look a little closer, and I am sure the Cheshire Cat smile has turned upside down because I am confused as heck right now. It must be clear that I don't recognize him because he gently guides me by my elbow, "Here, let's step into the light."

He begins to open up the gymnasium door, and I practically break my neck to block him.

"No!"

"Okaaay," he laughs, holding both hands up like everything will be okay.

"I mean, class is technically not over, and I was just on my way out, but you should probably go sign in."

"Oh, I didn't realize I was that late."

Before I can tell him that as sad as it may sound, yes, I am skipping out of class early on the first day of school, he has already pushed open the doors to the entranceway opposite of the gym doors. We step out of the dark hallway into the main entryway. Now it's too bright, so I try to adjust my vision by blinking repeatedly. By now, I am sure this guy has to think I need medical attention.

He is standing next to me, and I try to recall 1st grade, but all I see are tons of little sun dots that I would testify look exactly like baby angels dancing around his face. How did my long awaited tour of Kau turn into being caught skipping? *Snap out of it, Harbor. Your backpack probably knocked you upside your head.*

Finally able to focus, I see that whoever he is, his smile is calm. I notice his jacket, the one I practically french kissed. It is a soft, suede, caramel color and reminds me of the hue's in Fig's hair. But it's actually not a jacket I landed on, it's a velvety shirt that looks like a style from an old 70's music video. He isn't buff, yet he isn't skinny either. He was strong enough to hold me up, and you'd think I would remember vibrant eyes like his. That's what I do. I study people. I study faces. I'm going to have to find the page in dad's old FBI book on how to read your own body language. As awkward as this moment is, I feel oddly comfortable.

Okay this is weird Harbor. Compose yourself. But, a polite classmate is rare. A classmate who just so happens to smell like the bend - a never, ever kind of rare. A classmate with animal instincts to hold me up by my elbows using only his pinky fingers - super rare. I follow his peculiar gaze to be made bluntly aware that my own shirt is half sticking up, revealing a tad of my pale belly. I quickly pull it down and just as soon remember where I am and that I've been waiting to see this old building since grade school. Snapping back into consciousness, I smile and say, "Hi again. Do I know you?"

"It's me. Keyne! We were in 1st grade together. Mrs. Desai's class?" He can tell that I am completely at a loss of memory and what kind of heartless monster doesn't remember her first grade teacher? I can't blurt out the truth to a total stranger. *I have suffered numerous tragedies and have blocked out much of my childhood.* So instead I offer,"Oh yes, Keyne. Hi."

His laugh is warm and light. "You don't remember. It's fine." His response has a mixture of understanding and disappointment.

"I'm sorry. I feel like 1st grade was a lifetime ago. Did I have you for any other grades?"

"No, my family and I just moved back to the island." After a pause, he clarifies, "From California."

"Oh, wow. Well, welcome back. I didn't mean to make you late, and you probably should check in with the coaches."

I want so badly to stare at him, read his face, but instead, I concentrate on not arching my eyebrows. I've run through enough facial expressions for one day. Keyne's features are soft, soothing to look at, and I realize that he is looking at me also. For a slight moment, there is lumbering silence until he breaks it.

"Hope to see you around. I better go get my tardy," he smiles and returns to the other side, back into the dark hallway.

I could punch myself. Not because I felt my heart stop for a whole minute of my life. Not because I am a hell of a lot more animated than I previously thought. Not for anything, but the fact that it is rude not to remember someone. The FBI books don't outline what to do in these types of situations. And I, of all people, should know a face. Working the drive-thru window at The Shore, I not only recognize faces, but also the cars. I can tell who will pull up in front of the window before they even get there to pay, and I have a great track record. This guy wasn't in the window; he was actually in my class, yet I can't remember him. But 1st grade was a lifetime ago. It was a completely different life for me that included a mom and a dad. An innocent life where I didn't have to search for clues or study faces in pursuit of a murderer and missing mom.

CHAPTER 8

Taking a deep breath, I step out into the expansive foyer, excited to begin my tour. I wouldn't say I lost time in the corridor, but I definitely used it, so I have to move fast before the bell rings.

During summer orientation, incoming students were given badges that we are to wear on campus at all times. Kau High has a badge-in system, requiring staff and students to badge-in and out to gain access to the newer parts of the building. As I walk around Kau, the badging system is evident. I don't know if I should feel privileged and safe or unnecessarily guarded and overprotected.

Wearing it around my neck is irritating, so I keep my badge in a small pocket at the top of my backpack. This way, I can turn and bend slightly at the knees for my badge to scan. The bend and badge move works just fine for me.

I walk a few steps and stand I in awe. Clear, unblemished glass stands at least 50 feet high on parallel sides leading from the old building into the new. Our island has some of the most vibrant flowers in the world, and their beauty is displayed in high definition through Kau High's glass wall design. Colors I have seen my entire life, colors that some will never be aware existed in their lifetime, add a brilliant backdrop to the entrance hall.

The corridor is clean and long. Its depth mimics a large, pure ocean wave, the kind that can swallow a person whole in a heartbeat. Other than a recycle bin on each end, the corridor is free of objects, which makes me feel small, not insignificant, but rather impressed with how much bigger the life around me is. I like that there aren't options to create a buildup of gunk. Smart design.

Let's face it, every teenager is busy. Even if they aren't holding down a job, being a teen is hard work. I can admit that our world sometimes revolves around only one person. Our reflection. I stop for a moment to look up at the tall trees and kaleidoscope of colors and gasp when I see Honeycreepers nesting. If Kau High doesn't teach me anything else, I will be happy with the magnificence of this glass tunnel. I think it could brighten anyone's day, even making me smile. I think that's why I am smiling.

When I reach the door, I bend and badge. Seriously? The door slides open! I'm starting to think that the excitement of practicing my profiling is going to compete with all the perks of this spectacular new building.

I step over the threshold, hesitant to leave the amazing glass ocean wave. In a second, I find myself standing in an even more spectacular room. Out in front of me is a large oval lobby. The walls are shaped by tall, circular glass panels with a see-through summit. Sunlight washes over the wide room. Surrounding mountain ranges and beautiful wildlife dance in from every angle of the huge foyer. My jaw literally drops at the vast blue sky that arches over the school, its powerful hues forcing their way into every patch of the grand foyer. None of this was shown at our student orientation.

Computer work stations face the windows and are spaced evenly apart. There is a gap between each computer station that could easily fit 2 vending machines, yet the openings are left to be Zen zones.

The decor is soothing. It's a soft color scheme similar to the color of butter, and it runs throughout the carpet, chairs and computer stations. The bisque decor magnifies the many bursts of colors outdoors to be soaked in and viewed in a glance. I don't know where to begin. I want to lay in the middle of the floor and make a buttery carpet snow angel. I wouldn't dare though; especially after this morning's episode of 100 ways to make a face.

This section of Kau is so fresh and modern. It has the new car smell times ten.

The computers are thin, white monitors with 17 inch screens. Even the keyboards are sleek. I log on and immediately have internet access. No wait time! Can this get any better? Just as quickly as my search engine pops up, I notice Fig's school beyond the glass wall. I have great peripheral vision and realize that every day I will have a clear shot of her playground. I wonder what time the little butterbean has recess. Just as I am about to punch in Cheshire Cat in the search engine, the bell rings and it's time for my next class.

Walking away, I can't help but think - I like the new. I've been living in the old for too long.

CHAPTER 9

Most of my classes are in the old building. It appears the new building is reserved for the higher grades and select classes. Turns out, there are many new faces this year; introverts, extroverts, the haute, the haughty, malihini's and kama'aina's like myself. There is a fine line between profiling and casting judgement, and as long as I don't cross it, the many faces should keep me busy all school year.

The end of the school day is nearing, and I realize that my last class is in the brand new section of the campus. I will totally take that. It's History, my favorite subject. I want to savor the walk. After all, this is the coolest building I've ever been in. As I'm admiring my state-of-the-art surroundings, I feel a bump on my right elbow. I try not to gulp, but I do a little.

"Hi," I say to the guy with fluorescent eyes. *What was his name again? Oh, yeah. Keyne.*

It's not that I am a shy person I am just not a person of many words ever since…1st grade. Since then, all the words I had were questions. Questions that never received answers. I didn't want to place more burden on Tutu or Fig, so I resorted to being a quiet thinker. Dad's old books helped me understand that the unspoken language can be just as strong. I know lots of the kids in school, and I make small chit chat with customers at The Shore, but I prefer to stick to myself. I don't have a lot to say to people who don't really understand me. Instead, I prefer to see the words in others. You could say I am an extrovert turned introvert.

Keyne is walking alongside me, "Hi."

"Did you earn your tardy?"

He answers with a light laugh. "Yes, I earned my tardy. Told the coaches there was an emergency in the hall, and I was helping someone up." I raise my eyebrows and return the laugh.

In slow moving seconds, we are at the sliding door, but before I can turn, bend and badge, it's coasting right open. Keyne wears his badge around his neck. I am not positive, but I think he gulps as he extends his arm for me to go first.

"I am headed to History," his announcement sounds more like a question.

"Hey, I am too. Who do you have?"

"Mr. Reddy," we say almost in unison then both laugh. If nothing else, the name will provide enough entertainment. It dawns on me that this guy's presence is kind of like the buttery foyer. Airy and calm. We walk together. I think.

After the seamless round foyer, different doors take you to different sections of the building. There are 3 floors. I pull up my schedule to verify the room number of my next class, and Keyne says, "Three hundred, Room 300."

I must look puzzled. Here I am processing my schedule, and he is verifying it. This guy has probably seen every face I can make because he laughs and answers a question I never asked.

"We have the same class. Right there," he points to my phone and the enlarged picture of my schedule.

"Right," I say, but also, I think, *there isn't a we in my life*. Well, except for Fig and Tutu.

The campus map is blended seamlessly into the wall. Curious students are gathered in different pods referencing their schedules while looking at the walls, murmuring about their schedules. What first day can be perfect? I pretend to peer at the map in the wall, yet what I really want to do is discreetly confirm the scent I'm picking up from this guy. Clean, fresh, earthy scent, but not like cologne. He smells like a cross between soap and the bend.

"Keyne!" We both stand upright for a minute when we hear his name loud and clear. Looking around, I want to make sure I wasn't the one shouting it. But it's a blonde guy who called him. Phew. As he approaches, I realize he seems oddly familiar. Okay, how is it that I recognize him but not someone who was in my first grade class? The blonde isn't alone. It's only the first day of school, yet he is with a posse of older grade girls and guys. Keyne seems to know them all.

"Keyne. Let's walk together. What class do you have next?"

I begin to head to class and leave Keyne to his friends and just before I do, I notice his gentle, confident look fade into familiar discomfort. I am a people watcher. Transitions like that are not good. Then I feel a pull on my elbow. What is with this kid? No one has touched my elbow that much in, uh - ever.

"We have History together, and I promised I'd let her look at my syllabus. She didn't print one."

I am trying to suppress a shocked look on my face but can't seem to keep the Cheshire Cat grin from reappearing. I wasn't expecting this curve ball. The blonde analyzes the situation like he isn't sure if he should give Keyne permission to walk with me. I kind of nod as Keyne and I begin making our way to the stairs. Now we are definitely walking together. But why?

When we are finally at a landing in the stairwell, I break the silence. "Were we really supposed to print a syllabus?"

Keyne laughs, "Yes, and thank you."

Since normal people take an elevator, and Keyne and I are fairly alone, I ask him, "A fan club that followed you from California?"

He smiles, "No. Family of sorts."

We ascend the stairwell. It isn't as nice as the beautiful foyer we just left. The stairwell is made of wide, white concrete steps lined with black aluminum hand rails. I know a little about hand rails because we installed a cheaper version for our handicap ramp at The Shore this past summer. The stairwell was probably built for fire or tsunami protection. Little windows way up top, above the third floor landing provide enough light to illuminate the entire staircase.

Little reunions of students scatter the stairwell. Some are chatting, some holding hands, but all are on pause. After the long summer, they aren't quite prepared to submit to another school year. One couple is kissing. Not even awkward, it's kind of sad. A wartime bunker might provide more romance.

We push open the silver rectangle door together, and Keyne gestures me ahead. We find our class, and the teacher is vigorously chewing. I don't know if it's gum or the insides of his cheeks, but whatever it is will be disintegrated soon. He's greeting students at the door or pretending to do so because he doesn't say a word and only stops gnawing long enough to give a few slight smiles. He seems to be analyzing us more than he is welcoming us. Keyne and I glide over to the back row and take a seat - a little too much in sync. Then we both give a mini, nervous smile as to say, *I wasn't following you. No, I wasn't following you.*

The class is modern but simple. It has the same glass wall design, with one side doubling as a large window that provides a beautiful view of the old building and the overall school grounds and beyond. The tardy bell rings as a few more students shuffle in.

Once satisfied that we are tucked away in our desks, the teacher takes a brief pause from chewing and makes a lame joke about tardies, "My name is Mr. Reddy, and I am your History teacher. My number one pet peeve is any student who isn't ready." It's not a very funny joke, yet teachers tend to laugh even when the rest of the world isn't.

"Starting tomorrow, any student who is tardy and not ready will have homework all year to help them with timekeeping."

He seems to get a kick out of his own sense of humor, and I want to concentrate on what he is saying, but my mind keeps returning to the blonde, trying to recall where I know him from. Why did he appear weirdly possessive of Keyne? He is clearly in an older grade, but I just know he's new to the island as well. I usually remember customers from The Shore.

Keyne said *family of sorts.* Maybe close family friends or relatives moved to Hawaii from California with him? Or he moved with them? I catch myself falling deeper into a useless topic and tell myself, *Who cares?* Considering that our 1st grade school year has been deleted from my memory, I technically just met the guy.

This summer, I delved into my dad's FBI profiling books more intensely than when I was younger. Any break I had, I read. I tried to practice the techniques using the people that came through the drive-thru at The Shore. I've become pretty good at reading facial expressions and voice pitches, but matching them to motive isn't as easy. So when Keyne responded to the blonde kid, FBI rule #4 would have come in handy. FBI rule #4 is all about compare and contrast. Basically, look for deviations in the subject's patterns of behavior *compared to others in the same situation.* Yet how can I look for changes in Keyne's behavior if I don't know what he behaves like on any given day? The blonde, on the other hand, stands out against any teenager. He appeared almost dominating. In a high school of free spirited, independent teens, he is definitely swimming against the stream. That contrast is clear.

Becoming conscious of the fact that I drifted back into a non-subject about a 1st grade classmate I can't even remember, I decide that for the moment, I need to deviate from my own pattern.

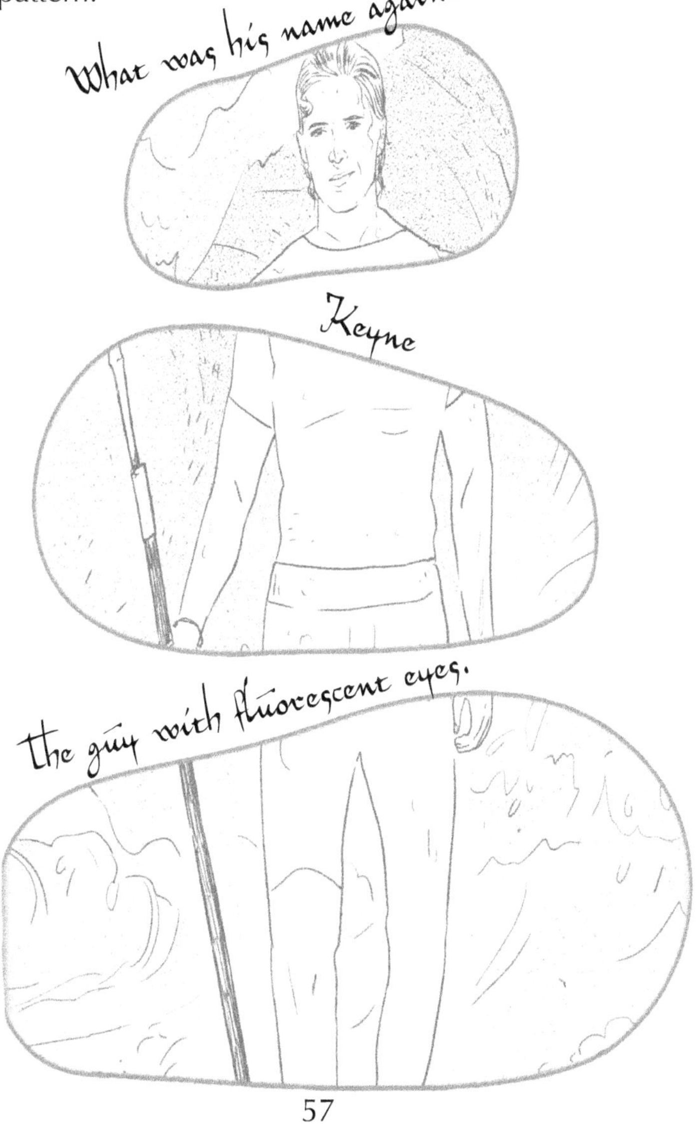

What was his name again?

Keyne

the guy with fluorescent eyes.

CHAPTER 10

Like a boomerang, my thoughts skid back
with the sudden laughter from the class. Mr.
Reddy must have made another joke, and it must
have actually been funny because the class is
going haywire. Reddy is in his middle 30's with
a needlepoint nose and medium length, reddish-
brown hair. A lot of surfers have long hair, but he
is pale with a sprinkle of freckles. I can't see the
surfer in him, but I can see the confidence. He
has a spunky presence about himself which is
probably why he received a laugh from a room
full of teenagers. Not an easy accomplishment.
If we stood side by side, I'd be taller than him. I
remember him from The Shore over the summer.
He'd stop in now and then to eat while working
on his laptop. He always ordered two cookies.
Can't blame him. Tutu's cookies are delicious.
I'd bet he was probably preparing the very
lessons he is about to teach us.

Reddy gives an overview of the syllabus and
in an animated voice explains that so much
excitement awaits us, "This class will be
different from all others. Who knows why?"

Oooh, I think. *Not* a smart question to ask a
classroom full of new high school kids. Sure
enough, a boy I recognize from the island shouts

out, "Because you give Friday Free Days and no homework!" Someone else calls out, "Because you bring us snacks, and we get to watch videos every day!" The wisecracks go on for a few seconds, but Mr. Reddy apparently has his wits about him because he didn't seem offended in the least. Instead, he jokingly responds with a smirk, "You just failed your first test. Guess when you make it up? Friday while I am eating a snack." Reddy's joke actually elicits a few more chuckles. Now that he has our attention, he informs us of why his class will be so different, "Learning about our past helps construct a very strong future."

I'm mulling over that thought when Keyne nudges my elbow and gestures that I can share his syllabus. It's my first day of school, and my elbows have been held, pulled, and nudged more than they have in my lifetime. I think my expression gives my thoughts away. *Did you do this in first grade? Maybe that's why I blocked you out?* Keyne may have read my thoughts because he sort of clears his throat, and we simultaneously turn our attention back to the lecture. But surprisingly, the bell rings! I can't believe the school day is over. Class felt like it was only 5 minutes long. Normally, I am ecstatic when the last bell rings, but today is out of the ordinary. Maybe because there is so much to soak in about a new school. Maybe because History class was awesome.

Mr. Reddy has already outlined our first project. He said we are diving right into the grizzliest crime in history. He said when we learn from history, we can prevent some horrors from ever occurring again. We will be studying the Holocaust beginning with an outline of events and a timeline. The syllabus lays out the projects and assignments to include dissecting the causes and then we will actually profile Hitler! I couldn't believe it when I heard Reddy announce it. The middle grades normally treat us with kid gloves, as though we are too fragile to discuss the root of the problem. He touched on some of the questions we will be examining. For example, how was a character like Hitler able to thrive? That is right up my alley! Sharing the syllabus with someone who smells like a warm sheet of fabric softener fresh out of the dryer wasn't bad either.

Keyne and I are the last ones filing out of class, and Mr. Reddy is busy organizing what appears to be an already organized desk. Keyne calls to me, "Harbor, hold up."

Almost at the door, I pause and turn toward Keyne. And then I see it - FBI rule #2. It focuses on deviations in the subjects pattern. Keyne is hunched over his desk trying to unzip and re-zip his backpack, and just over his shoulder, I can see Reddy standing at his desk.

He's no longer chewing. Instead, he's motionless. His head is facing down, his eyes obverse. Keyne can't see Reddy's swiveling glance from him to me or the smug smile on his face. An acute stare travels over his sharp nose and pierces our space. I return as close of a grin as I can muster. Peculiar man. Frankly, this entire day has been filled with the unexpected. Before I know it, Keyne is by my side, "Just so you know, I am not a perv."

I'm sure I look like I just stubbed my toe while being electrocuted. I don't know this guy, so his choice of words shocks me. However, stunned has been the theme of the day.

"I am sorry, what?"

"Your elbow. Elbows. I just didn't want you to think I have some fetish. I know it must have been weird me playing duck, duck goose with them. It's just the first time, I caught you. You know, when you were about to fall?"

"Uh-huh."

"Then later when I saw you, well, it was nice to see a familiar face. Also, I was surprised how soft your elbows are, so yeah, I nudged you again for the syllabus. I'm sorry if I over did it."

This is the oddest conversation I have ever had, and I am astonished that my lower jaw is still attached to my face. I definitely do not have his level of comfortability but manage to respond, "Sounds like a fetish."

Keyne's laugh is boisterous and hearty. He is clearly an easy going kind of guy. However, on top of the whole 1st grade memory loss, I will probably never be prepared for small talk about my elbows. Luckily, I won't have to be.

The blonde from earlier and a few others are outside our History class, and this time, they are the ones staring. Earlier, I thought his friends or whoever they are were wearing the same shirt as Keyne but dismissed it because it seemed too unlikely. Curiously, however, all of their shirts do match! They are not the same colors, but they are the same style, except Keyne's. He is wearing short sleeve. As confusing as this day has been, I'm interested in taking a closer look at their expressions. People have idiosyncrasies, all sorts that go unnoticed until we pay attention. To find out what theirs could mean will require FBI rule #1. FBI rule #1 helps establish a baseline.

Turning to bend and badge my way out, I clearly see Keyne look from them to me and back to them again. He's trying to make a decision. I don't remember Keyne from first grade, but even if I never see him again, I doubt I'll forget him after today.

My memory loss is justifiable. The last few years of my life have been filled with managed anger at the destruction of my family. My father was murdered and my mother, Aadya, seemed to die along with him. Then there's the sadness I have for Fig who deserves a mom, and for Tutu who shouldn't have to work so hard. This is why I refuse to play the role of a victim. I have too much to be grateful for and that allows me to cope. Even my almost-stepdad, Rob, is someone I'm lucky to have in my life. So, I made a pact with myself that even on the hard days, I will keep moving forward. Even though I know Ha'alele, I won't live in it. Every morning, I force myself to see the good, to see the light. Because the alternative is to fall into darkness.

So whatever struggle Keyne is having with his *family of sorts,* I don't have room to wait on it, even if it is masked by tapped elbows and the scent of a morning trail that leads to the ocean. I make my way down the hall, content in the fact that I don't even know this guy. First grade was forever ago. So by the time he makes his decision and turns back toward me, I've made my decision and wave good-bye.

CHAPTER 11

I load the Argo and drive to Ala to pick up Fig, yet the parking lot is full of parents excitedly waiting to pick up their kids. Luckily, the Argo can squeeze through the overcrowded parking lot. As I turn the key, I see Rob has already arrived. He is kneeling to help Fig with her backpack, but the little squirt instantly spots me. She runs over to give me one of her famous giant teddy bear hugs and practically pulls me off the Argo. Naturally, Rob walks over, "Hello, Harbor. Thanks for walking Makani to class this morning."

I smile and nod.

"She says she will prepare a surprise of toppings just for you," he laughs. That reminds me, I promised Fig she could pick my burger toppings. Everyone knows what you put on the burger makes or breaks the burger. One simple ingredient can change the entire taste profile. Spicy to sweet or bold to bland. Luckily, I am hungry and will chomp right through whatever concoction Fig creates.

Rob is a good father and tries to fill in as a good stepfather, but I was never really his daughter. No one, not even Rob, could answer the questions about my mother when she went missing. And in my world, if I didn't get answers from someone, there wasn't a reason to talk to them. So, Rob stopped trying to console me about Aadya long ago. We both loved her; we all loved her, and not one of us received the answers we searched for. The answers we deserved.

"Whata ya say, I drive you girls over to The Shore? I could use one of Bridie's famous papaya shakes." His grin is so big and a blueprint of Fig's. He is always happy to see Fig, and he is always hungry. Fig is jumping up and down and loves the idea, "We can load the Argo, Harbor!"

"Sure, I will take a ride home. But I'd like to freshen up and catch up to you guys at The Shore." Rob opens the tailgate of his truck and pulls down the ramp. After I drive the Argo up for storage, Rob secures it with two straps.

On the ride back, Fig talks about her day non-stop, and Rob listens intensively. He isn't like a lot of the parents I see at The Shore. Maybe I put a spotlight on other families more because my own has been under one for so long. Maybe the virtual slap hits a nerve. And sometimes, I feel like slapping back.

I'd do anything to have mine back. So when I notice parents who are so self-absorbed on their phones or other relationships that they are barely able to make eye contact with their kid, I want to scream. Obviously, some have to handle business or respond to a text. They have to divide their attention, but I am not talking about those parents. I am talking about the ones who don't hear half of what their kid is saying. Tutu says when you don't know what your kid is saying, you can't know what they're doing. Rob isn't like that. He and mom wanted Fig; they wanted our family, and I think Rob goes out of his way to make sure we remember. Once we are finally outside my house, Rob unloads the Argo while I talk to Fig.

"Tell Tutu I will be there in a bit."

"Are you taking your short cut?" Before I can answer her, Rob is calling out, "Harbor, I will gladly wait if you like." I don't want Rob to think I am ungrateful, so I contemplate his offer for a brief second. I can feel Fig's laser glare. If the kid could cast a spell to make me say yes - she would. But no spells today. I am eager to ride the bend, and the mere thought of the open road delights me. "Thanks, Rob. I will see you guys soon. Promise," I relay as I start to walk away.

Fig squishes her face to shoot me a you owe me look. She can be a ferocious little thing when she doesn't get her way. She isn't spoiled, but she has grown up worrying about me. The ripple effect results in her trying to keep tabs on my whereabouts.

In seconds, I've slid into my Teal Shore shirt and helmet. Aadya used to say that dad always wanted me to have the Argo. It's old, and the color is more rust than it is red these days, but I don't care. It provides refuge.

Aadya told stories about how dad rode to clear his mind, and when I was born, he often strapped my car seat in the Argo and rode around to help clear my mind. Apparently, it was the only way I could sleep. I have vague flashes where I will remember riding in the Argo when he dropped me off at school. As I zip away on the very same all-terrain vehicle, I often wish I could remember more.

My white tennis shoes take a beating when I ride, but it's okay. My style is pretty low key. I guess my sense of fashion never developed. My priorities sort of shifted when I lost both parents. I have about five staples: tennis shoes, shorts, a Shore shirt and Aadya's belt. I'm comfortable with those. Oh, and my contacts.

I have perfect vision, yet for years, my eyes would burn as if they were on fire, making anything I tried to focus on blurry. The doctors told Tutu that extreme stress can strain the vision. Between the death of my dad and loss of my mom, I've had my share of muck. The fever in my eyes never really went away. It's always simmering and always flares up during a dream.

My contacts don't match my actual eye color. Everything about me couldn't be more opposite of Fig's, from my height to my hair. I inherited my grandmother's lantern jaw and slenderness. The lady has some strong genes because I also have her narrow nose and eye color. By the time I was 12, I got tired of Tutu explaining to the busy-bodies at The Shore or school or wherever we went why her two granddaughters look so different. So, I began wearing contacts.

I don't like the term half-sister. Fig is my sister and since most people don't know a flick about profiling, they judge instead: so, I took it upon myself to make our lives easier. I opted for pretty brown contacts. Amber like Figs. Many of my features may take after Tutu's Irish side, but my height came from my dad. Aadya is to thank for my dark hair and eyelashes. Fig, on the other hand, is all Hawaiian. She is a sunny ray of light, yet the origin of her sass is still under debate.

It took years riding the Argo in shorts to get a barely visible tan, but I often wear long sleeve shirts. Arms get dark quickly when you work a drive-thru window most of your waking hours and sun cancer is no joke. Lots of islanders wear rash guards, but very few wear long sleeve suede shirts like Keyne and his *family of sorts* was wearing. Did they find a great sale? With practice, a person can grasp a lot from a glance, especially if they've learned another critical element in profiling. *Isolate the facts from emotion.* I have zero emotional investment in them, yet I still can't figure what other reasons they would have to cover their arms. I doubt they were trying to prevent sun cancer while inside the new school.

I kick off some dirt from my tennis shoes to slide my hand up my long sleeve Shore shirt. Hey, my elbows are soft. I never paid attention. I lotion after every bath but nothing more than average. And these days, Fig is trying to copy me, so I have to ration my lotion. If not, I find it disappears quickly, and she walks out of the restroom as slick as a baby seal.

Why can't I remember Keyne? How does he remember me? I didn't wear contacts in first grade, and my growth spurt wasn't until middle school. I've changed so much that at times, it's too much for me to remember myself.

CHAPTER 12

Every time I ride through the bend, I catch sight of a new detail. Honestly, the tracks of the Argo are deposited into a treasure trove full of massive trees, rainbows, ornate foliage and magnificent, dense greenery, all on display to the tunes of the uprising ocean, the gushing of waves, and the fizzle of the white foam tips. The black wings of the Honeycreepers often blend with the shadows of the passageway, but their plump, red bellies can be seen flickering in and out of the greenness, and their trill can be heard even over the ocean breeze. My pony tail whips in the wind. Daylight will be closing soon, and I want to soak in the last rays of sunlight that reach past their grasp, through the lush trees and help transport me to another era.

I know I can't find all the answers in dad's old FBI books, but I'm still drawn to them. I'm fascinated by the fact that the books give an outline of a person's psyche. They also allow me to challenge myself by forcing me to stay connected to my own past. Tragedy is part of my history, but I'm determined to not make it my future. And there's only one way to do that. Learn from it.

Take FBI rule #9, which opens the eyes to see how personality reflects behavior. Every human wears camouflage - our bodies. Rule #9 sees right through the camo and simply shows how to read a person's true motives and thoughts. Unfortunately though, it's not that simple. There are several layers, and mastering them can get complicated.

I had to really think about this and sharpen my skills on the ultimate lineup: body language, facial expressions, and the spoken word. The trifecta that reaches right into the window to the soul. For example, fidgeting and posture are huge clues. A classmate slouched over their desk may look like they just have bad posture, but that is a standout detail they are giving away. Slouching means a lack of confidence. In spite of that, my dad's old books are focused on Criminal Profiling, and since most people are not criminals, I make do and binge watch the customers in the drive-thru.

My dad's handwriting can best be described as jagged scribble, and proof is on the cover of one of his notebooks.

"Man's reach should exceed his grasp."

Sometimes I feel that quote comes to life in the bend and paves the road ahead. When I ride the bend, I am free. As crazy as it sounds, the bend is my favorite…okay…only hang-out.

When I first found the shortcut to The Shore, I was angry, and all the people I was angry with were dead or gone from my life. I was younger then and didn't have the easiest time processing how unfair the world can be. Tutu needed me at The Shore, and I subconsciously wanted to get lost. I wanted a reason *not to deal* with reality. I rode into the bend, and since then, it's a way for me to clear my mind, to think, or not think at all.

The passageway can definitely possess an eerie vibe, a feeling as though I am not alone. The road is smooth until you get to the trees, and that's where the road begins to curve and change into red dirt. The reddish soil reminds me of my history teachers' hair. I think it might be a perfect color match.

The wheels of the Argo grip the road and flatten clumps of dirt while guiding me through the passageway, not too fast, not too slow, but at a pace where I feel like I am part of the bend.

Then there are the waves. Growing up on the island, you can become acclimated to the sound of the ocean. It becomes harder to hear because it's part of everyday life and easy to drown out. Not for me though. Each time I ride the bend, I look forward to the delicate droplets of water carried by the wind to brush my face, hands, and legs. I feel born again with every ride.

I've never hit the curve in the bend without my heart racing, without a sensation grabbing hold of me as though I have arrived in another time, an ancient landscape. The thrill of my entire body moving at a sideways angle to match the curves of the bend has no competition. Nor does the ability to only see a few feet ahead, which forces me to live in the now. Then there is the darkness. Towering trees hide my shadow for as long as they can until pieces of light peer in.

When I get to the most convex angle of the bend, when the sound of the ocean waves are louder than the chirping of the Honeycreepers, I pull over to a clearing. My clearing. I found it the very first day I rode the bend and have been returning ever since. If I wasn't so familiar with this back road, I'd pass it right up because it's concealed by thick trees. You'd have to look for the tracks the Argo has forged over the years to know the clearing exists.

A jagged cliff overlooks the vast ocean. Foam waves rush into the sand, and in the near distance is a harbor. Down below, large rocks and boulders scatter along the beach. I have witnessed families of monk seals finding refuge amongst those boulders. Monk seals don't have ears that can be seen, but they have great hearing, so I have to be careful not to startle them even if I am more than 75 feet above sea level. The cliff is hidden yet sits directly above the beach, so I have an exceptional view. Every March or April, female monk seals deliver a pup. The first time I got a glimpse of the pups, I was awestruck. Baby monk seals are born with silky sable coats and have a shine that can be seen for miles, a true spectacle of wonder that I'll never forget. But their births also immediately reminded me of an old Hawaiian legend. The legend of the Mo'o.

I stopped believing in fairy tale games, rabbit holes and multi-verses long ago, so my theory on the Mo'o is grounded in logic.

According to legend, the Mo'o is an ancient lizard that has supernatural powers. It's a shapeshifter that can come for all of us. For centuries, the story has been whispered in the homes of Hawaiian families. *Be weary of the Mo'o.* Some islanders believe the Mo'o can summon an ancient form of sorcery. According to the elders, Tutu being one of them, the Mo'o can take the form of humans who call on them. Tutu learned the legends from my grandfather when they married on the island. She says the phrase, "make a deal with the devil," originated with the shape shifting lizards.

My theory, however, is that our ancestors mistook the monk seal for the ancient creature. After all, monk seals have been said to be the last living relative of the dinosaurs! For millions of years, monk seals have been part of the lineage of our land. Even today, they are intimidating, with hungry, large black eyes and eight pairs of teeth, so I'm sure when they dwelled in an undisturbed habitat, one without fancy hotels and coffee shops, they were much larger.

Monk seals are fiercely protective of their young. I think that's why they chose this spot to deliver. Aside from my secret attendance, it's a private beach, and I have no plans to give up my seat. I look forward to seeing the seals dive in and out of the water like torpedoes. They are especially fast during breeding seasons. They have adapted to hunt at night, so fisherman or boaters can only make out a sharp darkness cutting through the water; holograms of oil streaks that cut the Pacific. For centuries, these sightings have been the backbone, the catalyst for some very spooky tall tales. So, no. I do not believe that shapeshifting lizards live among us. I do believe that long before the internet, monk seals made a zealous entrance into our folklore and have toyed with the islanders ever since.

My eyes wander from the cliff to the boulders along the sand and then to the harbor across the ocean. "Harbor, naming a child is like a prayer over one's life…" I can hear Tutu's words even over the gushing waves. Aadya named me Harbor. I was too little when my mother was around to ask her why. What kind of name is Harbor? It's definitely not Hawaiian. I remember when she'd tuck me in at night. Aadya would whisper that I would always be protected from rough waters. I loved her, but as I stare down the cliff, as I hear the pressure of tons of water push against the surface, as I examine the harbor in the distance, I don't think she could have been more wrong.

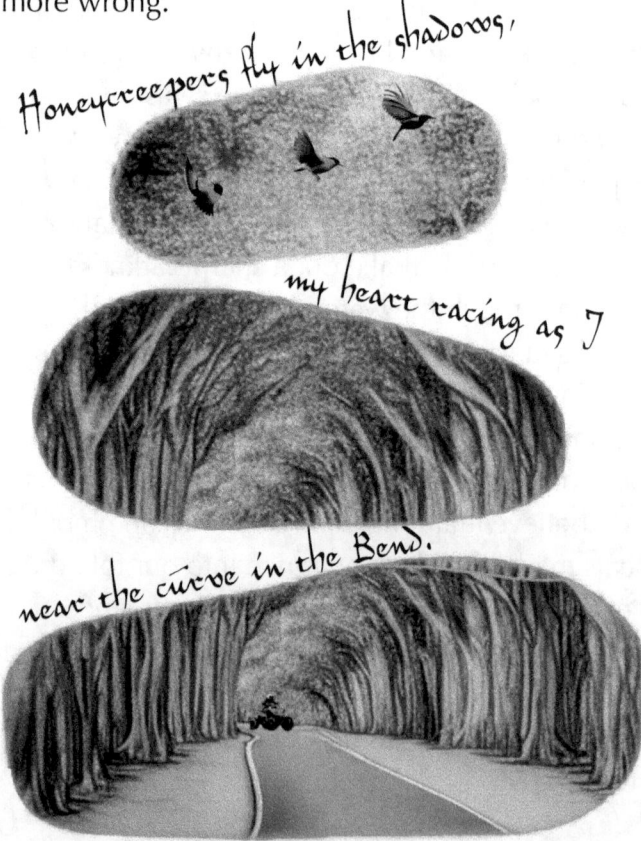

Honeycreepers fly in the shadows, my heart racing as I near the curve in the Bend.

CHAPTER 13

As soon as I park, I can hear the music flowing out of The Shore. Even over the hum of the Argo, the beach-themed music Tutu insist on playing cascades throughout the restaurant, into the parking lot and onto the surrounding beach.

Before I enter, I stop to knock off as much red dirt as I can from my tennis shoes. As much as she loves me, Tutu would have a fit if I stomped clay into her restaurant. I reach to open the door, but it is swung open by Fig who has a long french fry hanging out of her smile.

"Fig!" I say as I snatch the bottom half. She pulls me by the hand to a booth, "Surprise!"

She remembered my burger toppings. Of course she did. Fig may be as light as a kiwi fruit, but she has the memory as massive as the monk seal. I'm scared to look at what this child has added to my burger, but I dig in and take a huge bite. I can feel Fig's eyes fixated on me, waiting for my response. Oooh, I taste extra pineapple and pepper. I put my hand on my chin and make a face that says I'm undecided, and Rob and Fig break into a laugh. I fluff her pile of soft curls, "You remembered the pineapple, Fig! You do care," I say as I continue munching.

"You really like it?"

"Moderate the peppers in the future," I announce through a cough, my lips on fire.

"Okay," she laughs.

"Where's Tutu?"

"Working the window."

Apparently, Fig decided to add a dollop of barbecue sauce that is coating the toasted hamburger bun. With a juicy bite dripping from my lips, I take a napkin and make my way around the counter.

"Busy day?" I surprise Tutu.

"Harbor!" She's always happy to see me. And it's genuine too. She'd love Fig and I just as much, even if she hadn't been forced to step into the parenting role. She tries her best to make sure we are supported. Sure, Fig and I lost a mom, but I try to remember that Tutu lost her daughter. I know she misses Aadya.

The Shore helps her deal with the pain. Tutu is like one of the rocks in my clearing. She has remained a stable source of comfort. She has never shown an ounce of resentment that her retirement turned into two grandchildren being thrown on her. She lives her life around ours. Oh, and now she also has Sam.

Tutu recently started dating her number one short order cook. At first, I was a little grossed out. Sorry, but the idea of my grandmother in a romantic relationship would turn my tummy even if I had a perfect life. I was also skeptical about Sam in the beginning. He has no ties to the island, no history here, so what could he gain from a future at The Shore?

He's a retiree, probably in his late 60s, so a couple years older than Tutu. He used to be a railroad conductor up north. Now, he is Sam, who dates my Tutu. Ugh. But I can't complain. He takes good care of her, and they laugh a lot, plus he can make a mean burger. I guess when he moved out here, he fell in love with more than the island. Maybe it's proof, the heart doesn't stop working.

"Harbor, today has been packed!"

"The first day back at school must make everyone extra hungry."

"Parents have been in for lunch or picking up lunch to take to the schools. And it feels like every teenager on the island has come out for a burger!" I search The Shore from behind the counter. Not every teenager. Not Keyne.

"Tell me, Harbor, how was your day? And the new building, did you like? And where were you? Fig and Rob have been waiting for over an hour."

Tutu gave Fig her nickname based on her fresh, sweet nature and natural golden glow. She never gave me a one. I've always been Harbor.

"An hour?"

Tutu nods her head yes. I didn't realize I took that long. The passageway draws you in, and it's the only place I lose track of time.

"You took your shortcut, didn't you?"

I answer with a half apologetic smile because admittedly, I'd do it again and again.

"Oh Harbor, that's fine. It clearly makes you happy. But I don't want you riding at night," she flashes a look of concern, "It's not fair so much crime from the camps is being ignored. But it's spreading, and I don't want you and Fig out late."

"Tutu, let me work this week?"

"No dear, I want you to concentrate on school. The first year in high school is a big deal. It might be your year to join a sport or a club?"

Wishful thinking, but what I say is, "School was great, and you won't believe how nice the new building is."

"Really?"

"Yep, and btw, I am happy working the drive-thru," I withhold a small detail. *And practicing my profiling with books you don't know I stole out of Aadya's closet.*

"Besides, the first week of school is mostly getting used to our schedules. I can take a break from work when the real work starts rolling in."

Tutu sighs, placing her hands on her hips, so I jump right in with puppy dog eyes, "I can start right now, and you can go work on some of your crazy grindz," I tempt her.

She's hesitant but stares at me, reaching up to hold both my shoulders, "I miss your real eyes."

I am used to hearing this. She talks to me about my contacts every other week or so, and I've learned to let her. No response needed.

She huffs a louder sigh, "Okay, you can start tomorrow. I will take a quick break if you can mind the window for a few minutes."

"Done and done," I say, giving her a bear hug.

As she walks away, I hear her say, "You know a storm is on the way this week?"

Understanding that her questions are often rhetorical, I prepare to take my place at the drive-thru register.

A pair of wooden chopsticks lays over the card reader. Tutu is always creating new ideas to make the restaurant more hip, and I'm scared at what she has planned for these chopsticks.

We recently updated to a card reader because most customers pay with their credit cards. At first, Tutu complained that the card reader company was committing highway robbery by charging her 3% of every dollar we make. However, she now loves the reader because it's safer and so easy to use. She used to do all her bookkeeping by hand, and now, she simply logs into her account for her sales data.

As soon as I put on my headset, I have an order. Working the drive-thru is more than a job to me. It's more than a fun hobby. It's training. I witness hundreds of microcosms pass right before me like stories in a book. So, I expand on what I'm learning from dad's old FBI books while I make a little cash on the side.

Fifteen minutes of non-stop orders, and finally, I have a minute break. Tutu wasn't kidding: it is a busy day for The Shore. As I start to take off my headset, I hear an engine hissing in the drive-thru. I keep my headset in place and listen to the sound of air escaping from something internal in an older car. It's also a sound I vaguely remember. Oh well, I am the one who offered to work this week.

"Hi and welcome to The Shore." That is how Tutu expects me to greet customers. Then I am to add, "How can I help you?"

Silence, except for the fairly familiar rumble of that engine. No response. I think, *okay buddy this is still fast food*. I repeat The Shore lines, and a few seconds pass. Still silence. Maybe the driver thinks this is funny or fell asleep. Whatever it is, I feel like shouting through the intercom, "Order already!"

I can't wait for Tutu to add a camera so we can view the drive-thru live. I've been asking her for months, and she's warming up to the idea. It will also give me much more to analyze. Tutu's motives are a bit different. She is concerned about safety and thinks the cameras will be a great deterrent for crime.

Over the last half year, the main island has had a spike in crime, including a pair of child abductions. Islanders are suspicious that the kidnapper is a person who visits the island to stray not play.

"One water, no ice, a Shore burger, meat only, no Shore sauce," a rough, drawn out voice penetrates the intercom. The voice belongs to a man and sort of simulates the hissing evading his car. That is his order? He took all that time to decide on the most boring selection we have? Then, it hits me. I remember that boring order from this summer. I bet it's the same guy. Our food will be delicious no matter what, but it's practically a crime to eat here and not add a side of our Alea fries. Our hot fries are dusted in red sea salt with a dash of garlic and are irresistible! *Hey Mr. Boring, you are missing out!*

"Add a chocolate chip cookie," the gruffness of his voice travels through my headset and sits on my ears. *Okay, you're not a full robot yet. Robots don't need sweets.*

Mr. Boring drives almost as slow as he orders, and the jalopy that pulls up to the window confirms my speculations. He has been through the drive-thru a few times this past summer, and his order was always bland. But something is a bit different in his voice. It's heavier.

I repeat the price, and Mr. Boring hands me cold hard cash. Same as the summer. He is one of the few customers that still pays in paper money. I take the bill and can feel the heat rising from his hands. Maybe he was wearing work gloves before he stopped in for lunch, or maybe he has high blood pressure. Tutu takes medicine for high blood pressure, and one side effect is a rise in body temperature as blood is forced through the arteries. Her hands can get very warm too. It's a silent killer if you don't know the signs. The money he holds is generating so much heat, but I doubt this guy wants medical advice from a teenager at a drive-thru window.

It's a beautiful 80° outside, and most people echo the island sunniness, but this guy doesn't care for interaction. His gaze remains unchanged as he stares straight ahead. He doesn't smile. *Guess what, guy, I'm not looking for any new friends either.*

It's been a couple of months since I've seen Mr. Boring. I worked the drive-thru all summer, and he seemed to just drop off the face of the earth. Oh well, he doesn't disappoint, his same chilly soul travels along for the ride.

"Hello?" A woman's voice over the intercom interrupts my thoughts. Her voice is kind and matter of fact. It travels downward, so she may be driving an SUV.

"Harbor," Fig is at the counter wanting my attention, and Mr. Boring's order is up, and the nice lady is waiting to order. This job has taught me a lot, and at the top of the list is how to multi-task. I mute my mic.

"Just a minute, Fig, let me finish this order," I turn toward her briefly to make enough eye contact and raise my eyebrows so she can read my *give me just a minute* face. Turning my mic back on, I reach for Mr. Boring's order which is packed, all orders are, in Tutu's signature wax paper bag. The takeout bags match our work shirts; teal with a neon orange ocean wave that has the name The Shore written on top. I fold the bag twice while speaking to the customer at the menu board, "Hi and welcome to The Shore. How can I help you?" I hear what sounds like a couple of kids going back and forth, and I recognize the chatter. It's Soccer Mom! She requests a second, and I tell her to take her time as I hand over Mr. Boring's food and change. It's hard to ignore that the thick palm he collects his money with is as warm as the burger that just came off the grill. As he slides his arm back into his car window, the cuff from his sleeve brushes the edge of my wrist. It has a peculiar softness. Maybe it's a new trend because no one wears long sleeves. Okay, I do, but that's to prevent sun damage and my arms looking like an Oreo cookie after a week of working the drive-thru.

"Ma halo nui," Tutu demands we end every order with gratitude. No response. Mr. Boring looks straight ahead; he doesn't flinch. I'm beginning to wonder if he is hypnotized or sleep walking or rather, sleep driving.

Mr. Boring drives off, and now the lady at the window is ready to order.

"Yes, ma'am. How can I help you?"

Normally, I can guess who is in the drive-thru before I see them based on a number of factors using FBI rule #3. In this case, the amount of time the lady took to order and the babble in the backseat reminds me of a soccer family who ramps up their visits to The Shore during soccer season. If I'm correct, a brother and sister will be sitting in the backseat. But their vehicle sounds different, cleaner. There is barely an utterance of reverberation. Maybe they got a new vehicle.

FBI rule #3 is all about being attentive to the cluster of actions. So, even if I can't immediately observe who I am speaking to, I can try to match the noises with the movements in the car. Hands and arms shuffling around, fingers on a phone, the pitch of different voices and the pacing of voices all add to the profile. If it's the family I think it is, they always order a papaya shake and Alea fries. Soccer Mom's hurried voice breaks through the intercom and pierces my ear. I turn the volume down on my mic to take her order.

"Hi, can I get 4 kid size Papaya shakes and 2 Shore burgers with everything on them, but add pineapple to one and 2 orders of the special fries, hold the pepper on 1, please."

Bingo. I type in her order, so it will pop up on the kitchen screen, prompting Sam to prepare the meal fresh. Then I hear a noise that isn't from the intercom. My stomach is growling. That reminds me, Tutu was supposed to take a break. She has been gone longer than I expected. I still have Fig's burger waiting for me.

"Order up!" sings Sam.

I fold the teal bags and happily hand them to Soccer Mom and return her credit card. As it turns out, she is in a shiny, new SUV. It is the polar opposite of the Argo. Her new ride is polished and has soft interior lights and clean leather seats. Two kids are in a backseat wrestling match. That won't mix well with mouthwatering grindz, but when their mom passes the drinks back, the kids take a break from beating one another to eagerly start slurping their papaya shakes.

"Ma halo nui," I wave bye as the carload of commotion drives away.

I turn to look for Fig and realize she has been standing behind the counter this entire time. Poofs of honey tresses extend above the counter and lure a smile from me. The braids I make her never stay neatly in place. The poor kid has been waiting patiently for me to finish the burger she made me. I promised her, and unlike our mother, I'll keep my promises.

CHAPTER 14

"I texted you," Fig inserts. Patience is not her strong suit.

"What's up?"

"I texted you," she says again with her hands on her hip as though her texts are the only priority I should have.

I check my phone to appease her and laugh out loud. Her text isn't funny, she is. We have an inside joke Fig and I refer to as the sister emoji. With the busy weeks leading up to the start of school, she hasn't sent it in a while, nor was I expecting it today.

"He wants to go to school tomorrow. Will that be okay with you, Harbor?" Fig says while trying to pierce through my soul with her eyes. She always thinks I need her. Sure, I do, but I totally understand she needs time with her dad too.

I look over at Rob who is checking something on his cell phone and smile, "Of course, it's okay. I'll have the restroom all to myself."

She softens her analytical glare toward me. *Oh gosh, did I teach this to that poor child?* She is trying to read me the way I read strangers.

Rob walks over, and in his signature husky voice says, "Harbor, I have a three day layover.

Makani really wants to stay with you tonight. Whata ya say I pick her up in the morning and get her to school for the next couple of days if that's okay with you? Bridie has already checked off on it."

Is he asking me or telling me? I respect Rob, yet it is annoying how the grown-ups that are still left in my life treat me with kid gloves. Regrettably though, what's their other option? So even though I want to scream when they behave as though I'm a fragile, single snowflake, I try to be grateful that they care.

"Sounds great. I will make sure to have her ready." Rob gives me a hug over the counter then lifts Fig up, spins her around and tells her he will see her in the morning. Just before he pushes through the exit door, Rob turns to me, "Harbor, no short cuts home." I nod.

Rob has an astronomical view of the island as a pilot. He does plenty of tourist flights and has lots of stories. The most interesting are from tourists who have never been to America. The most unsettling come out of the homeless camps. He says most visitors to our island search for freedom and natural beauty, but that idealistic goal dies without hard work. I've memorized Rob's familiar lecture on why Fig and I need to always be mindful, "There is plenty of good among us, but the bad does lurk,

90

and lying about it will never make the truth go away."

The fact of the matter is that the news of child abductions has many of us on the island feeling unsettled. Tutu and Rob are on a safety kick, but Fig is really all I have left. So, I am always on high alert.

Tutu finishes up a conversation with Sam, then returns to the drive-thru where I remind her that I will be in to work tomorrow. She gives me a kiss on the cheek as her way of letting me know she remembers.

Fig and I hop on the Argo. I always keep an extra helmet for her in the storage compartment. She is forever asking me to give her the Argo when I'm done with it. Fig swears she already knows how to drive. I usually crack up and tell her Rob has a helicopter waiting for her. She's too young to hear the entire truth, too young to understand that I could never give away the Argo. It's the last flicker of light from my past.

"Take your short cut, Harbor," a warm whisper in my ear, a request from Fig that I am obligated to accept as a big sister, places us on the path toward the bend. It's not quite dark, so I think we will be perfectly safe.

Fig gives me a rundown of her day. She thinks her teacher is nice and pretty, but she doesn't believe the teacher will know who the mean kids are because she is too nice. Fig goes on to say how she already knows who the friendly kids are, and who the means kids are and the mean kids better not mess with her. Oh, might I mention, Fig is also feisty. I raise my voice above the wind and ask over my shoulder, "How are the mean kids mean?"

Apparently, a few of her classmates tried to scare the rest of the kids by saying that a giant lizard monster crawls out of the ocean at night and hides in the playground waiting for innocent children to eat. My ribs begin to hurt from laughter, "Fig, that is the oldest school yard prank! Even I remember that from first grade."

"Is it true? They said the water lizard waits to steal our strength."

"Of course it's not true."

"But kids have been missing, Harbor. You heard Tutu and Daddy."

"I'd already be in the belly of one if it were true, Fig."

By the time we enter the bend, Fig has moved on to her class project, "We are melting colors to make a self-portrait. I need more colors from the store."

Seconds later, we are completely enveloped in the bend, and other than the slow swish of waves below, there is complete silence. Even my little sister who talks nonstop is in awe.

Dusk is billowing in and with it, the gift of rare colors. The sheen of black and blue ripples over the ocean are flanked by looming trees with leaves the color of deep jade. We sit and soak it in. I braid Fig's wild hair while she re-arranges my stack of rocks.

By the time we arrive home, it's close to dark, "Fig, go get showered and then pack a bag for the week."

"I'm only leaving for a couple of days."

"It's better to have enough." Rob's family is from the island. It is a large family, and every now and then, they ask if Fig can extend her visit a day or two longer.

Once I hear the shower start, I pop open my computer to print my syllabus and turn on the news. If I watch TV with Fig in earshot, I usually can't hear a thing because she asks me a thousand questions. I'm waiting for any leads on a suspect in the kidnappings. Dad's books say the leads are credible information that will guide the investigator closer to the suspect. It makes me angry that a description has been given to the public, not one lead. But just as I think that, a well-dressed reporter goes into a story about another child abduction. What the actual hell!

This one happened earlier today! My heart
begins to race and I cling to every word.

Breaking News
*A toddler is missing tonight, taken right out of
his stroller. Police are trying to gather camera
footage from the surrounding area to put
together a sketch of possible suspects.*

The kid was taken from the front of a school. I
peer closely into the TV and realize it is an
elementary school! It's not Fig's, yet it can't be
too far away. The islands are all one hop away
from the next. I try to listen to the reporter over
my heaving breath. The crying family describes
their missing child while a picture of his smiling
face is juxtaposed on the screen. I can feel my
eyes starting to burn. I don't understand how
people can give an interview so soon after a
tragedy. I don't want to understand. If someone
had been so insensitive as to put a microphone
in my face when Aadya went missing, even at
my young age, I would have slapped it out of
their hands. The kid was taken from one island
over, and the reporter ends with the promise to
interrupt regular broadcasting with any new
information. A story about approaching storms is
up next. Usually, my heart skips a beat with
news of a storm, but I can't stop it from racing.

That poor kid. I hope he is found safe, and the person who did this rots in prison.

Fig runs out of our bathroom, and I shut off the TV. Surprisingly, she is already dried up and dressed in cozy pajamas. I compose myself. Fig must be excited to spend time with her dad tomorrow, and that makes me happy. I don't want her to leave thinking I am worried.

"Ready for a good night's sleep?" I ask as the twerp starts getting under the covers of my bed.

"We have to pack your visiting bag, Fig," I say as I stare at her. I know this little booger is trying to trick me. She wants me to pack her bag. My mind, however, is still absorbed by the image of the missing child. I couldn't bear it if something happened to my little sister.

The abductions seem to be getting closer to home, and the last time the kidnapper struck wasn't too long ago. Fig will be safe with Rob, though. I hear the printer stop. My syllabus. I must have slightly turned toward the sound because Fig, in her sweetest Fig voice, offers, "I'll get it for you, Harbor."

"Thanks, kid, but I'll toss it in my bag in the morning. Listen, I'll pack your bag *this time, and you're* not sleeping in here tonight."

She smiles as if her plan worked, "You know I always forget to pack something, and dad said he will take me to buy more colors tomorrow. To purchase more colors."

Fig has been working on expanding her vocabulary. She is a funny little thing and will probably run for president one day. I repeat to her that she will not sleep in my room tonight. She turns around and makes herself comfortable on my pillow.

I uncover her and carry her to her room. Her room is so much smaller than mine. It's cute and full of Figgy personality. The walls are painted a soft kiwi and are full of stuffed animals. Unlike mine, Fig's room has pictures of our mother. They are in a framed collage that includes snapshots of Rob, Aadya, Fig and me, and every time I pass them, I can't help but feel they are staring back at me. On her dresser, Fig keeps a glass jar full of candy. Colorful wrapped pieces, a variety of sour and hard sugar delights glimmer when I turn on her light. Helping myself to one, I open Fig's visiting bag and toss in 3 day's worth of outfits, one stuffed bear, a brush and rubber bands to keep her wild hair down. I wait on packing the toothbrush, so she can brush her teeth in the morning.

I eventually make it to the printer, but my eyes are already watering. No sense in trying to read through the syllabus tonight. I'll review it in the morning.

My thoughts return to the latest kidnapped kid as I tuck Fig in. That poor child wasn't the first victim, and if more details about the suspect aren't released soon, he won't be the last. The lady meteorologist said a storm was on the way.

When a storm is on the way, the open sea and surrounding terrain transform. The wind roars through the thick trees, the clouds become heavy with every shade of grey and blue, and the ocean mirrors all the beautiful fury of mother nature, washing ashore tumultuous, godlike waves. Tutu would never allow me to leave this late, but if I hurry to bed, I can wake up early and ride the bend for a morning glimpse before school starts. Hmm, how does a person hurry up and fall asleep?

Half asleep, Fig grabs my hand. I hold her hand a bit tighter to give her confidence that her big sister is still here. She wants to finish telling me about her day, and I let her as she drifts off to sleep. While she is talking, I reach for my belt and slide out the old photo I keep of Aadya, dad and me. That was a mistake. My eyes begin to burn, so I force it back in.

Lately, Fig's been mentioning our mom less and less when drifting off to sleep. More and more, she is remembering what happened in her day rather than in her life.

I can take a couple of pointers from this kid.

CHAPTER 15

I jolt awake. What time is it? Where is my phone? I look around in the dark and realize I must have dozed off in Fig's room.

It's early, and I try to convince myself that it was just a dream. Not falling asleep in Fig's tiny bed, but the nightmare I just had. My heart is pounding because it's the kind of dream where nothing makes sense and you wake up feeling as though there is no mercy. It's been so long since I've had a dream like that. I try to shake it, but my eyes are on fire. I hear my alarm in the other room, and in my slumber, sluggishly walk to my room to punch the snooze button as hard as I can. It doesn't sound like I woke Fig. Good. I need a moment to breathe in the dark silence before the day begins.

I hold my eyes, head down. Think, Harbor. My mom and my dad were in the dream. And just like the other times, I am always searching for them. Ironically, I can never find them.

This dream was a little different. There were more faces. People that I do not know and the profound feeling of grief that fills my heart. The bend was in the dream, but instead of riding the

Argo, I was being moved, almost floating through the bend at night. I don't know what was moving me. And the faces of people, including Aadya, were materializing in and out of the trees, but it was only their heads. They didn't have bodies, just normal size heads that gradually tripled in size then disappeared behind the murky trees. Processing time over. Fig is wide awake and suddenly standing near my bed with a brush in hand. No time to unpack the nightmare. Only time to start the day. "Let's fix your braids, kid."

A soft rumble travels up our driveway. Rob is taking Fig a little early. Thank goodness because I am on my toes, backpack ready with the Argo outside waiting to race the bend before I have to be in class. I make a mad dash to toss Fig's toothbrush in her bag and kind of feel like doing the same with her. She is moving like a snail this morning.

Rob started having early breakfast with Fig when she went to pre-school. He still carries on the tradition when he doesn't have to be at work. I can hear him practically yelling over the motor of his truck, "Harbor, want to join us for breakfast? I can drop you off at school."

"No thank-you!"

No, today I get to ride the bend and speak to the storm, to think my dream through. I wave goodbye from our front porch trying not to squeeze my eyes. I don't want Fig to worry. I ignore her beggar's face. She never stops looking over her shoulder when driving off, so I stand there waving continuously and partly smiling until she is out of the neighborhood and I am out of her sight.

I sprint to the Argo. Its faded scarlet red color and worn black tires appear a visual hazard that sit in stark contrast to the many hues of grandeur the island has to offer. But back in it's heyday, I understand this eight wheeler was one cool ride. The Argo is amphibious and can carry 10 times my weight. So I don't care how unsightly it may seem: it's a keeper. I insert the key, and the power in the twist throttles is like thunder in my hands. Go time.

One last mental checklist: phone, helmet and backpack. Ugh! My syllabus! I run back in the house and take the sheets from the printer then run to the fridge. Tutu leaves at 4:30 a.m., but her fresh papaya shakes are always on hand. One chug will hold me until lunch.

Finally on the Argo, I feel the breeze running alongside me and the dream and Ha'alele racing to catch up.

Most island mornings, the sun and clouds are the color of soft cotton candy, and the air around is diffused with cool, sparkling water.

But not island mornings before a storm. They are anything but soft, and I am no one to challenge Mother Nature. I'll be happy for a few moments alone in her grace.

Honeycreepers have left their nest and fly overhead. The wild things seem just as eager to enjoy the calm before the storm. If I didn't have the episodes that changed the course of my life, I don't know that I would appreciate the island the way I do.

Picking up speed along the curve, the Argo is in sync with my pulse. Once its fat wheels collect clumps from the cinnamon path, I take my cue and begin to steer left into my clearing, and it welcomes me. Thousands of rich green clusters on both sides of the harrowed entrance cheer in the strong winds. It isn't long before I'm overlooking the large expanse of water, standing high above the sounds of the mighty Pacific. I exhale, an instantaneous reflex and look at my phone, another instantaneous reflex. It's still early enough that I can sit and soak in the tranquility that encircles me. My butt print is molded into a rather nice groove in the ground next to my mound of rocks. As I take my seat, I can't help but smile. Fig re-arranged my simple collection into the shape of an emoji that we use on our sister thread. That booger.

Storm skies are on the horizon. And when they arrive, the world around will stand still to bathe in their beautiful fury. The ocean will mirror the heavens as they shout back and forth to one another, both demanding to be heard and both refusing to listen. Out on the edge of this cliff, I feel connected to something much bigger than me. For a long time, I did all I could to hide from Ha'alele, but each time, it found me. It would be easy for me to be mad at the world. My parents are gone, and I have tons of questions. Questions that might only have answers I don't like. Tough answers that I intend to find. But not as a victim. I refuse to be a victim. The world has enough.

I started making Fig watch TV with me once a week because if I don't, she will binge watch re-runs. It's not her fault she was forced to either watch the grown-ups she loved hurt or divert her attention to hundreds of the same cartoons. I want her to have something more, something positive. We usually log in to watch church services aired live. A statement the pastor said once shook me and it's a belief I carry to this day. He said, "When we look at all the creation around us, how can we not think there is a Creator?"

I remember driving the bend later that day and finding the clearing. I remember having so much hate in my heart, but no where to really direct it. Then as I sat there - *here*, I was able to breathe again, to see more than hate. Looking at the mountains, the wide trees, across the ocean, wondering what is underneath…made me look up. I've been looking up ever since. Besides, even when we choose to lie, to others or to ourselves, we can't ever choose to make the truth go away.

The wind picks up, and my ponytail whips in my face. The island's rainfall is as diverse as the millions of tourists that take the island by storm each year. When our climate is prepping for a downpour, nothing is quite as beautiful as the millions of tiny bits of light and water that fall through the trees. Weather that is a gift from the sea and clouds. From a Creator.

The splashing and roar of the ocean make me smile. The clearing where I park is on a high, grassy cliff full of lush, dark plants and Koa trees. It's stationed on a wall taller than Jack's beanstalk and made of slippery, jagged rocks that turn silver in the rain. I inhale as a few lazy monk seals take their time, a few minutes behind schedule, to re-enter their natural habitat. I watch them all the time. In the spring when they give birth to cubs, it is nothing less than miraculous. They have survived centuries in the dark harshness of the ocean, and somehow, they keep going, refusing to buy-in to the victim mentality as well.

The expanse of the sea is stunning. The good thing about not having anyone up here to talk to or disturb me is that I wouldn't have anything to say. All I want to do right now is listen. White foam tips have already begun a contest to see who can make it to the shore first. Pounding waves splash alongside the harbor in the distance. The harbor. My namesake. Bad joke or bad luck.

I need to process the dream. I want to completely forget about it but can't. It would only return worse tonight. I reach into my mom's old police belt without looking. I don't have to. I wear it everywhere. Just like my hair, it is practical. I've memorized the couple of small pockets on the inner most side. One is for the key to the Argo, and the other is for the picture. I slide my fingers along the inside of the belt and pull out the picture. I take a deep breath. My sigh parallels the crashing ocean below. Reaching for a nearby rock from my collection, I stare at the picture while clutching the smooth rock in my other hand. I think back to a time I had parents, a time when I didn't know real aching and absolute pain. It's an old photo, full of wrinkles from the many times it's been balled in my palms while I cried over it. When I was young, I thought if I closed my eyes and wished, wished so hard with all my heart, that maybe, when I opened them, I'd have my parents back. That they would jump out of the picture, so I could hug them one last time. I've cried enough tears to fill an ocean in my lifetime. So, I stopped. I stopped crying. As I grew older, I knew that if I cried anymore, I'd drown.

Years of crushing tears put pressure on my eyes and helped cause the damage that makes them burn. However, I don't cry anymore. So why do I feel like 2 torches are trapped inside?

I look at my tennis shoes packed with clumps from the red clay entrance and wonder if the Samoan crab's eyes ever burn with all that dirt on them, ever burn when their life is about to be turned upside down.

I'm 5 in the picture. Mom, dad and I are at a Fourth of July parade. It was the summer before 1st grade, before my 6th birthday and just months before my dad would be murdered in the line of duty.

Fireworks can be seen bursting across the background of the picture. Dad's eyes outshine the color of the fireworks. He was handsome. I can just faintly remember his hair early in the morning. It matched the coffee he poured, and all the waves of his hair lay flat, unlike this picture where it's styled casually back. I am sitting in the middle of him and my mother. Aadya. I apparently had just eaten cotton candy or a popsicle, something that turned my lips blue. Something that complimented my real eyes staring back at me from this old photo. Aadya was so pretty and strong. Her Hawaiian heritage made even more prominent by Tutu's sleek, Irish silhouette and an outline of toned muscles throughout her deep tan skin.

I keep photos of Aadya and my dad on my phone as well. I probably spend more time searching the past in the many pictures on my phone than I should. As though hunting for what I am missing will make my parents whole again.

I know most people on the island, but none are close friends. So, I don't do a lot of texting. Actually, Fig uses her phone more than me. I am often absorbed with what I'm learning and stay busy working or having fun trying to profile, so my phone is mostly for safety, and of course for school. It is almost impossible to balance school work and a job without it. I can research, download and upload assignments all within a few clicks. Speaking of school, I need to get there sometime today. But the dream. I need to try to remember some of the dream.

The dreams started when dad died, but I was too young to notice. It was Tutu and Aadya who talked me through the nightmares and *only after* breakfast. You can't be a Hawaiian and not take into account centuries of beliefs and folklore. They are passed down in each family like fine china. According to them, a person should *never, ever* share a deep dream until after their first meal of the day has been consumed.

Thanks to superstition, I was strictly prohibited from sharing a nightmare before breakfast, and even then, I had to process very slowly. Soon, the dreams just became a part of who I am. When Fig was born, they gradually went away. The burning in my eyes even stopped for a while. Hope and love slowly replaced the nightmares. Then when Aadya disappeared, everything returned with a fury, and this time, I refused to walk through them. Breakfast or no damn breakfast.

Tutu and Rob didn't know what to do and eventually made me speak to a therapist. Actually, for a long time, I *saw* the therapist. There wasn't anything I had to say to a complete stranger and even less that I wanted to hear from one. So he spoke to me. He started off with small talk, daily insignificant events like taking out the trash or yawning and eventually began talking about dreams. He explained how everyone has them. But what caught my attention and finally made me chime in was when he explained that all people have two minds. Every single person has two minds. A conscious mind and subconscious mind, and one doesn't always talk to the other and only one of them appears in our dreams. I learned that the dreams actually never went away. They were stored. And until I processed them, they would continue to control my day and even my life. I chose not to let them. That's why I process.

But Tutu sees things differently than the doctors. She is a strong believer that all things are intertwined, and energies cannot be ignored. Consequently, she has a habit of consulting ancient culture before she adheres to modern medicine. She says some people are born with *vision*. And she doesn't mean eyesight.

I remember one morning after a vivid dream, Tutu tried to comfort me, her gentle eyes looking at me almost apologetically, "…Until you learn to control this energy, you will never take hold of your own."

She says the dreams are helpful and can guide me if I embrace them. Different cultures call it different things. The Evil Eye, intuition, visions… We call it the Third Eye. It is the ability to see what is concealed.

Maybe this is why I respond so well on the eve of a storm. A dream for me is like an internal storm. When it is on the horizon, all you can do is be a good host. Whoever is right, Tutu or the doctors, why should any of us believe that a force of nature so strong can ever be guided?

What is the third Eye?

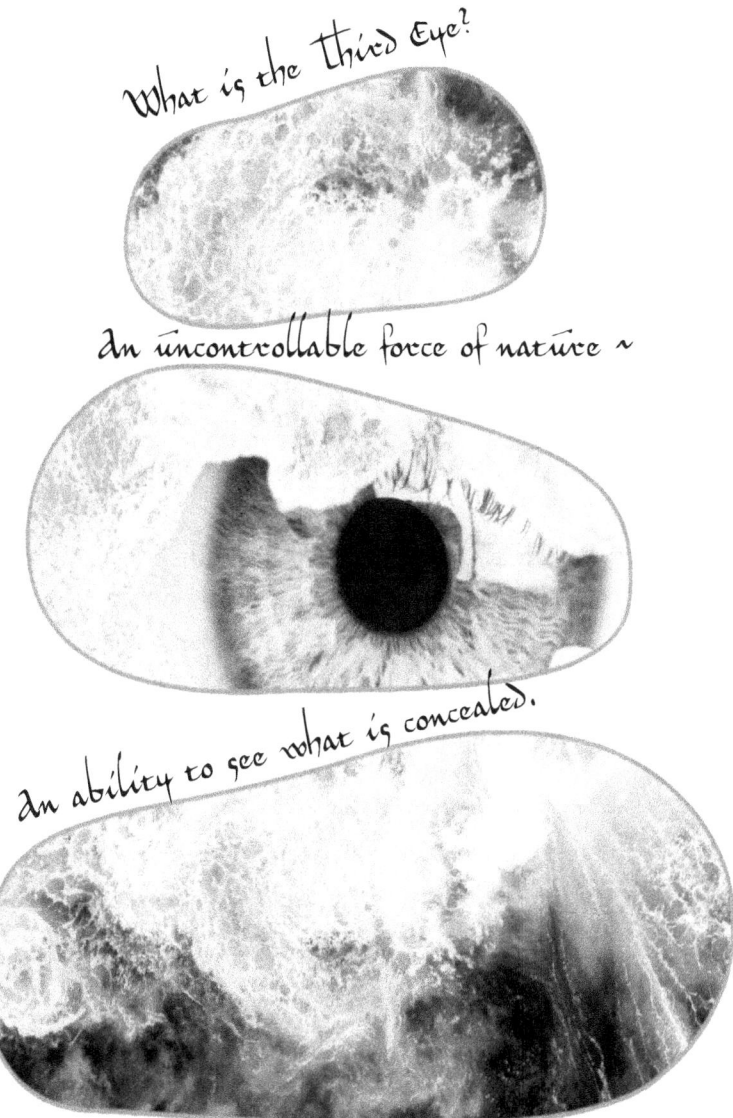

An uncontrollable force of nature ~

An ability to see what is concealed.

CHAPTER 16m

I make it to school on time, the Argo holding
the weight of not just me, but the thousands of
little bubbles of rain that have already begun to
fall and cover anything or anyone in their world.
This is one reason why I wear a ponytail 99% of
the time. My long hair pulled back is easier to
manage whether in a helmet, riding the Argo or
working the drive-thru. I roll past the main
entrance to Kau High, into the student parking
lot and into my assigned parking spot. The
Argo's cylinders disrupt the sound of laughter
and the scent of frothy morning lattes that fill the
atmosphere.

I practically tear the key out and slide it in my
belt pocket while slinging my backpack on. I
made it to school on time, but now I need to
make it to class on time. I truck it to first period,
and even though I am a minute late, the class
seems to barely be getting started. We don't
have to dress out this week. I can't express how
excited I am to finally have the opportunity to
sport the awkwardly long high school version of
P.E. shorts and scratchy shirt that I'm sure could
double as the heavy duty trash bags we use at
The Shore.

I step into the P.E. madness. Girls are on one side of the gym and boys are on the other, but we are both assigned calisthenics, and every student seems to have the routine down. I haven't seen Keyne yet. I'm not looking for him, but let's just say after yesterday, I haven't really forgotten him.

I look across the gym and notice the new boys' coach, the one with the butter yellow hair shouting instructions to the guys, then it dawns on me. His face is a carbon copy of the blonde kid who followed Keyne yesterday. The resemblance is undeniable. Obviously, there is an age and height difference, but they both have the same self-involved brusque look and mannerisms. I've become better at noticing more in a glance, even when I'm not looking for it.

The class begins to disperse, but a small group remains, and smack dab in the middle of them is Keyne. He is surrounded and based on the way he is smiling and talking, I don't think he minds. He just moved back to the island and already has more friends than I ever have.

This is a huge gymnasium, and I'd say there are at least 50 feet between us, but I can definitely see Keyne's smile. It's a nice smile. Well if I'm ever going to make a career in profiling, I'm going to need as much practice as I can get.

Keyne doesn't have the body of a jock nor of a gamer. He is muscular but not like the football players who throw back protein shakes like popcorn. He appears to be strong and lean, like the participants on those reality survivor shows.

FBI rule #5 concerns mirroring behavior. When we reciprocate what others around are doing, it shows a mutual respect. Keyne apparently has mutual respect for them. Or maybe they have a mutual respect for Keyne? I shake my head back to my reality. Calisthenics. I need to finish these exercises, so that I can have the body of a somewhat healthy person.

I make it through a fairly uneventful day, other than English class. We read a poem by a guy named D.H. Lawrence. I never thought one stanza could be so memorable. Maybe the bird in the poem was a Honeycreeper. Tomorrow, we research the poet and, Ms. Iona, my English teacher, says we will study many forms of literature, yet we will begin with the poem and end with it.

On my lunch break, I head directly over to the pale yellow foyer. I'm still obsessing over how soothing it is. I glance toward Fig's playground, and I see her immediately. The glint of her flaxen strands amid her cocoa curls bid for attention. Somehow, the braid I made her is still intact and whipping through the air as she rides the swing back and forth.

I feel a tap on my elbow and hear a voice behind me, "I think this is a nice view."

"Oh, hey," I say, startled. But this time, it's because I wasn't expecting anyone to be peering over my left shoulder.

"I'm not sure if you are aware, but freshmen are allowed to eat in the lunch room," Keyne says as a sweetly wry smile forms. The same smile I saw in the gym.

I laugh and shake my head, "I'm just checking on my little sister."

"Is this where you will eat lunch?"

I nod my head yes and say with a laugh, "Yep, hot glued to this very spot."

Keyne looks over my shoulder as I point out the kid who just face planted off the swing set. So now, Keyne is standing right behind me, peering over my shoulder as I lean in to observe Fig, aggressively willing her to her feet. A teacher runs over and plucks Fig's braids off her face.

Keyne sounds as surprised as I feel. "Ouch, sorry."

"Trust me. Fig is strong," I say as she gets right back on the swing. "She's also a stubborn little thing. Thanks though."

"Fig?" he ask.

"Makani. We call her Fig."

"Well, a couple of diving techniques would really help with her landings. I see that Fig loves the swings just like her big sister."

Certain that I am wearing a *what the hell did you just say,* confused kind of face, Keyne continues, "Remember racing out there at recess to see who got first dibs?"

I sigh, and I am about to apologize when Keyne interrupts, "I'm joking. You didn't race me. Us guys usually stayed on one side of the field, and you guys dominated the swings."

I laugh because I do remember that.

Keyne goes on, "We were in the same grade, not the same circle." He smiles, but this time it's a smile that says it's okay not to remember me.

"Still, I'm sorry I don't remember…you."

"Well, I do. No need for you to be sorry. Besides, we are kind of in the same circle now, wouldn't you say?" as he gestures with his hand to the large circular foyer we are standing in.

My eyes take in the sleekness encompassing us and back over to Fig, but I don't see her.

"Want half of my sandwich? It's not peanut butter." I give him a puzzled look, and I am certain my right eye is touching my eyebrow.

Apparently, this guy is a becoming a pro at reading my facial expressions because he answers a question that I didn't ask.

"I also remember you had to sit at another table...you were allergic to peanuts," he says as if trying to jog my memory.

I give a sigh of relief, but I know that I shook my head like a puppy drying off after running through an unexpected sprinkler.

"Sorry. I'm not trying to be creepy. I have a really good memory. It looks like your sister is better," he gestures toward the window.

Fig exits a small tunnel under the rock climbing wall and begins chasing a group of kids. The girl is never short of energy.

Smiling and reaching for Keyne's sandwich, I take a piece from half he offered. He looks surprised. Taking a bite, I think for a bit then say, "I'm not trying to be creepy. I was running late and forgot to pack a lunch." We both laugh, and in a glance, I notice FBI rule #5 again. Light hearted, mutual...mirroring.

And I thought it would be an uneventful day.

CHAPTER 17

Keyne and I walk together to the cafeteria talking about our upcoming History project, and somehow, the conversation shifts briefly to our teacher, Mr. Reddy. Keyne and I laugh because both noticed that Reddy has a slight twitch in his hips when he is writing on the board. It turns out we both have the same English teacher too, but not for the same period.

We are looking for a table when I hear a strong voice call, "Keyne!" It's the blonde. He's sitting with the same crew that was with him in the hallway yesterday. It's only the second day of school, but it's confirmed. They are wearing similar shirts. Long sleeve with pockets and discreet straps that look like camping gear could be attached at some point. Weird.

Keyne looks a bit distracted, the opposite of this mirroring I saw this morning.

"I will catch up to you later."

"No way," he says as though he's displeased, "save me a seat. I'll be right back."

In that moment, the blonde scans me quickly, his eyes a human metal detector. Keyne bends over slightly and appears to be explaining something to the blonde who doesn't look happy. Within a minute, Keyne is pulling another sandwich from his lunch bag and sitting next to me. He gestures for me to help myself.

"No thanks," I wave what is remaining from the half he already gave me. He then proceeds to dump out the rest of his lunch onto the table and a cookie I recognize is in his loot. He has torn off The Shore bag and broke it in half. I pull out a bottle of water from my backpack, noticing that he already is chewing through one half of the gooey, gooey greatness.

"How's the cookie?"

"Oh, my favorite," he says as the scent of the chocolate chips extends to my side of the table. "Have some," he offers.

"Oh, no thanks," I laugh. "I wasn't hinting. I was kind of fishing."

Now Keyne is the one with the puzzled look.

"I've already touched that cookie," I say. Keyne makes the funniest face and laughs, "Sorry, but I have to tell you - *that* is creepy."

Returning the laugh, I say, "My Tutu owns The Shore. We bake the cookies fresh every day."

"No kidding?"

"No kidding. When did you go by?"

"I didn't. Someone from home base will usually pick us up something to eat on their way back."

In a flash, Keyne looks nervous. I realize that up until this point, I have only seen a confident and laid back Keyne. FBI rule #8 zeroes in on action words and so will I, "Home base?"

"It's an inside joke, what we call home."

"We?"

"Lott is my cousin. Older cousin. Ever since mom passed, the family I have left is a bit protective of me."

"I'm sorry. I know how hard that had to be."

"It was."

Lord knows, I know all too well about losing family. Still, I'm uncertain if I should change the subject.

"Well, I should be working this week. Maybe I will see you there sometime?"

Because the school cafeteria isn't conducive for discussing family tragedy, Keyne goes along with the change in topic like a pro.

We spent the rest of lunch touching on topics like the Argo to his return back to the island. The bell rang in what felt like a heartbeat, and in sort of an organic manner, we began walking together when our conversation was interrupted by the blonde. Lott and a circle of friends or cousins or whoever they are, surround us. Lott wears a smile as though his patience is wearing thin, "Keyne, we should walk together. We've got a lot of Math homework to discuss."

Okay, that is either the lamest excuse I've ever heard, or Lott has clearly missed a few summer school notices because he is older and should be in a different math class.

"Keyne, I'll catch up to you later," I say emphatically to show the group that I don't care. But then I turn back and whisper to Keyne, "And by the way, I outgrew the peanut allergy."

He smiles. For a guy who was so talkative in our lunch conversation, he sure goes on mute around this clique.

Other than Lott, there are two other guys and two girls. All of whom model a pretty sort of seriousness. I realize that I've never seen any of them before. I'd remember their mashup of rock star meets lost kitten faces.

I pull over in the comforting school foyer to browse my news feed. I try to save the data on my phone because lately I've used a lot of it keeping up with the news, but I need to know if there are any new leads.

The baby that was kidnapped yesterday on the next island over was too close to home. I feel the anger growing inside me just thinking about it. If someone left the island with a kidnapped baby, it would be noticeable, so what does the mean? Could it mean the kidnapper is local? No way. They'd stick out like a sore thumb. Oh no! My stomach sours as a news headline reports another kidnapping.

Breaking News
A child was taken early this morning in the driveway of his family's home. A mother ran into the house for a backpack, but when she returned, the toddler was missing from his carseat. Police are looking for any leads.

The scrolling caption names the same island as the last kidnapping where the baby in the stroller was abducted. The suspect had to be watching! It's too small a window of time. This is surely going to cause mass panic. Maybe that's what it will take to catch the creep.

I try to resist the urge to look out the grand window with a perfect view of Fig's empty playground. *All the kids are back in class,* I tell myself. With a burning in my eyes, I think *what kind of evil person steals a child?*

CHAPTER 18

Just as I'm about to execute my pseudo-ballerina move to scan my I.D., a tug on my backpack startles me, and I'm certain my twirl could have broken a wrist. It's the blonde. It's only day two, but I can already feel that this dude isn't a fan of mine. So why the hell is he tugging me?

Lott. Keyne said his name was Lott. Well, Lott is giving me a hard stare while groups of students are badging in and shuffling along to class. So I ask, in a tone more daring than caring and definitely not in my helpful drive-thru window voice, "Did you need something?"

Lott takes a small step back, which tells me he understands that this is an uninvited meeting and with a slight smirk says, "Keyne has practice after school," he continues with counterfeit charm, "he can be hard headed sometimes, so if you could remind him that would be nice."

What the hell is this guy's problem? Examining his face, I see such a coldness, an emptiness in what would otherwise be a stoic, even handsome appearance.

"I'll pass it along, but in the future, text him or have him set an alarm. I have my own reminders to keep up with."

Lott smiles, satisfied with my answer and turns to walk away with his waiting groupies.

I bend and badge and the door to the corridor slides open. Keyne stands there. The passing time between classes is only 5 minutes, but I feel like time itself is standing still.

"Hi," Keyne says, smiling. "I thought we could walk to History together."

I stare at him briefly, trying to figure out how to tell him his cousin is an arrogant ass. I guess my stare isn't very brief because he notices that I am preoccupied.

"Did you see a ghost?" he asks jokingly. Snapping out of a fleeting daze, I give him Lott's message. Keyne appears surprised in a mindful kind of way as though what Lott says goes.

We read an excerpt in History from a Holocaust survivor then break into groups that Mr. Reddy pre-selected for us.

Keyne and I are in the same group. Mr. Reddy called the name of three others, but whoever the guy is, he is absent. Day two and already absent. The two others are girls who are having an entertaining conversation at their desk watching something on their phones.

"How about we begin, and they can just pick up when they're done?"

"Sure, but I wanted to tell you something if it's not too awkward?" Keyne sounds a little on the serious side. So, there is only one thing to do - not take it so seriously.

"Would you like to hold my elbow before you tell me?" I smile sarcastically, and Keyne reciprocates with a light laugh.

"I just wanted to say, talking to you was nice."

I can't help but look down for a brief second, trying my best to withhold a gulp. I know a lot of people from working at The Shore, but I'm not going to win any popularity contest, and if I did, it would be with Tutu's peers before my own. Sure, there are a few kids I grew up with on the island. Every year they invite me to their birthday parties, but by the time I turned 12, I didn't need the FBI rules to realize that they were pity invites. Their friendship wasn't because of who I am, but more about what happened to me. So I stopped going. As long as Tutu has Sam and Fig has Rob, I can spend more time searching for me.

So even if things sort of flowed with Keyne these last two days, the fact of the matter is - it's only been two days. He's a nice guy, though, who seems to get along with everyone.

We moved our desks side by side to work. He's close enough that I can smell the fresh scent of the outdoors on him. It's a combination of fresh cut trees and salt water. I want to ask him what deodorant he uses but figure the last two days have been weird enough.

"If you had told me that you are the one who saw a ghost, now that would have been awkward," I respond slightly laughing.

"Oh, the art of deflection!" Keyne laughs, seemingly motivated to get me to respond to his compliment.

"Well, if it makes up for not remembering first grade, yeah, talking to you was nice."

"Keep talking," Keyne playfully responds.

"We have an article to annotate," I say, deflecting again.

After a few minutes of annotating, I look over at Keyne, who is using a pen rather than a highlighter to make his notes. He is absorbed in the article, and I realize that from studying the Holocaust, to the loss of his mom and my parents that maybe he is searching for something more too. I can't help but wonder if maybe we are both searching for ghosts.

The next few weeks felt like they were the fastest I'd ever lived through, and an integral part of that was Keyne. I don't know how it happened, but somehow, we kind of naturally became lunch buddies. We have a lot in common, and it's a leisurely, at school kind of friendship.

Incidentally, time has flown by, and Fig already has her first school function. Today, I am to attend Ala Elementary to see her color project. "Harbor, you need to be on time. Just go with dad and me," she orders as I wrap together the last strands of her braids.

"Did you make my braids look like a goldfish this time?" Fig ask while she runs to the mirror, framing her face with her hands.

All I can do is chuckle, "Yep, perfect little goldfish."

"Please go with us? Dad misses you too."

"Rob," I say with emphasis, "needs to spend time with you as well. I'll meet you guys there."

"You are always running late."

"I will be on time. When am I not?"

Fig widens her eyes and tightens her lips, "When you take your shortcut."

I smile. This girl is growing up way too fast. Tonight, her grade is presenting their melting colors project; considering that it's taken them a month, it should be good.

I remember those days. Excited that mom and dad would both be at my school to see my work. They are just ghosts now. The kind that let you haunt yourself.

I'm going tonight to support Fig, yet Rob just returned from a two week exhibition. Even if we are some sort of odd family, Fig needs her dad to herself now and then, so I will ride solo.

Fig's mirror is so low, I practically have to kneel to put on my contacts.

"You don't have to wear those anymore, you know," Fig turns her gaze from me to the distant far left. This kid will do great in theater.

"Look, I will meet you there. Go say bye to Tutu before Rob arrives, or you are the one who will be late."

Fig gives me a hug and runs to find Tutu. When Tutu or I are not at work, The Shore is manned by a small staff that includes Sam. Aside from Sam, Tutu has about four other steady workers, but two of them; Lona and Guy, usually take part-time shifts due to school.

The big hotels have always been a rival to small island businesses. The large, fancy hotels have so many more amenities and are able to host huge, fantastic events. However, they made the news just a day ago, and it wasn't good. There was another kidnapping, and this time, it was from one of the nearby luxury hotels. My heart stopped when I read my news feed.

An Unsolved Mystery

The community is in desperate outrage as another kidnapping victim falls prey to an unknown predator. A three year old boy was strapped in the backseat of his family's van, asleep, when an unknown suspect pretending to be the valet drove off. No leads as of yet.

The family's rent a car was found dumped off the main road, the car seat straps cut and an empty car seat left behind. I squeeze my eyes shut. It takes a whole kind of different species to commit a crime like that. I can't imagine the terror that kid must be in, and as of today, none of the kidnapping victims have been found.

Nature on the island is sacred; abundant in lush landscapes, fruit and animals, but it lacks technology including traffic cameras. Whoever dumped the van and took the kid knew that there were not any cameras in the vicinity. Whoever or whatever it is can see us, but we can't see it.

The hotel posted a blurry image of what looks like a man running into the van. But the image is blurry not because of technology, but because of the fog. Fog is normal out here and can set in for days at a time. It doesn't affect my riding the bend. I'm used to it and can lay low on the handlebars to bypass the thickest parts. But the fog does some things very well. It can make your eyes play tricks on you, obscure everyday objects to look like monsters that don't exist sending chills up your spine. It can provide a sheer curtain of protection and keep hidden anything that wants to be invisible. Whoever is after our kids obviously knows this.

A month doesn't go by without one of the resorts hosting a large convention, wedding or tournament of some sort. Tourists attend from all over the world and The Shore gets a small percentage of that cash flow whenever visitors venture out and come across our quaint, less advertised beach. The latest kidnapped child was from somewhere in the states, and according to the news, the family had just arrived on the island for a convention.

The problem with how open our islands are is that some take advantage. We aren't overcrowded, yet what we lack in population, we make up with vast amounts of nooks and crannies, and densely packed forest, and lately, more and more have been infiltrated by homeless camps. I worry about Fig.

According to Tutu and Sam, these camps are filled with insane amounts of drug use. Sam says there are places for people to get clean, to get help, but too many people in the camps reject it. It's easier to feed off the people who replace logic with emotion. Sam says, "If people really cared, they'd balance their feelings with safety. Parents do it all the time."

Sam has children and grandchildren. They are all adults, and I don't think they have ever visited him on the island. Sometimes I wonder if it's difficult for a parent not to be able to speak to their kids, even if the kid is an adult. For all I know, Sam could talk to his family everyday in between flipping burgers, closing up The Shore and spending time with Tutu.

They go on a daily walk or shopping for the supplies The Shore needs. Tutu recently began ordering products online, but many cannot be delivered off the beaten path, so she and Sam often have to take a ferry to the main island to shop or pick up a shipment.

Luxury hotels line the main strips of the island, and their crowds often fill the larger beaches. From my spot in the clearing, I often can hear their party playlist dance along the air and see their twinkling lights skip across the ocean. Somehow, neither ever reaches the harbor. That section of the island is rarely used. But I doubt I would have been able to see the crime happen, the kid taken. The cliff is too far away.

I pull into the parking lot of Ala Elementary just as a text from Fig pops up. Of course, it's our sister emoji and even though I laugh, I know it's her way of telling me I better hurry. I see Rob and her walking in through the front doors holding hands. This puts a smile on my face. As I put my helmet in the storage of the Argo, I see Kau High. That makes me smile too.

Keyne and I also have a history project to present this week. Well, the group does, but Keyne and I did most of the work. He's a cool kid, and I've learned a lot about him. He's a busy kid too. He doesn't have a job like I do, but it turns out that he is a competitive swimmer and practices at least four days out of the week. Sounds exhausting just saying it. And that clique that always surrounds him is family and close family friends. All of whom are training on the same swim team. From what I understand, Keyne is only second to Lott. Lott hasn't warmed up to me yet, and what can I say, I am fine with that. Unlike the cool kid, Keyne, or like the tourists who come to the island looking for a new life, I'm just a local islander in search of my own. Also, I'm in search of my little sister's classroom because if I'm late for her presentation, she will never let me rest.

CHAPTER 19

The ride to The Shore doesn't disappoint.
Each curve around the bend clears my mind, the
path a giant eraser for anything that troubles me.
The Honeycreepers are hidden, and gray clouds
roll past the large trees, telling me a storm is on
the way.

Tutu reduced my shifts at work, but I plan on
picking up more hours now that I've proven to
her that I can handle the high school workload
and the drive-thru. My first report card was sent
home this week, and it made her happy. I think
my grades translate to her that I am safe, that
even on this road to recovery, I am taking care of
myself. She let me work the drive-thru yesterday
since business at The Shore has been great, and
Sam had to go on a fresh produce run. She
didn't want to be swamped and short staffed.

I arrive at The Shore early, and as soon as I
park the Argo, I can hear the beach music from
our little burger joint blaring out into the parking
lot. Each step I take into The Shore, I am closer
to the savory scent of fresh grilled burgers,
spiced fruits and seasoned fries. Perky customers
take part in chitter chatter while they chomp
down on their favorite grindz. Good food has a
way of bringing people together.

I have a few minutes before my shift begins, so I head to the break room to begin looking over my homework assignments. I try to organize not so much by priority, but by what I can take care of while manning the window. I toss Algebra aside. It would be wrong to go against tradition and not put that off until the last minute. History? Research the causes that led to Hitler's rise to power. We finished our class novel over the Holocaust and already presented one major grade. For our next project, the class has to combine the novel and our timelines to gather factual causes that led to the Holocaust. But I can answer it all in two words. Hateful rumors.

After reading the novel, I believe more than ever that had the horrible lies told about the victims been fact checked and condemned that maybe, just maybe their horror could have been preempted. Personally, it reminds me of drama that can spread at school like wildfire. It's traps you, making it hard to escape. I've seen some kids really suffer because of it. Hateful rumors cause real life problems, and that's why I talk to Fig all the time about staying away from the haters. Fig knows that our choices are our power, but I doubt that's the answer Mr. Reddy will accept for the entire assignment.

Keyne and I are still in the same group. He and I are doing the research, and the rest of our group is supposed to input what we find in a digital presentation. I can't do any of this at the window, so I return it to my backpack.

Keyne and I work well together and always seem to have something to talk about. I'm never bored when he's around. Maybe it's silly: maybe I should know the answer already, or maybe it's something that doesn't have an exact answer, but I'm still curious. How long does it take before you know someone likes you? As in more than a friend. Not that it matters. I like Keyne as a friend. I like that we can laugh together and talk about things of substance. Sometimes, it flows so well though that I have wondered if - and that's a big *if* - he liked me more than a friend, *wouldn't I know by now?*

Would he tell me? Would I tell him? I haven't had any genuine friends in so long if ever. What if what I really like is our friendship. The one thing that is indisputable, I like everything a bit more when Keyne is around. Ugh, high school needs to offer a class elective on *The Art of Romance*. Instead, today I will focus on the art of turning the drive-thru window of The Shore into my own personal, hands-on profile training. Detecting troubles in others allows me to put mine aside for a little while. I start toward the door to begin my shift, but I'm quickly interrupted by the local news.

Breaking News

Police report another abduction. A child was snatched from the swings in Coral Park while the mother changed the diaper of her baby in the car. The mother ran after the suspect with her infant in her arms screaming for help, but no one heard. A heartbreaking story.

Coral Park! That is only one island over. The report cuts to a live shot of the sobbing mom, "This has always been a safe place to play. I looked away for a second and when I looked back, my son was gone! I heard running and a car door slam! My son, my boy!"

The screen flashes to a blurred image, and the broadcast continues, asking anyone with information to come forward. Holy cow! The mom was able to use her phone to get a picture. But it's too blurry. A blue swish is in the center of the image among gray and orange colors.

I pace our small break room which is actually a cozy living room space Tutu calls our break room. My heartbeat is comparable to that of a race horse after its final lap. For a fleeting moment, I look from the worn tan couch to the wall, where a picture of The Shore's opening day is hung significantly crooked. Hoping to distract myself from the fact that the suspect struck again, I head out to the window to begin my shift.

"Hi and welcome to The Shore. How can I help you?" I'm distracted by the report but manage to let the words make it out of my mouth. I hear giggling followed by, "Hi, Harbor!"

I recognize the voice. Annie is about 5 years old now, and I've been serving her family for a couple of years. Her parents always roll down the window no matter which new car they're driving to let Annie retrieve the order. They currently own a blue truck. I'm lost in thought, but try to be as courteous as possible, "Hi, Annie. You started school this year, didn't you?" Annie ran with that question and starts a story before I can stop her.

"My teacher is nice. I have a new lunch kit, but guess who is in the class next door to mine! Harbor? Guess," Annie squeals in delight before I can play the game with her, "Makani! Hasn't she told you yet, Harbor?"

"Of course she has. That is so cool."

I smile as I hand her the 3 teal Shore bags. Their order is always the same: 3 Shore burgers loaded, 2 Papaya shakes, 1 Alea fries and a water bottle for Annie.

"Ma Halo."

"Ma Halo, Harbor!" Annie's voice trails off. It's nice when the regulars appreciate me, but right now, I'm so unsettled that all I can do is think of those kidnapped kids.

The intercom breaks through with another order ready to be given, and Tutu taps my shoulder then takes off my headset. She notices that the report frazzled me. I hand over the headset as Sam walks in with the produce and a bouquet of flowers for Tutu, "Do you gals need anything?"

The two of them discuss the menu and then both peek over at me with a concerned look. I head back to the break room thinking about the kidnapped kids. They must be frozen scared, out there with a stranger, confused at why their family hasn't saved them yet.

I grew up hearing locals brag about our island. Not just about the natural beauty and our rich culture, but compared to big city life, we have always been a safe haven. We didn't have the dangers of the concrete jungles. Apparently, that has changed. Little kids are being torn away from right under their parents noses. My back pocket vibrates, and I pull out my phone to scan the text.

I have practice, so putting my phone away for a couple of hours. Research ltr?

My heart is breaking for the missing kids. If I were forced to pick something positive in this tragedy, I guess I'd say, I'm relieved to know that my heart still works.

Fog can set in for days at a time.

It can hide what doesn't want to be seen.

Whoever is abducting kids - knows this.

CHAPTER 20

The sun is still at its summit on the ride home. Tutu made me leave work early, so I plan on taking my time riding the bend. Within what feels like minutes, I pull in and drive through an entrance that is ironically the perfect size for the Argo. Once I am on the opposite side of the gateway of rich forest green bramble that has not given into the approaching season, the familiar feeling of peace; my own little sanctuary grabs hold of me. My clearing.

A storm is brewing. Wasn't that breaking news, too? Dark clouds fill the far distance, but the sun isn't quite ready to depart and attempts to pierce the harbor in the skyline ahead. The big hotels are still bustling. Their music travels over the sea.

The ocean knows when a storm is on its way. Water splashes back and forth, thousands of little games of patty cake, while larger buckets of water propel past the rocks to seize the sand it wants, only returning what it doesn't. I pop open the lid to the hidden trunk of the Argo and take out a rock I found outside The Shore the other day. I've been holding onto it, found it the same day as the kidnapping from one of the big hotels on a nearby island. I wasn't paying attention and almost tripped over it. A person needs to be careful out here. My tennis shoe somehow caught the rock, causing me to stumble. My heart stopped because I thought I accidentally came across a Samoan crab. That would have been a dangerous step because I prefer to keep all my toes. Walking over to the escarpments edge, I take my seat on a barely visible patch of grass that I've worn in and can feel the temperament of fall. I gently place the rock in my collection.

I've looked over this edge so many times. A thousand-yard stare. From the highest point, where I sit, it's easily a 75 foot drop straight into the Pacific. There are multiple smaller precipices, protruding out, jagged, each one solitary, only big enough to hold one person at a time. To the foremost left are the glittering hotels, and further right, the beach, a haven for the monk seals and large boulders.

The rage in the ocean mimics how vicious I'd become if someone laid a hand on Fig. I screenshotted the article with the kid's picture. I wonder if screenshotted is a word. I look at the picture the family provided the media and push the image to expand the innocent face of a small boy. Maybe the bastard kidnapper is choosing kids based purely on size. It's easier to kidnap a smaller kid. The little boy is missing a front tooth, and his red hair matches the scattering of freckles on his nose. The sun on the island will do that to a person. Put a smile on your face and create freckles that were never on your family tree. Most islanders, like myself, have darker tones in our hair and skin. Tutu moved here decades ago, and even though I inherited her fair skin, meaning tanning is almost impossible, my Hawaiian side gifted me my dark hair.

I scroll over to pictures of my parents and decide to pull the picture of us out of my belt. I like the way the vintage photo paper feels in my hands. I know that at one point in time, both of my parents probably held this picture, held me, and I guess that's why I keep it so close. Looking at it, I can't help but think how some of us have had so much more stolen than others. I stopped asking why long ago, but when the kidnappings became closer to home, I realized a huge problem is *not knowing* why. Everybody deserves answers. I slide the picture back into my belt and begin to lay my phone on the ground when it vibrates. It's Keyne. Oops, I forgot to text him back, but I have a feeling he will totally understand why.

Whatcha doing?

I punch in, *Sitting.*

Where?

My spot

Is it invitation only?

I smile. Keyne and I have definitely become friends, so he's heard about the bend many times. But I've never invited him. I've never invited anyone. Fig invites herself.

I thought you had practice?

It was cut short. Doubt we can get much research done tonight tho

Invitation gif

Hands up emoji

How do I find you?

I think to myself, *you already did.*

I'll meet you at the old gas station

Clapping hands emoji. Happy face emoji.

I wait inside the corner gas station. This old gas station has been here for as long as I can remember. It's a two story, faded blue, grey washboard house turned gas station. The owners live upstairs and could win a cuteness contest. The Ferencz's are elderly, but they both still run the register, and Old Man Ferencz can usually be seen stocking the shelves with supplies. Natural resources are abundant on the island. Fruits and vegetables are never in shortage. But candies and canned goods can often run low. So, this gas station is a staple. I stop here all the time to re-fuel the Argo. And as old as it is, it is set against an ever-changing, amazing back drop of tall mountains that echo giant mounds of coffee.

I see Lott and a car full of his sidekicks pull into the parking lot. Keyne steps out, and the large, square, glass window of the gas station frames his every move. Keyne walks toward the gas station door, and I see he is wearing a black dive suit. He must have finished a swim and came straight here because his hair isn't fully dried. The soft waves that are normally folded in layers atop his head are now plastered on his face and forehead. The dark green t-shirt he is wearing looks like he quickly tossed it over his dive suit. Keyne is much taller than the car they drove in. Midway to the store door, he stops to read a text and rushes back to the small brown SUV that his friends are packed in. A cane or maybe a walking stick is fixed on his right thigh, and once at the car, Keyne slips out the long, sharp object and hands it to Lott, who was waiting for its return.

I wouldn't say I've ever formally met Lott. In the beginning of the school year, he would give me deafening glares. But as the seasons changed, my friendship with Keyne grew. Lott became used to seeing us study or eat lunch together and presumably felt I was a benign enough friend. So these days, I rarely earn even a glance from Lott. Besides, Lott is usually so preoccupied with his groupies that as long as I don't interrupt the practice they have after school, my existence seems to bore him. The joke is on him because I am not the kind of person to suffocate anyone. No way, not ever. I see a lot of people come through The Shore, and some look like they could use an escape plan on our menu.

I don't interfere with anything Keyne has going on, and he doesn't impose on my schedule either. As it turns out, the new blonde coach is, guess what, Lott's dad! He is also somehow related to Keyne and his swim coach. Keyne hasn't given many details about his family life. Since his mom died, I get the feeling his dad resorted to being a full-time workaholic who spends every waking moment on their new business. Supposedly, it will be a new wave in gyms. It is supposed to be a new concept in the next generation of fitness. Keyne's dad wants to break ground sometime next summer, so he has the Fam very busy coordinating and nailing down the logistics. Those matching shirts I noticed on day one of school are going to be part of the uniform, and Keyne's dad wants the team to start the trend. Other than that, Keyne doesn't speak a lot about his father. He was young when his mom died, and his dad, who already traveled a lot for business, became even more distant, choosing to work rather than parent. Maybe that's part of why we connected immediately. Absent parents seem to be the trend neither of us asked to follow.

Yeah, I practice the art of analyzing people, but I also respect privacy. I don't bombard Keyne with the hundreds of questions I have.

"Is this place abandoned?"

In the blink of an eye, he's walking around the store with me.

"Old Man Ferencz just went to the back. That can take a while. If I am in a hurry, I knock really loud on the counter."

"Rude?"

I nudge him with my elbow in his rib and can feel the dampness through his dry shirt. "His hearing isn't the best these days."

We walk around for a few minutes. Keyne has never been inside, and he is impressed by the old store. We pick up a couple of snacks, and it isn't long before we are on the Argo. We make a joke about Keyne needing to hold onto my elbows for the ride. Part of that laugh is nervousness on my part because no one other than my kid sis has ridden with me around the bend. No one but Fig has been on the back of the Argo, and a couple of months ago, I was a kid who's #1 hobby was getting lost in the faces of others. Now, I'm getting lost with a friend, and it feels good. And the fact that this friend is wearing Fig's helmet ups the mood a few notches.

Keyne says something, but with the churn of the Argo around the curve, the sound of the ocean, and the fact that my helmet is partially covering my ears, I didn't hear. I know he's done speaking because the warmth on my ear, that feeling that can only accompany a whisper, stops. I want to pull over to find out what he said, but we are almost at the bend, and it doesn't seem like it's an emergency.

Once I park and look at him, I get one last laugh, "I've only seen Fig in that helmet. What did you say back there?"

"Oh, you didn't hear?" he responds with the same sly smile I see practically every day in lunch.

"No. What were you trying to tell me?"

Keyne puts his hand to his chin and says, "I guess it got lost in the wind."

"Okaaay. Whatever. C'mon, let me show you the clearing." This time, I grab his elbow. I pull him into the hidden clearing. Now I'm the one wearing the sly smile. I see a bolt of shock flicker in his eyes as he smiles and follows me to the edge.

CHAPTER 21

An hour breezed by. Keyne and I talked about school, the people at school, the music we like and our dead parents. He confided a little more about his mom. One of the last memories of her was in her hospital bed. He said he replays her last words in his mind every night. I sigh to myself, hearing the grief in his voice.

"I was too young, naive. I wish I would have known to hug her more. I regret it. But there's more. She said something before she left. Actually, she repeated it, and it haunts me to this day that I couldn't understand her."

"It's okay if you don't want to tell me. I understand how personal it is."

"No, I want to. It helps me keep her alive."

Tell me about it. I think of the dreams I have of my own parents.

"She was so sick, so every breath she took mattered. She spent much of it apologizing *for the accident,* repeating for me to *find the accident. Find the accident.*"

I understand the solemn memories of lost parents and ask, "Have you spoken to your dad about what accident she could have meant?"

"I'd get more answers from a blank page."

I told Keyne I was sorry, and we both sort of moved on to other subjects including what we want to do when we're older. Keyne isn't sure.

"Why not use what you know?" I ask.

"What careers involve swimming? Funny, Mr. Reddy asked me that too," Keyne says taken aback.

"Reddy?"

"Yeah, you were on the computer, and he asked our group how we would escape Nazi Germany. I said I'd get to the first body of water and swim away."

"Assuming you could get to the Baltic or North Sea, uh, that would be a deadly journey."

"It's easy to sit here and talk about it, I know. We would have been starving and weak, but I know I could take on the water…"

"You forgot scared. Fear and being alone in the dark waters, I don't know."

"The dark doesn't bother me."

"Ever swim in a dark ocean, hiding for your life?"

Keyne tilted his head toward me and raised his eyebrows, "I was raised to be a swimmer. It's what I know, but I'm not sure if it's what I'd do, you know, for a living."

"Yeah, Mr. Reddy must have gone around to everyone and asked that question."

"What did you say?"

"I understood it as him asking what we - we as people *could do*."

With a slight shake of his head and a smile, Keyne says, "Well of course you did."

"What does that mean?"

"Just that you interpret things differently. I like that about you."

Taken a bit off guard, I turn toward the hoopla from the big hotels across the water and back to Keyne, "I do what?"

"You always see past the here and now, past you," Keyne says nudging me, "What did you tell Reddy?"

"Ignorance."

"You called our teacher dumb?"

"No, dummy. I told him the only escape was to destroy the ignorance and the hateful rumors it caused. Unjustified hatred kills. Besides, ignorance doesn't mean dumb."

"What does it mean then?"

"Not knowing any better."

Keyne looks out toward the water.

"So if there is unjustified hatred, do you believe there is justified hatred?"

I think of the kidnapped children and nod, "I told Reddy that if people saw, truly knew, how important it is to think for themselves, know the facts, then that is real freedom, and maybe we could have prevented the Holocaust."

Keyne turned his gaze back to me as though he was deep in thought, "You're right. The Holocaust started long before the genocide with propaganda."

"Exactly. A bad person and their propaganda are only as powerful as the number of people who follow blindly."

"That is scary. You know, how freedom can be stolen from right under our eyes? Something we need to be aware of."

"Not only aware of. Beware of."

We both look out over the waters, our bright mood changed to sullen, "Hey, you weren't taking a grade on that, were you?" I nudge him, but he wears an intense look and flicks the strap on his dive pants.

"I saw you run back to the car. Was that a cane you had?"

With a light laugh, he transfers his attention to the ocean and I take a closer look at his pant leg. A thin mesh pocket, approximately 5 inches long is stitched on the right thigh of his dive suit. It's either a loop or a strap, and it held the pointy staff he was carrying.

"Would you believe it's an early Halloween costume?"

"Halloween. The day you can be anything."

"What would you be...on the day you can be anything?"

I ponder his question, yet there is no sense entertaining a question that will never be fulfilled. *A daughter again.*

"I'm headed that way, to be anything I want. Why limit it to one day?" I say with a sobering smile.

"Ha-ha, of course."

"So what was that thing? An exclusive, limited edition light saber?"

"You don't know how I wish. No, it's a tool we use for night swims."

"A tool?"

And with a wink and nudge, Keyne says, "Yep. It helps me not be scared of the dark."

I give him a look that clearly says his explanation confuses me. Keyne laughs and says, "Seriously, you wouldn't believe me if I told you. Tell me about your future. What do you want to be?"

"Someone else is an expert at deflecting?" I tease, "I have some ideas."

"*Like?*"

"I have this trick that helps me when I'm confused."

"Okay, grown up, tell me."

"I can't. I can only ask you," Keyne positions his arms across his bent knees, smiling as though he is ready to play.

"What makes you smile every time you think of it and makes your heart beat a little faster when you're near it?"

A large wave crashes against the shoreline boulders and in the same beat, Keyne heaves. His chest is full and rises with his sigh. He slowly turns toward me and gives a quiet smile, "Such sound advice."

"Does that shock you?"

"Sometimes I am astounded by you, Harbor Haukea." Keyne looks down, pulls on the empty mesh strap on his pants again and allows it to snap back in place before slowly lifting his head back up and toward me as though he didn't mean to say those words. He used my middle name. Searching for my own words, I am not sure how to reply. I want to ask him what he means, but he interrupts the brief silence, "So tell me. What does the fierce and sound Harbor want to be when she grows up?"

Looking out over the cliff, the sky is starting to turn to dusk as I ponder his question. I remember being young and dumb. I remember eagerly wanting to follow in my parents footsteps. Then an evil man murdered my father. The little kid that thought justice was cool became drawn to tracking the bad guys. In a heartbeat, I had to grow up. The desire to stop evil is in my blood because it took my blood.

Aadya did all she could to keep the details of his death hidden, far away from me. I often felt like there was more to her motive than being a protective parent. I sometimes feel like she knew the truth and she was scared of it. She kept me away for a reason. Either way, she's gone and I can't demand answers. But, I can refuse to be afraid of the truth. And that reality will either propel me into a career I once thought I could love or keep me far, far away from it.

I feel a softness on my chin that startles me. I start to swat it away then realize it's Keyne. His fingers are gently lifting my head up and out of deep thought, "Checking on Harbor?" Our eyes meet, and I swear his emit light, the same light I saw that first day in the dark gym hallway. The colors in the atmosphere cast such a hue on the clearing, on him that I see for the first time the intensity in his eyes. Eyes that seem to consume anything in their path. Deep, dark turquoise mixed with a vibrant green. They are encircled by a dim gleam of blue, but the center, his pupil is so dark, it's pitch black. I see a lot of people through the drive-thru, lots of faces and lots of eyes, but none like his. Unless I'm imagining it, they glow softly. Shaking myself back to reality, my movement allows his hand to naturally slide away.

"Your heart beat and smile test?" Keyne reminds me.

"Riding the bend."

He smiles and pats my elbow, "For the rest of your life?"

"For a long time."

"Why?"

"I'm not trying to rush. Besides, growing old isn't growing up."

Our glances connect, and he opens his mouth as if to say something then pauses and says, "See what I mean? Way past the here and now," but he is interrupted by a text and wraps it up with an agitated, timid smile, "It's Lott. I've got to get going."

Still a bit shocked at the touch of his hand on my face, I nod to confirm that I understand.

"Sorry, I didn't mean to be too invasive."

Uncertain if he means about serving my question back at me or for holding my chin, he goes on, "My dad keeps us so busy with building the business, it's hard to break away."

"Yeah, I can imagine."

"Lott is the oldest and so it's even harder for him to take time to drop me off."

"You said Lott also swims?"

"He's tough in the water. One of the best."

"Compared to who?"

Keyne lifts his phone up toward the water then turns his long arm around, his phone pointed toward us and takes a picture. He shows me the selfie that includes the both of us and points to himself in the picture, "Compared to that dude."

He definitely makes me laugh. Keyne stands up and walks up to the edge of the cliff. He holds his hand out to me while walking back to help me up, "Here, let me show you."

"I've looked over the edge before."

Keyne laughs, bypassing my hand to pull me up by an elbow, "Okay, answer this question…"

I shrug with my hands signaling for him to bring it, "Ask."

"Do you know what it takes to enter the deep waters?"

We both stare out over the water. I slowly shake my head, "Tell me."

"Can I show you?"

I smile and shake my head again.

Keyne turns his full body toward me and takes both my hands. *Uh, are we about to dance?*

"It's a technique we use in diving," he says as he pulls my arms outward, "The goal is to make the smallest splash possible." Keyne places my right hand on top of my left hand then he slides my fingers wide open, "This hand has to be as flat as possible because it will make the opening into the water."

"Am I doing it right?"

He seems pleased and nods yes, "It's called a Rip Entry."

"Rip Entry?"

Another text interrupts.

Ugh, how do we always run out of time.

"You've gotta go," I say.

"It's Lott. Do you want him to pick me up here?"

The thought of that makes me jump. The clearing? My spot? No way will Lott pick him up here.

"Nope, I'll drive you back to Old Man Ferencz's station."

Keyne shoots Lott a text and puts on Fig's helmet. It's funny every time. Ready to board the Argo, I stop short of placing my helmet on my head and turn to Keyne, "You never answered the question. Your heartbeat and smile?"

Keyne pauses for a moment then points out over the cliff, "Harbor, do you know why I don't want anything to do with swimming when I'm older?"

I shrug slightly and shake my head no.

"I'm not interested in small splashes."

Satisfied that is the closest to an answer I am going to get from him, I affirm, "So we are both gonna bum around?"

He laughs and says, "Smiling bums."

"Are you ever going to tell me what you whispered on the ride in?"

I'm a bit stunned as he reaches toward my face and gently moves some hair caught on my lips. When dusk sets, the wind has a habit of flurrying across the cliff, so I'm use to hair in my face. But I'm not used to the weight of someone's hands touching my skin to help clear away the strands.

"It's something that puts a smile on my face," he says faintly before using my elbows as anchors as he takes his seat on the Argo.

CHAPTER 22

I shut down the engine before the Argo can embark on the long grassy driveway to my house. Every now and then, I take a moment in the quiet to remember when it felt more like home. I wish that the old saying had a sequel. *Home is where the heart is.* Really? And when the heart has been ripped to shreds, then what?

Aadya and I moved in with Tutu when my father was murdered. The white wooden planks of this solid, one story home welcomed us with open arms. It isn't very big. It's the size of a quaint bungalow, but it's cozy. A heavy duty hanging oak swing is perched above a spacious, hardwood porch. The porch is spotless and could easily double as a dance floor. Tutu insists that it stay clean and free of any objects ever since Fig tripped over a small planter when she was learning to walk. Her fall broke the planter in pieces and made a huge gash on her head that required stitches. Fig reminds us regularly how many stitches she has. *I have as many stitches as I do teeth!* Her hands immediately go to her hip in sassy mode when I respond, "And it is proof of how hard headed you are." The kid knows I'm kidding. Her scar is concealed beneath tons of swirly, rich brown hair. Seems like scars always find a way to hide.

I remember being so young. I'd lay a blanket out on the porch and do my homework while Aadya was at work, and Tutu cooked dinner. That was a lifetime ago.

The house is surrounded by tall palm trees that have not begun to shed and mid-sized shrubs sprouting bright, coral flowers that aren't ready to give in to autumn. And they've grown with me, tall and ready for change.

The air is crisp tonight as stratus clouds suspend themselves above the house. The walkway is gravel that was laid down a few years ago by Rob, but the driveway was formed by years of the Argo wearing in the sod, and tonight they are both gently illuminated by the rays of the moon that seem to have melted right into the path that leads up to our house. Four large pumpkins sit atop each one of the wide front porch steps. Tutu let Fig hang string lights shaped like candy corn over our shrubs and helped her hang a wreath shaped like a witch flying past the moon on our front door. I added an incandescent ghost. He's wearing an orange bow tie that glows, but the best part is that it looks like he has a dollop of whip cream on top of his head. I laugh every time I see it because he isn't much smaller than Fig, and she wakes up with her hair in very similar form.

Even with All Hallows' Eve creeping around the corner, even under the moody blue sky poked by a pitch fork allowing millions of stars to shine through, our house somehow projects innocence. The garage waits for the Argo, and the night is silent other than the sound of the nearby ocean. I see the warm glow in the window of Tutu's room. I know she'll be worried about today's news. Another kidnapped child is horrifying even if it didn't happen on our island. Pangs streak my stomach thinking about the missing kid. All I want to do is thrust my body onto my bed, maybe punch my pillow a few hundred times, but I know that won't do anyone any good. Hiding under nightfall won't help anyone either, so I put an end to my hesitation and slowly back The Argo into the pitch-dark garage.

When I walk inside, the distinct scent of Tutu's citrus shampoo fills the air, and sure enough, there she sits in her bathrobe waiting for me. Soft lighting escapes the two bell shades of our candlestick lamps that keep watch on each end of the couch. Tutu lights up when she sees me, "I made you a snack. Take care of your homework." And with a kiss, she is gone. She didn't give me a chance to respond, but that's because she said what she needed to. Her bedroom light flickers off. Her work days are long. I know she is tired but stayed up for me. I'm glad she is relieved that I made it home safe and that she wants to show me that she loves me. As soon as I step into my room, I see the tray of crackers, cheese and cup of hot tea she put on my bed. Good thing I didn't keep with my original plan to catapult into my pillow. The last thing I need on top of a day like today is to get burned by hot tea.

No sooner do I open my laptop when a Facetime from Keyne pops up. Within a ring and a half, his face appears on my screen. He changed and is now wearing a bright blue t-shirt and a huge smile.

"Hey, stranger."

"Ha-ha. I know it's too late to research, but just checking that you got home okay."

"Yep, thanks."

"I should be thanking you. The bend was awesome. I see why you go there."

"Let's catch up tomorrow,"

"Is everything okay," his eyebrows knit in concern.

"I'm sorry. Didn't mean to be rude. My mind is on that kidnapped kid."

"Today? Here?"

"Close enough. What kind of monster does that?"

Keyne sighs and squeezes his face with both of his hands. It reminds me that just a little while ago, one of those hands was on my chin. And for a little while, I forget about agony.

"Hey."

"Yeah?"

"I'm glad you found the bend today."

His smile returns, this time a bit washed out. Before he logs off, he says, "Try to get some sleep."

My screen goes black, and I whisper to myself, "That's what I'm scared of."

When I was little, Aadya taught me a trick, or rather, a technique to help with my dreams. She used to say that sometimes bad is just bad, and there's no changing that. She told me I had a choice to do something called re-focusing. I remember her voice like it was yesterday, "It forces us to remember that bad isn't the only thing in control."

The way it works, I don't have to ignore how I feel; all I have to do is recognize it. So, instead of crying about missing my father or being angry, she helped me focus on the wonderful memories we had and told me stories that helped keep his memory alive. This strategy doesn't take away pain, but it slowly helps to replace it. And it all worked just fine - until Aadya also went missing.

Working the drive-thru window at a very young age has been one of the best distractions for me. It's a fast paced job. There are a lot of parts to juggle, so it's taught me a lot. I've learned more about people than I have food. For the most part, we get plenty of happy customers. Sometimes, they are celebrating a birthday or winning a game. We get friends and family and customers who just want to sit and relax while munching on some first class, tasty grindz. Yet we also see our share of drama, and the one thing that all drama has in common - the fastest way to be wrong is always trying to be right.

I've witnessed too many arguments working the window or in The Shore. Each time a kid is arguing with his parent or a couple is fighting, or two friends get into it, the person forcing their will is usually on the losing end of the battle.

However, I've seen a lot of good too. Pet owners will drive through with small dogs on their lap and drive away feeding the pup one of Tutu's papaya shakes. Teammates pull through pumped up before a game to get a quick snack. Tons of busy customers eating for success, multi-task phone calls and emails, popping handfuls of Alea Fries. And I've also witnessed the gross. I see tons of kids doing everything from picking their nose to biting their feet. Ugh! Grown ups flossing and putting on deodorant is also common. And I see my share of the sneaky. Kids sitting in the backseat are the professionals. Unbeknownst to their parent up front, kids roll their eyes, mock their parents, play video games when they're not supposed to be on their phone or mumble under their breath while their parent talks to them. Some parents lecture, some scream, and some don't seem to know their kid is in the car. I don't know what's worse though; when I hear a kid curse and yell back or when the kid seems not to care one iota about what the grown up is saying. I've seen parents trying to speak to their kid while the kid completely zones out. In moments like that, I bite my lip to prevent myself from yelling out, "Life is short! Make some goddamn eye contact!" Those kids don't know the numbing, empty silence of Ha'alele. I'd give anything to make eye contact and smile at my parents just one more time.

Sure, sometimes I only see or hear part of the tense exchanges. Other times, I'm the lucky one to see an unrestricted series play out, a witness to the many disturbances. And drama is not my thing. Maybe that's why I often don't fit in. It's not society's fault. I am the one with the hang ups.

The definition of trauma is based on each individual's perception. I think about what we are learning in History this year. The death marches at Auschwitz. The Holocaust has made me even more aware of trauma verses drama.

I doubt the Jewish kids who were separated from their families and forced into grueling labor before marching to the crematorium would have wasted a millisecond on hallway drama. Or worse, social media drama. And as woeful as it is, my father was murdered. For all I know, my mother was too. I have to live with that. So I try to stay vigilant and not frame problems in the moment. I frame them against a bigger threshold. What constitutes real trauma? I think about the Holocaust and the scale is pretty high.

Oddly enough, I really am agreeable with most people. I am the one who chooses not to engage more than I need to. Maybe if disaster hadn't struck my family or if my parents were around today, my innocence wouldn't have eroded so soon. I wouldn't have to grow old with the *me, myself and I* attitude. Too late; it's a part of me, buried in my soul. But, spending time with Keyne today was a nice departure from simply growing old. It was a reminder that I am not completely shattered and maybe...I still have a chance at growing up.

CHAPTER 23

The storm hit full blast this week with winds reaching 30 miles an hour. It's too dangerous to ride the Argo, much less ride the bend. So, I car pool with Tutu or Rob to The Shore, which feels weirder and weirder the older I get.

I'm so used to driving the Argo alone, so I do my best to join in the car ride conversations. I'm usually on the other end of these, an eyewitness into the hundreds of microcosms I see through the window of The Shore. Passersby would ordinarily not notice The Shore, even though we sit off the main route in and out of the island, not far from the intersection that takes tourists to the big hotels. Unlike the vertical wall of rock where my clearing rest, The Shore sits atop a high, sandy peak tucked into the dynamic Hawaiian landscape. Even with modern technology, many sites in the region are still very secluded. Thankfully though, you can't seclude the light. It finds a way to break through.

Coral and teal beams of light from the neon sign above The Shore cast upon the height of surrounding Koa trees and bypass the massive trunks, rolling down the sandy ridge, illuminating enough of the highway below that it makes us impossible to miss. I could easily drive the Argo on the smooth pavement of the main road, but I would never pass up riding the bend. The bend is not just a shortcut. It's a retreat. And I miss it.

Luckily, the rain has finally turned to a light drizzle. By next week, I should be fully emerged back in my routine. But for now, I'm sharing approximately 50 inches of rolling cubic space and doing my best to not appear rude. I'm not only missing the bend, my mind is consumed with the child abductions. Preoccupied with disappearances for most of my life makes it difficult to break free from wanting the facts. Makes it difficult not to look moody.

Rob picked Fig and I up from The Shore after my shift. The three of us are going to Fig's school. Tonight is the Spooktacular, and luckily, the rain is holding up above Ala Elementary. Once we arrive, tunes of Monster Mash and other Halloween classics welcome us as we follow Fig, who is spiraling in and around the food and game booths set up outside her school.

Fig couldn't decide on her costume. She was torn between an ice princess and a butterfly. So, she dressed as both. Out on the islands, only the tippy tops of the highest volcanoes will feel the snow. But butterflies are a frequent sight. I wonder if Fig's costume is a combination of what she wishes she could see and what she

166

sees all the time. Aren't we all drawn to what we can't have? Then I remember the FBI Profiling rules. Kids cannot be profiled. They are too young. So, Fig's costume mash-up and that of the hundreds of wild animals trampling every inch of the Spooktacular weren't chosen because they are crazy little brats, even though sometimes they act like it. They were chosen because they are curious little twerps who are learning to be themselves and navigate all the tempting choices put in front of them.

A person that can be profiled and needs to be is the kidnapper. Where are the missing kids? Who is taking them? And why? The victims are so young, so they can't weigh much. The kidnapper wouldn't have to cold-cock them because one large hand can cup a kid's mouth. Is this why kids are being chosen? No matter what the answers are, they can't be good.

On a day like today, I would normally have a blast in the late night drive-thru. Halloween can bring out some sinister behavior, but I only worked half a shift. I didn't get to see the entire array of creepy peeps that normally set the scene. The Shore was busy though, and the drive-thru had its share of traffic. I easily swiped close to a hundred digital fingerprints. Hungry families picked up food for their festivities, and friends dressed up and grabbed their grindz before their parties. Sliding credit cards in and out speeds up the transactions but cuts down on my profiling time. I can think of very few customers who still pay in cash. Mr. Boring does. In fact, he swung by today with the same bland, plain order. In place of digital fingerprint, he leaves a spine chilling effect. Who doesn't make eye contact? Well, actually, Lana fits the no eye contact policy too because she's always on her phone. She called in tonight probably to go party, and I doubt she's attending Ala Elementary's Spooktacular. Guy and Sam filled in for us.

Fig had a blast, and now, the four of us are driving back home. After Pumpkin Ping Pong and a Marshmallow Toss, Fig used her sharp baby teeth to win first prize in the Root beer Apple Bobbing contest. Her prize: a useless goldfish. Fig could have been a vampire for Halloween, and we would have saved money on a costume. Goldie, on the other hand, is a bit dull on the gold, making me think he was once someone's classroom pet who coincidentally became a prize. Either way, the floating nugget is on the road home with us.

You would think the ice princess butterfly would be tired, but no. Fig is talking her dad's ear off, which gives me a small window of mental downtime. I miss the breeze in the bend. The last time I was there, Keyne was also.

Fig is going on and on about the mean kids at school. Rob reassures her, "Makani, stay busy, ignore those kids. They don't know what they are talking about." He should know by now, Fig is a persistent little thing, "Well, is it true? Is there a giant lizard that lives in the ocean? Does it take little kids?"

Rob is from the island, which makes him kama'aina or locally born. So are Fig and I, but since our Tutu and my dad are from other countries, sometimes I am looked at differently. Wearing contacts helps to blend my more northern features, but I am just as much a part of the island as any other kama'aina. And one thing that is true for those of us born here, we know every story of Aina, our land. However, it's Rob's responsibility to explain island lore to Fig, and she knows it because innate to all islanders is kuleana. Translation, *our right to know*. All of us know the stories of our land, no matter how far-fetched. I should wish Rob luck.

"Makani, it's just a legend."

"Tell meeeee. I have the right to know."

"And if you don't sleep tonight? Huh, Harbor, what do you think? Should I tell her since you are the one who will be left with any aftermath?" Rob teases with a laugh.

I re-enter their world for a brief second and attempt to look amused, "Sure, tell her. What she imagines will only be much worse."

"Okay then," Rob gives in. I know this story by heart. Fig, on the other hand, is transfixed.

"Long ago. A long time ago before the big hotels and planes, our islands were untainted. Our ancestors shared the land with the animals. We respected one another, and this allowed us to co-exist for centuries. But it is said that some violated a Heiau, an underwater ancient worship site. Well, this Heiau was sacred to the animals who possessed it. They were called the Mo'o, the lizards your friends speak of. The trespassing angered the Mo'o..."

Fig sat in complete silence, glued to her seat. A rare feat to say the least, "Dad, tell me. I know you're not telling me everything. What did the lizards do when they got mad?"

"Tribal chiefs made a solemn promise that their people would not invade the Heiau ever again. But for the Mo'o, the damage had cut too deep. Animals are not like us. They could not accept this truce."

"So what did they do?"

"Began to pray," Rob hesitates, and I doubt he wants to finish the rest of the legend. It gets a bit dark. Giant water lizards vowed vengeance to feed and seek the souls of islanders. And how they sought them - well, there were *a few* parameters. Turns out, even vicious lizards can abide by some morals. The Mo'o didn't prey on random islanders. They sought humans with ill intent, those who could be as fiendish as the Mo'o themselves. Then they marked them.

Every islander at one time completely and totally believed this. The Mo'o had full reign over islanders who chose evil over good. Any islander who willingly chose to cause harm to another was subject to the wrath of the Mo'o. And what did the slimy suckers get in return? Souls. Life lines to walk the island again, freeing them from the isolation of the sea. According to legend, ancient tribes permitted this behavior once a year and agreed to not hunt the Mo'o. The water lizards that are said to have survived the Cretaceous now held a new purpose. When the Mo'o took an evil soul, our ancestors believed the monster was also drawing out poisons from Aina. To them, it was a win, win. I'm glad I wasn't born in the dark ages. But even as a little girl, I understood the story of the Mo'o to be a grim lesson about making better choices. And what better prop to play the role of a giant sea monster than one that is in constant view? Monk seals. The legend of the Mo'o has been terrifying kids on the playground since *forever*. Even today, when I watch the monk seals from my clearing atop the cliff, I am amazed at their velocity and swiftness. Nestled in their resting place among the jagged screes, their huge bodies can easily be categorized as clumsy, but I have seen how smoothly they enter the rough waters like a massive fleet, they control the ocean. They make propelling through millions of tons of water look easy. The habits of their world parallel ours and long ago, these seals had to be even more humongous. They could easily be mistaken for gigantic sea creatures.

Rob gives an appropriate finish to the story; enough to quell Fig's curiosity, "For many years, long, long ago, ancient priests watched the stars and the movement of the sky to foresee the return of the Mo'o. Islanders, like your great ancestors, allowed the land to be foraged for only one day each year. They knew that the Mo'o would enter onto land for one night, taking their share of the harvest, just as islanders took from the sea. And they all got along happily ever after."

But Fig isn't having it. She's old enough now to know that not every story can end in happily ever after. She's not going to let him off the hook until she feels she knows the entire legend. How else will she be able to educate every other kid on the playground? Rob can expect to be answering these questions for a long time.

I drown out Fig's inquisition. The drive-thru was extra busy today, and I'm tired. It happens that way when storms are on the horizon. More people want to stay dry and order on the go. This means the herds of families that normally stop in, drive through. My left arm sleeve is still wet from opening and closing the window.

Fig did her homework in the diner, making sure to finish in time to go to the Spooktacular. She likes to take up the corner booth closest to the front register where customers order. The same booth she colored in as a toddler; the same booth she waited for our mom to magically re-appear in one day, to slide in next to her and finish the picture. Now, I think she chooses that booth primarily because she is nosy. She likes to hear what people say.

Nowadays Fig lays out her backpack, pencils, and scatters of worksheets, dividing her time between staring at other families or sending me text messages full of emojis and doing her homework. The homework part takes her 30 minutes max. She's a smart little kid. I can't blame her for watching people. So many interesting characters stop into The Shore, some regulars and some one-stop shoppers. And the drive-thru is even more eventful. I can't help but peer into the cars. I like to practice my profiling, but frankly, some people are simply batshit crazy and that's its own puzzle. Profiling not required.

I'm trying to teach Fig to be discreet about staring at people. Sometimes I even have to remind myself to do the same. Each car features a mini movie trailer in motion, and no two scenes are alike. I read in dad's FBI books that there are only eight basic emotions. They act like a portal because all the other hundreds of feelings are filtered through the basic eight. Well, I guarantee that I have witnessed all eight multiplied by hundreds of directors' creative cuts working the drive-thru. It's a nice perk when surprise and joy occupy a car, but when fear and sadness rear their ugly heads, I force myself not to turn away. Not to turn a blind eye. I want to know what I'm looking at. Who knows? One day, I may need to look for it.

Sometimes I wonder if the best way to prevent crime is to monitor the drive-thru window. So many of the simple moments in our lives happen on a car ride. Yet not every car contains simplicity. Still, I try not to stare. I try to profile. But when I work the drive-thru at night, profiling takes on several twist and turns. Nightfall conceals, so it's not always about what I see. It's about what I hear.

The Shore drive-thru is open late on the weekend, and the after-hours customers are not the carloads of families that visit in the day. Instead, orders are from tourists leaving a concert venue or those who aren't ready for the fun to stop. Often, the police and paramedics stop in for a quick refuel. And then there are the hitchhikers and transients that make a pit stop off the main highway for their late night rendezvous.

Sounds that creep in through the window during a night shift don't require it to be Halloween to be eerie. The wilderness camouflages hungry animals whose ferocious grunts and groans are muffled only by the crashing of the ocean. And the always invisible wind shows itself through a tirade of gusts through the window, off-set by residual big band music that fills the air from one of the nearby fancy hotels.

Fig and I are now home, a normally quiet spot. But not tonight. The sound of splashing interrupts my thoughts, and this time, it's not coming from the ocean. The carrot stick Fig won at the Spooktacular is dipping up and down in its round fish bowl, making a dripping water noise. Guess there's no escaping animals that want to play a game of psychological manipulation.

Chapter 24

"Don't you love him, Harbor?" Fig practically squeals over her prize goldfish. Maybe I should join in her and Rob's conversations more often. We'd have a cute puppy instead of a floating tangerine.

I fluff my pillow and catch a glimpse of the orange ball flapping it's spiky fins. I'd swear its eyes were bulging. With each happy step Fig takes, a splish and splash of water travels up either side of the glass bowl, causing even a fish to seem uncomfortable. Apparently, it is a task trying to stay in the bowl. Welcome to the family, Fishy. We are both going to have a learning curve.

"Fig take him or her to your room, please."

"Fine, but I want you two to get along."

I stare into the bowl and see the fish is idle, staring straight ahead. Is he dead already? Then almost as if to taunt me, the little troll dives right, and I jump back. Fig thinks this is hysterical, and with a hug, I push them both out of my room, "Goodnight, squirt."

"I hope the storm doesn't scare him," Fig says as she is leaving my room.

"Try putting his fishbowl by the window to see if the lightning will strike him," I smile.

"Harbor!"

"I love you. Now get out. Your little turkey is safe and sound. Go to bed." Hesitantly and with squinted eyes, Fig exits my room, and I rush to shut the door, which means nothing because she will still burst in at her will. But it's late, and she will probably conk out soon. Finally alone, I pull out dad's old box. Maybe there is something in here to help me profile the kidnapper. To find out why. Why that monster steals little kids.

The cover of the box has warped with time. I've learned to gingerly jiggle the top loose. Dad's profiling book is on top, "Motive and Forensics." I slide my hand across the dark green cover. It's soothing to know that my dad used this book. It's heavy, and as many times as I've searched it, I've barely made a dent in the information. I'm decent at the FBI profiling rules, but it isn't enough. I need more. There is a dirtbag stealing kids, and no one seems to have a clue how to stop him.

Using voice control on the remote, I turn on the TV to masquerade the sound of the pages I'm flipping through. If I don't, Fig will hear me. I've made her believe that I fall asleep with the TV on. I'm not proud of it, but sometimes a little white lie serves a purpose. Okay, I actually am proud of it. She's not an easy kid to fool.

I sift through the book and back to the table of contents. All of this looks like it applies. Using my finger as a marker, I scroll the various names of different sections in the book. My eyes land in the middle.

"Types of Crimes and Who Commits Them"

Bingo. Involuntarily holding my breath, I tear through the pages. The chapter is divided into sections: Terrorism, Corruption, Organized Crime, Sovereign Nations, Major thefts, Kidnapping and Murder. And Nestled between Major Thefts and Murder is my guy. Can you have Bingo twice?

With trembling hands and the sounds of the news and distant thunder in the background, I turn to the subsection on Child Kidnappings. It says here that the location of the young victim is usually a key factor, and abductors often know the victims. No. I dismiss that notion because some of the kids were visiting neighboring islands. I turn the page to read the remainder of the section when the words jump out at me.

Traits of a Child Kidnapper:

1. Often socially isolated
2. Seeks power. The act of kidnapping puts them in charge.
3. Narcissistic behavior
4. Males, often between 30-40 years old
5. Deviant past relationships particularly with women
6. May or may not have a criminal history

This guy has definitely stayed under the radar. A flash of lightning in my window signals me to put the book away. I've had a long day and need to ponder what I read, but it sure would help if the police could obtain a clear picture or description of the suspect. I was so focused on reading that it wasn't until I put the box back that I noticed the news. And then my heart really stops. Another kid was kidnapped! I rewind the broadcast. OMG. There is evidence, and this time, I won't need the book to help. I recognize that car! Then a thought hits me like a Mack truck. My mind is transported in a split second from the kidnapper's car frozen on the screen to where I remember it from. I know that car and saw it today! Today in the drive-thru!

My stomach lurches as I try to call 9-1-1. My hands are shaking, causing my phone to slide off my bed. *Calm down, Harbor!* I don't want to alarm Fig, but I need to let Tutu know. Taking a closer look at the screen, I need to verify that it's definitely the car from the drive-thru. I press play to hear the reporter.

Police need your help identifying the owner of this car wanted for questioning in the abduction of a 4 year old boy taken from an outdoor school function. A Boo Bash gone bad as a night of festivities has left one family devastated. School cameras captured this photo.

I feel weak in the legs. This kidnaping happened tonight, on our island! Fearful that I might faint, I have to call the police, but what do I tell the them? I pay attention to faces, people and cars, so even though I don't know the guy's name or where to find him, you will just have to trust me? I fumble my phone again.

It didn't happen at Fig's school, but it occurred closer to home than any of the other kidnappings. The image on the TV shows a car with a blurred license plate, but the color of the car is undeniable. Silvery, ice blue. It's a 4 door, older vehicle. A pencil sketch of a man wearing a hat is on a split screen next to the car. But the sketch is not of the man's face. It's only of his backside, walking away. I can't do much with a pencil sketch, but I am certain I know the cold, blue car. Most of our customers have regular drive-thru or stop in schedules, even if they don't realize it. Not this guy. The person who drives that car doesn't have a regular schedule. He has a regular order. One water, no ice, a Shore burger, meat only, no Shore sauce.

Get a grip, Harbor. Call the police! It's late, but I doubt the police department has closing hours. I need to call now so Fig will not listen in.

I finally get through, and a steady voice answers, "9-1-1, what's your emergency?"

"The kidnapped boy. I know the car! I saw the car tonight!"

"Calm down, ma'am. Are you referring to the Boo Bash kidnapping?" The 9-1-1 operator's voice is unwavering and clear like she's in the room with me and not on the other end of the line trying to make sense of my gibberish.

I balance my voice, "Yes, that's the one. I work at The Shore, and I took an order today from a man driving that car."

The operator thanks me and gets my name and location. She says she will send an officer out right away, "Stay put."

I pace my room a bit and for some reason place my hair back in a ponytail before I wake Tutu. She has been rudely awakened too many times in the middle of the night by officers of the law delivering bad news.

I'd swear I could hear the wagging caudal of Fig's fish making loud thumping noises in his water. But it could also be my heart. I knock on Tutu's door.

"Harbor, calm down. Relax. Are you sure you have seen this car?" Tutu slightly moves imaginary strands of hair out of my face and looks at my eyes to assess whether or not I may finally be having the break down they've all anticipated.

"Yes. I'm sure!" I firmly reassure.

"Okay, I will call Rob to stay with Fig. Let's meet the police at The Shore," she must have determined I'm sane and reaches up to kiss my forehead before she gets her keys.

A knock on the break room door makes me jump up. I run to open the door and what I see makes me gasp. The officer is speaking to Sam with his back turned to me. But the uniform shoved me back in time by a few years, to a picture of my mother when she wore the island's uniform, just before she disappeared.

The officer heard my gasp, "Hello, I'm Officer Lam. I understand you might have some information for me."

"It took you so long. There's a kid missing." Oops. I said that in a more quarrelsome tone than I meant. Sure, I'm frustrated about a kidnapper on the loose, but I also realize that part of my angst is also about my anger for Aadya. The uniform added another layer of emotion, and I know my cheeks are red hot as my accusation slipped out into public earshot.

"I'm sorry, Officer Lam," I invite him into the break room, "I feel so badly for the family of that little boy. For all of the missing kids."

"It's okay and normal to be distressed. Let's begin by talking about what information you have," he pulls out a pen and a little blue notebook from his front shirt pocket.

I explain to him that I work the drive-thru window and remember that car. "I recognize the blue color and squarish shape of the rear." I refrain from mentioning that I also read my deceased father's FBI books and make it a point to profile our customers.

"I'm positive that car came through here this past summer and today. I know because he orders the same thing all the time. Well, lately he's been adding a cookie," I gasp again, "Do you think the cookies are for the kidnapped kids?"

Officer Lam seems to be jotting down what I am spewing, but tilts his head when he hears my question, "Let's not get ahead of ourselves. Can you show me the security footage?"

"The security footage? You're looking at it." He raises his eyebrows, and I clarify before he thinks I'm a loon because I'm sure I sound like one, "We've never had cameras because we've never needed any. I'm the eyes of this place."

He looks disappointed and asks if I can recall anything else about who was in the vehicle.

"The driver is a light skinned man. He doesn't look Hawaiian. This may sound weird, but I've never seen the front of his face. He stares straight ahead and doesn't seem to want to socialize."

"Okay, if you think of…" Before he can finish, I reflexively jump up, pointing my hands at Officer Lam, startling him. Before he reaches for his taser, I quickly explain what I remembered, "He only pays with cash!"

Officer Lam appears relieved, "Any chance you still have the money he paid with?"

I waste no time. I'm out the door and at the register asking Tutu.

"I took it out and put it in the money bag in my office," Tutu says, and I could kiss her. I run back to her office, which is a corner of the break room. Tutu and Sam follow me, and she retrieves the money bag for the officer, "We only go to the bank to deposit actual cash once a month since most people pay with a debit or credit card these days. Times have changed, and I have to keep up with the big hotels," her voice trails off, and all I want is to find the scum who did this.

Officer Lam explains that he will need to collect the money bag to be fingerprinted with a special machine, but often times there are overlapping prints or stains that interfere with the print lifting.

"Harbor," Tutu asks, "do you remember what that man paid with, and did you give any change?"

"Yes. He gave me a ten dollar bill."

Tutu beams then looks at Officer Lam. I'm wondering if she realizes this is not an appropriate time to smile, but she quickly adds, "Harbor is an excellent observer. Trust her memory. If she is saying she saw it, she did."

I'm so worried she is going to begin to tell him the story of The Third Eye and she'll be the one who is arrested, but luckily, Tutu tells the officer that she lifted the money tray in its entirety and dumped the contents of the slots into the money bag.

I want to jump up and down for joy, but I think I've used up my allotment of spontaneous movements for one day.

"Since I didn't count the money, officer, and there wasn't much in the money bag to add it to, maybe we have a good chance," she smiles as though we are all part of the same detective agency. Officer Lam returns her smile and says he will contact us as soon as he has information. Then he turns to me, "Anything else you'd like to add?"

"I don't know if this is important, but each time I've seen him, he wears a long sleeve shirt. Not many people wear a long sleeve shirt in the summer."

"Harbor, dear, what color was his shirt?" Tutu ask, but I draw a blank. I can't seem to recall, and before I can admit this, Officer Lam reassures me that it may come to me later, "Besides, right now we have to focus on finding the car. We'd like to find the driver also, but we are only certain about the car that was involved." He closes the little flip notebook with all our information and slides it back into his uniform pocket. It reminds me of my dad's old notebooks.

I feel a bit of relief to know that maybe we can help save the missing kids and stop a coward from hurting anyone else. Sam and Tutu wait in the car while I walk Officer Lam out, and as he is in mid-reverse, I hold up my hand and wave to get the officer's attention. Lam rolls

186

down his window. For a split second, I imagine my mom and dad as young rookies. Officer Lam seems young, maybe 24 years old.

"Be careful out there, and please, let us know if you find out anything new, please? No matter how small."

"Okay, thank you. Will do. You and your grandmother have my number," he raises his eyebrows and says in a firm voice, "If you remember anything, call me."

Officer Lam drives away, and I return to my heightened state of emotions. On the drive home, my mind whirls and the rain picks up again. *Think of the bend. Erase the emotions.*

Safe, sound and settled back at home, a loud strike of thunder advances as my head simultaneously hits the pillow.

CHAPTER 25

It's been over a week, and I haven't heard back from Officer Lam. The dreams have returned. And Fig still has a dysfunctional goldfish for a pet.

Each night since I called 9-1-1, I've fallen asleep to the sound of the scaly butterball stirring in its mini toilet bowl at an unnaturally rapid speed. Burying my head in the pillow doesn't work. Thank God for the storm last night.

The downpours come and go as winter approaches. I can still hear the rainfall outside my window. As peaceful as it sounds, as much as it makes me feel at home, my mind drifts back to the nightmare. I've been staying up late reading about child kidnappers, and that task has instigated the old nightmares. My alarm is set to go off in a few minutes, and every minute counts. I need these few extra moments to sleep, my dark room cozy compared to the thoughts that raced through my mind last night. Ha'alele made an appearance, and even in the dream, it made all the guest appearances desperately hollow and internally empty. That's a feat even in a nightmare.

A large animal, an angry, bloodthirsty animal in the unrelenting sea and an evil person waiting in the dark, staring at the crowds of people were the main characters. Then there was me. I was also in the dream. I was the dark. Present but invisible.

Other faces shifted in and out of the darkness, the dark that was me. Above the darkness, above me, the rough waters of a black ocean became the sky. Only I and the angry monster could see in the dark. All the others, even with their eyes wide open, were lost.

I need to stop falling asleep reading these old books, yet my dad wasn't one of the faces in the dream. But Aadya was. She made a brief debut and spoke in fragments, screaming at me. *Wear the belt! Pull yourself out!*

The alarm jolts me up, my eyelids still heavy. I want so badly to shake free of the nightmare but know that it doesn't work that way. I have to process the dream. I take the rubber band off my wrist and wrap it around a length of my hair, not so much a ponytail but more of a way to pull enough of my hair back to counteract the headache.

Tutu says the dreams are meant to make me see what can't be seen. She said some people are born with a vision to see into the minds of others, into the future. To see beyond what is in front of them. She calls it the Third Eye. I've asked her a thousand times, "How can you be certain? Who's to say it's not another freak legend?"

Instead of a logical explanation, it became a separate nightmare trying to figure out what she meant, "Some will know, and some never will."

She said people like me are aware at a young age, but others often dismiss us as having a good imagination. Or that what we put forth is simply coincidence, "Therefore, as they grow older, it's easy for those with the Third Eye to cast their powers away, but not you, Harbor."

I've heard this hundreds of times, yet each time, I feel more confused than the first. I've thought about banging my head against a wall to make that so-called Third Eye pop out. Today, I settle for placing my head in both hands with my morning ponytail hanging over. What good is this Third Eye, this so-called power, if I don't know how to find it or use it? All my eyes are going to be today *is red*. With my head in my hands, I listen to the finale of pitter, patter and realize that it sounds like it's inside my room. My head practically swivels around toward the window. Worried that I may have left it open, I reach over and find that the window is dry and perfectly sealed. Although, when my fingers almost knock over the cold bowl, I see that the sound of water is coming from Fig's paddling meatball. She left her goldfish in my room. When does that kid sneak in?

"You're gonna be late, Harbor. It's time change. Did you set your alarm?" The sound of her voice startles me as I realize she's been in my room this entire time. Maybe *she* causes my nightmares.

Exiting my closet with my clothes, she tosses an outfit on the bed with my phone. The kid leaves me speechless. I pick up my phone and see that the battery is dying, "Fig, take your fish, or I will use his bowl as my tip jar," I smile as Fig gives me a *you wouldn't dare* kind of look.

"His name is Wasabi, and he doesn't appreciate his big sister speaking like that."

We both laugh because despite all the pain we've had in our lives, that's what we can do for each other.

"I've got to get ready. You ride with Rob, and I'll see you later."

I'm on the Argo in minutes, racing a light drizzle to school. If I'm tardy again, I'm in for a lecture. I don't want anything to interfere with swaying Tutu into letting me drop out of school to work every shift until the kidnapper is caught. Okay, dropping out is a bit extreme, but I must persuade her to give me more work hours. If that asshole goes through our drive-thru one more time, I want to be there. Maybe he doesn't leave a digital fingerprint, but there is still a way to track him if I can somehow get his real ones.

I park the Argo and pop a stick of gum in my mouth. I pleasantly walk into the front office to collect my tardy slip. Morning announcements have begun. Turkeys, pilgrim hats and burnt orange and rust colored dried florals line the office. My phone vibrates, but it will have to wait. Phones are not allowed unless they are being used for specific class assignments, and since I already have enough attention due to the tardy, the text will have to wait. A handful of students have gathered in the office, also late, and we are given the universal hand signature for quiet until the announcements are finished.

Tickets for the Winter Dance will be on sale starting next week in the cafeteria. Now please join me in the saying of the pledge.

Towards the end of the pledge, it dawns on me that the dance is a perfect cover! I can use it to persuade Tutu to give me more work hours. I'll tell her I'd really like to go and that I want to buy my own new dress and shoes for the dance.

"With liberty and justice for all," I proudly declare with my hand over my heart, pleased with my idea. The attendance secretary asks my reason for being late because she has to select one of the boxes on the yellow tardy slip. I'd like to tell her to pick any box she likes. It won't matter because I guarantee night terrors, murdered parents and criminal profiling are not options on that checklist. Instead I blurt out, "Car trouble," and smile politely as I'm handed the unnecessarily large, neon tardy pass. Walking out, I can finally sneak a peek at the incoming text. It's Keyne.

Shocked emoji, "Absent?"

I smile but can't text back because I need to hurry to class. He will see me race into P.E., and we usually sit together at lunch. Also, we've been partnered in History class since the beginning of the year. Every now and then, he eats with Lott and their group, but I'd swear it looks more like a meeting than eating.

I really enjoy working with Keyne. Not everyone in the class nor in our group pulls their own weight. It's clear to everyone, even Mr. Reddy, that the two girls he paired us with are more occupied with their social media lives to put any real effort into a group project. And the other guy in our group is absent more than he is present.

Lately, when Keyne stands close to me or when we work together, I'm kind of happy. I guess it's true friendship, and if I ever start dating, I want it to feel like that. Positive. Life is too short for anything less. Sorry, not sorry.

Before Keyne though, I never really thought about friends or what kind of person I wanted to date. I've been occupied with lost family members for so long that it never occurred to me to think about new relationships. Maybe it's something that you're not supposed to think about: maybe the whole dating thing happens naturally. It's not that I'm ready to date. It's not even like I've thought about dating Keyne, and *it's not that I haven't.*

When he doesn't have practice or when I'm not working, Keyne and I have a good time together. I think. But it's when we hug hello. Something happens, and I have a hard time ignoring it.

It's a toastiness. An energy like peeling off a sheet of fabric softener from clothes that are fresh out of the dryer, and the zing that runs up the arms before tantalizing your whole body. The soft warmth that makes you inhale and take a big whiff of the hot off the press threads. The fresh electricity that zaps your hands before you want to pull the load close and cuddle right up with it, throwing them on. And during those fleeting friend hugs, I can't imagine that Keyne hasn't felt the energy too.

194

It's like everyone else is a dirty pile of laundry, and Keyne is a basket of freshly laundered duds. Even though I can't ignore the sensation, I don't go around advertising it. I'd be mortified if Keyne thought I liked him as much as I do clean clothes. Still, sometimes I wish I really could summon that Third Eye. Then I'd see if he feels the static cling too.

And Keyne hasn't ever tried to impose himself on me. Over the years, I've been aware of a crush or two that thought I was their perfect match. In those instances, people can be extremely pushy! They naively seem to believe that because they like you, you are obligated to like them back or that you are somehow required to respond to their teen affections. Nope! Sorry, not sorry! I see teens play Ring Around the Rosy with their partners more than we did on the first grade playground.

But talking to Keyne is always easy despite the most awkward way in which met. Well, as Keyne reminds me, the way we reunited. But something happened the other day. We were in the middle of a conversation and walking to class as we normally do. Keyne reached for my elbow, which has totally become an inside joke, yet in the moment while I was returning from my bend and badge, his hand slid down my arm, causing him to accidentally hold my hand. It lasted a whole second, and it was definitely unintentional, but it felt...powerful. Either way, we are both busy with school and our family obligations. All we may ever have is static cling.

When I look at other couples though, whether at The Shore or at the grocery store or even in our packed school hallways, I see a lot of unnecessary turmoil. My life has had too much loss and stolen love, so I won't entertain unnecessary drama. And I see others, just when they crack through one barrier like dating who they want, it isn't enough. There is a bigger pressure. Knowing when to stop dating, knowing when the relationship isn't a positive one. So, I keep my head clear. Although yes, sometimes when I'm at work, I wish Keyne would stop by. And yes, I have *briefly* wondered if he ever thinks about me.

When we do talk, I'm not nervous at all. But when I reflect on our conversations or when I read an incoming text is from him, I catch myself smiling. Every time. Maybe I am the one hiding it well. Maybe the only thing that's real is what we hide.

My phone vibrates, and this time, it's Fig. The little kid gets all of 5 minutes a day of free technology time, and she uses it on me.

Wasabi's new name is Ember. Don't call her Wasabi anymore. It's Ember.

Oooh, I'm so relieved Fig clarified that. I want to have the right name of the chunky fish I imagine flying off in a gust of wind. Turns out, that makes me smile too.

I need those shifts. One eye, two eyes or a Third Eye, I'm not going to see anything if I don't work the window every chance I have.

Only I and a large

angry, soul ~ thirsty

Monster could see in the dark.

CHAPTER 26

English class was eventful. I turned in the rough draft assignment I wrote. Ms. Iona had us write an ending or new stanza for a poem by D.H. Lawrence. It's titled "Self Pity." Lawrence's words: *"I never saw a wild thing sorry for itself. A small bird will drop frozen dead from a bough without ever having felt sorry for itself."*

My experience:

For sorrow, even in the coldest winter,
is Breath from bough to
unchartered swell
and the wild things know this well

I think it fits well.

Thankfully, no group work in this class. All solo. It's been a pretty smooth day. Before I head to lunch, I decide to pull over in the grand foyer and call Officer Lam again.

No more delaying. This suspect is prowling too close to home. Enough is enough. The abductor may not be working alone. Whoever he is, he's picked up the pace on the kidnappings. If he comes through The Shore again, I will be there. And if the car matches, I am going to get a better description. I don't know exactly how, but the police need more information than just a blue car. Whoever this phantom kidnapper is, it's time for him to be haunted.

According to dad's police profiling books, the kidnapper won't be able to lay low for long. He wants control and will keep seizing kids until he gets it. The kidnapped children are feeding his internal struggle.

Tutu has told me time and time again that I have an internal struggle. She said when people like me most need help, we refuse to invite it in. And that's when either help or hurt forces its way in. She says it's why I have headaches and the nightmares, "It will take time to learn how to read your dreams."

"What if I don't want to learn to read them?"

I remember her answer like it was yesterday, "Those born with vision will never have the choice *not* to see. The only choice will be what to do with what you see."

I use to make jokes, "Most people have vision, Tutu."

She'd laugh right back and say, "Not the kind to see what is *beyond them*. The kind that is held in the mind. Learn to use your intuition, Harbor. It will protect more than you."

"How?"

"Even if you don't understand now, you will one day, and you only prolong confusion by not trying."

WTH? This is my real internal struggle. Not a murdered dad and missing mom, but my loving yet crazy grandmother and her cryptic messages.

As much as I love her, I really do think Tutu is the one who is confused. C'mon, the woman is inventing a chopstick burger to reveal by next summer. It's going to be her newest way to deal with *her* internal struggle, competing with the resort hotels.

As I look onto the playground of Fig's elementary, Officer Lam finally picks up and before he could say much, I broke in.

"Hi, this is Harbor Ludovic."

"Oh, hello, Harbor. Haven't had a chance to touch base with you. Is it okay if I stop in today to speak to you and your grandmother?"

"Of course. Did you want to come by The Shore, or would you like our home address?"

"I will go by the restaurant. Your grandmother has a winner in those papaya shakes. How does 5 P.M. sound?"

"Great. I will plan my break for that time. See you then, Officer Lam."

Ending the call and stuffing the phone in my bag, I can't help but think of my little sister as I look at the empty field, vacant swings and barren slide at Ala Elementary. No recess due to lightning, so the playground is abandoned, but the swings still move eerily back and forth as though happy children could never desert them.

Staring into gray quiet is welcoming. Last night's dream gave me a massive headache that is playing tag with the pain in my eyes. I remember now that Fig was in the dream, running on the playground, her long braids like syrup in the wind. She ran towards the edge of the playground to a steep cliff. My cliff. And out of the muddy ground, a huge, snake-like creature appeared. It was vicious and snapped at Fig. In that moment, the dark shielded Fig and traded her for itself. This made the reptile hiss loudly, and the dream paused like an old photo frozen in time. And for what seemed like an eternity, I was in a stare-down with this blood thirsty creature. Its slimy mouth drooled and unlocked. Opened wide, it was ready to soak its two rows of triangular, pronged, serrated teeth the color of chicken broth into me. But it couldn't because I was the darkness. You can't bite into the darkness. The toothmarks won't show.

I lay in bed terrified, unable to open my eyes. I forced myself to look up from the monster's decrepit fangs and then I saw her. Aadya stood there, and the thought of her paralyzed me. I woke up shaking uncontrollably, but not from the outside. I was shaking internally, my own heartbeat louder than the thunder. Now, how in the hell do I make sense of that?

A tap on my elbow startles the memory of the nightmare and halts my processing. It's Keyne. In an attempt to shift gears from the flashback of the nightmare, I ask, "So, how'd you know where to find me?"

"You are only in this same spot every day at the same time," he laughs.

"You are a master detective," I half-laugh.

He gives me a *what's going on* stare, and I see concern in his eyes, "Where's Fig?"

Keyne is more animated than I am, and his facial expressions have grown on me.

"Can't have kids struck by lightning. No recess today."

"So, is everything ok? Thought you were gonna be absent?"

"More like absent-minded. Remember that police report I told you about?"

"Yeah, the kidnapped kids?"

"I called the officer back just now. I can't accept that there aren't any updates."

"Yeah, with cameras everywhere, that is odd. By the way, I have extra swim practice, but do not worry, I'm going to do my end of the project…"

Keyne's voice begins to trail off because in a matter of milliseconds, a memory rushes through me like a strong current. Maybe I was so caught up in the anger of the last abduction. Maybe all the newness of the school year or my homework had me so utterly pre-occupied that I only now remembered that the suspect had on a shirt I recognize.

Thin slivers of sun rays have managed to escape the looming storm clouds. They penetrate the glass walls, bounce off the creamy furniture, and right into Keyne's brilliant, smiling eyes and the fabric of his shirt. The shirt. The suspect wore a similar shirt, except Keyne's is short sleeve.

I reach out my hand and run my fingers over Keyne's chest. The buttons, the pockets, the soft suede material, yes, very similar. My stomach reels in an undertow. I know I've felt the same fleeciness on the cuff of the suspect when I returned his change that day at The Shore.

Keyne looks both concerned and surprised. He turns his head to both sides with a nervous grin, but he doesn't stop me. Instead, his mousy look has composed itself into one of pleased relaxation. My panic swaps reasons as I remember where I am, "Keyne?"

My hand is still on his chest, and I feel his heartbeat on my palm. I'm used to Keyne grabbing my elbow, our inside joke, but now he is holding both my elbows and I feel a gentle pressure, then a squeeze on my arms.

Oh no! I think. No! Maybe, one day. I don't know, but not now. That's not it. *He thinks I was making a move on him!* Seriously, here in the grand foyer?

"Keyne," I use my bend and badge move and wiggle my elbows free. Keyne's expression flashes back to confused and his cheeks blush a downy pink. I'll have to address this later. My heart is racing and, once again, I'm shaking internally.

"Keyne, your shirt. Where did you get it?"

"What?" Keyne leans closer to me, puzzled, and attempts to touch my arm again, "Harbor, what are you talking about?"

I move away, trying to recall everything I can about what the kidnapper wore. Just then, the bell rings, and we both kind of appear to be in a daze.

"Nothing. Okay, actually it's something, but we can talk about it later," I say as I stare at the design of his shirt.

His eyebrows are raised, and his eyes changed from lighthearted to uneasy, yet he still manages to offer, "Okay, can I walk with you to class?"

Keyne hasn't ever offered to walk me to class. Sure, it naturally so happens that we walk together, but that's because we are usually talking or have homework to discuss. But now, he wears a look of uncertainty as if he isn't sure that I can walk myself.

"I'm fine. I'll catch up with you later," I turn and quickly pick up the pace.

What just happened? I've got to get my mind wrapped around this. Lots of people have the same shirts. I bet I could walk down the hall right now and count 5 people wearing shirts that look close to identical. I make it to class and didn't count one. So, I turn to a blank page in the back of my journal, grab a pencil and take a deep breath.

Try to remember everything you can about the kidnapper before you go blow things out of proportion. I attempt to sketch what I can remember about the suspect and his damn shirt, but a competing memory pushes through. I can't help but remember the feeling of Keyne's heartbeat through his shirt. The rhythmic strength and friendly forcefulness vibrating from his chest onto my fingers, resonating from my hand into my arm.

Wait. Why was Keyne holding both of my elbows? I can feel my stomach flip. Maybe he thought I was going to faint. *Or did he like my hand on his chest?* Was he holding me to bring me closer or trying to create distance? There's no time for this now! I force those thoughts away as well. *Think Harbor.* No time for feelings.

CHAPTER 27

Trembling, I make two columns on an empty sheet of paper in my journal. Straining to write every detail I can recall, my arm quivers from anger, but I know writing it on actual paper is the best way for me to line up the facts. As I begin to make my list, I feel a cold sweat encroaching. In the first column, I jot down what I remember. I'll save the second column for what the news has reported. If this doesn't help me, maybe it will help Office Lam.

By the time class is over, my sketch is as complete as it can be for now, but I didn't hear half of what the teacher said. The crackling of the speaker startles me, forcing me to snap back.

Tickets for our Winter Dance will be on sale in the cafeteria starting next week. We've had a great season of hard work, Kau High, and now it's time for the Sea Turtles to celebrate! Don't forget to buy your tickets.

The Winter Dance. I remember being in the lower grades, wondering how much fun a high school dance could be. I never imagined I'd be using it as a cover to get closer to a kidnapper. My phone vibrates, and when I check my text, I smile at the line of bright heart emojis. Tutu responded to my request to work a few extra shifts to save for the dance.

Harbor, I will get your dress. You don't need to work more

Tutu, I want to earn it myself.

I am conscious of the fact that the grown-ups left in my life are committed to having me socialize more, so I know she will want me to go to this dance. I just need to gain access to the drive-thru. It's a win-win.

Waiting on her response, I can't believe I'm so bugged by that stupid shirt. I remember the first day I literally ran into Keyne in the gym corridor. I fell on him, and he helped peel my face off his warm chest. So I know the fabric by heart, but he doesn't wear the shirt often. He only flaunts it periodically because they are part of the business. Maybe Keyne and his cousins share shirts. Now that I think about it, Lott's shirt is long sleeve too. Fig is always in my closet, and I know she would wear anything of mine if I let her. Even if it is 3 sizes too big.

Assuming Keyne isn't completely terror-stricken by the fact that I practically tickled his rib cage and rubbed his bosom out of the blue, I'll ask him. It doesn't matter how weird he thinks I am. All that matters are those missing kids. I've read that if a suspect can be connected to an uncommon store or location, they can be tracked. Online stores should be even easier. But then again, so should The Shore.

Tutu responds. *Sure dear, we can speak about it later. Enjoy your day.* I click to like the message and look down at the scribble I sketched. The way it's laid out, I have to wonder if this monster is from the island or an outsider. I put away my phone and briefly wish that packing away my feelings was as simple.

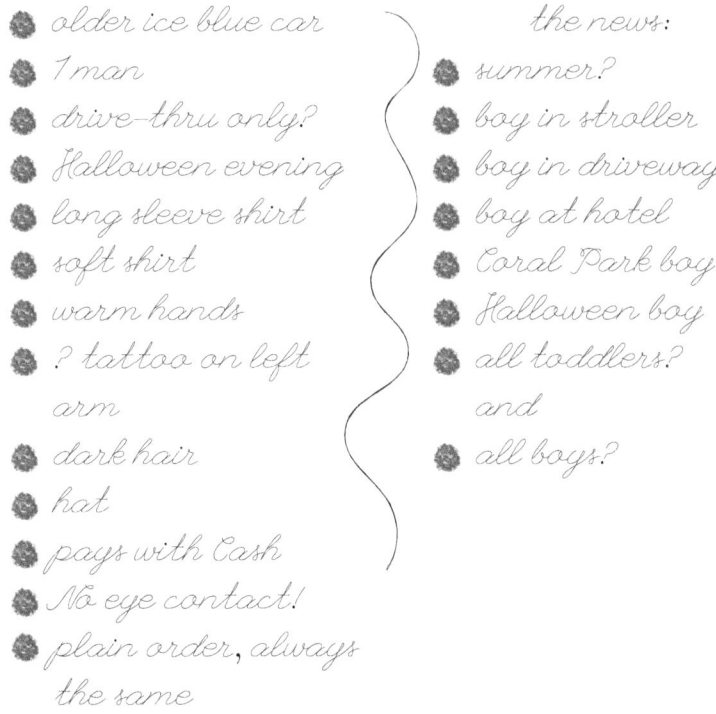

- older ice blue car
- 1 man
- drive-thru only?
- Halloween evening
- long sleeve shirt
- soft shirt
- warm hands
- ? tattoo on left arm
- dark hair
- hat
- pays with Cash
- No eye contact!
- plain order, always the same

the news:
- summer?
- boy in stroller
- boy in driveway
- boy at hotel
- Coral Park boy
- Halloween boy
- all toddlers?
- and
- all boys?

I hop on The Argo after school with the intent to speed. I need to get to The Shore, but the vibration from my phone stops me. I have to check it incase Tutu or Fig need something. But it's 2 different messages. One is from Keyne.

Hey, I didn't see you after class. Do you have a minute?

Even though I am in a hurry, I can feel the smile slowly form on my face. I begin to respond but stop when I feel a pang in my shoulder. I must have pulled a muscle in the rush of the day, or maybe it's the stress of the kidnappings. I rotate my shoulder a few times and try to text back using my pointer finger. Wow, I can't imagine having to text like this all the time. I've seen Tutu text with one finger but never tried it myself. I squeeze my shoulder again when I feel a grab on my elbow. I scream in surprise and turn so fast my ponytail whips Keyne right across the face.

Keyne looks stunned and scared.

"Are you okay? I've been working out, but I didn't think my grip was that strong."

Semi-laughing, "I must have hurt my shoulder earlier. I was about to text back."

"Hi."

"What are you doing?" I ask, "Don't you have practice?"

"I do, but you seemed to have so much on your mind earlier. I wanted to check on you."

"I did. I do, yeah. I'm fine, headed to work."

"Earlier, you kind of left me hanging. I felt like you wanted to ask me something," Keyne sighs, his eyebrows arch as he looks at his shoes and back again into my eyes. That's another oddity about Keyne; his eyes are mesmerizing. It's a feature I rarely see, not just the bold color, but the softness behind his eyes that is always on the verge of something more serious. Eyes occupied by a rhythm of daring and tenderhearted innocence. I can't help but look down at his shirt. I fight the urge to touch it again and decide that now isn't the time to ask him where he bought it. Gee, I wear white tennis. What if the kidnapper wore white tennis shoes? Should I be a suspect too? I need to narrow my facts and make sure I am correct before I start an inquisition.

"Maybe we can catch up later?"

"Sounds good because there is something I want to ask you."

I'm certain I raised my eyebrows, and as tempting as it is to know what Keyne wants, I have to go to meet with Officer Lam soon.

"Okay. For sure. Later," I assure him as I drive away. Keyne waves goodbye, and I realize that he only let go of my elbow when I drove away.

211

As I hit the main road, I can still feel the static cling. *Focus, Harbor.* I push on, determined to get a handle on these kidnappings. Maybe I care so much because I've already lost too much. And I won't lose more. Fig fits the age group of the abductions, and they are getting closer to home. I pray Officer Lam can offer new information tonight.

The rain has stopped, and a special sort of transformation occurs in the bend after a storm. As I make the drive through, I want so badly to stop, but I have to prioritize. I've got to get my name on the schedule at The Shore before Tutu changes her mind or Lona or Guy take the shifts.

That car hasn't been through the drive-thru often. Tutu is not going to let me work every night, so I am going to need to narrow down the driver's feeding pattern.

The bend is sobering and helps me compose my thoughts. When they run free, I find myself wondering what Keyne wants to ask me. Maybe he will ask me why I attacked him at lunch. I doubt he wants to question me about my Shore shirts, and if it were that, the answer is easy. Tutu sells them at the restaurant. Who am I kidding? I veer off the bend and roll the Argo through the brush to park. The ocean stretches for as long as the eye can see and immediately washes away the day's problems.

A brief tug of war with my backpack results in pulling my journal out while loading my news feed. Reception can be iffy inside the bend. Good, it's working today. I click on the face of the latest kidnapping victim. A little boy. I scroll down on the link to other victims. A boy at the park. My heart starts to race again. I know there were other kidnappings. I've got to find them. I hit a link and the victim is another innocent little boy. What the hell does this mean? I go back and forth from my news feed to my journal. He takes them when they are all alone! But how would he know? Does he wait? Does he watch?

I make notes in the 2nd column of my sketch. After the summer victims, the stroller kidnapping happened in August. The hotel was a month into the new school year. September. My hands begin to tremor, shaking so much that I drop my pencil. *The monster does have a feeding pattern!*

Staring down at my notations, the tangled truth ties in the simple fact that this creep is abducting a kid or two every month! What the hell is he doing the rest of the month? Planning the next victim? I can't be the only one who has noticed this! Surely the police have seen his pattern. I have to speak to Officer Lam! And I have to be careful not to let Tutu see me frayed. The new revelations have thrown me off balance. If she gets wind that I am under

213

pressure, she will never let me work extra hours, and the window may be the only way into this psycho's soul.

I click on the other blue highlighted links in my news feed. Scanning the articles, I realize that 2 children were taken from a homeless camp. They've been missing since midsummer, yet this is the first I've heard about them. I click on an updated post.

Captor Unknown, Kids Unknown

While police can't confirm that two missing children known as John and Jane Doe are connected to a string of recent child abductions, the similarities in the crimes are alarming. The Doe's are possibly near three and could be twins. Authorities believe they were homeless. No known family records exist. No one has come forward on their behalf. Police ask for anyone with information to call.

Jane Doe? She's the first girl. I scribble both their names in my sketchbook and draw a faded heart around hers. Camp kids often raise themselves. It's bullshit. No one really looks out for them or takes care of their needs. I've seen it myself when we used to donate food to the shelters. I remember during a class discussion on homelessness last year, the kids, even the

214

teacher treated me like a leper after I was called on to answer a question. I sat quietly in my desk, preferring to stay to myself. I listened to everyone's views. But no one wanted to listen to mine. The teacher asked me how we can help the homeless crisis. I answered, "Realizing our emotions are not everyone's facts. What we feel *is real*, but it's not the only reality. A lot of people are hurting in these camps because they don't use or don't know about the resources."

Needless to say, the already unpopular me became a heartless monster according to the superficial murmurs. Not one person asked what I meant. Not one person cared. So much for emotions. I sat alone the rest of the year and paid no attention to the bandwagon the class rode. But now, I'm furious! No one, not a parent, not family, not a friend came forward to claim John or Jane Doe. All these kids get is a lame snippet in the paper! A pitiful sketch! Where is the emotion now? Kids who live on the streets have hard lives. They're often victims. There's no way to sugar coat it. I guarantee John and Jane Doe didn't feel safe. A stranger's pity didn't keep them safe. I'm young - not dumb. I see the hypocrisy. We need to do better for them. Tutu and her staff used to hand out pamphlets with bus routes and locations for shelters that accepted anyone who needed a hot meal, medicine and a safe bed to sleep in. John and Jane Doe deserved at least that!

When their help was denied, it was always because the person simply didn't want to go to a shelter. Sometimes it was mental illness preventing them from understanding the assistance, but other times it was because they couldn't get high in a shelter nor avoid taking their meds. Or because criminal records are checked, and on the street - no one checks on you. That's the sad truth.

Then there were those with compunction held at the border of their eyes. They wanted to get clean. They accepted our help. They wanted a way to work toward real freedom. A vet suffering from pain and PTSD. A hurt, misguided runaway. A victim of violence or someone down on their luck. And this made our sacrifices worth it. But kids can't make those decisions! Having to go to sleep at night in a homeless camp is bad enough, but not having anyone recognize you is heartbreaking. Maybe this infuriates me because I also know a little something about being dealt a bad hand. I understand what it means to fight demons. I understand enough about battling for my own freedom to not let it be my future.

Sam and Rob say these pop up communities are drenched with drugs. Many of the vagrants living in the squalor are just a few years older than me. The new generation of unsheltered people learned that they can refuse to go to shelters: they can turn away civil help, and no one will bat an eye. Not all encampments are rot. Not all the people in them are rotten. But they do attract aggressive goons. They do draw in deadly drugs and duplicitous ways. This puts everyone in danger. No kid should be forced to live in illness, hour to hour unpredictability, garbage. Why don't these kids get the spotlight they need? My eyes begin to burn. Who keeps up the charade? You can't trick the world. Well, unless the world *doesn't want to see John and Jane Doe*. Who benefits from lies? Living on the street is not freedom. No one is spared.

Authorities were only able to get a sketch of the two kids. Not one person was able to identify them! I don't know who it helps to ignore these problems. I only see who it hurts.

Rob sees. He has been commissioned on flights with doctors who specialize in disease control and has flown psychiatrists working on unsheltered people studies. He is the pilot who gives them a birds-eye view of the real deal. He has lots of stories and says each time an organization tries to clean up the camps, a crowd of supposed activists fill the news, chanting that society is cruel to the homeless. I used to think he was too strict, but as I got older,

I began to see the suffering myself. Where are the crowds of yelling activists chanting to help John and Jane Doe?

These are the thoughts that keep me from hating Aadya so much. These are the thoughts that make me try to come to terms with my dad's murder. John and Jane Doe and I have something in common. We are victims of circumstance. I inhale and glance at the picture in my belt. The difference is, when my childhood ended abruptly, it had been short and sweet. Theirs was just short. The Doe's deserve to be more than a vague, outdated sketch.

People can choose to live a lie, but they shouldn't expect others to believe it or go down with them. Now more than ever, I believe no one should be allowed to live on the street. People need tools to live independently, to have access to learning a skill, to stay clean. Saving even one John or Jane Doe is worth it. They are true freedom.

Dad's FBI books say to always look for a consistent behavior pattern. I look from my sketch to the articles. Why the monthly pattern? I'll have to confirm with each article, but it appears the suspect prefers the end of the month. *I need every shift I can get for the end of the month.*

CHAPTER 28

Taking the backwoods off the bend, I bypass the main highway and cut through the massive reddish brown Koa trees. In this passage, under the cover of the mighty Koa boughs, I can be free, wild and invisible. Until the path runs out, the bend is a place where even Ha'alele cannot exist.

When I exit, the forest curtain opens into a picturesque view of our charming little restaurant and the seascape just beyond. The heavy wheels of the Argo maneuver the crowded, white sandy gravel parking lot of The Shore, and I pull into my parking spot, parallel parking the Argo to be flush with the side of The Shore. Pulling my teal Shore shirt out of my backpack, I shake it off and look across the beach. The Shore sits off the main road and on a private stretch of beach that is a mile or so long. To get to the big fancy hotels and to leave the big fancy hotels, you have to pass The Shore... unless you know the back way. Very few people know the back way. Ocean waves calmly make their way on and off the sand. The Pacific blue is pristine.

I store my backpack in the compartment of the Argo and make my way past the front porch, past the white wood chalkboard easel that stands guard. The paint looks like it has been scraped off the frame, yet the board is displayed proudly and serves its purpose loyally. This chalkboard is where Tutu writes her daily specials, each accompanied by a picture meant to represent the food that has been drawn in teal, coral, pink, yellow and lime chalk.

Today, she wrote Shore Cheeseburger, Alea fries, fresh baked chocolate chip cookies and sweet papaya shakes. That is also what she writes most days of the week. Mouthwatering staples of her signature creations. However, Tutu is also known to delve out one of a kind recipes to invigorate customers and compete with the big hotels. A few times a year, she offers new on-the-go dishes. My stomach growls thinking of the many delicious meals I've taste tested over the years. Mind over matter though. Right now, my job is to get my hands on more work hours. Grindz later. Catch a kidnapper now.

I walk in through the coral framed screen door in the rear of The Shore and find Tutu in the kitchen slicing tomatoes and Sam seasoning juicy, hand tossed burger patties. Past the kitchen, I see Lona on her phone. Lona is 18 or 19 years old and has probably spent 17 and a half years on her phone. She is a senior at Kau High and works the counter at The Shore part-time. As I look over to her, I notice her smiling, which is rare! Maybe someone tickled her. I rarely see her at school, and honestly, if I did, she may not even recognize me because she barely notices me at work. Once, I asked her where she would like to go to college. She answered in a two-second glance that told me her time was precious, so beat it. That's been the extent of our dialogue.

Past the counter, Guy is cleaning tables, the strings of his white apron too short to tie in the back. Guy isn't out of shape. He's solid. He's a grade above me and puppy dog nice. The accumulation of the last couple of years, Guy has all but admitted that he has a crush on me. It was obvious that I couldn't reciprocate his affections, so thankfully, he transitioned from lucidly gushing over my every move into an amiable, at a distance respect. He recently said he was going to ask Tutu for full-time hours because he is saving for a car. He went on to say that he is using his uncle's car for now and that anytime I need a ride to work, he'd be glad to bring me even if he doesn't have a shift. When I first started at Kau, Guy wasn't exactly inconspicuous when he'd hover near me in lunch or the halls. Yet my friendship with Keyne kicked off both oddly and quickly, and Guy never seems interested in speaking to me when

Keyne is around. As he tries to wiggle out of a booth he finished wiping, I apparently catch his eye, and his exuberant shout across the restaurant startles sitting patrons. They return to eating happily once they realize it's just Guy. "Hey, Harbor! Do you have a minute?"

Most busboys wear black aprons, but Tutu insist on white aprons. Guy is wearing a long sleeve Shore shirt today and a napkin has somehow gotten stuck to the left sleeve of his Shore shirt. I laughingly shake my head while pointing at the snafu. The kidnapper wears long sleeve. Mind over matter. Sorry, Guy. Car savings or not, I've got to beat you to those extra work hours. With Guy frozen in the booth, I shout back with a smile, "Maybe later, Guy, gotta get to the window." He begins to respond, but I've already turned back toward the kitchen.

Giving Tutu a hug, I ask if she needs help slicing the tomatoes. Tutu laughs, "Oh, Harbor dear, last time you sliced tomatoes, they looked more like ketchup." I laugh because she's right. I love food, but my strong suit isn't handling it.

"You know, Tutu, as I mentioned earlier today, there is going to be a dance at school."

She stops slicing for a moment and looks at me curiously. I've caught her interest. Now, I need to keep it, "I haven't been to a real school dance, and I was thinking it would be nice to start taking part in more school activities."

Tutu places the knife on the cutting board and turns her entire body toward me, "That makes me so happy. Guy mentioned that you haven't gone to one Kau football game this year, and I was a bit concerned. School spirit is very important." For a fleeting moment, I'm puzzled why Guy is talking to Tutu about me, then I remember that Guy plays on the football team, but how would he know if I've been to a game? Oh well, it doesn't matter. Returning to the mission, I lay the groundwork for Tutu, "The cost for a ticket, a dress and shoes," I see she is about to interrupt, and she will probably insist on paying, so I pull out my pre-emptive strike, "I want to pay for myself. I want to feel good about paying for myself, if you can give me some extra hours at the window?" Not a total lie.

Tutu sighs and looks directly into my eyes and asks, "Will you buy a dress to match your real eyes?" I smile back and see Guy passing with his grey tub of dirty papaya shake glasses and empty Shore baskets that once held yummy deliciousness that vanished into the bellies of Shore customers. With a side glance, he begins loading the large dishwasher.

"Yes."

We both turn as we hear a crackle at the drive-thru intercom. Tutu smiles and says, "There goes your first customer."

I jump into my Shore shirt, putting it right over the blouse I wore to school.

I'm on cloud nine! I secured the work hours I need to get closer to the suspect, yet I'm also on pins and needles waiting for Officer Lam. Talk about a roller coaster of emotions. Still, taking matters into my own hands is liberating. It provides me relief to know that the person I can most depend on, myself, is actually going to do what she said. If the police can't draw out the suspect, maybe the window can. The profiler and the profilee. Designed to work in sync.

I left my notebook in the Argo. I need to review my notes from earlier to see if there is anything I missed. The drive-thru runs steady, and when it finally simmers down, I take off my headset for a quick break. I want my journal and need to beat the second wave of hungry customers. I hear Tutu and turn to see what she needs. What I see instead is Officer Lam. He is standing outside the wide break room door speaking to Tutu.

I still can't help but notice how young he looks. I wouldn't doubt that four or five years ago, he was in high school.

"Hi, Harbor. How are you?"

"Hi," through my peripheral vision, I can see that Lona has actually looked up from her phone long enough to pass an order to a customer while smiling at Officer Lam. Two smiles in one shift. Totally FBI rule #3! Totally unlike Lona.

After my invite, "Why don't we go into the break room?" I'm certain I hear Lona sigh.

I walk over to turn off the noisy fan and listen as Officer Lam asks, "So, you have additional information?" He pulls out a small notebook from his front shirt pocket. *Should I get my journal?* My sketch could prove useful or that I'm crazy. I decide that Officer Lam is surely aware of all the facts I jotted down, so I'll go at this alone. Where do I begin?

"I remembered," I stall, contemplating what I want to tell him. His expression suspended, Officer Lam prompts me back from my subconscious thoughts, "Remember what, Harbor? What did you remember?"

"When I saw the suspect."

"Great. Tell me what you remember."

"This past summer, in the night drive-thru he came by, and there was a passenger in the car. He was with someone. Both men, I think. They both wore hats. The driver doesn't make eye contact, and the other guy might have blonde hair. A snippet hung out of his cap, but it was also dark outside."

225

Officer Lam takes copious notes and stops short to ask, "What color hair do you think the driver has?"

"Dark. His hair is dark. And he was in the same ice blue 4 door car. Same silver trim from the news and the same car and driver that came by the window on Halloween night."

"All of this is helpful, Harbor. Remember not to let this stress you out. Witnesses often remember key details in stages."

"That's not all. I think the driver has a tattoo or maybe an odd shaped bruise on his left arm. It's close to his wrist and raised like a welt."

Officer Lam seems a bit surprised but pleased, raising his eyebrows and opening his eyes wide as he jots down my words.

"Any chance you can describe it? If it's a tattoo, it will have ink color. Any words or names?"

I shake my head and hesitate, "Dark ink. Like his hair. It's swollen."

Realizing that I have nothing to lose, I go for it, "Officer Lam?"

"Yes?" he obligingly responds.

"If the suspect's car is so distinctive, why are you guys, why are the police having such a hard time catching him?"

"Harbor, I want you to know that we have officers on the ground dedicated to bringing these kids home. I'm sure you saw the search parties on the news."

"How many kidnappings have there been?"

"We can't commit to a number yet," he pauses, "but Harbor, many criminals try to outrun their crimes. This guy seems to have a different goal. He's not running. He's hiding."

Surprised that he is sharing extraneous information with me, I respond quickly before he changes his tune, "What do you mean?"

"This crook seems to be trying to outrun society."

"What does that mean, Officer Lam?"

"It means that even if you can't see all the details, you need to trust that we are conducting a top notch investigation to stop him. But when a person like him has found a way to stay off the grid, we've got to find the grid before we set the traps."

Well, Officer Lam may be young, but he seems to share the gift of the elderly. His analogies confuse the hell out of me as much as Tutu's do.

"Does he live on our island?"

"Not 100%, but he obviously has access. The road to your Tutu's restaurant is on the main highway. If this guy is stopping in, why haven't our traffic cameras been able to capture him?"

"He's taking the back roads," but as I say it, I know that very few people know how to navigate the back roads. They aren't even roads really. They are natural pathways that have been worn in by islanders like me.

Office Lam wore an expression that said he knew more. It was clear that he wouldn't be sharing to appease me. I read in dad's old books that if the investigator allows a long pause, the suspect will usually give in and fill it. Officer Lam is no suspect, yet he did give into the silence and ended with, "He may not be a local, but he is definitely familiar with the local areas."

"Do you think that's why he stops in here? We don't have cameras."

"We are looking at every possible lead, kid." He ends the meeting and heads toward the door to leave. It crosses my mind that he is the one who looks like a kid.

I walk Officer Lam to his car and again notice that Lona has taken a long enough break from her phone to stare as we say our goodbyes. If she smiles a third time, I may have to call 9-1-1 again.

I return to the window as quickly as I can. Headset on. I'm determined to be the eyes and ears the next time that asshole wants a camera-free glass of water. I feel the vibration of my phone and see an incoming text from Keyne.

Swim tonight but want to tty

Smiling, I return a thumbs up emoji.

John, Jane Doe and myself.

We share something.

Your Dream Vacation awaits

We are victims of tragic circumstance.

CHAPTER 29

"Unlike your last project which merely touched the surface, this time your group is to delve deeper. Find out the reasons why and connect your explanations to real world solutions. What we do today can prevent damage tomorrow," Mr. Reddy addresses the class, and Keyne and I share a quick giggle because Reddy had that twitch in his hips as he turns to write the assignment on the board. Then Reddy spins around quickly, and I'd swear he directs his eye contact at Keyne and I, but says to everyone, "This will be the last major grade on the upcoming report card."

Half the class is busy complaining because our projects are due the day before the school dance. I don't see what the big deal is.

Mr. Reddy puts his dry erase marker in his front pocket, a pocket already loaded with bright color grading pens, and then dismisses us to work in our groups. Keyne immediately turns his desk toward mine, and we both look around for our other group members, but we are used to the routine. One seems to be absent, and the other two are engaged in an exuberant conversation.

Keyne laughs and says, "Déjà vu."

"What?"

"Déjà vu. Don't tell me you haven't heard of déjà vu?"

"I have. Kind of, sort of."

"Well, you know what they say about it?"

"What?"

"It's a second chance."

"What? I don't know about that."

"Yeah, it's an experience that you've had already, a place you've already been, a time you've already lived through."

"Drinking sugary drinks all day? You don't seem to be thinking straight."

Keyne laughs, "Seriously. Think about it. How else do you explain people of all races, cultures, religions being familiar with, *knowing* that eerie feeling that tells them they've done this before?"

I pause to a flashback of all of Tutu's conversations about visions. "I have these dreams. Sometimes, I feel bits and pieces of them have already occurred, yet it isn't until later that they actually do."

"Yeah, it's your second chance!"

"Why? For what?"

"To fix what you didn't do right the first time."

"Well, you're definitely a true believer or experiencing a sugar rush," I chuckle.

"Oh, I believe. Like running into you in the gym after so many years after first grade."

"I don't think that counts."

"It might," Keyne smiles and turns to the page in his history book that Reddy wrote on the board then asks, "What about re-incarnation?"

I look up from writing my name and date on my journal page, "What about it?"

"Do you believe in it?"

"No way. I don't believe in anything that has me return to this life as a bug or a tree stump."

Keyne's lighthearted nature shifts to lost in heavy thought.

"Keyne?"

He clears his throat, "Yeah, yeah. Let's do this project. I need an A if I ever plan on getting free time."

"Do you have practice tonight?"

"Yes."

"Do you swim in a heated pool? I've never understood how the human body can perform summer sports in the winter."

"I wouldn't call it a pool, and the only heat in it is from the team begging for warmth."

Not sure if he's joking, I shrug away his comment. Keyne and I haven't been able to catch up ever since my hand slid down his chest. I'm not avoiding him completely, but I am staying away from the subject of his shirt and the fact that I scared the hell out of him when I ran my hand across his left breast. I can feel a private rise in temperature causing my cheeks to turn red just thinking about it. Ugh. It's a dumb shirt, and even if it is similar, that doesn't give me permission to assault him or conduct a full blown investigative search in public. And he doesn't wear it often, so the right time to examine it hasn't come up.

"How about you begin research, and I will summarize the argument? When the others make time for class, they will get the leftover jobs, citing and presenting."

Keyne raises his eyebrows and says, "Genius."

By the end of class, we have a decent amount of research accumulated, and as I'm packing my backpack, I feel a bump on my elbow. I'm used to it and give him a *go ahead* look. Keyne dives in, "So, not sure if you remember. I want to touch base with you on something."

"Sure, go ahead. Just been busy. I spoke with the officer again. The one who took the report on Halloween night."

"No kidding? How did that go?"

The bell rings, and we both look up. It seems like all our time is cut short. There just isn't enough time in school to include our personal lives. Each time we get started on a real conversation, the bell rings. We are literally forced to choose between social life or school life.

Lott is outside the classroom door. Man, he gets here fast, "Got a message for you. From coach about practice." Lott's voice carries a menacing tone.

I interject and tell Keyne, "How about we catch up later?"

"Sounds good," he smiles, and I practically race to the crowded school parking lot. Little splashes of water from the wet pavement cover my once snow white tennis shoes.

I miss the bend, but I've got to get to the drive-thru. The last couple of weeks have included homework, dodging Keyne, and an intimate Thanksgiving feast. With the end of the month upon us, there is a trap to set.

The Shore is relaxing and pleasant. It agrees with the crisp, cool outdoors. I toss my backpack in the break room after taking out my journal. Turning to my list, I mull it over. What am I missing? I can hear Tutu humming along to the jolly Christmas music playing on the speakers. Holidays are the only time the woman takes a break from her beach soundtrack. My phone vibrates. It's Fig. She is constantly sending pictures of Ember. Delete.

Where are you, Harbor?

Working.

Dad brought me home to feed Ember then I'm going with you and Tutu.

See you soon.

Transported. He transported me home.

I laugh. Fig is still working on her vocabulary.

Okay kid, ltr

That is what Officer Lam called me. Kid. Tugging on my belt, I briefly pull out the picture of mom, dad and me. That's the last time I was a kid. The last time I was allowed to really be a kid. I place the picture back, I am never able to look at it for too long. Concentrating on my journal, my eyes are drawn to the long sleeve shirt. I decide to scribble in his name.

Mr. Boring

Tapping the journal, I feel something isn't right, so I re-read my notes.

soft shirt
warm hands

Why do I call him Mr. Boring? I read over the list of his regular order.

water

1 Shore burger

Then it dawns on me. *Warm hands! Warm cookie!* Mr. Boring began adding a chocolate chip cookie. I told Officer Lam, but I didn't write it in my notes. Every detail matters and often the smallest ones are the most important.

But so what? It's not like the police can follow cookie crumbs. I heave a sigh of impatience and tuck my journal into my backpack. I need to get to the window. Need a uniform. I walk over to the closet where Tutu keeps extra Shore shirts. As I'm pulling one off a hanger, Guy walks in wearing his uniform and smiles.

"Hey, Guy."

"Hi," he says. His outward appearance seems to be without a purpose. He is standing idle, looking straight at me and it doesn't appear that he has blinked. He doesn't say much more and I'm not sure what he wants, so I excuse myself, "Gotta go get ready for the window."

He delivers a chortle, even though I don't see or hear anything remotely funny. Then Lona walks in, looks at both of us, and laughs out loud. Maybe I'm having another nightmare. I close the dressing room door and hear the rare sound of Lona's voice. *She can speak in complete sentences, whoa.* She tells Guy, "Just do it already."

I don't know what's going on, but by the time I'm done changing, they have both begun their shift. Ready to begin mine, I move the pair of chopsticks Tutu left on the drive-thru headset.

What is this lady planning? She has been working on some new menu items again. The drive-thru is empty, and I'm grateful for a moment to myself. Literally a moment because a sudden noise rattles my Zen. It sounds like a bullfrog coughing. I turn to see if the window was left open, but I see quickly that it's Guy clearing his throat. He is standing still, staring at me again. Now this is déjà vu .

"Hi, Guy."

"Hi, Harbor."

"Harbor," Tutu walks up. You have a friend here to see you. Guy looks just as surprised as I do. There are so many things wrong with that sentence.

"Officer Lam?" I ask Tutu.

She laughs, "No dear. Officer Lam is an adult. If he were your friend, *he'd* need the police."

I shake my head at her and place my headset on the chopsticks. I walk to the counter and smile. Keyne is standing by a back booth, his green eyes, chock-full of light, stare right past Lona and rest on me.

He seems taller in this setting. His dark hair is brushed back, and he wears the same generous smile that makes me glad to be his friend.

"Keyne. Hi?"

He looks even more confident outside of school; maybe it's because Lott isn't sweating him. His long sleeve rash guard roughly outlines the muscles in his arms, and he lifts one hand from his pocket to wave hi. I walk over as a small family walks up to the counter to order. I can feel Lona's eyes following. Keyne and I take a seat in the booth.

"You came all the way down here to work on our project?" I laugh.

"You look so responsible in your uniform."

"Looks can be deceiving."

Keyne's eyes almost seem to reflect my shirt, so bright and welcoming completely contrary to the winter days.

"So, that thing I wanted to run by you?"

Surprised, I say, "Yeah, what is it?"

"I was wondering what you thought about us going to the Winter Dance together?"

Completely taken off guard because the dance is my decoy to get more work hours, I hadn't even thought about really going, and

Keyne and I are always running out of time, so I haven't updated him on my plan. My moment of shock wasn't intended, and Keyne asks a bit embarrassed, "Did I just ruin a friendship?"

"Noooo. Of course not," but because it's absolutely adorable watching him try, I playfully smirk, "Are you asking me to go with you?" Keyne laughs and reaches across the booth to cradle my elbow, "You're killing me."

"Do you dance?"

"I have several versions of the Rip Entry I can show off."

We both laugh, and that seems to irritate Guy, who is a couple of booths adjacent to us. He is harshly scrubbing an already clean table. It couldn't be more obvious that he is listening. So, I tactfully move my head up and down with a smile. Keyne lights up with my answer and stands to leave. When he does, his hand slips off my elbow, and the playful strong hold I've come to enjoy vanishes.

"I'll get our tickets."

Hoping Tutu didn't hear that because I need her to think I need all the extra money I can get, I say thank you.

Guy is now scraping the already sparkling clean booth.

"I'll walk you out."

Lott and his posse are waiting outside the car in the parking lot. The chill in the air doesn't seem to disturb them one bit. Together they possess a cavalier quality. They are self-absorbed in conversation until they see Keyne. It's hard not to notice that they are all wearing matching rash guards and that they ceased their heart-to-hearts and await Keyne's next move.

"We have practice."

"Nearby?" I ask.

"Not too far off the shore. Not your Shore," he points to the large neon sign cheerfully afloat the restaurant, one letter still on the fritz.

"You swim outdoors?" I ask with surprise, a facial expression that Keyne surely has memorized by now.

He walks steadily backwards while answering, "What better training than swimming with sharks?" he laughs, and his crew follows his cue and begins loading the same small brown SUV I've seen them in before. The two girls conspire as they hold a steady stare toward me before they disappear into the vehicle. I could swear one of them resembles a dorsal fin. The front passenger seat is left available for Keyne.

FBI rule #9 is look at personality clues. Most islanders use the Shaka hand signal to say hi. It is a friendly greeting, but none of Keyne's peeps present their hand. They are not from the island.

Keyne's personality is full of natural magnetism. He's likable. Yet there is a hint of esteem that he possesses in that razor sharp circle. Swimming with the sharks is an understatement. Wonder what they substitute for shark bait? Speaking of bait, the window!

I race back inside ready to hook my own predator.

CHAPTER 30

Time has flown by and there hasn't been any new signs of the kidnapper. I can't discuss my plans with Tutu or Rob because they will freak out, so all I have to go on is that the news has not reported any new kidnappings and even with my extra shifts, I haven't seen the car. But this assignment will have to wait for at least a few hours because tonight I am committed to the Winter Dance. And I'm not sure how, yet somehow, my dance decoy turned into a Tutu and Fig adventure.

I've basically been a guinea pig for two giggly groupies, one 3 times my age and the other not even half. Both had a wonderful time choosing my dress and accessories. And similar to a gingerbread cookie being decorated, they added more color to me than I've ever worn in my life. To show appreciation for their help, I played along with the game of dress up. I sashayed and shimmied, turned and twisted on command until they were pleased with my attire. Truth be told, they took the hassle out of preparing for tonight's dance. My mind has been occupied with the drive-thru, yet I really am excited to finally have a couple of hours with Keyne, neither of us bound to homework, practice or profiling.

Tutu and Fig settled on a blush pink dress for me to wear. It has long sleeves sewn beside a delicate lace bodice. The bottom half is a soft, satin mini gown. Its wispy bloom compliments the intricate v-neckline. After some discussion, the two were content with letting me keep my ponytail. Both little ladies approved a pair of rose gold double teardrop earrings, and the youngest stylist was thrilled to declare, "They go perfect with your long hair, Harbor."

As I am ushered to the mirror, I complain, "Tutu, it's winter. I'm going to be freezing."

"Harbor, dear, it's modern day America. We have heat." For a sweet old lady, she sure is candid.

Standing in front of the full length mirror in Tutu's bedroom, I smile. Tutu and Fig just might know magic. My skin glows, and my ponytail has been given a chic and elegant vibe. The bronzed oil mirror frames a sophisticated reflection I barely recognize. One without Aadya's belt around my waist or Ha'alele in my eyes.

It is rare that I am without her belt. It holds the image of family I once had; my father, her and I. Tutu and Fig join me in the mirror. Tutu stands to my left and is a whole four inches shorter than my shoulders. Fig stands on my right holding her fishbowl, and she barely reaches my waist. I have no doubt they are scrutinizing any last possible alterations, but within a minute, they both don the sweetest grin, notifying me that I passed inspection.

"You shouldn't wear contacts anymore, Harbor," Fig holds my hand while Ember chooses to swim to the opposite side of the bowl. The image of the 3 us in the mirror is beautiful to me. Not one of us looks so similar that you would automatically know we are family, yet there is a sacred and undeniable likeness. It's not in our skin color or hair. It's not in our eyes or bone structure, but in the most fundamental element of family. Simply standing together. Being together. I inhale peacefully, "So ladies, how am I supposed to ride the Argo dressed like this?"

Tutu gives me a sly look to show she isn't amused, "Rob will be taking you, dear."

I laugh and walk back to my room to find a jacket. I already knew that Rob is driving me, and of course, Fig would be going along to document every detail.

Tutu is aware that Keyne is my friend, yet she insists on referring to him as my date, "And if your date decides to offer you a ride home, please text me."

I humor her by bending down to place a kiss on the top of her head, and downy tufts of gray

244

hair remove some of my lip gloss. I reapply a dab of pink sliding my finger on my mouth. The creamy gloss is so lightweight that it glides effortlessly across my lips. Much nicer than my everyday gunk. I decide I like the subtle boldness this adds to my smile.

I offered to pick up Keyne, but he declined, saying it would be too complicated. When he said that, his eyes seemed to indicate there was more to the story, but I didn't press him. I know he is riding with Lott and the posse.

Keyne alluded a number of times that his dad can be withdrawn, and they still take it one day at a time since the death of his mom. In a way, Keyne and I have both been involuntarily detached from traditional child-parent relationships. With his heavy swim schedule and the new business, I get the impression that Keyne reveres his father more as a boss than a loving parent. Anyhow, since that first day he visited the bend, he doesn't talk about his parents much, and I don't ask. It seems his real family, the people he depends on, are Lott and the school of sharks that are always splashing around, and I don't fit in their plans.

Keyne and I are friends. Not an easy accomplishment for our busy schedules and the fact that the last few years of my life have been incommunicado. Our friendship has been a learning curve for me, and tonight, I am happy to have some extra time learning even more. It will be weird not to have our conversations interrupted by the sound of tardy bells, practice or Lott. But I can't promise that it won't be cut short by work. I have a sinking feeling that the monster will prey again soon, so if I can get to the window, I will.

"Time to go, Harbor," Fig squeaks, running into the room with her fish bowl.

"That Christmas chestnut is gonna dart right out, Fig. It's not a puppy you can carry around."

"Should I take...let me rephrase that, should Ember accompany us for the ride?"

"Sure, if you want to see if the floating nugget can fly."

Rob pulls in front of Kau High. The sound of music travels on the wind, and lights sparkle through the massive glass window. Crowds of teens are huddled in various circles, taking pictures and moving to the beats. I see a few people from my classes and The Shore. Guy is talking with a group of football players. No sign of Keyne. Fig has rolled down her window and is straining her neck to take in every detail. I ruffle her hair and laugh to myself. I guarantee Fig isn't profiling. She is judging. Since she is years away from a night out on her very own, curiosity is consuming every ounce of her tiny body.

"Thanks, Rob. I appreciate the ride *and* that you made Fig leave the fish," I giggle as Fig turns to give me a mean glare.

"Harbor Haukea," hearing my middle stops me short. Rob insists on using our full names. A word of caution follows, "Be careful. Have fun, but there is still a kidnapper out there. You need to be aware at all times."

I'd love to come face to face with that monster, but that's not what Rob wants to hear, "Of course, Rob. Promise."

"I will be back to pick you up in a couple of hours. Unless you've decided to stay later?"

"Two hours," I confirm. As the huge truck drives off, I catch a glimpse of Fig's wide eyes absorbing all she can. Turning toward the music blasting through the school speakers, I make my way through packs of cackling kids. If it's this crowded outside, I can only imagine how many are inside already dancing the night away. I walk a few feet, smoothing my dress, hoping it won't blow up in the wind. Maybe I should text Keyne. I pull over and lean against one of the columns, so I won't bump into anyone while texting. Ugh, it might be time for a new phone, my screen is locked again. I try to place it back in my jacket pocket, but my arms are cemented. I turn around and when I do, the hands that were cupping my elbows in place fall with my motion and slip right across my waist.

The column which was holding me up is now blocking my view. However, very little can mask the rugged scent of sea water floating off layers of volcanic brown hair. Keyne and I take a step almost as if choreographed and stand there face to face until he lets go and lets out a sudden gasp. This catches me off guard, and I drop my phone. When I bend to pick it up, I make sure to try and quickly turn on my camera to check to see if I have a booger in my nose or food in my teeth. Ugh! The damn thing is still frozen. I rub my nose and roll my tongue across my teeth when a strong breeze nearly raises my dress above my head. This is not the entrance I envisioned for my first real dance.

Keyne kneels down, and once again, we are face to face. He stares into my eyes for a second and I'm certain I see him gulp. A look I've seen before, "I'm sorry, Harbor." Keyne says as he takes my elbow to help me back up.

"For what? I should have a case on it. Lesson learned."

Keyne is staring again and now I'm starting to wonder if the punch is spiked. Not sure if I should leave him outside while I go smell the bowl for booze, he breaks his concentration in a heaving sigh, "Sorry, it's just your eyes. Your real eyes."

I nudge him, relieved that it wasn't snot or food on my face that startled him, "Let's go have some fun."

We cross under a huge, hand painted poster hanging above the entrance.

Welcome Turtles to the Makahiki!

And then it's my turn to gasp. The grand foyer has been transformed into a Hawaiian winter holiday theme! Two long candy tables greet guests with an array of sweets in varying shades of powder blue. Past that, a winter wonderland of trees decorated with tiny, soft amber lights line the walls with snowcapped shrubbery snuck in between. The delicate twinkling bounces off the dance floor and my dress.

The center of the room boasts a long table with an elaborate ice sculpture shaped like an ocean wave and a typical punch bowl has been swapped for an illuminated drink fountain that welcomes thirsty students. Classy.

Amid the subtle warmth of the lights are Kau High staff members, the older Sea Turtles and Lord help them. They are dancing and dressed up. I think. They did the best they could considering that each of them is wearing a school shirt.

"Look, Mr. Reddy," I half point, but apparently, we already caught Reddy's eyes because he waves at Keyne and I.

"Is he staring at us?" Keyne asks.

"Nope, you are just paranoid," I laugh, "See? Ms. Iona is here too."

On second glance, however, it does appear that Reddy, though fully engrossed in the music and conversation, does have his gaze fixed squarely on Keyne and I.

Keyne notices too, "Look again."

"I saw. He is probably thinking, *those 2 are my only A+ students*," I joke. I want to shake Keyne and tell him that I only have 2 hours, and I've wanted to see the inside of a Makahiki dance since grade school! I haven't told Keyne my plans yet, so he doesn't know I'm leaving the dance early.

On another end of the room, snowy branches tied in glittery blue ribbon lay on a long table among the spread of fruit and veggie trays, chips, and cheeses divided by a tall tier of cupcakes. My mouth waters at the mound of fluffy pale blue frosting swirled atop each dessert. Each blue cupcake dawns a sugary snowflake at its summit. I'm willing to trade my new lip gloss for buttercream in a heartbeat.

Circular tables are scattered around the room covered in Cinderella blue gowns. Each table has a can't miss, tall, glass vase planted in the center. The centerpieces are filled with iridescent pearls and seashells resting on tiny mounds of sand covered by blue water. A floating candle that acts as a small moon above the miniature island flickers in each vase.

The large glass walls of the foyer open up to the outside, and the music flows in. An outdoor dance floor is kept alive by a D.J. spinning awesome beats. Three radiant, ice blue Christmas trees are set by a snow-covered bench and a light post for pictures.

"How did we not know that the walls slide open? So impressive, it's gorgeous," I turn to Keyne who is smiling from ear to ear, and I don't think it's because he is as enamored with the decorations as I am, "Is everything ok?"

"Oh, yeah, I totally agree. Impressive and *gorgeous*."

"Ok, weirdo. C'mon, let's get a seat. We finally have time to talk. Did you get permission from Lott?"

"Ha. Ha!" he cocks one eyebrow, "Very funny. *Not*."

CHAPTER 31

The Winter Dance is rocking, bringing Kau High's soul to life. Everyone is merry, dancing, eating, and laughing. Fun is in the air. Twisting around to pull Keyne's hands, I walk backwards a couple of steps while shouting over the music, "Let's get a drink first."

But when I whirl back around, I barely miss bumping into Guy, who is making his way outdoors with a girl in his grade. By the way she was holding him, I'd guess it's his date. My body barely misses Guy's, yet I tugged on Keyne so hard that he clashes right into him. Keyne would have smashed into Guy's date too if she hadn't jumped out of the way.

"Dude, I'm so sorry!" Keyne apologizes to them but turns toward me, laughing and shaking his head.

Guy doesn't respond. He doesn't even check on his date. He stands in place staring at Keyne and me, so Keyne tries one more time while Guy's date repositions herself on his hip, "Sorry, guys. That was an accident."

Guy still doesn't respond, so Keyne reaches for my hand as we try to maneuver around the lovebirds. Yet Guy, in defensive lineman mode, blocks us, finally speaking, "Hi, Harbor."

"Hey, Guy. That was my fault. Sorry," I look to him and his date who purses her lips into a forced smile then looks at her phone.

"Maybe we can sit together?" Guy asks.

Taken a bit off guard, I say, "Sure, maybe we will see you in there," as Keyne and I bypass Guy and his girl. Nonetheless, I still feel the weight of a heavy presence, so I turn to look over my shoulder and sure enough, Guy is still standing idle and staring our way.

Keyne and I make it to the glistening punch fountain and fill our cups. We are yakking back and forth as we find a seat, yet as I'm about to actually sit, Keyne goes mute. He sets his punch on the table and grips my elbow, preventing me from sitting. Maybe tonight is a full moon.

"What is it?" I ask.

Keyne reaches inside his coat and reveals a little something I wasn't expecting, "This is for you. I hope you don't think it's weird."

A light giggle escapes me. This is the nicest gesture, "It's so pretty. Purely tradition, right?"

"Of course," he smiles, seemingly relieved.

"So, what's the tradition?"

"Whether or not the girl you give it to crushes it beneath her feet determines the giver's fortune," he smirks wittily.

"Well, I don't want to ruin these new shoes. Took me a whole shift to buy," I smile and give him my hand. Keyne carefully slips the corsage onto my wrist, and I feel the static cling. He takes his time placing it on me as I take a closer look. The corsage is made from two pieces of rustic, khaki colored rope, each about half an inch wide. The strands are intertwined and hold two pure white flowers, each with six petals. I recognize them instantly, "Nanu?" I ask, surprised.

"Excuse me?"

"The flowers. Are they Nanu?"

"I don't know. They reminded me of you."

"These are rare."

"Then you understand why I chose them."

The corsage fits like a bracelet, and as I take a closer look, I'm surprised to find tiny, light blue flower petals and a seashell tucked in.

"The shell is from a swim I did not too long ago. Since I didn't know the color of your dress, I tried to match your corsage to the night. One of Lott's friends is on the decorating committee."

"You made this?"

His nod answers yes.

"Keyne, it's so pretty. It's amazing. I wish I had something for you."

"You do."

I look up at him for clarity.

"I haven't seen those eyes since first grade."

I inhale not knowing how to respond. Luckily, Keyne saves the moment with good old fashioned deflection, "Hey, do you want a snack before they all disappear?"

"I want to stick my face in one of those cupcakes."

He laughs, "What are friends for? I'll be back."

Running my fingers along the miniature ridges of the seashell, I can't believe he found this during a swim meet. I thought he was joking about swimming outdoors.

"Harbor!" The shout of my name startles me, and I look up to find that Guy took a seat in the chair that Keyne left vacant.

"Where's your date?"

"She's around. Are you having a good time?"

"Yeah, you?"

"I'm so glad we all got the night off."

"Lona is here also?"

"Yeah, she's around here somewhere."

I didn't realize we deserted Tutu and Sam to handle the entire diner. Sure, they can handle it, but I still feel bad, especially with the kidnapper still out on the loose.

"Your friend," Guy interrupts my thoughts.

"What?" I say, distracted by the thought of The Shore being short staffed.

"I saw him and his cousins."

"Okay?" I respond a bit annoyed and realize that I see Guy enough at work. Why is he in Keyne's chair?

"Did you know he hangs out off Old 99?"

"Uh, nooo," I say. Every local knows that Old 99 is a rugged strip of highway that is often closed. Even on a gorgeous day, it is known for dangerous driving conditions. Newer roads have practically all but replaced it, but for those who know what they are doing, navigating it can get you to some of the most pristine and rarely seen beaches and pools on the island, "I'm not sure what your point is."

"That's a deserted stretch of land."

"Maybe you saw wrong, or he was returning from a swim? Either way, that's his business."

"I saw them tonight, Harbor. On the way here."

"Okay, what are you getting at? What were you doing up there?"

"Hanging out."

"Thought you wanted to play college ball. Maybe you should pick habits that won't kill your dreams." Guy knows full well that I am referring to the fact that Old 99 is also where some kids go to smoke and drink.

"Do you think your grandmother would let me work at The Shore if I had a problem?"

My deafening silence answers for me.

"I'm looking out for you, Harbor. No one dresses up to visit 99."

"Apparently you do." My stomach turns at the idea of Keyne being some low life druggie, then I snap out of it. Keyne is a clean person. He cares about his future and wouldn't mess that up.

"I'm sure he has his reasons," I tell him, looking down to send Rob a text asking him to pick me up early. It has nothing to do with what Guy just said. I just can't stand the thought of Tutu working alone, but not only that, I have a gut feeling. I need to be in the window tonight. The kidnapper hasn't struck in a while, and according to my dad's FBI books, criminals will have a pattern. Like a gamer on a streak, they become addicted and develop a length of time they can't surpass. They can't resist. So the intervals of time to re-offend won't span longer than the last. And it often shortens. Meaning, the monster strikes again in less than two weeks.

Lost in thought, I jump when I feel someone brush my shoulder. Keyne sets down a cupcake and a plate of chips and dip. Guy is still occupying a seat that he was never invited to take, and he doesn't appear eager to move.

"Hey, man. So soon, it's like I just saw you," Keyne quips.

"See you guys around," Guy raises his eyebrows as he pulls himself out of Keyne's chair, but before he walks off, he gives me a warning glance and adds, "Harbor, you look amazing. As usual. It was nice catching up with you."

Guy doesn't acknowledge Keyne, yet the friction in the air speaks loudly. Besides, the last thing I want are compliments from Guy, but since we work together, I sacrifice half a smile and turn toward the real star of the night, the lovely cupcake. I am eye level with a small mountain of pale blue frosting.

"Enjoy it already. I think I see your mouth actually watering," Keyne laughs.

I return the chuckle and waste no time running my finger across the silky piping and take a lick. The cupcake is just as velvety delicious as it looks.

"Don't you work at a diner?" Keyne jokes.

"We have crazy awesome burgers, but we don't make luxurious cupcakes like this," I say popping the fondant snowflake in my mouth.

Keyne and I are engaged in our usual quick moving, light hearted conversation until an announcement is made for all students to enter the dance floor. Once again, we are interrupted. Turns out we had been talking for almost an hour. Keyne is finishing up a story about how he was once on a swim and his dad was timing him and how his dad takes the times seriously, but when under water, Keyne remembered something funny and laughed out loud.

"The worse place to laugh out loud is underwater!"

"Or if someone is trying to murder you, and you need to hide," I say instinctively.

Keyne looks at me, and we both laugh.

"Sorry, that was a bit extreme. I've been hitting the books pretty hard lately. Back to your story. So, I see you didn't drown."

"No, but I did get my head dunked to teach me a lesson." Keyne makes a motion with his hand as if pushing an object down and yells, "Focus!" I assumed he was joking, yet the tone he placed on the word *focus* is more the way a person would impersonate another.

"My lips were as blue as yours."

I quickly wipe my hand across my lips, "You let me talk this entire time with blue frosting on my lips!"

Keyne tenderly brushes his thumb across my chin, and we are eye to eye. His lips begin to move, but a crackling sound from the microphone overpowers the moment. We hesitantly turn our attention to the hubbub and clearly see Mr. Reddy standing across from us on the other side of the dance floor. He is sharing the provisional stage with the D.J. and holding a mic, "Sea Turtles! As we enter a new year, remember to glance back in order to proudly forge ahead. On this magical night, we celebrate the Makahiki."

Keyne grabs my elbow and whispers into my ear, "Is he speaking in riddles again?"

I almost snort, but notice through the crowd of students, Mr. Reddy appears to be speaking directly to Keyne and I. I don't want to call attention to it, so I decide to wait to ask Keyne if he noticed that, "Why did our great ancestors turn to the eastern sky? Because within the constellations is an ancient guide that can lead you anywhere."

"I think we call that GPS today," Keyne jokes, so I nudge him and realize that he never let go of my elbow.

I look up at the sky. It will be dead of night soon, and I worry about the missing kids. That reminds me, Keyne doesn't know I'm leaving the dance early, "Keyne." I stop short, abruptly interrupted by his eyes. Maybe it's standing out under the stars or amidst so many decorative lights, but it is hard to ignore that his eyes hold the light. I have seen over a thousand pairs of eyes through the drive-thru window but none like this. The bold and deep green somehow cast a bright and dusky hue at the same time. A stare that arrests you. I lean in to take a closer look and when I do, I feel it again. But it's more than just the static cling: it's Keyne's warmth. A steady, slow swell moves in my chest, as if the rising tide itself could hush my breath. The scent of salt water, fresh air and the briny sea seizes me. I'm not an avid swimmer, yet when you live on the island, you learn both the beauty and the dangers of the ocean. What I feel now is a combination of both. A tidal wave. One body of water running into another. Turbulence and power spinning until it encloses us, granting us permission to stand under the wave for a small moment in time. The music, the other students, Ha'alele are drowned in this second, the seafloor removed and all we can do is hold on. The world is so calm under the wave. Keyne cradles both my elbows, and I feel his tempered strength. He gently, slowly walks in to me and stares down into my eyes, and I hear the single distinct sound of pounding and crashing. My heart. And then the loud snap, crackle, pop of the microphone. The sound of Reddy's voice makes us starkly aware that we've been washed up and returned back to the middle of the dance floor. The clamor and reverberation of Reddy's voice in the microphone causes other students to cover their ears. I am jolted back to the end of his speech, "…and a prosperous year to all! Let's boogie!" The D.J. cuts in with a fast paced mash-up, and all the students jump, cheer and begin dancing.

Keyne hasn't let go of my elbows, and I don't want him to. He is standing closer to me than he's ever been, well, except for the first day of school when I face planted on his chest. This is different though. This isn't rushed or accidental. This is intentional and we are both willing. Everything around us is a flurry as we stand motionless under the peak of a tidal wave that resists crashing down on us. Until Lott does.

Lott crash lands into Keyne with such force that Keyne's hands slip off my elbows, and he has to catch his balance. Suddenly, it's Lott who is standing in front of me. Not the picture I want in the yearbook.

"Dude, sorry. My dance moves aren't as smooth as I thought," Lott exclaims nonchalantly rather than apologizes.

In the past few months, I have witnessed Keyne treat Lott with numero uno respect. Yet in this second, the normally cheerful Keyne holds daggers in his eyes. His firm stare turns the mood serious, and there is a detectable erosion between the two. With a slight rise in his voice, Lott responds to it, "I said I was sorry."

With a long sigh that doesn't break his stare, Keyne concludes, "Okay, in the future that's not the way you cut in to dance."

Dorsal fin walks up and places her hand on Lott's shoulders, turning him toward her and leads him away before she glares toward Keyne. In a blink of an eye, she made sure Keyne understood her disapproval. Okay, it has got to be a full moon. Keyne holds out his hand to me with an apologetic smile. I take it.

We walk to the terrace behind the D.J. booth overlooking the ocean. Everything on the island is never far from the ocean. My heartbeat still moving with the sound of crashing waves, my phone vibrates.

Outside waiting

"Seriously! Seriously?" I murmur to myself.

"I'm sorry. I have to leave."

"What? Why? If it's Lott, I can handle that."

"No, of course not. It's work. I promised to work a shift tonight," I hold up my phone.

Keyne looks at me in disbelief. I understand we had a moment, but I have to get to that window, "My step-dad is outside waiting."

"Can I walk with you?" he looks around as though something is gnawing at him.

Reaching up, I give him a hug, and over his shoulder, I have a view of the dance floor. Lott and his friends see our hug. They are definitely looking our way, but I sort of expect that. What really catches my attention is that among the D.J. and other students jamming out, Reddy also has his eyes fixed on us. I don't want to let on that I notice, so I take Keyne's hand, "Let's go."

At the front exit, I stop him.

"Are you too big to have help out?"

"Trust me, it will be too many questions. I'll take it from here and you still earn a gentleman's stripe."

He laughs, "Can I text you later?"

"Have you ever not?"

"True."

Heaving a heavy sigh, I don't want the night to end either. But there is a monster in a deadly game of kidnapping and it *has to* end. I know he will push it to the edge. Because monsters never stop on their own.

Our great, wise ancestors turned to the Eastern sky
for within the constellations is an ancient guide ~

CHAPTER 32

I almost black out when I hear the reports that the monster struck again. This time it was a little girl taken on the night of the Winter Dance.

Tutu didn't make the connection until the morning news, and we called Officer Lam immediately. She recalls taking a drive-thru order from a man matching the description I gave Officer Lam. Once again, no one saw the kidnapper. They only caught a glimpse of the blue car screeching away.

"All our customers are cordial with me, but he has a coldness. He never looks my way, as if to say I am nothing, as if I am not even standing there."

My eyes burn and head aches to hear my grandmother was that close to this monster. He struck again, and maybe if I hadn't wasted time at the dance, I might have been able to help.

"What does this mean?" I asked Officer Lam, "Why is he coming through the drive-thru? Does he take the kid before or after? And how does he choose the child? He wasn't supposed to do this again until the end of the month!"

My comment stupefies everyone. Quickly, in an attempt to quell the pensive looks, I say with an ounce of ignorance, "It just *seems like* he's picking up the pace." I left out the fact that I have a sketchbook in my backpack with his demonic profile, his menu order and the dates and newspaper clippings of every kidnapping.

Then what Officer Lam says next is like a punch in the gut, "He is increasing in the number of kids, too. He tried to pick up 2 that night. A brother and a sister, but the boy escaped, and it's his screams that alerted the adults."

Officer Lam goes on to say that the money we gave him didn't have useable fingerprints.

The rest of the holiday break passed in a humdrum. Fig decorated Ember's fishbowl like a fat Santa Claus before she visited Rob's family for a week. Nothing much happened at The Shore, and I had a lot of time to read over dad's old FBI books and reflect on the night of the dance. I remembered that after I got home from my shift that night, Keyne called me on a video chat. Even looking back at our conversation was a welcome pause to all the bad news.

"You changed?"

"A pink dress and heels hasn't been adopted as The Shore uniform yet," I say as I let down my hair. "If you're sleepy, we can catch up later."

With a light laugh, Keyne confesses, "I'm wide awake. Stoked."

"What does that mean?"

His finger magnified on my screen, he is pointing toward me, "Messy lawlessness."

I shake my head in confusion.

"Your hair. It has no rules. Just like you."

"What do you mean?"

"You have a delicate strength, Harbor. One that I've never seen in others."

He constantly diverts my thoughts, "That's why I wear it up. To control it."

"I like it down. The way if falls around your face, wild and graceful. Reminds me of a night swim. The flower."

A warm feeling on my cheeks grew with a smile. The rest of the night, we exchanged talk that revolved around my blue lips, how Keyne ate too much junk food, and how Reddy's dance moves were a pumped up version of how he writes on the board, "Reddy make anymore announcements?"

"I don't know. He left after you did."

"That's odd. Thought he was a chaperone."

"He's a teacher. They're all odd."

We had great conversation sticking to safe topics, staying away from the fact that for a little while, we held hands, we held each other.

Keyne was going on a swimming retreat where phones weren't allowed. The last night we spoke passed so fast, I didn't ask him details. I figure if he wants to tell me, he will. The fact of the matter is, we always get interrupted. I haven't even mentioned much about the kidnappings. Somehow, our friendship has survived despite being cut-off all the time, a nice escape from Ha'alele. That's why I can't stop thinking about how secure I felt standing close to him. It was not the same closeness as squishing our desks together to work on group projects or the kind of closeness when we sit next to each other scarfing down our lunch. This closeness stirred me inside. For a split second, we were more than just friends. If Lott hadn't slid across the dance floor and practically broken Keyne's ribs, I'm certain Keyne was going to try to kiss me.

That moment under the wave was filled with a tender intensity, a new feeling I didn't know existed. Goosebumps crawl up my arm. Why did we both stay away from talking about it? I wouldn't even know where to begin. *Hey, Keyne do you think that was first love we felt or a high from the sugar and chips?* Yeah, I'm growing up, but maybe there is something about growing older that will make this easier. If Keyne really wanted to kiss me or if I really wanted to kiss him, wouldn't we have by now?

Returning to present time, I wonder if it will be weird when we return to school. I will see him tomorrow for the first time since holiday break. Did we pass a point of no return? It's not like holding hands and staring into each other's eyes is a common thing for friends to do. Ugh, why did my hand fit so perfectly in his? And how can an entire world spinning on edge, with rapid undercurrents, always ready to knock us off balance slow down so much? Slow down enough to give us a moment where we stood together, Harbor and Keyne, as one. No dead parents, no kidnappings, no problems. In that moment, life was simple again. A complicated simplicity.

Either way, Lott collided with Keyne, and in an instant, the wave came crashing down. That's the real problem. The apex of a tidal wave can't last forever. It will always come crashing down.

Before I turn in for the night, I want to verify something I read in dad's books. I open Traits of a Child Kidnapper and flip through the pages until I find what I'm looking for.

Child kidnappers tend to be socially isolated, luring those who cannot defend themselves.

A sharp pang cuts through my head. My face and my eyes burn. I think about the recent news

Officer Lam gave me, and pure rage fills my heart. Was the abduction of the little girl an accident? If so, what will he do with her?

According to the FBI, all criminals have a signature. Their signature is different from their M.O. It's a stamp they leave at the crime scene that tells us a key part of who they are. It's their personality. The motive, the M.O., is necessary to commit the crime. *The signature is not.*

A criminal who breaks into two story homes through a window and only steals expensive electronics has both an M.O. and a signature. They need a window to enter, so that is the way they operate or their M.O. But why a two story home? Why only electronics? One of those is their signature. Electronics are easy money and can be resold or pawned. Two story homes, however, are harder to enter. This criminal doesn't have a fear of heights. As a matter of fact, *they enjoy it.* And that's their signature.

Up until now, the kidnapper seems to prefer abducting little boys. Why now a little girl? What is his real signature? His M.O. is obvious. He is a wolf in sheep's clothing. A monster.

Where are you hiding, Mr. Boring? It's only a matter of time before you prey again, and I will be waiting. At least now the entire island is finally on alert, demanding justice. Their signature, not to care until the crime hits home so hard they've been kicked in the gut. It reminds me of studying the Holocaust in our class projects this year. That, in retrospect, we should have acted sooner. We shouldn't *ever* give monsters an inch. Nor an excuse. But Hitler was practiced in the art of propaganda. Maybe this wolf is too. Maybe the next full moon will bring him out, and when he's ready to hunt again, he will be the one devoured.

Slamming the book shut, I grab my pillow and place it over my face with all my strength so it can lasso in my scream. I need to try and get some sleep though not suffocate myself. I curl up next to my pillow and decide to focus on the tidal wave. A tidal wave has a way of washing away the bad dreams.

CHAPTER 33

The parking lot of Kau High is buzzing. As I park, the bright eyed and bushy tailed vibe is evident. The new year offers a clean slate, and old friends catch up while new friends catch on. For so long, the new year meant a continuance of old pain for me. But not this year. I can feel the difference. I feel alive.

Shaking out my ponytail from the flattened state my helmet leaves it in, I realize I haven't had a haircut in a long time. Even worn up, my hair falls past my shoulder blades. When I turn around to get my backpack, I see the smile I missed. Keyne is standing there, relaxed, his hands in his pockets, and waiting for me. How long has he been waiting?

"Good morning," he says.

"Hey, good morning."

How did this friendship shape-shift into a labyrinth? The last time Keyne and I stood together, we held hands and stared into each other's eyes. What turn do we take next? I use both my of hands to grab the straps of my backpack, so there isn't an option for my hands to be free. Keyne's hands fly out of his pockets and he cups his mouth. Was I that obvious?

"You're not wearing your contacts?"

273

"It's a new year. Trying out the old me."

Standing transfixed, he moves in closer to my face, probing my eyes, "Alluring blue…until you swim under and see the jet black center."

"*Awkward?*" I ask tentatively.

"I'm sorry. They stood out at the dance, but in the sunlight, they're bewildering like the ocean. Okay, I'll stop being weird."

Keyne and I immerse ourselves into the first day back from holiday break, each step I take more buoyant than the last, my heart a single plume from a Honeycreeper on the high sea. He is still gaping but manages to plunge into a story about how glad he is to be back.

"Why?" I stop short distracted by his shirt. He is wearing that shirt again. The soft shirt from the first day of school, the shirt Lott wears now and then and the one that eerily reminds me of Mr. Boring.

"Why am I glad to be back?" he attempts to finish his story, but I have to interrupt his enthusiasm.

"Why the long shirt?"

He looks down at what he is wearing and back at me, "Uh, this. It's part of our uniforms. Keeps us warm after a cold swim."

My thoughts are frozen. Keyne stops walking and turns toward me, grabbing my elbow. Oh, I haven't felt his touch in so long, "Harbor, are you okay?"

"No. I mean, yes. Is that Reddy at the vending machine?" I stopped myself from revealing a crazy notion. *Hey Keyne, your shirt reminds me of a psychopath. Are you one?* Thankfully, Reddy is a distraction. He is in a battle with his nemesis, an old vending machine. New building. Outdated, clunky machine.

"Throwing money away?" Keyne walks up to Reddy, and they shake hands.

"Keyne! Harbor! How was the winter break?"

"Cold," Keyne says as he sets down his backpack and approaches the vending machine.

I shrug, "Mostly worked. How was yours?" I finish the question just in time to see Keyne tilt the entire vending machine forward. He made it look as easy as pulling a cereal box off the top shelf of a pantry. I've always known he was strong, yet the muscle mass he just exhibited is a new level.

"Happy New Year," Keyne hands Reddy the candy bar and picks up his backpack.

"Thanks," Reddy's beam is overt. He doesn't seem as surprised as I do that Keyne handled that vending machine like it was a toy. It's almost as though Reddy was aware that Keyne was capable of such strength.

"Keyne, what did you do over the break that you were so cold?"

"Free dive," Keyne smiles.

Bubbly passersby fill the hall and a few stand in line behind Reddy waiting to take their chance with the vending machine. Gleefully, Reddy turns to the crowd, "Oh, excuse me."

By the time he returns his attention to us, we are making our way through the masses. Keyne shouts back as politely as he can, "Catch you later, Mr. Reddy!"

"Every day swim. That's one reason I'm so glad to be back! School will be a break."

"Glad to be back? Homework and tight schedules?"

Holding up his phone and shaking it for emphasis, "On land and cell phone."

We both smile, and I part with, "Well, maybe I'll see you in gym," and we go our separate ways to dress out.

Normally, the boys work out in one gym and the girls in the other, but today, the coaches are loudly scrolling through an announcement. We don't need to dress out. As a matter of fact, they tell us we can walk the length of the gym twice, then do one of the light circuits set up across the two gyms. Good, I can't stand the P.E. uniform. A few of the girls tell me they love my new look, pointing to their own eyes. I forget how long it's been since I've stepped out uncovered. You know, Reddy didn't seem to notice my eye color. However, Keyne lifting a 500 pound clunker over his shoulders was a distraction.

I place my backpack in the locker room before heading out to the gym. When I do, I see Keyne and the blonde coach off to the side. I can't hear, but I can see. Keyne and the coach are very familiar with one another. And why wouldn't they be? The blonde coach is Lott's dad and Keyne's coach outside of school too. But there is something more and I think about FBI rule #6.

FBI rule #6 is never mistake the loudest voice for the strongest one. The person who wears the more esteemed title is not always the leader. Keyne is on the other end of the gym, yet his smile is broadcast atop his confident posture. His entire disposition conveys control. Profiling 101, the blonde coach gets along with Keyne quite well and respects him. Hmm. Odd. I don't think the blonde coach has looked my way once. Who cares? I need to concentrate on applying these profiling rules on the kidnapper. A monster who doesn't seem to have any rules. It's only a matter of time before he rears his ugly head through the window again.

I walk over to the lone bean bag toss station and Keyne runs over, picking up two bean bags and tossing me one.

"So, free diving? Where?"

"Remote spots where we can train without interrupting anyone. Not too far from old 99."

That explains why Guy saw him the night of the dance!

"So, you do compete? Or is this all for the family business?"

"You could say we compete, within our own team. But yeah we are going to offer Free Dive certifications."

"Exciting."

"Wanna sign up?" Keyne gives me a mischievous look.

I laugh, asking, "Sounds dangerous. What height do you jump from?"

"If you score the next point, I'll tell you."

"If?" I scoff playfully, taking both bags, tossing them in a row and scoring top points. I turn back to Keyne with my own mischievous look.

"Impress me over and over," he mumbles.

"So how high?"

"It's definitely in the double digits."

"Now I'm impressed."

His loud laugh is confirmation that I did hear what he mumbled correctly.

"How long before you hit the sunlight zone?"

"Oh, you do know a little something about the ocean!"

"We go over this every year in science."

"Okay, Blue Eyes, how many layers of ocean water are there?" Keyne tests me.

Startled at the new nickname, I stutter, "Do you know?"

He moves in toward me, taking a bean bag and with an unwavering stare, confesses, "Of course, I swim them." His hand grazes mine before he turns and shoots for the top hole. He scored.

Now I test him, "No one swims in the trenches."

An oddly occupied expression just short of a grimace looms over him, "Like I said, always impressive."

And there, I saw it again. A soft flicker, a penetrating glow in the green of his eyes.

Keyne explains that he officially started training at age 10. Now that he is older, his priority is building endurance by slowly pushing his limits.

"Why?"

"To develop stamina, to bear the weight of the water."

"Again, why?"

279

He nudges me, "I'm better at *how*."

He tells me that the team trains their muscles to contract and expand. This conditions their lungs to take in more oxygen. By the end of class, I know more about free diving than I can remember. Making our way out of the gym, I remind him, "You still didn't tell me how deep?" I know there is a level of concern in my voice.

Every year, islanders are warned to use caution on free dives, and every year, there are deaths from people pushing the limits, thinking they can go against mother nature.

"With my suit and mask, I will near the Twilight Zone soon."

I stop in my tracks, stunned, "That's impossible."

The grand foyer is bustling with students making their way this way and that. Keyne grabs my elbow, "Get to class. You don't want to start this semester off with a tardy," as he waves bye with a sobering smile.

Throughout the day, I thought more about Keyne than I did my classes or profiling the monster. New login information for every student had to be verified during our lunch break so I didn't see him, but I couldn't stop thinking about him. Well, actually it was little Keyne that was on my mind.

The young boy who grew up in a cold, dark ocean while most families were enjoying cozy holidays. The small kid who's mom was replaced with disciplined training. By the time I made it to Mr. Reddy's class, Keyne was sharpening his pencil by the window and speaking with a couple of classmates. Seeing my friend in a new light, framed by the window, I smiled in admiration.

Mr. Reddy assigned some group reading, and of course, Keyne and I partnered up giving him a chance to ask, "Do you want to talk about it now?"

"What?" I think, wondering if he read my thoughts and knew I was thinking about him.

"My shirt?" he reminds me looking down at the suede green garment.

"Sure, just not here. It's silly anyway. When can we talk?"

"Any day that ends in a Y," he winks.

Again, I can't help but smile, "There is something I want to ask you."

"Anything."

I try not to look surprised.

"Free diving…so deep, so often. Is that how you enjoy spending your time?"

Keyne gives a contemplative look, "I was raised to be a swimmer. It's a way of life."

Mr. Reddy asks a kid to handout a paper and instructs us, "Have your parents sign this permission slip," but in a knee jerk reaction, looks directly at Keyne and adds, "Or your guardians. We are taking a field trip for those of you who can keep your grades up."

Why would Reddy look at us after saying *parents*? He doesn't know my history.

FBI rule #3 takes note of new gestures in clusters. One or two differences in behavior may not mean a lot, yet when a person acts out of character multiple times, especially in a short period of time, it means they are up to something. I don't have time to figure out what one weirdo teacher might be up to. More than likely, he heard the rumors about my parents and is aware of my many misfortunes. I decide to be a bit more cautious of what I say or do around him.

By the time the bell rang, I was still pre-occupied with the thought of the hurt little boy who was once Keyne. I know more than anyone what the pain of losing a parent can do to a kid. What I don't know is if dunking an already traumatized kid in treacherous waters helps any or hurts even more.

The bell rang, and Keyne stood, ready to leave class, yet I was still lost in deep thought and stayed seated. Keyne took his seat again and leaned in forward over my desk, "It makes my heart beat a little faster. But no, it doesn't make me smile."

Stunned that he remembered *my quiz*, I'm coaxed into showing my amusement, "What does then? Makes you smile?"

"Now *the answer to that* is what scares me."

A raucous clearing of a throat prompts us both out of our seats. Together, we realize it's Reddy who is making a point to clamor about his desk, shuffling papers around to purposely interrupt our conversation. Once we are a few feet out the door, Keyne stops me, a tantalizing grip on my elbow, "I want to finish our conversation. I haven't heard your voice in what seems like forever."

"Me too."

"Do you work today?"

Lott's timing is impeccable. There he stood eliciting a sigh from both Keyne and I. Does this guy wait in the shadows for us to step out of class? Does he even go to class?

"Text when you get a chance," he says, releasing my elbow. I wave goodbye.

I ride the bend to The Shore and with each inch of the road, I am eased back into a free state of mind, not bogged down by burdens or old scars. The hum of the Argo plays backup for

283

the coal black and scarlet feathered creatures flying above. With the winter comes seclusion. But the Honeycreepers don't retreat. They don't hide from the cold. I wonder where monsters hide.

No recorded kidnappings since the night of the Winter Dance. According to his profile, the suspect will strike again and soon. If the drive-thru window makes that socially isolated coward emerge, *perfect*. I will be waiting to make sure he's isolated until the end of time. In prison.

Pulling into The Shore, a light breeze from the ocean travels up and fluffs my ponytail as soon as my helmet is released. I look at a picture of me and the lady I use to call mom. I think of the kid version of Keyne again, without a mom. What accident did she mean? Why would she tell her son about it on her death bed? The vibration of my phone stops my mental interrogation. All I want to do is reach out to Keyne.

Any chance you can meet tonight?

Immediate response.

I wish. Training, you know one of the things that scares me. Laughing emoji. Swim emoji.

Well, don't get lost in the darkness.

The reason I train is to see through it. Winky face emoji.

Toying with the idea of adding a heart emoji, I'm saved by a commotion. It's Fig running out of The Shore, "Harbor!"

Ringlets of soft caramel hair chase after my little sister in her in excitement, "Harbor, you gotta see what Tutu added to the menu."

"Please don't say it involves chopsticks."

Her giant grin and tiny hand grabs me, and before I know it, I'm in our bustling little hamburger joint. It's the place I work, but it always feels like home. Lona and Guy are adding new menu inserts. Clings and clangs from the kitchen staff vibrate through the walls, and savory scents from the grill waft through the air. Fig lights up as she hands me one of the menus. I read it, shaking my head, "Chopstick Cheeseburgers?!?"

Fig bobs her head, "Tutu added burgers you eat with chopsticks! Told you."

Looking closer at the bright pictures on our new menu, I'm intrigued. Four mini, flattened meatballs topped with melted cheese wrapped in a fluffy baked dough are accompanied by a selection of four dipping sauces. The little cheeseburger ball comes with a choice of sweet and tangy ketchup, spicy mayo, buffalo or pineapple bacon barbecue. I peer closer at the picture on the menu and see that customers have a choice between teal or coral chopsticks. In disbelief, I look up at Tutu who is waiting for my response.

"Harbor, we have to compete with these big hotels."

"Tutu..." I hug her and look down at Fig, who I'm sure is trying to read my mind, "I love it! My mouth is watering."

Tutu's proud smile mirrors Fig's, "I'm gonna change. Prepare to sell out of those Chopstick Cheeseburgers. And I want my own set of chopsticks."

Guy walks into the break room behind me, "How was the first day back?"

"Good," I turn away. Sorry, not sorry that I don't care to ask him the same. As I try to head into the bathroom, Guy stops me by clutching my arm. I glare down at his arm and back at him with a look that clearly directs him to move his hand *now*.

"Sorry," he says letting go of my arm, and after an involuntary pause declares, "Your friend is crazy, you know."

"Excuse me?" I say pretending I don't know who he is talking about.

"Keyne," Guy says in a terse, flat manner.

I feel my face get hot. Who is Guy to be talking about Keyne? I turn toward him, expecting some breaking news even though deep down, I know Guy is jealous of my new friendship. He seems intent on giving me rumor mill shocking news that will make me pull away from Keyne.

"I saw him and his buddies cliff jumping off 99 the other day."

"So what? Lots of people do that."

"It was midnight, Harbor."

Trying to conceal my alarm, I question what Guy was doing out off 99 at midnight, always seeming to be in the wrong place at the right time, "Do you have a problem with Keyne?"

"I was with some friends, star-gazing," Guy punts back.

"Whatever, Guy."

"Harbor, this new guy appears out of nowhere and you, who won't go out or have fun with anyone in years, becomes his best friend? Someone that's not even from our island?"

Clenching my jaw at his loaded remark, I keep my poise. Guy is testing my patience. But, even if he sounds like a jerk in this moment, I know he is apprehensive because he has seen the pain my family has suffered. He's protective of my pain. He doesn't know you can't protect someone else's pain.

"Guy, Keyne *is* from the island. He moved away for a while, but that's beside the point. He's a friend, doesn't matter where he's from."

"Well, if that's the case, I guess you won't care that he's hanging out with some of the kids from school. Seems real close to some of the girls at night, but at school, you wouldn't have a clue since he only wants to be around you."

"Rumors are a waste of time, Guy. He's a friend and I don't know why I'm entertaining this conversation. I've got to get to the window."

"I saw it. And I didn't have a window blocking my view. Those girls hang all over him!"

Guy walks away, having stolen a hunk of some of my good new year vibes.

The window is busy. Tutu's Chopstick Cheeseburgers are a hit! Lord knows, I needed the distraction. I didn't acknowledge Guy for the entire shift, and even though I refuse to be influenced by his ranting, I admit, I am secretly irritated but not at Guy. Guy may be a lot of things, but he won't lie to me.

Keyne can talk to whoever he wants when he wants. So why would he hide how close he is to other girls? Why would I care? *Why would he care that I care? We're friends. Right?* Friends don't need to put on acts for each other. *Yeah,* I think to myself, *they also don't hold hands and stare into each other's eyes.*

Fig lights up as she hands me the new menu.

Chopstick Cheeseburgers?!?

"Tutu says to compete with the big hotels."

289

CHAPTER 34

Another nightmare. Someone I knew…
someone I loved was wrestling with the water
monster. Others waited in the shadows watching
me, avoiding me. They didn't help. They were
observers. Attentive spectators betting on my
distress, gambling on my next move. Whether I
would sink or swim against the terrifying giant
lizard. It conjured evil while I tried to summon
myself, but my eyes stung with a torrid burn.
From its pores oozed a molten drip, a dross that
blistered my skin and scalded my eyes. It
wanted possession of my loved one, and it
wanted to brand me. Even if it meant going
blind, I wasn't going to let that happen.

The worst nightmare yet. It was so realistic
that if the aroma of bitter and sweet steamed
espresso had not floated through the house and
right into my nostrils, I may have fallen prey to
the monster. Rob makes coffee when he arrives
early to take Fig to school. I'm glad. He can
handle Fig this morning, I need to leave early
today. That's a good thing about having an easy
wardrobe, I can be ready in seconds.

My head is still ringing from the so-called
dream that when Rob offers me a ride to school,
the best I can do is decline with a shake of my

head and a wave good-bye. Rob will get the hint. I need to clear my head before school, and there's only one place I can do that.

Approaching the curve of the bend, the bad dream falls behind me, splattering into the volcanic ash pavement. I'm enveloped in towering trees where the sunrise can only faintly announce its presence, and the whistles of the Honeycreepers irrefutably mark the morning.

The whir of the Argo comes to a halt once I enter the clearing, and the sound of crashing waves below says hello. I walk to the edge of the cliff and inhale deeply. Pure, fresh air is abundant and planks the titanic ocean for as far as the eye can see. From the edge where I stand, I have a bewitching vantage point. A sky the color of cotton candy is an umbrella over the blue green expanse, and it is breathtaking. As I look down over the steep cliff, I realize that in a couple months, the landscape will change again. Monk seals will fill the beach as they begin to deliver their pups. In that moment, I'm jolted back to the water monster. It was colossal. Could I have somehow dreamt of the monk seals? Who was in the dream with me? Why can't I see their faces, and what the hell was I thinking fighting a drippy lizard? If this is what Tutu calls a vision, are the nightmares the Third Eye? If so, what should I be seeing?

I take one last look across the massive sea, out toward the harbor. I tell myself it was just a dream. *It was just a dream.* Maybe by the time I get to school, I can convince myself of just that. Turning to walk away, I stop to look back over my shoulder once more and inhale deeply.

Turning the handles of the Argo, it turns on, then shuts off immediately. Oh no, remembering to fuel up is not my strong suit. I won't have time to stop at Old Man Ferencz'. Using my thumb, I rub the small window to the gas gauge making short, high pitched squeaking sounds before I realize that I have enough to get to school and back. I can put gas later. Phew.

Keyne texted last night, but I was so busy lobbing Chopstick Cheeseburgers out the drive-thru window, I didn't get home until late. By the time I showered and said goodnight to Fig, who somehow tricked me into humming along to a bedtime song to Ember, I was pooped. Even though Keyne had texted again, which is rare, I was too tired to answer. He asked some random question.

Tattoos? Thumbs up or thumbs down emoji. It wasn't until I woke up that I saw a missed call from him. But as I pull into the school parking lot, I notice something else about Keyne. He's there.

Waiting near my parking space, he stands, waiting with both hands in his pocket. Same confident stance, same silky, wavy dark hair, same subtle strength. He is talking to his posse of tiger sharks and turns to wave hi to me when he hears the Argo. He waves a *catch-up-with-you-later* gesture to the group, who look from his hand to me. In a displeased fashion, they change course and dart away. Keyne takes a few steps toward me, "Good Morning, stranger." Forget any plans I had of trying to avoid this guy.

Barely responding with a hey, I distract myself from the smoulder in his green eyes. I pack my helmet, put on my backpack and immediately occupy both my hands with my backpack straps, but Keyne doesn't move. He is standing so close to the Argo with a puzzled look on his face. Looking down at me, directly into my eyes, he asks, "Is everything ok?"

His gaze is sharp and deep. Delicate flashes of blue twinkle from within, making it hard to look away. I take a huge sigh to prevent myself from going beyond the edge, from being drawn in any deeper. The sigh allows me enough motion to unlock from his stare. I know that I have no right to be irritated with Keyne. We are cool with each other, and he's a good guy, so I can see how other girls would totally want to hang out with him. I shake my head, wondering how I ever let myself care this much about someone I have no intention of ever telling.

"I'm wearing a different shirt," he jokes.

I nod my head and start walking, which naturally moves Keyne from my path.

"Ok, so this is different," he says, now walking beside me. I don't say anything.

"Harbor," he stops me by gently grabbing my elbow, causing a couple of kids to stop mid-walk and bump into us. "Hey, what's going on?"

"What do you mean?" I say, moving my elbow. Keyne looks down at his empty hand and back at me.

"I'm not really sure what myself. Things always seem to flow with us, and you're not talking to me, so, yeah, it's kind of weird."

Keyne is right. And I am wrong. I let what Guy said get in my head. It probably isn't even totally true, and even if it were, so what? Deep down, I know that's the real problem. The so what?

"Keyne, I just have a lot on my mind. It's nothing."

"Harbor, we're friends. You can talk to me." *Exactly. We are friends.*

"I'm good," I smile, "besides, I can't tempt chance with another tardy."

Leaving my smile with Keyne, I begin to walk off but stop short when I hear him say, "Well, if it means I'm with you, I'll take the chance."

I fling around and find myself locked in his gaze once again. Keyne looks serious, and this confuses the hell out of me. Before I can stop myself, I blurt out, "What does that even mean, Keyne?"

Oh, how I wish I could go back in time and chomp those words to smithereens. But it's too late. It's out there. All I had to do was pretend I don't care. I feel the burn on my cheeks, and a surge of anger rushes through my veins. I'm half angry at Keyne's unclear signals like accidentally holding my hand or how he remembers things about me from years ago or why he is so freakin nice, but I'm more angry at myself for caring.

"I wasn't planning on saying that…"

"Let's pretend you didn't," I cut him off and walk to class.

In P.E., the coaches have the girls' and guys' rotate from inside calisthenics and outside sprints. I don't run into Keyne until after I race out of the girls locker room to make it to class in time. He's standing outside waiting. Ugh. Thank God there isn't an echo in here because my heart would make someone bust a move. Keyne smiles almost sympathetically, and I decide to smile back. Why bother being mad? We are friends, plain and simple.

"Was it a full moon last night?" he asks jokingly. I put out my hand as if to say *truce* and he takes it, but instead of shaking it, he holds it. Okay, I am about to slap this boy! I start to pull my hand away but don't have to because Lott is exiting the gymnasium and walks right between us, breaking our hands apart.

Keyne and I both laugh at Lott as he walks on talking to a group that was waiting for him.

"Your cousin sure isn't a people person."

"Lott is a really good guy, but yeah, he's all work. Hey, did you get my text last night?" Keyne's coy smile acts like a magic wand. I don't want to be mad at him, especially when he doesn't even know why. I feel good that our friendship is still in tact. We begin making our way through the grand foyer.

"Yeah, the tattoo?"

"Soooo?"

"Tattoos or teen tattoos?"

Keyne's laugh is as warm as his hands, "What's the difference?"

"How about we catch up at lunch?" I bend and badge and leave Keyne in the foyer. As the door slides open, I catch a glimpse of a lateral line led by Lott approaching him and realize that everyone in the group except Keyne is wearing long sleeve shirts. Yeah, it's winter but on the island that just means beautiful weather.

With the nightmare, working late, Guy's stupid comments and my stupid feelings, I need a little peace and quiet and decide to skip lunch and go to the library. I send Keyne a polite text.

Catch up with you later

He texts back an emoji with a confused face.

Yeah, welcome to the club, I think.

I decide to check out a book we need for English next week. Apparently, the English and History departments are teaming up for a novel study, and we will get the English part from Ms. Iona and the History lesson from Reddy. Getting the book out of the way will be a good distraction.

The aisles of the library remind me of our front porch. Clean and quiet. My hand glides over rows and rows of books, looking for the one I need, but I succumb to another distraction and allow my hand to fall and slide into my belt. I take out the picture of mom, dad, and me. If they were here today, could I talk to them about whatever this is I've been feeling? Would I? Would they also say I have the Third Eye? I return our picture back in Aadya's belt and force myself to place my efforts back to looking for the book I need. Within minutes of actual effort, I find a few copies. I sift through a couple of pages but tuck it under my arm when I get a text. It's from Tutu asking me if I want her or Rob to pick me up because it is 50% chance of afternoon showers.

No thanks, Tutu. I have a rain coat. Need to stop for gas anyway.

I feel a tap on my shoulder and practically jump into the turn. I don't know why I was so startled because when I look down, I see a gray-haired woman looking up at me, "Excuse me, the library is a no phone zone."

Oh, I forgot to turn down my volume, so even the keys make an annoying ticking sound when texting. I give an apologetic smile to the librarian and turn down the volume. I turn around, and this time, I do jump. Why am I so jumpy? This time I have good reason. Keyne is standing in front of me. Boy, after an entire holiday break of complete silence, he is popping up everywhere.

"Well, you just break the rules everywhere you go, don't you?"

I softly hit him with the book, telling him he needs to check one out before they are all gone. He follows as I show him where the copies are and he whispers, "So, about the tattoo?"

"Are you seriously thinking of getting one?"

His facial expression is clear.

"And you're asking me because…?"

"I want your opinion."

"Yeah, I doubt that."

"What do you mean?"

"I mean, you might not like what I think."

"I'm not asking for permission," Keyne says sarcastically, "I want to know how you feel."

Uh, I highly doubt that too.

"Okay, just for the heck of it, what is your dream tattoo?"

Keyne opens his mouth to answer but stops short and instead makes an aha gesture, guiding me by my elbow to the couch. Taking out a pen from his backpack, he lightly draws a figure on his left forearm. I laugh and say, "A baked potato?"

He laughs and shakes his head then gestures for me to wait as he prances back towards the rows of books. He disappears into the library for as long as it takes me to turn down the volume on my phone and returns with a giant book. Taking a seat across from me, he turns to a page with a huge, black sea creature on it. My eyes begin to burn, and it's like I am transported back into a memory I can't exactly recall. It compels me to reach for my temples.

"Harbor, are you okay?"

I try to dismiss it; old dreams run a marathon through my mind. Unable to escape the flashbacks, I do what I learned a long time ago. Go with it. When I was younger, I'd have blackouts. Doctors attributed this to the trauma I suffered from losing my parents. Both suddenly. Both without explanation.

With my forehead cradled in my right hand, I'm back in the dream. I see the outlines of dark figures, rotating around the faces of people, some I know, some are too young, too little. The dark figures move slowly, almost as if they are guarding a hunt, protecting their cache. They are so big, yet swim in sync, an odd grace to their cumbersome masses.

Keyne is calling me. His voice sounds muffled as though he is under water. I know he is outside the dream, but I'm stuck inside. And then I see, I see me. My vision is of me! I bolt up from the couch in an effort to escape. It's a stupid dream! Then loud and crystal clear, I hear the depth of concern and cracking of Keyne's voice, "Harbor, what happened?"

I see the librarian walking toward us, maybe he does too. His arm cushions my elbow as he leads me out of the library.

The fresh air of the grand foyer, the birds singing outside the large glass windows, and the beautiful colors of the landscape are a welcome contrast to the dream. I try to focus on that for a moment and breath slowly. Feeling his hand on my elbow, I turn toward Keyne and the most bewildered look I've ever seen.

"I'm sorry," I say.

"Don't be," he responds. "Are you okay? Do you need the nurse?"

"The nurse can't help."

"What happened? Is the word tattoo a trigger word?"

Rubbing my eyes, I laugh. He meant it as a joke, but I am in no condition to dissect it. I walk over to the window facing Fig's school and set my backpack down to lighten my load when I realize that Keyne has been in step with me the whole time.

I explain to him that this sometimes happened in the lower grades, and my doctor said it's the fight or flight mode. She said that all of us have it. It's our own safety mechanism from stressful situations.

"Well, the library isn't my favorite room either, but…"

I laugh and nudge him, and his huge smile comforts me. He asks, "Which are you, fight or flight?"

"Complicated," I say matter of factly.

"That, *I know*."

I nudge him again and explain that the doctor described it as me fighting myself. When I try to suppress my natural impulses, I sort of short circuit.

"But what were you trying to fight or not fight just now? "

"I don't know."

"If it means no headaches, why not flight, why not run further away?"

"I'm a slow runner."

Keyne shells out another reassuring smile, and I turn to see Fig's class headed out for recess. The bell rings, and her class breaks out of their line. Kids set free on the playground are running like hungry little ferrets. Then our bell rings. And I wish with all my heart that I could feel that sort of innocent freedom again.

CHAPTER 35

For the next couple of weeks, I work long hours. Tutu releasing her Chopsticks Cheeseburgers early was a smart choice. They've taken the island by storm. With Valentine's Day approaching, she is preparing a re-release of one of her sweet treats and has been occupied planning the marketing. So the extra work is good for me, especially after that episode in the library. My brain needed a re-coup and my mind needed a safe place to cooperate. I decided it was time to diagnose my headaches. To give this whole Third Eye thing an opportunity. After all, I'd rather control the dreams than have them control me. I began by writing down what I saw, what I could remember, and as it turns out, it's not that far removed from profiling a suspect. Just this time, I'm looking into my own subconscious.

And even though I haven't heard from Officer Lam, I am still waiting to hear from the suspect. I've read and re-read Traits of a Child Kidnapper. According to professionals, the suspect will be socially isolated. But from the outside, I'm sure I appear that way too.

"Order up!"

Sam's loud voice and the ding of the bell almost knock me out of my chair. I fold over three teal Shore bags and hand them to the father driving the mini-van, but he is engrossed with his phone. I see two empty car-seats and a kid buckled in between playing on his iPad. I recognize the van and know how busy this family stays. The third row holds a violin case and a flute.

"Excuse me sir."

"Oh, I'm sorry. The only time I have to check email...when I'm not driving," he says taking the wax bags full of mouthwatering grindz.

"Ma halo," I offer, and he waves good-bye. We serve fast food, but we aren't like the bigger chains. We stand out for preparing our food fresh. Sure, Tutu is always trying new ideas, but we keep our menu simple and sell only what we do well. *Menu simple.* My mind drifts back to the suspect. He may be the only order I serve that is so simple and plain. Simple and plain. I take out my journal and look at my notes on his previous orders. Re-reading it, simple and plain definitely jumps out.

Shore burger plain. Well, he's ordered a chocolate chip cookie at least once. It doesn't fit. Everything else about this guy is stale. I don't know why, but this has to be important. I scribbled a small star by the word cookie.

My newsfeed hasn't had any new leads on the missing kids, and that is bullshit. It makes me sick that we live in a modern world yet can't catch a monster.

Fig left early with Rob today, and Tutu said she and Sam are going to take the late evening shift, so I should go home and rest because she may need my help in the next couple of days.

"Are you sure, Tutu?"

"Yes. Lona and Guy are helping close today."

"Okay," I give-in hesitantly.

"Harbor, dear," Tutu seems to have hesitation in her voice too,"…you seem quite distracted lately. Is there anything you want to talk about?"

Not completely thrown off-guard because Tutu has always been an anchor in my upside down life, I sigh and answer as honestly as I can, "Nope."

Placing her hands on her hips, "Anymore dreams?"

"I have big dreams, Tutu, getting into college, seeing the world…"

She arches her brows and says, "Be serious, dear."

I can't help but laugh, "No more bad dreams, Tutu." My phone vibrates, and I see a text from Keyne. I give her a kiss and head out, "Talk to you later, Tutu."

Hi
Hi back
Can we talk?
What's up?
Where?
???
Can we talk in person?
I'm not home
I will go to you
Meet me at Old Man Ferencz'

The Argo is practically on empty, and I need to fill the fuel tank anyway, so I head that way.

Old Man Ferencz wears a funny face while he hands me my change. As I try to make sense of why he is smiling and crinkling his nose up, I feel a tug on my elbow. Simultaneously, the distinct scent of fabric softener wafts in the air, producing a carefree, woozy feeling, and I know Keyne is standing behind me. Gee, what if it weren't Keyne? For all Old Man Ferencz knew, I could have been robbed, and he didn't even warn me. I turn around and somehow Keyne's hand stays cupped over my elbow.

Valentine's Day is around the corner and I want to be careful. I'm not interested in joining the googly-eyed mad rush to hook up before V-Day. Unlike many of my peers, I don't have free time to prioritize caging a lovebird. Maybe the chirpy girls Keyne hangs out with do. Who cares?

"Hey," I say peeking past him. A clear view through the window shows an empty parking lot other than he Argo.

"Lott dropped me off while he ran a quick errand," Keyne responds to my look of curiosity.

"Wanna go on a ride?"

"One hundred percent, absolutely."

In no time, we are riding the bend.

The curves in the bend force our bodies to move in unison and the pristine ocean breeze feels like a thousand kisses escorting us into the clearing. I pull in, and Keyne walks straight to the edge of the cliff. Looking down, he says, "One hundred feet."

"What?"

"We are 100 feet up," he states matter of factly, as though he has measured the cliff.

"I never thought about it that way."

"How do you think of it?"

"High enough to see what I want and hidden enough to get away when I don't want to be seen."

He laughs walking over to me, "What is it you want to see?"

I take my seat in the clearing, and Keyne follows. I feel the weight lifted off my chest and exhale. That answer is easy, "A pure ocean, the dusk, the dawn. Oh, the monk seals. When they have pups, it's pretty spectacular. This will be my 3rd year to catch it."

"Awesome. So, what are you hiding from?"

With a firmness, I look at him and say, "I didn't say I was hiding."

Grabbing one of my rocks and rolling it between my hands, "I said I prefer to be unseen now and then."

"Like your eyes?"

"I thought you wanted to talk not interrogate," I say playfully.

"You've been kind of quiet lately, and I just want to make sure you are okay?"

"Yeah, of course I am. Again, I'm sorry about the library. That hasn't happened in so long."

"What happens exactly?" Keyne asks, but I'm not ready to dive into that subject. *Well, my grandmother says I have a Third Eye.* Yeah, not something said easily, if ever at all.

"What makes you so confident we are 100 feet up?"

He goes along with my deflection. Standing up, he holds out his hand to me. My upper teeth bite my bottom lip, and I inhale because these are exactly the type of mixed messages that confuse the hell out of me. Before my lip starts bleeding, I slowly release my pearly whites back up and take his hand, allowing him to help lift me up. And there they are again. Eyes like I've never seen before, flares that pull you in. His hand feels just like it did the night of the dance, but this time he doesn't let go. He guides me, and as we near the edge of the cliff, he uses his free hand to point out over the ocean and back to the bottom of the cliff.

"When we dive, we learn how to gauge the depth using the entire landscape," he says as though he is having trouble breathing or getting his words out. He turns from the water to me and uses his free hand to move my hair from my cheek. A few minutes ago, I was handing burgers out a drive-thru window and now I'm on the edge of a cliff, holding hands and staring into the eyes of someone who makes me feel happy, safe, alive and furious at the same time. No wonder I have nightmares.

Keyne and I stand together, our eyes smiling at an unknown fear. He seems to be breathing slow and heavy too. I've felt something like this once before when I was caught in a tidal wave. The water around you moves so fast, and it's so powerful that for a brief moment in time, it locks out the world, the noise and allows you to live in the intimate fear of its protection. At any moment, the heavy powerful waters can come crashing down on you, and all you can do is keep your composure, seize the rare moment and get ready to ride the wave. Or find a way to push yourself out, which is exactly what I do.

I begin to walk away, but Keyne doesn't let go of my hand. He gently brings me back, and I let him. We are standing closer than we ever have, a magnetic force between two friends. Our eyes lock once again, and he places his forehead on mine. I hug him.

"Thank you."

"For?"

"I forgot what a real hug felt like."

I open my mouth to respond yet stammer on my words. How can someone forget the closeness of a real hug? Not sure what to say, I decide what to do. I wrap my arms around him a little tighter. His sigh crushes me. It's hollow and dense at the same time. It makes my heart heavy, "Keyne…"

"Don't," His cheek touches the top of my ear, and I feel the warmth of his voice travel behind me, "I want your friendship, not your pity." He squeezes me a little tighter, and a surge of bittersweet energy travels through my veins. My breath is audible. I want to tell him how sorry I am but decide to let the wind do the talking.

Our friendship revolves around more than our losses. Keyne and I have fun together, working and laughing, yet beneath the surface there is a heightened comprehension that we share. One that very few will ever share. One that no one should. It's taboo.

We both had our childhood uprooted when we lost a parent and both of us have felt cavernous suffering. Even though I don't admit it, sometimes the only thing to get you through the toughest days are the real hugs. I have Tutu, Fig, and even Rob for that, and I actually dodge their hugs! Who does Keyne have? A school of sharks and an absent dad whose sole focus is building a business? I may choose to fight mine daily, but Keyne was forced to bury his sorrow along with his mom. How far can that make a person sink? Like the burrowed Samoan crab, does it only come up when it's provoked? Ha'alele.

The wind picks up, thrashing my ponytail across Keyne's face and onto his shoulder, "Keyne…"

He interrupts me by re-iterating, "Harbor, please don't…," He lifts his head and pulls back, sliding his hand down my arm to take my elbow. My hair slips off his shoulder as he turns toward the direction of the open waters.

I can feel my eyes begin to swell, imagining a little boy, a young Keyne, with no one to hug, maybe even no one to tell him that he's loved.

He studies the expanse then sighs in contentment, "Out there, Harbor...when I'm in deep, the ocean carries me, and life is so simple for that moment in time. I'm one body clinging tightly to another. That's gotta count as a hug, right?"

"You don't live in the water."

He laughs, "Sometimes I feel like I do. Besides, if I wanted a hug, they seem to be everywhere. A dime a dozen."

I squint, my sympathy shocked by his arrogance, "What does that mean?" I ask to the tune of his ring tone.

"Nooo, not you. This was amazing. I don't mean you," he says looking down at his incoming call.

"Hugs are everywhere? Easy?" I say with particles of Guy's accusation lingering in my question.

"Harbor, that came out wrong. It's Lott," Keyne says holding up his phone. "Can we talk later?"

I walk away, slipping my elbow out of his hand, "It's okay. Seriously. We both need to get back. Let's just enjoy the ride."

We arrive at the gas station, and Lott is waiting with a carload of roadies. The Dorsal Fin girls greet Keyne like lures on a hook, and I don't doubt they are part of those easy hugs. I've convinced myself that I don't care; that I won't ever take part in anyone's drama. Yet what do I do if it's my own internal drama that is the real hazard?

The Argo hugs the road tightly on my ride home, and with each curve, I focus on the bend. The bend is always better than focusing on what I don't understand. Like the fact that, just because you stare someone right in their eyes doesn't mean that they will see you.

CHAPTER 36

At school, Keyne and I spoke, but stayed away from the subject of hugs...until we didn't.

On the way out of History, he catches up with me at the Argo, "Harbor!"

"I'm headed to work."

He says he wants to give me something then makes a joke about how it wasn't another headache, "Things have been kind of weird since that day at the bend."

I raise my eyebrows withholding an emphasis on my thoughts. *You Think?*

"It shouldn't be weird. We're friends. Can we meet up tomorrow? If you can, I'll find a way to get out of practice."

"No other hugs available?"

"What?"

In that moment, I'm angry by how confused he looks. How can he not see that his mixed messages muddle the hell out of this friendship? Instead of pledging an oath that I don't care who he hugs or dates, a slur of emotions spills out of my mouth, onto the concrete pavement of the school parking lot and all over Keyne.

"Guy's seen you, Keyne. Hanging out at midnight, laughing, living it up! All that is fine, but what I don't understand is if we are friends, maybe," I re-iterate, "*Maaaybe*, it gets under my skin a little because friends usually talk about nights like that. Instead, all I hear is that you have practice. Really, Keyne? Practice sounds a hell of a lot like a party." I release my clutch on the throttles of the Argo and see Keyne's eyes, widen to twice their size.

"Party?" he asks, bewildered. Then as if barely able to breathe, he laughs so loud, it mimics a small explosion. I feel my cheeks blush, "Maybe you like it casual, call it hanging out, partying, easy hugs, whatever, Keyne."

"Harbor, I don't know where to begin. I train."

"Late nights with some girls up off 99 swimming in the moonlight sounds like a real rigorous program," I don't try to hide my sarcasm.

Keyne and I began our friendship on an awkward footing. After I slammed into him in the hall on the first day of school, I would never have guessed we would become friends. He's seen me for who I am, and maybe I'm angry because I thought I saw him too. Now Keyne and I stand idle while carloads of students try to escape Kau High.

"You can date whoever you want. That's not the problem I have."

Then he does something I've never seen him do. He begins shaking, one arm around his stomach, the other slapping his knee before he doubles forward, laughing so loud that I swear the busy parking lot paused for a second. My blushing turns to a short burn.

"Harbor, we reeaaaally need to talk," he grabs my elbow to hold himself from falling because he is winded by his own laugher. I yank my elbow back, causing him to lose his balance then I hop on the Argo, "Later."

"Wait," Keyne has managed to tame his atomic laughter to a slight giggle under his breath, "Sorry, but I'm not dating anyone. It's funny because…"

"Keyne, you can do what you want. You said it yourself. Hugs are a dime a dozen."

"Harbor, girls are on our swim team too."

Because interrogation is natural to me and not because I care, I mention a critical detail, "At midnight?"

"Yeah, you know we train at night. I didn't know you cared?"

Is he asking me?

"It's not your training that's the problem. It's…"

"What?"

"If it's that easy to get your hugs…I'm not easy."

"That's what this is about? Harbor, half of what I want to say to you gets mangled from when I'm thinking of it underwater to when we actually have a moment alone."

I replay the series of his words. Did Keyne just say that he thinks of me on his swims?

"Harbor, this isn't the place I imagined I'd give you this," he says looking around at the dreary, half empty lot then reaches into his backpack, "I'd like you to have this."

He takes my hand, and dammit, I let him. He places a small bundle, hardly bigger than my cell phone into my palm. It is wrapped in an exquisite, soft blue tissue and fastened with a thin, weathered rope. The package feels heavier than it looks. Keyne arches one eyebrow up, hinting for me to open it. I untie the twisted strand to unwrap the paper. Staring down at the object inside, I'm speechless. Beneath the blue, a smooth, dark rock is revealed. And without thinking, I allow my fingers to glide over the silky smooth texture. It's so dark that I can practically see my reflection. It's just a rock, but it has a distinct beauty, almost like a charm. A car pulls up and blows its horn, breaking my attention and grip. I bunch up the tissue, distracted by the music blasting and see that Lott and the so-called team are waiting.

"Thanks?"

"I saw that you collect them at the bend. This one is from my deepest dive, so it's not a common find."

I smile contently, but Keyne is already halfway to the car and yells over his shoulder, "We'll talk later, okay?"

He drives away, and I start to pack the rock, but my eye catches writing on the flip side. It's the date. Tomorrow's date. Then I realize, tomorrow is Valentine's Day. More confused than ever, I drive to work. My short burn reverts back to a blush.

The Shore is gridlocked. Midway through my shift, Tutu gives me a break. She smiles at the rock laying in blue tissue by the register. I stationed it there hoping to examine it a bit closer, but the window was so busy, I haven't had a chance. I grab my rock and head to the break room to slurp up our seasonal Sweetheart Smoothie while knocking out my Math homework.

This time of year, rambutan and strawberry are plentiful, and Tutu capitalizes on their harvest. It's a luscious smoothie. Pureed berries add a subtle sweetness and give it a bubblegum pink color that pairs nicely with our teal Shore straws. And it taste great with Tutu's other Valentine specialty; Cupids' Crush.

Cupid's Crush is a generous portion of crispy french fries with 3 dipping sauces: a pink sauce that combines house made ketchup and ranch dressing, a bright red sauce composed of a handful of crushed cherry tomatoes and see-thru thin radishes sprinkled with pink Himalayan salt and a white sauce that is house made ranch dressing mixed with horse radish and a dash of red pepper. Simple, but boy, does it bring in the crowds. This is also the only time of year she bakes her chocolate chip cookies with pink, white and red chips.

Fig enters the break room to say good-bye to me, but that develops into a long chat about how she is attempting to train her goldfish and how I should help. Then she says that Rob may take her on one of his helicopter runs over Spring Break and how the kids at school are dumb. Before I know it, my break is over, and I stash my half-complete Math assignment and rock from Keyne in my bag. Of course, Fig zeroes in on the tissue.

"Ooh-la-la. What is that?"

"An old rock someone gave me."

"Harbor, it's wrapped in pretty tissue."

I shrug, but Fig, who was born to look for a scandal says, "That means it's a gift."

Thinking about that for a second, I'm not sure what surprises me more, the fact that Fig could possibly be right or how young she is to be right.

"Is that writing on it, Harbor?"

I hesitate then nod yes. Fig squeals and pokes my ribs, "Someone wanted you to remember the date."

"How old are you?" I ask putting the rock away. That reminds me, Keyne wanted to meet tomorrow. Tomorrow is Valentine's Day. I'm tempted to ask Fig if that changes a meeting to a date but realize I should not be getting advice from someone a third my height and age.

I put my earpiece back on and hear the crackling of an engine. I stop halfway back to the window. My stomach immediately becomes nauseous. A strong feeling like I've lived this exact moment before. I did just chug a Sweetheart Smoothie in record time, but as I take a few more steps and take my place in the window, a familiar, eerie sound bleeds through the intercom. My breathing becomes heavy. A rapid, carsick attack grabs me. It isn't the Sweetheart Smoothie. It's a second chance. A chance to fix what I didn't before.

I listen intently to the raspiness of the engine, and my heart and breath stop. I fumble for my cell phone and wait for the voice, trying to steady my own, "Hi and welcome to The Shore."

320

Barely able to muster the words, I bite my lip to prevent myself from screaming out: *Talk bastard! Say something.*

"How can I help you?"

A heavy, brutish voice belonging to a man orders, and I silently mouth along verbatim, "One water, no ice. A Shore burger. Meat only, no Shore sauce."

It's him! My heart races. It's now or never. A second chance.

"Add a cookie."

My cell phone slips out of my sweaty palms. Why call 9-1-1 now? What will I tell them? Mr. Boring is back? He won't look at me, and I read these books, so since he drives a blue car, yeah, he is the kidnapper. I'll be the one escorted away in cuffs.

Get a hold of yourself, Harbor! Follow the plan! Trying to control the trembling in my breathing, I punch in his order and wait for him to drive up, my heart beating so hard it could break through the orange wave on my shirt.

Mr. Boring pulls forward, and even though it's almost dark, the faded steel blue of the car is crystal clear and so is the capped silhouette of this monster. He hands me a ten dollar bill, and the heat generating off his hand could set fire to mine. He doesn't bother to turn his head: he doesn't look my way, and I don't take the money. This is the only chance left. I have to make him look at me. I have to see the tattoo. I have to get his prints.

I can feel my eyes burning. I stall, moving as slowly as I can, pretending his order is too much for me to balance. Yet, he still won't look my way. Why? I have no choice now but to take his money. I have to make sure he touches the cup.

I place the drink in his hand, and for a few nanoseconds, we hold the cup together. Fiery pangs from his hand transcends to mine. I inhale as I squeeze the Styrofoam using my ring finger to puncture a hole in the side of the cup. It works. Mr. Boring flinches as the water gushes over his sleeve, but not before I retrieve the cup, trying to distract him with my apologies.

"E kala mai! I'm so sorry," I grab a napkin to dry off his arm, and as if orchestrated by a higher being, the tempo of my nervousness melts into the mission. I lift the cuff of his sleeve. On his wrist, I feel ridges, a contusion of dark ink that travels up his left forearm. It's a figure, an animal. It has a tail and sharp claws and a tongue, a long, forked tongue. But my scope is shattered as he tears his arm away, seething in his seat and still avoiding eye contact. Acting as ignorant as I can, I make my false apologies and try to hand him more napkins. And then he does it. In a stark second, he glances my way. He rips his order from the window, and through his fumes, a nefarious evil flashes as he peers at me before he speeds away.

I toss the empty broken cup and money into two separate Shore bags then run out telling Lona to watch the drive-thru. Pulling the key from my belt, I hop on the Argo. I try to follow him, but his taillights have already faded in the distance by the time the Argo pulls to the end of the lot. I call 9-1-1 and within half an hour, Officer Lam is in front of me.

Needless to say, neither he nor Tutu are very happy with me. I received a double lecture about how dangerous that stunt was and that I shouldn't ever do anything like that again.

"Harbor, *if* that was the kidnapper, you could have been seriously hurt. You have to let this play out."

"How can you say that, Officer Lam!" I can't help but raise my voice, "Innocent kids are missing, and we are supposed to let it play out? That is bullshit!"

"Harbor!" Tutu corrects me, but Officer Lam interrupts, "What you did was brave, don't get me wrong. But if those kids are going to be found, we can't have another one hurt."

Too furious to respond, I turn around. "She won't be working the window again until he is caught, Officer."

I whip around so fast, my ponytail grazes Officer Lam's badge, "Tutu!"

"That is it, dear! If that horrible man saw you chase him or caught on to what you were doing...Fig and I cannot lose another family member!"

Silence fills the low lit break room, and I realize that Tutu is right. What was I thinking? Satisfied that I got a look at part of the tattoo and the prints on the broken cup and money, I ask Officer Lam, "How soon can you check the fingerprints?"

"I'll get them to the lab tonight, and hopefully, they will get processed within a couple of weeks."

"A couple of weeks!? Why so long?"

"It takes time, Harbor, for fingerprints to be lifted properly then compared in national databases."

"These kids don't have 2 weeks! This guy is close to striking again!"

Both Tutu and Officer Lam seem taken aback by my statement, so I clean it up faster than the water on Mr. Boring's sleeve, "What if he strikes again?"

Tutu turns her attention to Officer Lam's response, "This case will take priority, and we have undercover officers in the field trying to prevent any more kidnappings."

Undercover officers in the field? I grab my forehead and squeeze my eyes.

Tutu walks Officer Lam out and calls Rob to take me home. After Rob loads the Argo, we drive home in complete silence. Rob is good about giving me my space. He once said that even if he flies helicopters for a living, Fig and I are the real whirlybirds in his life that constantly challenge him. He said when we are ready to talk, all Fig or I have to do is tap him on the shoulder. Fig interpreted that like a happy woodpecker on a tall tree. Guess I have to admit, Aadya picked a good guy. He is part of my little sister, and I, will forever be grateful to him. He could have easily separated Fig and I, taken her to live with his family and left me behind. Instead, he's kept us together. I can't imagine my life if my sister was raised by strangers, growing up in one home, and I in another. So I try to show respect even when I feel completely detached from the world.

Fig is asleep in the backseat, and as I stare at the open road, I replay the events. The kidnapped kids weren't given a choice. They aren't sleeping soundly in the backseat after a productive day at school. No, they were separated by force. Where are they now?

Mr. Boring's hands were hot, even when the ice cold drink fell on him, they were boiling hot. But his tattoo, it was cold. The image on his forearm was cold and slippery. I'm certain. And like I told Officer Lam, it seemed to be scarred artwork of an animal, maybe something with fins, a piercing eye. I'm glad I didn't overthink it at the time. I may not have been able to capture his fingerprints. Officer Lam said the department has undercover officers in the field. That's new information. Where are they, and why haven't they caught the monster? I wanted to ask Officer Lam, but he sees me as a kid. Well, this twerp kid got her hands on real evidence tonight.

Once home, I wash up and unpack my bag. I smile when my hands find Keyne's rock. Ugh, to think a few hours ago, I actually wasted time spilling my guts to Keyne about who he hugs. I could slam this rock on my head. What was I thinking? Even Keyne made it clear, *we are friends*. I start to place the rock on my nightstand but hesitate to take a closer look when I notice it has a vague shape. Running my finger along the two equal curves on top, I tap the point where they connect and see my reflection in the ebony gloss. It's shaped like a heart.

I place my hand over the date before I set it down and turn off my light. And then I immediately sit up in bed. The rock glows! It's a subtle, soft radiance. I peer closer and see fragments of my reflection caught among the specks of starlight, "Huh," I tell myself not to overthink it. Just like the window tonight. Yeah, well, I had a mission at the window. *Don't overthink it.*

I exhale and place the rock on my pillow. It's been a long day. Maybe sleeping near it will keep me grounded, anchor me so I won't dive so far into the bad dreams.

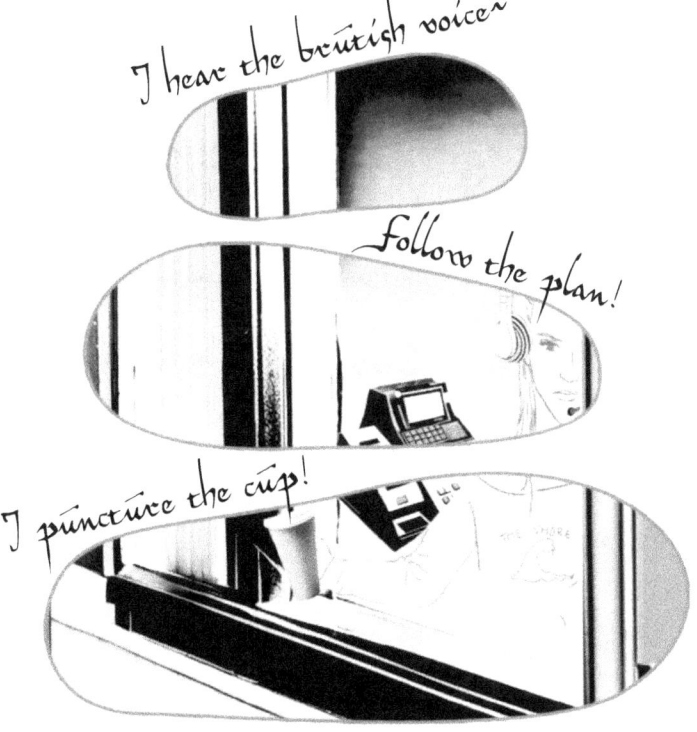

I hear the brutish voice

Follow the plan!

I puncture the cup!

CHAPTER 37

I woke up to more breaking news. Tutu grounded me.

She agreed to let me ride the Argo to school and work, but nowhere else. She also cut my hours in the drive-thru until the police catch the suspect. She didn't take my phone away, probably because it doesn't vibrate with excitement like Lona's. What could I do? I told her I understood and gave her a hug.

I glance around at Kau High's bustling parking lot. I don't see Keyne. I compete for elbow space as I walk to class in the Valentine's Day hustle. The halls are overflowing with right hand Shakas, new couples, candy boxes and successions of heart balloons tied to cute little teddy bears. Love is in the air. It is too early in the morning for so much fluff. Maybe that's the point. Not the love, but the fluff?

Announcements begin as I enter the grand foyer. In the background, past the mylar and chocolates, I catch sight of Keyne. He is talking to Guy outside the gymnasium.

Remember to pick up all your trash.

The crackle of the announcement is a laundry list of Valentine's do's and don'ts. Neither Keyne nor Guy seem to care. Both seem invested in the conversation.

Keyne is a tall dude, so he has to look down to speak to Guy, who isn't short: he's just not as tall as Keyne. Star crossed lovers stifle my view, so I strain my neck to get a better look. Something in their juxtaposition appears tense. Escorted by a couple of fuzzy teddy bears as cover, I inch closer. Keyne and Guy either noticed the bears or my hard stare because both of them simultaneously turn to me. In a heartbeat, they shake hands. Guy walks off, and Keyne walks toward me.

"What was that about?"

"Tell you later, don't want another tardy." Keyne guides me by my elbow as we navigate the extravagant treats filling the foyer.

The day flew by. I am glad to finally plop down next to Keyne in lunch. I eagerly open my lunch, "Starving."

"I need your help with the English assignment. Why does she give so much homework?"

"I have so much to tell you."

"Hey, any chance we can meet up later?"

I sigh, "Can't. I'm grounded."

"What? You grounded? Why?"

"It's a long story. But hey, before I get into that, why…" Then my words halt and all my thoughts are interrupted as Keyne pulls a cookie out of his lunch bag. It has pink, white and red chocolate chips.

"Did you go by The Shore this week?"

"Didn't you see me?" he laughs.

"No, seriously. I worked all last night, well, most of it. Anyway, we bake those."

"Yeah, one of the guys must have gone by."

"When?"

Keyne looks at me with a puzzled expression and shrugs laughing, "I don't see their every move. You know, most of my time is here or under water. Why?"

"Sorry," I continue with an unsettled feeling, "It's just, I know most of my customers. If they went by this week, maybe I served them. I'd remember Coach. Haven't seen him lately."

"Maybe. What about my question? Any chance we can meet?"

I shake my head, "Groouunded."

"If I ask a third time, you gotta make it happen?"

"Why?"

"Three's a charm."

"You believe too many myths. When I explain why I'm grounded, you will understand. But

330

first, I want to know what was going on between you and Guy?"

Keyne shrugs his shoulders naively.

"What were you two talking about? I didn't realize you were friends?"

"Uh, we're not."

"Okay, so what then?"

"We are both passionate about early morning prayer," Keyne smirks, and I shove him.

I jokingly offer, "You pray with your enemies?"

"I pray for them," his words cue Lott, who appears with a small crew before us. Their smug faces and even glares could flatten a tire. Keyne's mood clearly deflates as Lott tells him that there has been a schedule change, and they need to talk. So as usual, our time runs out.

"I'll see you in History."

"No, you don't have to leave, Harbor."

"I know," I smile at Keyne and walk off.

And History was the theme of the next couple of weeks. I barely had a chance to speak to Keyne, much less meet up. With homework and practice, our schedules never aligned. There was also the small fact that I was banished to the kitchen at The Shore where Tutu gave me tutorials on her secret recipes. In the evening, I am occupied with Fig, which is usually no biggie, but tonight she needs help cleaning her fish bowl. The highlight of my week is holding Ember over the drain of the sink as I fight the urge to let her slip out of my hand, accidentally of course. The sushi roll won, though. Fig got Ember back safely into a clean bowl.

School seems even busier. Most days, Keyne and I try to catch up in lunch or class, but it's never enough time to finish a conversation. Girls and boys transition out of different drills and try-outs in P.E. It's almost as if the blonde coach goes out of his way to make sure we are separated. All our teachers, including Mr. Reddy, bombard us with homework. Reddy says he is giving us the structure that he knows deep down we all so desperately want. Lott seems to set a timer as a matter of sport to interrupt our lunch. The culmination simply sucks. So the brief time Keyne and I have, we keep the convo light. I stay away from subjects like easy hugs, mixed messages, heart shaped rocks and midnight cliff dives. Plus, a few spare minutes in a crowded cafeteria never seem like the best place to discuss the details of why I am grounded. Keyne knew I called the police, but that's all I've told him. It's going to take a while to explain the whole FBI profile thing.

Weeks pass in the blink of an eye. I called Officer Lam every week and haven't heard back.

I've been more than patient, and using Keyne's logic, decide that three is a charm. I will use today's lunch break to ask for an update on the fingerprints. I'll need to find somewhere quiet to call. Spring Break is around the corner, and Kau High students are thrilled. From this point on, pristine beaches, laughter and music, fun and delicious grindz will cheer us on into the summer. Needless to say, there aren't many quiet spots available.

Hopefully, my punishment for doing the right thing will be over soon. But until then, the only waves I'll be seeing will be Fig's hairdo when she walks up to the counter after school. The least I deserve is an answer on the evidence that I collected.

After lunch, I perform the quickest bend and badge ever and almost trip in the process because my bag is too heavy. The only thing preventing my fall - my elbow. It is being held up by a warm, strapping hand.

"Maybe you are the one meant for the water. Falling down doesn't hurt as much."

"Whatever."

"C'mon, let's go eat. I've got to tell you what happened in the hall. I bumped into Mr. Reddy."

"I can't, Keyne. I have to make a call."

"Again? Trying to win a radio contest?"

"I'll be in the library for a few minutes. I'll meet you as soon as I can."

Keyne heads off to lunch and I faintly see him blend in with a group of higher graders. They act like they are old buddies catching up. That kid has no problem making friends. I head to the rear of the library and keep my head down. I don't want to be chased off again. No sign of the librarian, so I enter a well-hidden secret, the cleanest restrooms in the building.

Tucked away in the far corner of the library are the most sanitary and spotless facilities. There aren't any windows in this back corner, yet somehow it is still brightly lit. Cell service will be a roll of the dice. The couches aren't too far away, but I wouldn't dare try to call out in the open. I pull open the wide door and take an available stall. I scroll through my contacts, and just as I'm about to press call, I stop when I hear noises that sound like a baby dinosaur being hatched. What the hell is that? Ew. It's coming from the stall next to me. I have no choice but to wait. Finally, by the fourth flush of the toilet, the lady exits. I quietly stay put and listen to the dawdle of footsteps. C'mon! Through the half inch slit in the door, I see the faded black, slip-on loafers. No FBI book necessary. The feet in those shoes belong to the librarian. Uuuughhh! I want to puke. Thank God there are automatic air fresheners on two corners of the ceiling. At least she washes her hands, but after what I heard, she could probably use a shower. As soon as the savage noises end, I make the call. On the third ring, Officer Lam answers.

We have a brief conversation where he apologizes again for being so busy. The bad news, the water may have ruined any fingerprints that may have been on the cup the suspect held. The good news, Hawaii PD sent what they thought was salvageable, including the money, out to a national lab for further analysis.

"When will have answers?"

"Those national labs have more resources than us and can turn a case around in a week."

Officer Lam promises to stop by The Shore soon and makes some small talk. I'm not listening. I'm over small talk.

"I'll call you next week, Officer Lam," and with 10 minutes left to eat, I hang up and slip back out into the library, my appetite ruined. I doubt I will have time to catch up with Keyne, but then realize I won't have to. He is sitting on the library couches reading a book.

"Hey," I sit next to him. He quickly closes the book.

"What? The pictures are rated R?"

He laughs, "It is that book from a few weeks ago. I wanted to check up on something, but don't want to give you a headache again."

"I highly doubt it was the book. It was just a stressful week. So, what are you reading?"

Keyne opens the book to a page dog-eared by his thumb. On his lap is a two page spread, titled *Legend of the Mo'o*. And I don't know why, but the encore begins. My stomach lurches, and my head tingles, but I hide it, "Fascinated with a kiddie legend?"

"I'm not so sure I want the tattoo, but just for the record, it is not a kiddie legend."

"Keyne, the first thing we learn in grade school is the myth about the Mo'o. Even Fig is going through that now, kids teasing about the monster coming to shore."

"It must be nice having a sibling, someone to share stories with and always have around," he sighs before he brags, "By the way, I don't forget anything," Keyne's smile turns dark as a shadow looms over us, covering the illustration. We look up to be greeted by the librarian, a scowl on her face. She apparently isn't happy that we are happy. She places her pointer finger on her lips just as the bell rings. Trying not to laugh, we set the book down and practically run out of the library busting into laughter in the Grand Foyer.

"When are we going to get a chance to have an entire conversation?" Keyne asks.

"I didn't even have time to eat today."

Lott walks up to us like clockwork, and as I start to say bye, hoping I can sneak in a couple of bites of my sandwich before class, Keyne grabs my elbow.

"Harbor, wait," then he turns to Lott, "I'll catch up with you later, man."

Lott looks surprised too, but I'm more concerned with pulling my sandwich out of my bag. Keyne and I begin walking.

"So, any chance we can meet before we head out for Spring Break?"

"I'm grounded, Keyne."

"We are going out of town for the week."

I stop chewing the piece of sandwich I tore into as I realize that Keyne and I are in a forever cycle of catching up between tardy bells.

When we are at the door of my next class, Keyne leaves me with a thought, "Maybe one day, we won't be tardy. Maybe we will just be absent."

It was hard to concentrate the rest of the day. I'm pretty sure Keyne was hinting that we skip school. How dare he think that I'd do that! Even if I miss the bend, and the monk seals will be delivering soon. This was supposed to be my third time watching them. But skip school for it?

When we get into History, Mr. Reddy immediately begins class with a lecture and puts up notes for us to copy, "You will need these for next week's test."

All our teachers are giving us a test before the break. I think it's the only way they can manage all the excitement busting at the seams of Kau High.

"Are you seriously asking me to skip?" Two kids whip around with their eyebrows arched. They study Keyne and I up and down before returning back to their notes with a smirk. Kau High is the premiere hub for eavesdroppers.

Taking his voice down a decibel, Keyne sounds serious, "I'm asking that we finally take a chance. We never get one."

"Skip school?"

"Maybe just part of the day? Enough to have a full conversation before I leave."

Nervous excitement races through my veins at the thought of bending the rules a little, "We can do it after testing."

Keyne stares at me, motionless, his pencil hovering above his partially written page. For a second, it was like looking at a still photo.

"Breathe."

"Sorry, a bit thunderstruck."

Before I can respond, Reddy walks up to us, "Did you guys have any questions?"

A million! But not for you. Keyne and I shake our heads, noticing that the two eavesdroppers are gawking our way, waiting for Act II.

After class, Keyne and I walk to the parking lot because he is finishing up a story about Mr. Reddy that he has been trying to tell me forever, but I have to interrupt it again, "Keyne. Are you sure?"

"Yes! He thought it was me who made the noise!" He bowls over laughing.

"No, not Reddy. Are you sure skipping is the right thing to do?"

My question seems to slow him down, which is not an everyday occurrence for Keyne. He gulps, looks down at his tennis shoes and then back up at me, "I think it's wrong to do nothing."

"How long will you be gone?"

"The entire break."

"Okay then. Besides, there is a book I need to show you too."

"Ooh, myths and monsters?"

"Uh, actually you're half right."

On the ride home, I consider aiming the Argo toward the bend, but decide that today I will follow the rules.

Chapter 38

For the first time in a long time, life is calm, even pleasant. With the spring arrives a renewed energy. It can put a bounce in the step even if the foot is chained to an unchangeable hell.

No new kidnappings have been reported, but that does nothing for the kids that are still missing, and I'm still waiting for Officer Lam to call back.

According to the FBI profile, any change can throw a suspect off their game. Maybe when I played peekaboo with his tattoo, it disrupted his pattern? Good. My entire life has been disrupted. For a change, I don't mind taking on the role of disrupter.

Picking up the kitchen duties became an easy chore, and even Ember became somewhat tolerable...after I almost murdered her. I tried to do something nice for the scaly paper wad and feed it, but when Fig got home, she panicked. Apparently, she had already fed Ember, and I poured in too much fish food. Definitely not one of my prouder moments. C'mon, how was I to know the goldfish feeding rule was never feed it more than the size of one of its eyes? I'm use to rolling food out to hungry customers who would tear the roof off The Shore if their meal was eyeball sized burgers and fries.

Riding to work with Rob or back home hasn't been so bad either. The past few weeks have given the three of us more moments together. It sort of feels like family time rather than a schedule. But I have this thing called stubborn pride, and Rob is not at parent level DEFCON yet. So when he asked if there was anything new in my life, I resisted telling him: *Um, I'm a teenager. There is always something new.* For example, I'm skipping a few classes to hang out with a friend who might like me as more than a friend, but I'm not positive. He gave me some snazzy rope at the Winter Dance and a rock for Valentine's Day, so either he is attracted to me, or I'm unknowingly concealing evidence of a crime. On top of that, how can a person really know when they truly want to be with someone? Am I supposed to do a few hair flips to start a spark? What does sweet-talk sound like? Yeah, questions Rob is *not* prepared to answer and dilemmas that would entice Fig to flush Ember if it meant she could listen in.

Two days until Spring Break. When I arrive to work, Tutu asks to speak to me.

"Yes, I just have to make a quick call to Officer Lam first if that's okay?"

After I leave a message for Officer Lam, I go to find Tutu, but Sam says she stepped out to pick up a delivery. I flinch when catch sight of a bandage on his arm, "What happened?" I ask.

He pauses and I swear I see him clench his jaw before he answers.

"Grease fire. Next time I won't put it out with my arm," he laughs and the firmness in his face vanishes.

"Ouch. Sorry. I'll wash and slice these potatoes if that helps."

Sam nods, and Guy walks in. He asks Sam a question and completely ignores me. He's been in an ornery mood ever since I saw him and Keyne talking that morning. There is a lot of ground to cover with Keyne, and I want to find out the full story. What were he and Guy hashing out? And what the hell is up with cliff diving at midnight with mermaids? Okay, that's a bit of an exaggeration. Most importantly though, I needed to fill Keyne in on the suspect and the window stunt that got me grounded.

I've been feeling slightly guilty because I haven't told a lie of this magnitude. Technically, I lie daily. If Tutu or Rob, Sam or a Shore customer asks how my day is going, I always answer good.

Tutu walks in with a wide brown box that covers her entire upper body. Sam rushes over to help her, lifting the huge box and letting it rest on his arms. He doesn't seem bothered in the least that pressure has been applied on top of his bandage. Tutu pulls up a stool next to me. It registers to me that I haven't had much time alone with her. Sure, we live together: we work together, but when was the last time I actually looked in her eyes to have a conversation I didn't try to avoid? At work, we help customers, cook and clean. By the time we get home, it's already late for homework and time to rest or sleep before we wake up to do it all over again. Sitting next to her is a nice reminder of the softness that she contributes to any room she occupies. When she is at The Shore, Tutu wraps her medium length white hair into a thin bun. And sitting this close to her, I can see the tint of pastel pink that hugs her high cheekbones and the shine in her eyes that reminds me of rock sugar candy. When I was little, I used to think my grandmother was a living sugar cookie. Back when life was sweet.

"Did you get a hold of Officer Lam?"

"I left a message."

"It wasn't easy to ground you, but it's even harder to think of how badly you could have been hurt. Why did you pursue that dangerous man?"

"The missing kids."

Tutu tenderly grabs my hand, "You've had to grow up so fast, but you are not those little kids."

I'm not sure what she means, so I try not to glower as she goes on, "Maybe a part of you that is still healing wanted to save those kids...so you can save yourself from your own pain."

I don't know why, but I slide my hand away and stand up to walk away, then stop myself. I return to the round stool next to her and slide the tub of uncut potatoes out of reach, "Maybe you are right, but I don't know how to look away."

"Don't."

"What do you mean?"

"You don't have to look away, you just have to learn how to use your superpower safely."

"Tutu, you've got to stop talking like that. I don't have any superpowers!" I didn't mean to raise my voice, but it caught Sam's attention. He and the kitchen staff moved to the back of the kitchen, apparently to give us a minute.

"Tutu, stop! I appreciate everything you've done for me, but these stories about the Third Eye, visions, superpowers is too much! I'm just a girl! Okay? A girl whose parents were replaced with pity. Everywhere I go, it's pity. Waiting for me. Teachers who remember, customers, old friends! They wear it in their eyes. That's not a

344

superpower, Tutu. It's the sad truth!" I bite my lip when I see the bits of rock sugar in her eyes begin to melt. I try to apologize, but she chimes in, "It can't be the truth if you refuse to recognize both sides."

"I'm sorry," Her words cut off my apology.

"Some people are born different, Harbor. Some are placed into horrible events that force indelible marks on their soul. You have been assigned both fates. Now you must make a choice. I'm sorry if that confuses you, but it's true."

"A choice?"

"Give up, or give in. It is said for those who embrace their fate, that they evolve and adapt so rapidly, an inevitable transformation occurs. A powerful reshaping of the psyche that stokes advance stages. Their mind races, and their life force kindles, connecting to all. It is said that this is the origin of power."

I want to ask Tutu two questions. One: Are you drunk? And two: If you're not, can you slap me because maybe I am?

How did I go from sorting potatoes to listening to my grandmother's half-baked scenario of my life? Sure, I've suffered unthinkable tragedy, but to believe that I have powers is looney to say the least. Confused, I hold my head and wait for the burn, but no singe. My eyes aren't ignited despite the fact that Tutu interpreted my request to *stop* as keep going, "When I was a little girl, I heard tales of the sorties."

The pit in my stomach grows, "Sorties? Like the bedtime stories you would tell us?"

Tutu nods with a lighthearted smile, "The meaning has changed over time. Like all things do. Nowadays, a sortie is a mission in war, but that's not how the story began."

"I remember the stories, but you never told us how they began."

"Oh, they began long before I was born, dear. Their tales are from the old isles. Very few can grasp a Sortie's power or understand them."

Scared to ask, I do anyway, "What do you mean?"

"Sorties excel in skill and knowledge. They are vessels of wisdom but took an oath not to arouse suspicion. Every Sortie's strength is veiled: it's invisible until it must be used."

I remember the verses of legendary ancient people, creatures of magic who fought in epic battles to destroy evil. But that was make believe, stories to amuse a child, right? I want to walk away, I do, but now I'm wondering if the little old lady I love needs to be hospitalized. Maybe she is confusing fiction with reality because I acted like a brat, "Tutu, listen, I was wrong. I have a lot to be grateful for. You, Fig. Don't worry about me because I don't worry about myself. No pity here."

She moved a few strands of hair that fell on my forehead, "No Sortie does, dear."

I don't want to accuse her out loud of being a wacko, so I shake my head to refocus. Mind over matter. This lady raised me. She is one of the most sane people I know. If the FBI profiled her, they'd have a sketch of an angel. So, I humor her, "What's the point of the Sortie?"

Asking this aloud is so strange. I can't believe I'm having this conversation, but with optimistic conviction, Tutu makes clear, "They vow valor. They flourish in defense of justice."

I check her head for a fever, and she playfully slaps my hand away. I laugh, having had enough of kid stories, "I can't lie, Tutu. You tell a great story. I'm sorry I raised my voice. Maybe because you love me so much, you have convinced yourself that I am perfect. Maybe that's why you want to believe I have powers. Or maybe, all along, I've been raised by a lunatic?"

Tutu squeezes my shoulders and looks up into my eyes, and I can see into hers. She is as levelheaded as ever, "Oh, Harbor, dear. A power doesn't make a person perfect. As a matter of fact, it can be the biggest flaw of the few who possess it."

She goes on to say I am no longer grounded and that she trust me to learn from what she referred to as hunting at the window. She starts to step away, but I stop her, "Wait. That's it?"

"Oh, the window is still off limits, dear, even if the customers do miss you." She walks away smiling, not a care in the world that she piqued my interest and left me with a thousand questions, one being, *What kind of crap was that? What did she mean by born different? Did she do a DNA test? And has she lost her damn mind?*

Today of all the days, she tells me she trusts me. The nerve! Well, I already planned a skip day with Keyne, and I'm not bailing. Recruiting him to help catch a kidnapper is practically a public service. Plus, our plan is decently benign. Big whoop, we want to finish a conversation. We pre-decided that if we couldn't, maybe we weren't meant to. I am starting to question why I thought for a second that today would be calm and pleasant.

I dozed off right away last night and woke to a morning of lively chirps. The Honeycreepers know that spring has arrived. Don't be fooled, red winged beauties! Tutu may fly in and burst your bubble too. I wake up a bit early to pack a

swimsuit and some extra lunch and sodas.
Keyne and I won't be able to go by Old Man
Ferencz's for snacks because he would know we
were supposed to be in school, and if Fig saw
me, she'd go straight into Spy Kid mode. I don't
feel as bad anymore about skipping because it
isn't a full day and technically, I am no longer
grounded. Brushing my teeth, twice, I stared
back at my reflection in the mirror. It looks
different. I pulled my upper eyelid up with my
index finger and my lower eyelid downward,
trying not to blink as I insert my contacts. But
once the first is in, it obstructs my view.
Extracting it, I see someone in place of the angry
little girl, and it's not the girl who ached, or the
one swallowed by Ha'alele. My once sad eyes
are now filled with the familiar Pacific blue. I
see me. And Keyne is right. At the center, they
hold a darkness. One that challenges the tone in
the monk seals. What did Tutu call me? A Sortie?
I breathe a laugh. Talk about going to extremes
to help lift someone up. What was it she said?
Placed into horrible events? What does that
mean? FBI rule #8: pay attention to action
words. Essentially, they are the fastest way into
someone's head. *Placed into horrible events?*
Placed? There were horrific blows in my life, no
doubt, but I wasn't the one placed in them. My
dead parents were. Tutu knows that.

I'll process this later. A new sense of strength fills my veins, a resolve to be better than my circumstances and more than my dreams. And I have no intention of disguising it. I drop my contacts, slide on some lip gloss, wrap my belt around my waist and place a kiss on top of Fig's wispy head. I'm not only saying good-bye before I head out the door, I'm saying hello to the first day of my Spring Break.

CHAPTER 39

Lunch can't happen fast enough. Keyne and I place our helmets on halfway out of the parking lot and are on open road, riding the sun rays as fast as the Argo will take us. I show him the shortcut from school to the bend and the amphibious side of the Argo. The shortcut from Kau High contains a shallow tarn, which is why it's my shortcut. No one knows it's beyond the thick brush, and even if they did, most aren't going to wade through water.

"I swim for a living so this is hilarious," Keyne says into my ear.

When we get to the bend, I turn the wheels of the Argo, navigating the huge trees that somehow grew their roots on top of a cliff, a cliff that Keyne says is 100 feet high. I slowly descend to the right and sunlight fades to darkness.

"Where are you taking me?" Keyne asks hesitantly.

I laugh, "It's just a little darkness. Don't be scared."

"It's not the darkness I'm scared of," he says in my ear. Breaking through the wood pillars, the Argo treading over the last of the rocky cliff, the sun reappears, and the sound of the ocean greets us as we make our way to the sand. The waves loudly brush the shore, and large seabirds gawk above the water, looking for a lunch of their own.

Keyne and I kick off our shoes and run to the water line. He scoops up water with both his hands and pours it over his hair and face. And then in a weird, but somehow cute boyhood rite of passage, Keyne lifts both his hands up in the air and starts to bay at the absent moon. He has competition. A harem of monk seals line the beach opposite us. Taking our phones out, we both try to get a picture. I zoom in and focus on a couple of monstrous monks sunning on the boulders.

"I've never been this close," I whisper to Keyne. "We need to be careful. They're ashore to deliver pups."

Keyne raises his eyebrows and looks from the seals to me and back.

"I usually watch from above," I say pointing up the center of the steep cliff, it's height so due north that it strains my neck. Keyne follows my hand. His eyes crawl up the rock wall and over its razor sharp edges that lead to the clearing, then draws his breath, "Awesome."

The coastline of the island is an uneven loop that bends at the will of an expansive sea. Deep blue and green ombre hues turn into extraordinary shades that wash over the terrain. And in doing so, it's white cap waves create the curves that contain a terrain so varied that in only a matter of steps, soft sand manifolds into impenetrable stone walls.

In the far distance, I can see the lights of the big hotel chains. Even in broad daylight, they glitter. I'm reminded of the scared kidnapped kids that are somewhere out there. I pray they are still alive. Turning to Keyne, I make a simple request, "Let's eat. There's a lot I have to fill you in on, and we are going to run out of time."

"Uh, let's swim," Keyne says enthusiastically and guides my hand in the direction of the Pacific. A cool swash covers our feet, and Keyne stops to take off his shirt and throw it back to land. I follow. Pulling down my shorts, I toss them ashore to uncover my full bikini and my pale white skin. Keyne paddles out a few feet, breaching the sea and moves so fast that his long body easily mimics a large aquatic animal. I walk out to hip level but stop to tip my head to the baby blue sky and breathe in the crisp, fresh air. I turn, ready to immerse myself into the cool waters and stop when I see a torpedo propelling toward me. In seconds, I'm staring at the back of Keyne's head. I'm not floating, I am being moved across the water, carried on his back. I laugh loudly and go along for the ride. We are in deep. My ponytail whips in the air, my fingers glide along Keyne's stride and the world around disappears. I lean forward not sure if I'm hallucinating, but Keyne's wet hair is so black that I see a partial reflection of myself and the sky above and as I peer closer. Keyne changes course and throws me off balance. I fall into the water and for a moment, I am suspended above the ocean floor. My body is weightless, and my thoughts move in slow motion in the soothing dimness. I'm only conscious of a sense of peace and purification and not the fact that I am being lured deeper. What if I stayed here? In that moment, two radiant eyes stare back. Below me, Keyne comes into view. I feel his long arm wrap around my waist and begin to carry me upward. I try to place my arms around him, yet they slip off his mighty chest. His wet upper body is filled with power. Unable to clasp my wrists, I slide them upward with the water until they are around his neck and lay my head on his shoulders until we break the surface. Once above water, I gasp in the world again, breathing loudly. Ocean waves, singing birds and the barking of monk seals in the distance muffle what sounds like static.

"Harbor? Harbor! Are you okay?" Fortitude in his voice cracks the atmosphere. When I turn to look at Keyne, I spit up more water than I could drink in a sitting. Relieved when the episode is over, I laugh, but weakness is in my voice, "Race me." Together, we dive back under and swim to shore, yet it's obvious my strokes are being flanked by Keyne. Once we reach the shallow edge of the ocean, he helps bolster me up by my elbow, and together, we walk back onto land and take a seat on the plush, white sand.

"Harbor, are you okay?"

"Yeah, I'm fine. I didn't know you were into synchronized swimming," I close my eyes and aim my face upward toward the wide blue sky, allowing the sun to gather what moisture my skin won't absorb. Keyne sighs loud enough for me to hear. I glance toward him in time to see him shake his head then jump up to pull his shirt over his head covering his face long enough to absorb a loud exhale. The muscular bulge of his chest and arms pushes through his t-shirt. He returns with our backpacks and takes out his lunch, twisting off the top of a water bottle.

"Drink."

I shake my head and ask for a soda. Keyne laughs and snaps off the metal tab, and the fizz begins to escape. I place my mouth right over it and take a long sip. We lay out our backpacks and use them as a makeshift picnic table to share a midday munch.

"Hey, thanks for bringing me back up."

"Yeah, thanks for not dragging me down," he laughs, and I give him a light nudge with my elbow. He catches my elbow long enough to ask, "So, what did you want to tell me?"

Keyne mimics a large aquatic animal

propelling toward me.

In seconds, I'm being carried.

"Some of it's kind of dark. Why don't you go first?"

"I thought I was pretty clear. I'm not scared of the dark," Keyne winks then adds, "What do you want to know?"

"Tell me what you were talking to Guy about."

"You."

"What? Why me?" I ask spitting up a bit of carbonation.

"C'mon, Harbor. It's no secret your friend is totally into you."

"Uh, we work together, but I can't say we are really friends. He's a nice guy. No pun intended."

"He likes you."

"Okay sensei."

"I'm just stating a fact."

"Okay, so what if he did like me, why would you speak to him about it?"

"He lied about me. To you. That was a mistake." He side glance meets my eyes with an unwavering assuredness.

Certain my jaw has dropped an inch, this wasn't the conversation I was expecting. Setting down the unfinished half of my sandwich and standing up, I walk a few steps back into the water, "So what did you say to him?"

"The truth. If he is so interested in my life, he needs to get the facts straight before he goes around spreading rumors."

My eyes widen alerting Keyne of my disapproval.

"Well, Harbor? Weren't you bothered by what he told you?"

Inhaling deeply, I toy with the idea of lying before I deflect, "That's not the point, Keyne."

"Okay, then what is?"

"I was a *tiny* bit upset that you didn't share with me that you are dating. Don't friends talk?" The words always sound so much sillier exiting my mouth than when they are rolling around in my head.

"Let me get this straight, you didn't have a problem with me dating someone, you just wanted to know?"

Crossing my arms and looking toward the monk seals, I yell, "Keyne, quick!" I run to find my clothes and toss our food and backpacks into the Argo. A few of the seals scooch along the sand in our direction. They are massive and moving in fast.

"Nursing seals smell our food! I'm not going to be the next Deadliest Catch!"

His demeanor and the tempo in his voice are so calm, "And, I'm not going anywhere until you answer me."

"Keyne, they will swallow us whole!"

"Like the water almost did you? Answer me, Harbor. Please?"

"Okay, fine, maybe, maaaaybe, I care a *little*."

Keyne smiles, and in seconds, we are on the Argo headed up the rocky bluff. The ascent takes the Argo longer than the descent. Good, I need this extra time to pretend that's really a sunburn on my cheeks and not utter embarrassment from basically admitting to Keyne that I like him.

Once we reach the bend, we look over the edge of the cliff, and sure enough, out to the distant right, two monk seals are mauling half a sandwich we dropped. Keyne reaches for my elbow and leans into my ear, "Harbor, I care a lot."

"Why?"

"Well, that leads me to what I've been wanting to talk to you about."

CHAPTER 40

"First, I want to clear up the whole tattoo thing."

Well, no one can accuse us of wasting our conversation time. Keyne raises the long sleeve over his left arm and shows me what looks to be a red lined tattoo on his forearm. How did I miss that on our little fishing expedition?

"You got it?!"

"Nooo. It's a stencil to prep my skin for the real thing."

"The real thing?"

He shrugs, explaining that it's a weird family tradition, "My dad wants me to carry it on."

"How is a tattoo a family tradition?" I ask, unable to conceal my distaste.

"My dad's old school. He believes the tattoo is powerful."

All this talk about powers lately makes me wonder if something is in the water.

"A lot of people believe the tattoo is sacred, that it emulates ancient powers."

I think back to the day in the library, "That sea creature? The Mo'o?"

Keyne confirms with a nod that is almost regrettable.

"Sacred? It's a stupid legend."

"Have you ever researched it? It dates back almost 2,000 years."

"How do you know that?"

"Cave paintings, stories handed down," Keyne answers with a confidence that tells me he knows more. FBI rules and experience taught me this. Aadya would answer the same way when I asked about my father. She always knew more than she admitted.

"A lot of islanders don't believe the Mo'o is *just a legend*. They believe they are from a line of ancient warriors."

"Are they intoxicated when they say it?"

"Haha. Look, I don't even want the tattoo."

My stomach churns, and I stammer to respond, "Then why get it?"

Keyne explains that his dad's father had one and his father has one. Now the lizard has been incorporated into their new business logo. He goes on to talk about his family and tradition. Apparently he is from a line of lifelong outdoorsmen who can be traced back to the island for generations.

"And when my mom died, my dad was so angry, he had to do something to try and save his soul. He started the business. So see? It could be worse. He sees the Mo'o as a savior, a symbol that gives him power."

"Keyne, getting a logo on a company shirt is a hell of a lot different from permanently etching it into your body."

"I know. That's why I wanted a second opinion. Lott was given his at Christmas. I'm supposed to get mine next week."

"Can't you just tell your dad no thanks?"

Keyne shakes his head no, "Tradition is too strong."

My heart sinks, "I'm sorry."

"It's not so bad," he smiles and nudges me. "Legend says the water lizard can be summoned, and its strength harnessed. So I'll have that."

"You seem to know a lot about the legend."

"I might be an expert" he chuckles, "It's the only story I heard growing up."

I pause, his explanation can't be any crazier than the one my grandmother told me. *Oh yeah, Keyne. That superpower thing. I have it too, bro. I'm a Sortie.*

"Do tell," I say hesitantly.

"Around our neck of the woods, the story goes that before the islands rose from the sea bed and separated, they belonged to the Mo'o, you know, the ancient water beast."

"Yeah, sure. Let's go with that."

"When man came along, the Mo'o learned to share land and food. But, in power and love, the Mo'o were given no place. Islanders saw the agitation in the lizards and knew they had to control the population before it was too late. The Mo'o were intuitive creatures, having lived with mankind for so long, they knew how to read their intent, even if buried deep in their hearts. So the Mo'o retreated into the sea, abandoning their portions on land."

"Yeah, that's where sea lizards should be."

"These weren't just any sea lizards though. The Mo'o were considered ancestors. The first beings in Hawaii."

"Are you giving me your family's version of the legend or what you read in that book?"

Keyne begins to answer, but my phone vibrates, and he stops when I jump up. It's Officer Lam! I walk a few feet away from Keyne to take the call.

"Hi, Officer Lam?"

"Hi, Harbor. I wanted to give you a bit of good news. After all, you are the real hero here."

"You guys caught him!" I exclaim.

"No, not yet. But we got partial prints."

"That's great, so then you guys know who he is?"

"No, not yet," Officer Lam explains that the national lab will be working on putting the partial prints together to make one useable print that they will compare with their databases to see if the guy has a record or even if he applied for a job that required a criminal background check, "Sometimes these criminals don't have any prints on file because they've never been caught, so the civilian background checks are a separate database. But, Harbor, they promised a 24 hour turn-around."

My heart thumps a bit faster at the thought of finally getting this guy off the streets and behind bars.

"I'll be in touch when I know more. You be safe. Let us handle it from here."

"Thanks, Officer Lam," when we hang up, I realize Keyne has been listening. It's about time we move on from that stupid legend to some bigger gaps I should probably fill in.

Staring down at him sitting in my spot, playing with my little mound of collected rocks, I know I have to tell him what my parents did for a living, maybe show him the picture I keep in my belt, so he can understand why I inserted myself in this police investigation. But as I slide the picture out from my belt, Keyne stands up and walks a little closer, "No doubt, Harbor, I am curious about that call," he gives a light smile then grabs my elbow, "But we have to be back in less than an hour and there is something I've got to tell you."

I move the picture back to its spot and give Keyne my full attention. He guides me toward the edge of the cliff. The sound of water below us has turned into a passionate torrent unlike the halcyon sea waves that welcomed us. Using the arm that will soon have a permanent scar, Keyne points outward, never letting go of my elbow, "When we go on dives, we are training to navigate the water, to go deeper, learning how to make more oxygen and use it wisely when adapting to pressure changes."

I slowly nod my head, not sure where Keyne is going with this.

"And for the past year, we've been working on night dives, building endurance with our vision to adapt to the darkness below."

He sounds so serious, but it's hard to concentrate because I have exciting news. I want to yell! *Keyne, I have secretly been chasing a bad guy, and now, we are finally closing in on him!* Ugh, now is when he decides to share about his swim team.

"Can you imagine being out there at night, under the weight of the dark waters?"

I pause and look toward the horizon that I've sat and watched so many hundreds of times and the truth is no. I've seen and heard the dark waves. They will still the heart but no, I can't imagine the weight of total darkness, "Guess that would be daunting."

"It is. But there is one thought that shields me on every dive," Keyne shifts my attention out to the distant right to an inlet that dots the shore, "Look closely."

Sighing because I'm fired up to share what Officer Lam said, I give in and peer across, but only see a forgotten port. Boats used it ages ago.

"Abandoned territory?" Struggling to decode his target, I look to Keyne for the answer.

"The harbor."

I look across at the harbor and breathe out in a semiconscious state, "The harbor?"

Keyne slides his hand from my elbow into my hand.

I don't surf much, rarely actually. But growing up on the island, there is no way to avoid being part of the ocean. There is this moment that anyone who has ever surfed has felt. A moment when your heart picks up the pace because you are on top of the world, riding a wave knowing that at any moment you could wipe out. Wrapping my fingers into Keyne's hands, I am back in the tidal wave.

366

Keyne's dark hair has begun to dry and rustles in the breeze, causing long layers to fall above captivating eyes. Eyes I've been waiting to see uninterrupted. With a tender stroke from the back of his fingers, Keyne skims my lips to move long strands of my hair but doesn't stop there. He follows the strands along my back and then moves upward, mounting my ponytail holder. I let him slide off my rubber band. His mouth opens slightly as if to speak, but only an exhale is heard. Standing in front of him, my untamed mane released, my heart throbbing, I speak, "So why the harbor?"

He takes my other hand, "Do you think I'd make anyone a corsage? Give anyone *that* rock? Doesn't that tell you something?"

"You're on a budget?"

"Wow, that is cold, but funny."

I am always impressed how Keyne can let a joke roll off his shoulders, "I took that rock from my deepest dive."

"Keyne…I don't want vague messages. Rocks shaped like a heart? What does that mean?"

"I mean what I said. Even the thought of you makes me smile. I think about you, like all the time, and it puts a smile on my face every time. Even under water."

I know now what the moment feels like, the moment when friendship takes a sudden turn into more. I want the chance to explore this uncharted territory. I want to hug him, hold him, kiss him, but I also want to hear him.

"Harbor, even when I am in the dark ocean, alone, oh my God, *you*! I smile remembering a conversation we had or a look you gave me. A couple of times, I laughed out loud in an underwater training! Do you know how dangerous that is?"

"I'm glad you didn't drown," laughing, I lean in to hug him, and as we embrace, the tidal wave swells. A spark rushes in the air surrounding us, and with our upper bodies pressed against one another, we hold on. We stand, unwavering, in the middle of the tidal wave.

Keyne's phone starts to move along the sod, ringing, "Sorry," he bends to press ignore without picking it up or looking to see who's calling. He walks back to me, and stops about a foot away from me, on the edge of the cliff. He looks down then walks closer, standing directly in front of me and asks, "Do you remember what it takes to make the smallest splash possible?"

I smile and motion yes, "Can I show you?"

He smiles and whispers, "Yes." Stretching out both my arms, palm over palm, I walk closer to him. The opening in my arms is just enough for his tall, muscular body to slide in. Once he is tucked in my embrace, he grins his approval. I feel the heat from his body. He wraps both arms around my waist, and I watch his smile turn into a content furrow before he places his head on mine, "Harbor, with you, I want to make the biggest splash possible."

Looking up at him, our gaze locked, I see the strong fluorescent colors in his eyes, and they make it hard to turn away. Why would I at this point? Keyne does though because his phone rings again, and he walks over to the incessant ringing. Yanking up his phone, he presses ignore again and tosses the phone near the back tire of the Argo. Both of us holding on to the other's hand, we simultaneously gravitate to the ground, sitting closer than cafeteria rules would ever allow. But when we try to turn our attention back to us, the mood is interrupted again by his ringing phone.

"Maybe answer it?" I say softly.

Keyne reluctantly jumps up to retrieve his phone but turns back around, offering his hand out to me. I cross my arms and put a finger on my chin attempting to make a thinking gesture, but the ringing is ruining the joke. I take his hand, and we walk over to pick it up. Keyne scans the call, and his smile swiftly turns to a concerned frown. He answers, "What's up? I'm kind of busy."

"Where are you?"

The voice on the other end of the line is unquestionably Lott. Even with the noise from the light wind and the crashing waves below, I'd recognize Lott's hounding voice anywhere.

We were supposed to be back 10 minutes ago! This isn't a problem for me. I'm not grounded anymore, so all I have to do is head to The Shore. Rob is picking up Fig from school, but Keyne seems to be in trouble. I hurriedly pick up our bags and helmets and hear Keyne direct Lott, "Tell him you dropped me off to check out a new dive spot."

I can't hear Lott's response because I'm firing up the Argo, but Keyne hangs up after giving Lott directions, "Pick me up at that old gas station. Yes, that one."

Wondering how many old gas stations Keyne visits, I start to turn the Argo around in the direction of our exit, but Keyne stands to block my movement. He stops me to place both his hands on the handle bars of the Argo to cover mine. Hunched to make eye contact, he says, "So, I owe you the most supreme apology in the world."

With a simper, I tell him, "I'll wait for it."

"I'm not an expert at this, but whatever we were in the middle of…I'm not ready to let it go."

"What was that move the expert diver taught me again? Oh, the Rip Entry," I remove my hands from under his and get off the Argo. Moving my hands over his, I allow them to slide up the bulk of his shoulders then close them together, "I think this is right."

Keyne looks a bit amused and then I insert myself in between the opening of his arms, "Is that right? Because I'm not an expert either."

Keyne pulls me in and gives me a hold, pushing me into him with a gentle strength. Say goodbye to the friend hug. Running through every part of my body is that surge, an ebb and flow, a rush of energy so strong it makes me tremble. I don't want him to let go, yet his call sounded urgent. I know he has to leave. How can we be so young yet always have time against us?

"We don't have to be experts, Keyne."

Looking down at me, he slowly runs his fingers through my hair then he sighs, "There is so much I want to tell you. I just don't want to rush, I don't want to rush anything with you."

The dogged chiming of his phone continues. We take the hint and together we climb aboard the Argo.

Under the dark waters,

one thought shields me.

Look closely, Harbor.

Chapter 41

We exit the bend with a coagulated cloud of red and black hovering above us, the procession of the Honeycreepers seem to shadow the Argo. Lott hasn't arrived, so Keyne and I wait inside the empty gas station. I'm low on fuel again and figure I might as well fill-up before the weeklong break begins. I pay Old Man Ferencz who goes to the back to make change. He shuffles through a door that says employees only, and I wait by the counter. Keyne is taking another call by the large window that looks out from the store of the gas station. He seems upset. No sign of Old Man Ferencz and since I'm use to him taking a while, I walk over to Keyne.

"Is everything okay?"

He turns toward me and takes an elbow, "They're here. Are you gonna be all right getting home?"

"Of course. I'm just gonna wait for my change then head to The Shore."

"Can I call you later?"

"How else are you going to begin that outstanding apology?" I reach up, placing my arms on the muscular ridges of his shoulders to hug him good-bye and have a clear view through the wide window. My hands fall from him to my side as dread and horror stampede through my chest. Keyne's back is turned to the window, but I can see right through it.

I try not to panic, but my phone falls out of my hand. My mind is reeling as I hear it thwack on the ground. I'm dizzy as though I have just been kicked in the head. I can't match what I see in the parking lot with reality. Keyne bends to pick up my phone, speaking to me, but I can barely hear him. His voice sounds like it did when I was under water, "You might need this."

Pushing past Keyne, I walk closer to the window and see Lott reversing into an empty parking space. He is driving an ice blue car. I'd recognize it anywhere, "Call the police," I reach to clutch my phone from Keyne, but I'm so lightheaded, I inadvertently knock it out of his hands. Images are swarming through my mind, making me woozy. Keyne catches me by my elbow, and I can hear his concern, "Harbor, Harbor? Are you okay?"

"Call the police, Keyne!"

"What? Why?"

"Keyne, that's the kidnapper's car!"

I know it didn't happen in slow motion, yet it seemed that way. Keyne looked from me to the window and back to me, "No, Harbor. That is my dad and Lott." But I detect an uneasiness in his voice.

Hearing him vouch for that man is a metal ball with spikes lobbed into my stomach, my chest barely able to decompress to allow air to flow. Almost choking on the words, I muster out, "Keyne, I recognize it. That is the car from the news! That is the car from The Shore!"

And like the sounds that get turned up to high volume when you exit the water, I am suddenly blasted with all the noises surrounding me. The doddle of Old Man Ferencz walking back to the counter, the sound of the ice machine, the engine of the blue car, Keyne's voice and my own breath are in high definition. I know time is against us because the passenger side door is opening. Out steps a tall man. He is wearing a long sleeve shirt and a dark ball cap. He surveys the store, and for the first time, I have a straightforward view of Mr. Boring. The metal ball with spikes takes a second swing into my gut, "It's him."

He will remember me. I spilled water all over him and basically tried to take a selfie with his tattoo before chasing after him out of The Shore parking lot. I have to get out of here. Even with my eyes burning, the confusion and fear in Keyne's eyes is easy to decipher, "I'm sorry, Keyne," I say with a mournful last glance as I run back to the counter, tapping it loudly, screaming for Old Man Ferencz to call the police, "Call 9-1-1!"

With no time to spare, I run to retrieve my phone from Keyne, "That man is the kidnapper!"

Keyne is processing a million thoughts at once. Seeing the man light a cigarette and take a long drag while still having his eyes fixed on the front door of the store, I fumble to call 9-1-1.

"It's not safe here."

"Harbor, stop,"and in a grieving plea, Keyne begs, "Let me go talk to him. That's my dad. I'll show you."

9-1-1, what's your emergency

"The kidnapper! The kidnapper, the one who took all the kids is at the gas station off Old 99!"

Does he see you? Can you hide somewhere safe? Officers are on the way.

Screaming into the phone, I pray the dispatcher listens, "Officer Lam, call Officer Lam and tell him this is Harbor!"

What is your exact location? Can you hide? Is he alone?

I think about running out the back, but I'd still have to go around to the front to get the Argo unless my get away plan is rolling off a steep cliff.

Normally, I park the Argo on the side of the store, but today it's smack dab in front, waiting at the gas pumps. I can't hide here, but I also can't get to the Argo without being seen.

Tossing his cigarette onto the sandy gravel lot, Mr. Boring puts out the light with his boot. He takes a step forward approaching the store. Lott opens the door. And then I see them. *The tools.* Both of them have a long spear attached to their right thigh. It's just like the one Keyne wore.

And then as though he finally resigned himself to a buried truth, Keyne moves me behind him, "Harbor, get out of here."

Regaining his wits, Keyne flings open the store doors and confronts his dad.

This is it. It's my only chance. I run out back and alongside the store then dash out to the Argo. I start it up and turn tail toward the bend.

I didn't see the entire scene play out, but it was clear that I caught Mr. Boring's attention. His glare aimed at me, he is being held back by Keyne. Rampant thumps from my heartbeat block out fragments of shouting in the distant.

The thunder in my chest is deafening, I can barely make out Keyne's plea, "Hide! Go!"

The throttles of the Argo burn into my hand as I twist the handles to ignite as much power in the old engine as it will take. Clutching the Argo, I begin to roll into my shortcut and pause when a heavy whack collides with the Argo.

"Drive!"

Keyne shifts to gain balance on the back of the Argo as we make our way through the trees.

I look over my shoulder and through the leaves, I can see Lott peering our way while acting as barrier. He is holding the kidnapper back.

Lurching the Argo forward, I dip into the brush, and Keyne jumps off. In a voice that is more apologetic than fearful, he warns me, "Don't stop!"

Then, as though this were a football game, Keyne runs defense behind me. He knows Lott will not be able to hold Mr. Boring.

Cutting past the trees faster than I ever have, I hear someone running behind me. No one knows this spot. Winded, I exhale loudly when Keyne emerges from the thick. He hops on the Argo just as it plows through a small hot spring. Warm water splashes all around us, but the Argo makes its way out of the crevice, an entrance is visible. I never thought my shortcut would have to act as my escape route. I have two choices. Continue to descend or enter the bend to make it to the clearing. If I descend, I may not be able to hide, and I'll run out of beach before the monk seals catch me. If I drive the bend, I will be vulnerable, out in the open. I decide to enter the bend and navigate clusters of large trees, but I am not the only one clearing the path. Standing at the rear of the Argo, Keyne's arm is extended. He is slashing open a path before us with a long, thin rod. Branches fall at our sides until I arrive at the crossroads. *It's the fastest way.* Exiting from behind the cover of the rainforest, I am exposed. The large wheels of the Argo grumble along the main road. A smoother road. A fleeting thought crosses my mind. *Can I make it all the way to The Shore?* No. Fig and Tutu are there, and I don't want that monster near them. I have to get to the clearing. It's impassable for a full size car, so whoever tries to find us will have to do it on foot. I pray that the police use my cellphone pings to find me.

I've made hundreds of drives down this road. I know every curve, every sound, but never have I carried all these emotions nor could I have predicted that they would all merge onto the bend. Anger, loneliness, fear, peace and even love are all a part of this journey.

Frantic Honeycreepers scatter as the Argo parts the bramble to make its way to our destination. I silence it with the turn of the key and then push Keyne off.

"I'm sorry, Harbor. I'm sorry!"

Trying to stabilize my breathing, I attempt to call 9-1-1 again, but slam my phone on the Argo when I lose reception. The pressure in my eyes is almost unbearable. Raising my head to look at Keyne's, my stomach twisted in a knot, I peer into his eyes. Even before the books, I've always been able to read people. I didn't know how to put it into words, but I could see uneasiness, distress, anger. Maybe it's because I was around those attributes more often than most. Body language gives away secrets, but the eyes hold the evidence.

"Did you know?"

He reaches for both my elbows, and I instinctively launch myself back, "Harbor, you know I didn't. I still don't! He has problems! But a kidnapper? No!"

"That's the car, Keyne! That's the car from the drive-thru and the news! Didn't you notice little kids popping up at your house!" My head reeling, I utter the worst, "Or are they dead? Oh my God, maybe you never saw them."

Holding his head in his hand, Keyne cries out, "I don't live in a house! Okay! I live in a camp!" he shouts as though he just opened a wound. He walks in a circle around the Argo, and I try to process what he said.

"A camp? A homeless camp?"

Keyne walks around to me to take my elbows, and I let him. I don't know if I'm too stunned to move or maybe I don't want to.

"Harbor, I wanted to tell you, but there was never the right time. I don't have a choice: my dad has issues, ever since my mom died, but I swear, I swear, I know nothing about missing kids."

"Not missing kids, Keyne! They were kidnapped! Ripped away from their parents, ripped away from their lives!"

"It can't be! There has to be a mistake. If he had something to do with it, I'd know! Right?"

"How could you not?"

"Harbor, I rarely talk to him. He doesn't talk to me other than to give me orders."

"It's been all over the news, Keyne!"

"I know it sounds crazy, maybe it is, but we don't even have a TV. I don't watch the news! I really only know the little you've told me about the kidnappings."

"You have a phone, Keyne. We Facetime! And all phones get Amber alerts. "

"I sneak in FaceTime ,so I can talk to you. All the rest of my life is spent training!"

I am about to hurl and walk a few feet away to allow the downpour to fall in the dense wooded area.

Just moments ago, Keyne and I stood in this clearing holding each other. I held my breath as we willingly embraced for whatever might happen next. Not a snowball's chance in hell did I think it would be this. Holding our breath for our lives should the suspect find us before the police do.

Then in an instant, we freeze. Keyne holds his hand up and motions me not to speak.

A car slowly rolls in and stops just outside the clearing.

CHAPTER 42

"No one knows about this place. Maybe it's the police," I whisper to Keyne.

In what has to be purposeful stealth mode, the car on the other side of the thick foliage crawls closer, no sound of a motor. Whoever it is must have put it in neutral. Why would the police do that? A car door opens, provoking Keyne to grab my elbow tighter than he ever has and yank me behind him. In a hushed tone, he guides me to hunch down behind the Argo, "Don't kill me."

I don't know where my Third Eye is, but the two on my face feel like they are twitching and definitely have a look that will kill, "What?"

Keyne's voice is low and apprehensive, "I wanted to surprise you, leave flowers or carve our initials in a tree, so I came out here…"

My glare switching to confusion, Keyne admits, "Lott drove me."

His announcement sinks my heart into the sour acid rising in my stomach. They know we're in here.

Plodding that could wake the dead dwarfs our heavy breathing. Someone big is entering the clearing. Heavy, slow steps move in. According to FBI rule #7 those are not the steps of someone trying to get from point A to point B. The pressure in each step is a clue to the pressure in the brain, a strain on the mind. This person is dangerous.

A dark figure steps through the forestry, its looming shadow splinters the shadow of the Koa's, and Keyne stands to confront it. In his direct line of sight is his father. Mr. Boring.

"Dad, leave! We can talk about this at camp."

Following right behind the suspect, Lott makes an uneasy entrance, dusting leaves off his blonde hair. Both of them have Keyne and I in their scope.

"Dad, there has to be an explanation. Tell me there is an explanation!" The magnitude of pain in Keyne's voice fills the clearing. And then a similar octave, one much lower, answers in protest, "You don't understand the struggle for power, son. You don't understand that I am doing this for you."

Mr. Boring walks toward us in a doomful trance. I dig for my rocks with such force that clumps of soil get trapped in my nails. All I have to latch on to now is the scooped up dirt and two of my biggest rocks as Keyne zeroes in on the intruders.

Lott's eyes sink with worry as he attempts to cut off Mr. Boring by standing in front of him while screaming to Keyne, "It's not worth it, bro! C'mon, leave her! You put the whole family at risk, Keyne. Let's go!"

Mr. Boring is taller than Lott, and looks right past him. It's clear his attention is laser focused on me. Lott implores him to retreat, but Mr. Boring ignores him and begins to walk methodically toward me. Neither Lott nor Keyne are visible to the suspect.

Without taking his eyes off his father, and in an unshakeable resolve, Keyne's voice overrides the others, "Get on the Argo and go," he throws me his phone, "Try to call again. Now!"

The urgency in his voice propels me onto the Argo: I grip the throttles only to hear the rattle an empty belly makes. *Dammit! I'm out of gas.*

"Run!" Keyne commands with finality. Taking the rocks, I sprint past a shield of Koa trees through tall grass and downward. I need to make it to the shoreline, but the slant is slippery, and unless I want to tumble to my death, I need to decrease my pace. I have to try to get a signal. Sliding the screen on Keyne's phone to call 9-1-1, a picture pops up, and it stops me in my tracks. It is a picture of Keyne and a girl.

It's me. It's the selfie Keyne took of us on this cliff. That seems like forever ago. I am the girl he saved on his screen. I grapple with what to do next, and I look over my left shoulder. In a continuous blur, I see Keyne's dad lunge forward in a rage. His sights are set on finding me. Then, in what looks like a production of a slow motion video, Lott lurches in front of the suspect. Something won't let me run away. With my tennis shoes dug into the ground, I turn completely back around. I exit the thick, protective canopy and walk back into the living nightmare. And what I watch unfold before me is horrific.

Mr. Boring plucks Lott upward as thought Lott is simply a dirty piece of laundry. For a mere second, Lott hovers above Mr. Boring's head until he's thrown onto the fertile ground. I hear something crack and Lott lays motionless. Momentarily breaking his stare from the wooded area, Mr. Boring looks around. He knows I ran in here, but he can't see me. Then his next move numbs me. He does something that forces both my hands over my mouth to clamp it shut to prevent me from screaming out. Mr. Boring repeatedly lifts his boot and pummels it into the stomach of the unmoving body beneath him. An amplified screech of pain exits Lott's lungs, causing my tears to push through. I want to cry out to Keyne, but it's too late. And like a switch that can be flicked up and down on a whim, the suspect's fierce aggressiveness toward Lott reverts back to an almost sedated march, but not toward his son. His glare is steady on the patch of woods I'm hiding in. He wants me. Hot tears wet my eyelashes, but before they can flow down my cheeks, I wipe them away and feel the mud, the sting and the rawness of the rocks graze my face. I hate this man. Not just for the kids he kidnapped, but for the kid that was his. The desperate kid who looked him right in the eyes when he didn't even notice. He didn't see his own son standing in front of him *suffering*.

Then in what looks like an attempt to divert Keyne, Mr. Boring strolls toward the exit of the clearing. It's a trick!

The Argo now divides them, Keyne on one side and his dad on the other, and Keyne begins to close in. It is too late. Mr. Boring thrusts forward into a run toward me!

I can't move. I can't gasp. Maybe I don't want to. My stance is glued in fury as Keyne unflinchingly pole vaults over the Argo, diving into his dad's charge. Both are knocked to the ground as they struggle in matched strength. I know I've wasted time. Compelled to help, I move forward. If he catches me, then what? The best way out is to try to make it to his car. Then I can get help. Gripping both rocks, I step out of the cover of darkness and reveal myself.

The car is just outside on the main road. If I run, I can make it, but what if I can't find the keys? *You have to try, Harbor!* My mad dash, however, is foiled when I hear Keyne's howl. Not like the one that sang to me a few hours ago when we were basking in the sun. No, this was the sound of agony. I turn to see Keyne pinned under his father, and I can't leave him with that beast.

Taking one a rock, I throw it as hard as I can at Mr. Boring's back, but my hands are so full of sweat, the rock slips. Instead of knocking him out, all it does is make him angrier, more violent. Keyne's moans grow louder. His long legs are wrapped around his dad's back, trying to hold him down. *No!* I don't know if I thought it or screamed it out loud, but *No! You've already caused too much pain. And you don't get to keep causing it!*

I place my own rage and confusion into the last rock. The images of each of the kidnapped kids seem to harness an energy that surges down my arm into my hand. I lift my arm, and with an unearthly forcefulness allow it to bash into the back of Mr. Boring's head. My strike narrowly misses Keyne's face. Mr. Boring is hit hard causing their manic, ungovernable percussions to pause. He momentarily stops moving, and I see a dark trickle of blood on the back of his head. His face is buried, but his feverish hands, hands that hold a sickness even when they crossed the threshold of The Shore window, begin clawing the dirt. Keyne slips out and immediately reaches for the long rod, the one he called a swimming tool. Distracted by the object Keyne holds is my own downfall, and like the 4D movies where the image seems to escape the screen, Mr. Boring stands before me, bigger than ever.

He flings his torso toward me, and I can't escape in time. With one arm, he reaches out and grabs my bare leg, causing me to hit the ground so hard, the cheekbone on the right side of my face feels like it caved in. I don't know how long I am out or if this is even real. Some part of it feels like I have been here before. The darkness, the struggle, the pain were all familiar. And just like after the dreams, I come to with a splitting headache, but this time, instead of my head buried in my pillow, my face is covered in dirt, and somehow, the ground is moving under me. Then I feel it. The strong grip, the hot density of a hand sears into my ankle. It makes my blood run cold. Mr. Boring is dragging me… towards the edge of the cliff!

I exert all the power I have left, ripping, pulling my leg away until I feel Mr. Boring's hand slowly peel away, leaving only nuked skin.

I wipe at the dirt in my eyes and try to see through the haze that is my own dizziness.

Keyne has risen from the mucky ground and is standing between me and the evil that is his father. Even though he has regained control of his stature and voice, I can tell he is wounded too, but his arms flare anyway like two giant pincers. A infernal wrath flows out of his roar, "Let her go!"

The abductor pauses for a second but not because he cares about anything his own kid has to say. Keyne must have done something to him. Mr. Boring walks sluggishly toward his son. *Don't fall for it, Keyne!* He wants to appear weak, so he can strike. A wolf in sheep's clothing, just like he did to gain access to the missing kids. As the animal slinks closer, I see his full face. For the first time, I have a clear view of his entire face; his dominion over Keyne and the sunken void in his eyes. There is no soul in those eyes. Just unsympathetic, mechanical control that seeps out in a husky, broken drawl, "Son, you wouldn't understand! I have to do this."

"Don't call me son. You've never treated me like a son!"

However, Keyne's sadness is only a nuisance to Mr. Boring who continues to creep forward, "Keyne, you will never understand. I tried to protect you."

"You never tried to protect me. Or mom! You didn't protect either of us!"

"Shut up! You don't know what you are saying!" Mr. Boring's response is vehement. He doesn't try to clear up any confusion or apologize. No, instead the villain strikes out at his son as though he wants to knock the words right out of Keyne's mouth. It is evident that Keyne has been let down many times by this man, but even in his heartache, he fights back. Keyne blocks the heartless slap with his forearm and uses his open hand to chop down at Mr. Boring's neck. What ensues next are an array of explosive blows. Both father and son are familiar with the fight.

Barbaric knee kicks, elbow punches, rapid hand strikes and jabs. The kid and the kidnapper are now opponents in a ferocious battle. And somehow, in the brutal exchange, Keyne is able to use his attacker's momentum and a series of turning motions to create distance - away from me. He has lured his dad to the cliff's edge. But the very risk Keyne takes to draw the monster there, puts him in peril as well. And now, because neither of them has the advantage, each tries to outmaneuver the other, their moves conducted with strict precision, nothing owed, nothing felt in the merciless match that plays out before my stunned eyes.

"Casimero, don't!" Lott, still a few yards away, tries to untangle himself from the coiled knot he was body slammed into.

Casimero? Who is that? Mr. Boring?

Lott regains consciousness and pleads from the ground, "Casimero! Sir! Please don't!"

The reverence in Lott's voice toward this foul man, this false superiority adds shock to an already infuriating scene. How did my clearing become an arena? Nonetheless, Lott's timely entreaty does divert Mr. Boring's attention. The sparring halted gives me a chance to make it to my feet. I know I have to make a run for it, but Lott struggles to his feet at the same time I do. Mr. Boring is seething, his cutthroat fuming prongs the air.

The split screen before me stiffens my blood. One side displays the monster's head lowered, his back arched. The other, the low angle of Lott rushing at me, both his arms in full wing span. In unison, both of the gutless cowards zero in on the ambush. I make a run for it, but my escape is obstructed once again. This time, a paralyzing pressure covers my back. Lott lays across me.

"Get off of me!" I punch and hit as hard as I can, but he doesn't hit back. A searing sensation on my ankles makes me aware of what he is doing. Lott is protecting me. His body mass is a shield, a human paperweight. The suspect's monstrous hands boil over my skin as he drags both of us. Even with the added weight of Lott, who is also digging his hands into the dirt to slow Mr. Boring down, we are being hauled closer to the edge of the cliff.

Together, we try to unclasp the suspects hands from my kicking legs, but we are unable to break the grip. Without one misstep, Mr. Boring's huff produces a long, destructive smirk as he stares down at his prey, simultaneously delivering a twisted message to his son, "I'm doing this for you."

Lifting my head to look back at Keyne, maybe for the last time, our eyes lock. Even in my rage, fear, and disorientation, all I see is love.

A jolt on my leg is yanked so hard that it feels as though my entire limb will come loose from my hip socket, and I realize I am too close to the edge. The bayonet hangs from a strap along Mr. Boring's thigh. Besieged with pain, it's all I have left to defend myself. I grab for it but fall short. I reach again and again until finally, three fingers clasp it. I rip backwards as hard as I can removing the spear. With the harpoon now in my possession, I summon all my tenacity. Despite being dampened by the weight of Lott, I am able to rise long enough to thrust the spear into Mr. Boring's thigh. Who is the prey now! With the spear stabbed into his thigh, Mr. Boring releases his hold, and before my legs can hit the ground, I feel a current of air rush above me. It's Keyne. Both of his arms are extended, and he has one hand in front of the other, his palms are facing up, and he flies over Lott and me. In the blink of an eye, he seizes his father in between his strong, long arms, and I no longer can contain my screams. We are too close to the edge. There can only be one ending. With the threat gripped firmly in his hold, Keyne dives over the cliff, submerging the danger with him.

Heaving, dizzy and nauseous at what I witnessed, I push Lott off and balance myself to my knees. The dark waters below only reveal the remains of the deadly splash. Lott grabs my shoulders and tries to hold me back, but my screams for Keyne nearly dislocate my throat as I cast them over the peak's fringe.

Even the monk seals in the far distance wail a honking alarm along with a new sound advancing closer and closer. The echo of sirens is amplified in the night air.

CHAPTER 43

In a split second, Keyne is gone. I continue to look over the edge, searching for any signs of life. Examining the dark waters below, I can't move. Part of me feels so faint, I know that if I peer into the obscurity any closer, I will fall in. I begin to pray that Keyne will emerge from the water when the loud voice of a woman causes me to blink, "Show me your hands! This is the police! Show me your hands, now!" She gives the command, her voice cogent, yet I can't move. I have only one goal. Find Keyne.

"Show me your hands, or I will have to tase…"

"Tara! She's the one who called, the one who got the prints."

I recognize Officer Lam's voice and alert him as fast as I can, pointing down below, "He's down there! The kidnapper's down there! But someone's with him who needs help! He needs an ambulance!"

As I'm saying this, I feel my right wrist jerked from under me and placed behind my back. Startled, livid that Keyne's life is at stake, my reflexes cause me to do the one thing I know is the worst. I resist. Or rather, I try to resist. Both of my wrists are now in handcuffs.

"She is just going to give you a quick pat down. It's protocol, Harbor. For everyone's safety," Officer Lam calms me by placing his hand on my shoulder. I can feel her gloves enter the pockets of my shorts, my waistband and my bra straps. Then she shakes out my hair. What could I hide in my hair? When she doesn't find any weapons, she ends her search by reluctantly releasing my wrists.

"Can you do your job now? The kidnapper went over…" But as she lifts me up and turns me around, my thoughts are cut short when I see Lott in handcuffs, facing the ground. I forgot he was here.

"It's just safety protocol, Harbor," Officer Lam assures me.

"You think I care about that! That bastard, the kidnapper is down there!"

"We have units combing the entire area. He's not going to get away. I understand what you care about, but we have to care about *everything*," he turns to the female officer he called Tara, and though his words are directed at me, he consciously looks at her, "Follow Officer Sullivan to the ambulance. I need to get a statement from the beta," before he heads toward Lott.

The hours that follow seem like days. Since The Shore is nearby, it becomes a temporary command post filled with squad cars, ambulances, a fire truck and swarms of news reporters in the parking lot. I can hear the helicopter above as Officer Lam and Officer Sullivan take my statement. They give me a photo line up and it doesn't take three winks for me to identify the bastard, "That one."

Mr. Boring is easy to pick out. Even in his mug shot, his eyes are like empty graves. Officer Lam asks to speak to Tutu outside, and Officer Sullivan stays with me in the break room.

My eyes attempt to fill with water, remembering the murderous drop, but I squeeze them shut. I'm doing everything so not to be afraid of the truth, but I know. I know that no matter how great a diver someone is, a jump like that is treacherous. Keyne sacrificed himself. He saved me. He saved Lott. He may have even saved the kidnapped kids.

The paramedics tell Tutu that I am in shock from the incident and that she needs to monitor me through the night. I have icky medicated gel on my legs and arms, but I don't remember getting the cuts nor being treated. Too many feelings have left me emotionally depleted. I need a sanctuary, some privacy. I take the worn golden streaked blanket from the couch in the break room and drape it around me. It's going to have to do.

Officer Lam steps back in and whispers something to Officer Sullivan. Both turn to look at me and stand silent. I've seen enough sorrow to recognize it anywhere.

"Is it Keyne? You found him?"

Before they can respond, Tutu walks in. She breaks ranks and stands in front of Officer Lam and Sullivan. She is my grandmother, yet I've never seen her look as old as she does now. I worried her sick and deserve any punishment she issues. But in this moment, I've lost another person I care about and have nothing left to give.

Deep down, I know I owe her an apology. She also sacrificed; raising me when no one else would. Emotionally void or not, I drag the drab, once golden cloak and walk over to hug her. I raise the blanket over her shoulders, and at the same time, a third officer walks into the room. It's a woman who stands by the door, a few feet behind Tutu and begins speaking to the officers. She is shorter than the other two, but I can still see her small frame through their huddle. She wears a police jacket and plain clothes, and the way she speaks to Lam and Sullivan steals my attention away from Tutu. This new officer has a command presence about herself. Maybe she is the police spokesperson I always see on the news. She also dresses in plain clothes. No, this woman is not getting information from the other two. She's giving it.

I peer in and listen closely. There is something oddly familiar in her voice. She is definitely from the island.

"Harbor," I lower my glance to restore my attention back to Tutu, and I see heavy tears slowly spilling out of her eyes. Not sure how to begin apologizing, not sure I can talk right now, I wrap my arms around her, and the old, flaxen blanket follows. Tutu is a small woman, but very strong. Yet in this moment, she is helplessly fragile. I open my mouth to apologize, but once again, I'm distracted by the officers just beyond her. My grandmother is crying, and yet, I can't pull my attention away from the discussion by the break room door.

Officer Lam steps out, and Officer Sullivan follows. My view is no longer blocked. All the gravity in the room, in The Shore, in the world weighs me down forcing me to release my hold on Tutu. A giant suction cup absorbs my mind and body. All the agony from the cliff, the bruising, the cuts, and the sharp stabbing in my leg return at once. Too weak to move, the most I can do is let my arms fall to my side, the faded, gilded blanket carried on my back. Staring ahead, unable to breathe, I have a crystal clear view of Aadya. She stands firm, staring right back at me.

Sorties were never fairies.

As the faded, gilded blanket cloaks me,

I think of the old land. Free of self-pity.

Chapter 44

How hard did I hit my head out on the cliff? Dumbfounded, I look away, thinking maybe when I look back, the hallucination will be gone. Returning my view only proved that the figure standing there didn't vanish, and it still looks like her. Sometimes we see what we want to see. It can't be her.

This lady officer isn't smiling. She is waiting. Her stature is guarded not maternal. But her tan, smooth skin is the same as Aadya's. Her hair is worn in a tight bun and she's aged a bit.

I test the waters to make sure I am not stuck in another nightmare, "Aadya?"

With a gulp, the female detective takes a step forward and slowly holds out her arms to me. Her firm expression softens into a smile. "Yes," she answers as though I just got the answer correct for the big prize on a game show.

I call for Tutu, and when I don't see her, I yell for her, "Tutu!"

"I asked them to wait outside. I wanted a moment with you."

Rage burns in my eyes. I can't believe this woman thinks she has the right to speak to me.

"You've been missing over 2 years and you want a goddamned moment!"

"I am sorry, Harbor, but I can explain."

"You can explain?"

What shimmer is left in the beige blanket shields the blow, yet the sound of my punch into the break room wall cannot be muted. I want to pull the blanket over my head and cry. I'm in another nightmare!

"Harbor?"

"Shut up!"

"I know you are angry. You should be. But I am still your mother. I had to leave! It was the only way!"

"You have the nerve to think, to make yourself believe there exists a good enough explanation for abandoning your daughters?"

"Whether any of us like the truth or not, we are going to have to accept it. I did what I had to protect both of you! All of you! I'm the lead detective on this case."

For so many nights, I dreamt of running up to Aadya again. I used to wish I could wrap my arms around her, hug her and never let go. I tried to remember her scent and her laugh. I'd look at that picture of my parents. I missed them so much that I'd cry myself to sleep, until one day, I ran out of tears. Now, I want to run at her and knock that smug bun off her head. Instead, I barrel over and grab my stomach. How is it I haven't thrown up everything I've eaten in the last year?

"Did Tutu know?"

"No one did. Not your grandmother, not Rob. It had to be done this way to protect you and Fig."

Cutting her off, I yell, "Don't say her name. You left her! You have no right to waltz back in here like you know her!"

"Harbor, you are right. You are. But you are right in a situation that went very, horribly wrong."

Does she seriously think this is a time to reason? My look of disgust must alert her to the fact that I don't know what the hell she means. Unfazed, she continues, "I don't know how we are going to repair the damage, but we are," she says trying to hug me.

Reeling with fury, I move away from her, my fist clenching the sides of the blanket as I try to make sense of what is happening. There is nothing more I have to say to her.

"Harbor, we are not the only ones hurt."

"We? We! You have the nerve to include yourself in the hurt and suffering?"

"The kidnapped kids, your father, your sister, Keyne were all hurt…"

Her words confuse and alert me, "What do

you know about Keyne?"

"Harbor, please. Just sit with me for a moment. I only have a few minutes."

"Oh poor you. Poor you!"

She grabs hold of my arms and sits me down. "Be as mad as you want. But know that I am so proud of you. You are a big part of this."

I jerk my arms back. I am sitting so close to the mother I missed for so long, and yet, I feel farther away than ever.

"I want to stop the world and hug my girls and explain to you why I did what I did. But right now, others need us desperately. We are near the end of the operation, and those kids still need to be rescued."

Aadya looks so strong in her police jacket, an image that any daughter should be proud of, but I can only filter in absence and pain.

"Harbor, Officer Lam and Officer Sullivan and others I had in place have filled me in, but I need to hear certain details from you. Tell me your involvement with the kidnapper."

Hesitant, I understand that something bigger than me requires my cooperation. I muster out the story of the drive-thru and the pattern of kidnappings. Dad's books and my journal. I tell Aadya how I retrieved his description and the finger prints.

Her smile holds a sense of pride, "So smart for you to preserve them in one of our wax Shore bags."

She can't see my disbelief, "Stop. Don't ever say *ours* again! You have nothing to do with this place or how hard Tutu worked while raising Fig and me!"

"I'm sorry. All I meant is this has been a harrowing event, and I'm proud of you. Because of your bravery, we were able to have the national lab match his fingerprints. All of our surveillance was useless without hard evidence linking him to each count."

The makeshift cloak clings to my shoulders as I rise from the couch. I don't want any compliments from her. I want answers, "What do you know about Keyne?"

She caresses the blanket as though she isn't sure if she wants to pet it or shine it, so I rip it off and throw it on the floor. Aadya gently places it back on the couch, her expression conflicted, "He is the son of the kidnapper."

I figured that out on the cliff. I was winded by it, but I need to hear the official report.

"He is innocent, Harbor." My eyes clamp shut as an overwhelming gratefulness fills me. *I knew Keyne was good.*

"Too many have lost in this battle. I know that I have taken so much from you, and I promise, one day very soon, I will explain."

I can hear her excuse forming, and sure enough, Aadya executes it with precision, "I am not ready for your sister and Rob to know."

Puzzled, I shake my head, giving her permission to continue.

"Not until they are safe, until we all our safe. We need to put this guy behind bars before we can be together again, before they know that I am home."

"I don't care what you do. Fig is fine with us. Abandoning your kids seems to be your M.O."

"Harbor, before he kidnapped the kids, he murdered your father."

CHAPTER 45

If I had done one thorough internet search, I would have uncovered that the night my dad was murdered, I was with him.

I wasn't spared in the terrible crime. My father hid me. He saved me. The news articles tell a story of a young agent assassinated, a monster yet to be captured, and the one eye witness, a little girl placed in heart-rending chance.

All these years later, an arrest has finally been made. It was Keyne's father who had slain mine. I would have preferred the burial of a monster, yet Mr. Boring would now rot in prison for the rest of his life, freeing Aadya to re-enter ours.

Rob and Tutu carefully informed Fig that her mother was coming home. Aadya immersed herself into our lives, acting like she didn't miss a beat, like she could just pick up where she left off. I couldn't hide my disdain. I didn't.

She wasn't around when Tutu and I had to take Fig to the emergency room with a flaming earache. She didn't know what kind of candles Fig had on her last birthday cake or that Rob and I had to go to 3 stores to find the right ones. She missed Fig's first day of school, and she wasn't a part of my growing up. She missed everything - but us. If she had, she wouldn't have left. That was the drum I was set on beating.

The news flashed for weeks with the suspect's face and follow-up interviews with sobbing parents, grateful for the safe return of their children. But not all of the kids' stories had a happy ending. John and Jane Doe were never found. Victims of the homeless camps, now subjects of a cruel crime.

I remember the first night Fig found out she would have her mom back, she fell asleep holding my hand, "Harbor, mom is coming home. I told you she would come home. I just know she is going to love Ember, and I know she loves us. Don't be mad, Harbor."

Fig is young, but she knows. I do my best to play along in the weeks that follow in front of Fig who is beside herself with happiness. The kid has both her parents back and is riding a rainbow of new energy and hope. I wasn't going to steal her pot of gold.

Old news articles can't satisfy all the questions I have. So, after a few weeks of shunning Aadya, I knew the only way I am going to get the answers I need is from her.

She is still handling police business, even weeks after her return from the dead. So, Officer

Lam and Officer Sullivan are almost regulars at our house. With each briefing, it is clear the two younger officers revere their supervisor. They look at me a differently too. They have the case files in front of them. They're familiar with the investigation and know what laws were broken. However, not one of them could ever understand the full extent of the offenses committed. The suspect is an evil villain who broke the law. No one denies this. It is Aadya's crime that no one takes notice of.

When I learn that Keyne survived, I am in a free fall for days. I haven't heard from him. He didn't return to school, and the memories of seeing him at Kau, laughing with him, eating with him are so far away. I know I may never see him again, yet knowing he is alive gives me a conflicting inner peace.

His father is responsible for kidnapping those kids. His father murdered mine. So yeah, I have questions, and as much as I don't want to talk to Aadya, she has the leverage, the answers I need. When I approach her, she acts more than happy to talk with me.

She explains that once the department got a lead on the man who murdered my father, she was pregnant with Fig. She claims that she tried to distance herself from the case, but every time our new happiness as a family reached a new peak, it was overshadowed by the one stolen from her former one. She initiated being placed on the assignment because she couldn't marry a new man until she could properly, and with closure, bury the other.

She insists that she loves Fig and I with all her heart and knew Rob was strong enough to care for us. The murder was related to other serious crimes with ties to the island, and it was imperative she not reveal her position on the case, or our lives would be in jeopardy, "You had trouble remembering, and I couldn't add more torment to your life."

The name that Lott yelled out on the cliff is Keyne's father. Casimero. My dad was closing in on an arrest that would have put Casimero in prison for a minimum of 30 years. My dad, Alexander, had been working long hours and was suffering from insomnia. The investigation stole all his time, and he hadn't been able to spend much time with me during those days. So, right after his shift that night, he surprised me and took me for a ride on the Argo. I wasn't supposed to be there; in the bend at the witching hour.

As Aadya speaks, she unlocks pitch black memories, freeing them from a hiding place they found in my dreams. The abysmal gloom. The ride. The admiration I held in my heart for my family. I even remember school and Keyne. First grade Keyne. I remember him standing by the swings waiting his turn. Now I know, he was pretending. He didn't want a swing. He was waiting to be my friend.

Aadya confirms that Keyne didn't know Casimero had stepped that far away from reality. Like so many of us who have a problem with our parents, Keyne figured his dad had become sick, isolated, grieving from the death of his mom.

Keyne's mom was deathly ill at the time of my dad's murder. Casimero escaped, gathering up his small family and fleeing to California, one to hide and two to seek medical treatment for his wife, unbeknownst to his innocent little boy. Keyne's mom was in and out of hospitals for a year, and this was extraordinarily hard on Keyne. He loved his mother, and Casimero was distant and uncaring.

When Keyne's mother passed, Casimero blamed the hospitals and accused modern technology of being a sham because they couldn't keep her alive. He was on a volatile trajectory and became further obsessed with crime and power. He exploited Keyne's pain and the death as an excuse to refuse to hold a steady job or seek help. Unable to function in society, Casimero went so far into a life of crime that the financial strain found young Keyne living out of a car, moving from rest stop to rest stop until they found a home of like-minded people.

When it was time for school to begin again, Casimero had Keyne stay with their new family, people like the blonde haired coach and Lott. Keyne grew up thinking they were his dad's business partners. Casimero left Keyne under the guise that he was buying land to start up a new business, a modern training facility, but in actuality, he was building a very different, sinister kind of camp - right under their noses.

Casimero was a fanatic who believed the island should be his. He pledged to never lose again like he had his wife, his fortune, and his home. Through exploitation and cunning, he became the leader of a sovereign nation.

Casimero returned to his old stomping ground, the place where he cowardly gunned down a man who was protecting this island. *My dad.*

The island camps were rapidly increasing and ripe for someone to corral them. Casimero took advantage of this. He gained power quickly because he prospered off the pain of others. He seized their grief as an opportunity for his grand plan. His mission was financial expansion through the ultimate theft. He plundered a rare, new mineral, hidden deep in the ocean trenches; water jewels said to contain power.

The technical name for the jewels is Ocean Nodules. They are said to be worth billions.

And the tattoos that were ordered on his faithful soldiers were of the giant water lizard known as the Mo'o. And these weren't ordinary tattoos. They were injected with ocean minerals, a filler that was their lifeline to the legend that was deemed their ancestral guardian. Casimero believed the fierce monster, the Mo'o, is the guardian of the water jewels.

The account Aadya shared left me with one word, "How?"

"In some twisted way, he believes the Mo'o exist and that their powers can be harnessed."

Barely able to comprehend, I hesitate to ask, "What is a nodule? What's a sovereign nation? How can one man accomplish all that?"

"Using mercenaries. He wanted what no human should ever have. Full power. And he was willing to take any measures necessary. Kidnapping. Brain washing. Stealing. He isn't exactly cooperative. You could say his communication skills are lacking."

No kidding, I think. *He didn't earn the name Mr. Boring because of his lively personality.*

Casimero returned to visit Keyne periodically and eventually sent for him and the rest of their California camp a summer ago.

"Are you saying that Keyne lived among mercenaries?"

Aadya reaches over and takes my hand. Something tells me that whatever she is about to say requires me to not pull away, to sit still and listen, "I'm saying that Keyne *is one*, Harbor. A soldier in training. Even if he didn't fully realize it."

I flounder to my feet, my hands flying out from under hers, and walk to the large window in the living room. How could I not see that? Was Keyne ever a threat to me? Shouldn't the title 'mercenary' scare anyone shitless?

"Harbor, there's more."

I turn toward her with the expression *of course there is*.

"Harbor, you may feel that I don't have a right to parent you, but I promise I won't ever steer you wrong."

"Where are you going with this?"

"Keyne."

"What about him?"

"Harbor, I'm sorry. This is too much too soon."

"No, it's too much - too late. Tell me now."

"I know Keyne. He knows me."

My head vibrates at this revelation, and all I can do is hold my eyes for fear they might actually pop out of my skull.

"I can't tell you everything just yet. Some things are still extremely confidential due to the severity of the case. But I was undercover in the camp. Keyne doesn't know I'm your mother."

"You've been on this island all along!"

"No. I infiltrated their California camp."

My fist strikes the table so hard, Aadya jumps. She holds my balled fists. She is as strong as I remember, but I've also become stronger and rip my hands away from her. Here my long lost mother stands, and I can't even bear to look at her. All I see is the air she is sucking up. The space she is standing in belongs to me, to Tutu, and to Fig. Not to this lady!

"Harbor, I am sorry. I am telling you because you need to know. You need to know how proud I am of you."

"Stop!"

"No. No, I won't stop! If you don't take the compliment from your mother, then take it from a high ranking officer. What you did was heroic! It took guts and brains, Harbor. The lengths you went to saved those kids' lives. Yes, it was dangerous, and I ask that you use extreme caution from now on, but oh my…you have the heart of justice. But if you had been hurt…"

"You wouldn't have known!" I respond loud enough for my words to slice her sentence in half.

"That's not true," she retorts in a resolute tone.

"What do you mean?"

"This has been a huge undercover operation spanning two states. Do you think I'd leave and not have eyes on you?"

"Okay, so what? You put an App on my phone that I couldn't detect? Oh, don't tell me, you put a camera on the tree outside?" I point to the window and wave hi, "Or, hold on, hold on, you peered through my window every night to make sure I was tucked in safely and still expected a Mother's Day card!"

"I know you are mad. You have every right, but I'm here now, and at some point, we are going to need to move forward."

Huffing, I ask as sincerely as I can, "What then? How could you know what was going on in my life?"

"Agent Reddy."

I think I'll be in a neck brace for sure after my double take. I thought I heard her say the name of my nerd history teacher, Mr. Reddy.

"What the hell did you just say?"

"He is one of us, Harbor. He worked with your father."

She lowers her head and as exasperated, as furious as I am, I see it. I see a flash of anguish in her expression that can't be ignored. She misses my father too.

In spite of that, I am still not going to hand Aadya an ounce of empathy. Regaining her thoughts, she continues, "He's worked the case since the beginning."

My knees feel weak, bloodless. If I don't sit down, I will fall down. I return to my seat at the table with the mother I want nothing to do with. Like the dreams, a flashback of the school year almost makes sense now. Mr. Reddy's disappearance at the Winter Dance, his odd glances at Keyne and me; always making sure we were grouped together, his long work meals at The Shore. What a fool I've been! I knew something was peculiar. I feel so violated, "You left us, but didn't want the guilt that came with that choice. So you hired a babysitter?"

Then Aadya says something that I cannot not turn a deaf ear to. I hold my eyes shut and listen, "Keyne is going to need time to heal. He suffered traumatic events. Yet we feel certain he never hurt anyone *intentionally*."

"Intentionally?"

"The crimes Casimero committed are only unconscionable to people with a conscious."

"Keyne is a good person. He has a conscious."

"You still need to be careful. He was raised by a person without one."

Remembering the murderous drop,

made the line up easy.

Just look for the eyes that hold empty graves.

CHAPTER 46

Keyne didn't return to school and neither did Lott or the blonde coach. A substitute replaced Reddy and I completed most of my classwork online. Remote learning. More like lonely, dejected learning.

Many of the camps were cleared out and cleaned away. But, John and Jane Doe still haven't been found. Aadya witnessed how the camps were a safe haven for criminals, a cover for the sovereign nations that breed victims. She says this is how Casimero was able to hide for so long.

Each new detail concerning the case history is like a 50,000 volt taser to my back. And just when I think nothing can ever shock me again, Aadya informs me that there was more to the investigation, "Harbor, we can't compromise evidence that took years to gather."

"Yeah, I know a little about that. Tell me what you can."

"Keyne has a brother."

As is customary when receiving information that rattles you to the core, I pause for a minute, "He never mentioned a brother. Is it Lott?"

"He didn't know."

"Is it Lott?"

"No."

I think about young Keyne, alone, trying to tranquilize the pain from a cruel upbringing. A brother could have provided an anchor, a comfort. I am grateful to have Fig. Happy that she is my sister. She has helped lighten the burden without even knowing it.

"Is his brother here on the island?"

Silence.

"What is his name?"

"I'm limited at this juncture on what I can reveal."

"Aadya? You brought this to me!"

She contemplates my demand and places her hands on my shoulders, "Soon. I will tell you as soon as I can."

I know not to try and swindle more information from her. Aadya is managing her time with the various crime scenes and immersing herself back in our lives. She and Rob are like a new couple again. Both embrace parenting. Rob never seems angry with Aadya. He is too stunned like the rest of us, and somehow they both still seem very much in love. It isn't long before they start looking for their own home, and of course, insist that Fig and I move with them. Fig has no choice, but I haven't made up my mind. I'm angry with Aadya and have my own learning curve. Coping with the aftermath for Fig's sake is an effort I make, but I'm not fooling myself. I'm not going to be running into Aadya's arms anytime soon and calling her Mommy.

Quiet fills most of my days. I decide that whatever a Sortie is, I better find out what I can. But my research is often interrupted by thoughts of Keyne. None of the scenarios I contemplate are good. Keyne is a smart, standup guy. How could he not have seen the warning signs? How could he not know he has a brother?

Refocusing on school and working the window helps. And there is still the ultimate distraction, riding the bend. Even after everything that happened in the clearing, I haven't once regretted my role. The bend never became this horrible place where I saw my first kiss jump off a cliff. Instead, it's where I saw my first love.

I still sit and watch the monk seals and their pups. Aadya told me that when my dad was stuck on a case, he enjoyed a drive on the Argo to watch the monk seals, "Actually, it was working this case that piqued his interest in the seals. He studied them for hours."

Maybe that is why I find peace in the seals myself. Monk seals can live up to thirty years. I like to think that I'm watching the same monk seals my dad surveilled. And that the monk who see me, remember his spirit, and see it close by, see it in me.

In the struggle, all my rocks were scattered or lost. The only rock remaining is the shimmery one Keyne gave me. I often contemplate if there was more I could have done to help him. It's silly, yet if I had accepted the visions of The Third Eye and Tutu's story about the power in the Sortie, would things have been different?

All those years, Keyne was raised in a regime. Aadya can't tell me what will happen next, but she and Rob make it clear that if Keyne tries to contact me, I must let them know. I find out that Casimero branded his so-called soldiers with a tattoo of the Mo'o because the shapeshifter, the evil lizard was his maniacal signature. A perfect match. One evil for another.

On top of this, one day out of the clear blue sky, Aadya initiates a conversation about the Sorties.

"You can't tell me that you believe in fairytales too?"

"True, I don't. However, the Sorties were never fairies."

"What is with you and Tutu? I don't understand what you want me to take from this conversation."

"Don't view it as a conversation. View it as knowledge, as history."

"Okay, Aadya. Humor me."

"The Sorties date back to the old land. They were a species revered for their delicate strength. Recognized by their slender height, billowing crowns and their Third Eye."

I'm momentarily caught off guard. *Delicate strength.* Keyne said that, too. Why does that stand out more than a crazy Third Eye?

"Don't tell me, Sorties also worked the drive-thru window at fast food restaurants?"

"I know it's a lot to take in, Harbor."

"Look, if you are trying to make up for lost time, I'm too old for kids stories. Try Fig."

"Harbor, I've known since you were in my belly. And my prayer for you is in your name. The ancestral blood that flows in the veins of the Sortie protects us all."

After 50,000 more watts fry my spinal column, I inhale, "Okay, Aadya. What do you want me to do with this so-called history?"

"Embrace your refuge, Harbor."

CHAPTER 47

Summer arrives. Fun for everyone on the island except me. School is out, and the tourists parties are in full swing. The big hotels throw huge parties with live bands and nightly fireworks, and I get a birds eye view from my clearing. I still stop in before my shift. Tutu hired more staff for the summer rush. This will free her up to finally take a small vacation to visit family back in her homeland. She hasn't seen them in decades and mentioned that she would like me to accompany her.

Security cameras are finally installed in The Shore. I still get first dibs on working the window. Although I have to admit, it's not as fun profiling now that I have a live view into every car that comes through. I cringed earlier tonight during a few orders. Customers scratch and poke some unreachable places when they think no one is watching. A few could give lessons on how to pull a wedgie out in the blink of an eye. I am glad when my shift is over.

"Go straight home. Your mom will be waiting."

"Tutu, you know it's impossible for me to drive in a straight line. It's so hard to see with three eyes." My humor doesn't amuse her.

"It's almost dark, dear. Make your visit quick and get home."

Kissing her cheek, I run out to load the Argo and feel my phone vibrate. These days, Fig tries to map my every move.

Can we meet? Emoji wave.

With arrested sensibilities, I am transported from the parking lot of The Shore into Keyne's magnetic eyes. My heart putters uncontrollably at the text on my phone. It's him. I haven't seen him in months. Aadya and Rob warned me, but Keyne was my friend long before he was their concern.

Where?

Where else?

When?

Now?

I set the Argo on the open road, and my heart pulsates rapidly with every inch of the curve. I don't know why, but the stanza I wrote for my English assignment, the only one that the teacher chose to display on the board, replays over and over in my mind. Its distraction comforts me as I arrive in the bend. The lights of the Argo cut through the trees toward the clearing, creating shadows on the empty path ahead. There is an obscure flicker of light creeping up. Maybe the hotel fireworks started early. I cautiously roll into the clearing to park in my usual spot when an insuppressible gasp seizes me. Overlooking the ocean, the harbor, and the island inlet is a jaw-dropping display made of tiny bulbs, and my heart stops.

An intricate arrangement of soft-glow string lights has been hung along the lingering branches of the trees on either side of the clearing. They are strung in such a way that they form a huge illuminated spiral. Tranquil beams of light touch my face and lure me closer. A bit nervous, I walk into the center in awe.

Cascading string lights sway in the breeze, soothing my soul. My hand traces the teeny meteors as high as my fingers can reach, and I laugh out loud when I realize, the shape is an exceptional, majestic tidal wave! Enough light is emitted that a figure slowly stepping out from the darkness is visible, yet I'm not apprehensive. I realize more than ever that his presence could never frighten me.

"Keyne."

"I thought it was kind of late for a picnic and too dark to see carved initials."

Nearly breathless, the view fills my heart with elation, "So many lights. I thought you weren't scared of the dark."

"I'm not. I'm just adding a little more light to my life."

Keyne takes a step closer to me and the moonlight reveals a checkerboard of mending scrapes and cuts on his tough, rigid skin. A laceration runs down his left arm and even in the twilight, its subterranean imprint is exposed. Unable to restrain my alarm, I utter, "I'm sorry."

"They'll heal. I'm here to talk about you. About us."

I breath in and nod in agreement gesturing the night ambiance, "Why?"

"A token. A way to show you."

"Show me what?"

The rays in his green eyes cast a warmth over me equal to melted butter on fresh baked bread. "That we are going to make the biggest splash."

I exhale as he joins me at the core of the tidal wave. He takes both my elbows, kindling a sensation that turns mind and matter into puppets. His steady downward gaze lays on me, delivering his face closer to mine than it's ever been. His words dance on my mouth.

I've always heard there is nothing like your first love. For so long, I wondered how I'd know, curious if Keyne's hold and lips would make me like him more. As my hands slide into his, I no longer have to wonder.

Turns out, there isn't a formula. There is a seismic softness, a waning pull, an internal rapture. All transport you to a terrific plane of existence. Breathing virtually halts, yet you feel more alive than ever. The loud, crowded world blurs. The noise about fades into a moment that will crush all others. Every ounce within you is electrified and lingers in an ebb and flow between two bodies who hold on in that rare, cherished lull under the wave, together ready to conquer the wipeout.

I run my hands over the steeled contours of Keyne's back, careful with his wounds as he gently squeezes my waist. The rims of our chins delicately touch and an untamed sweetness deliquesces over our lips. Surfing, in synchrony.

I don't know how long we stood in the clearing under the twinkling lights, yet it is a summer night I will remember forever. What began as a chance journey along the bend turned into an uncharted, unforgettable wavelength, a crest of one wave that swelled into the next. A tidal wave I wanted to ride onto the next.

Hang loose for the release of Book Two:
Keyne

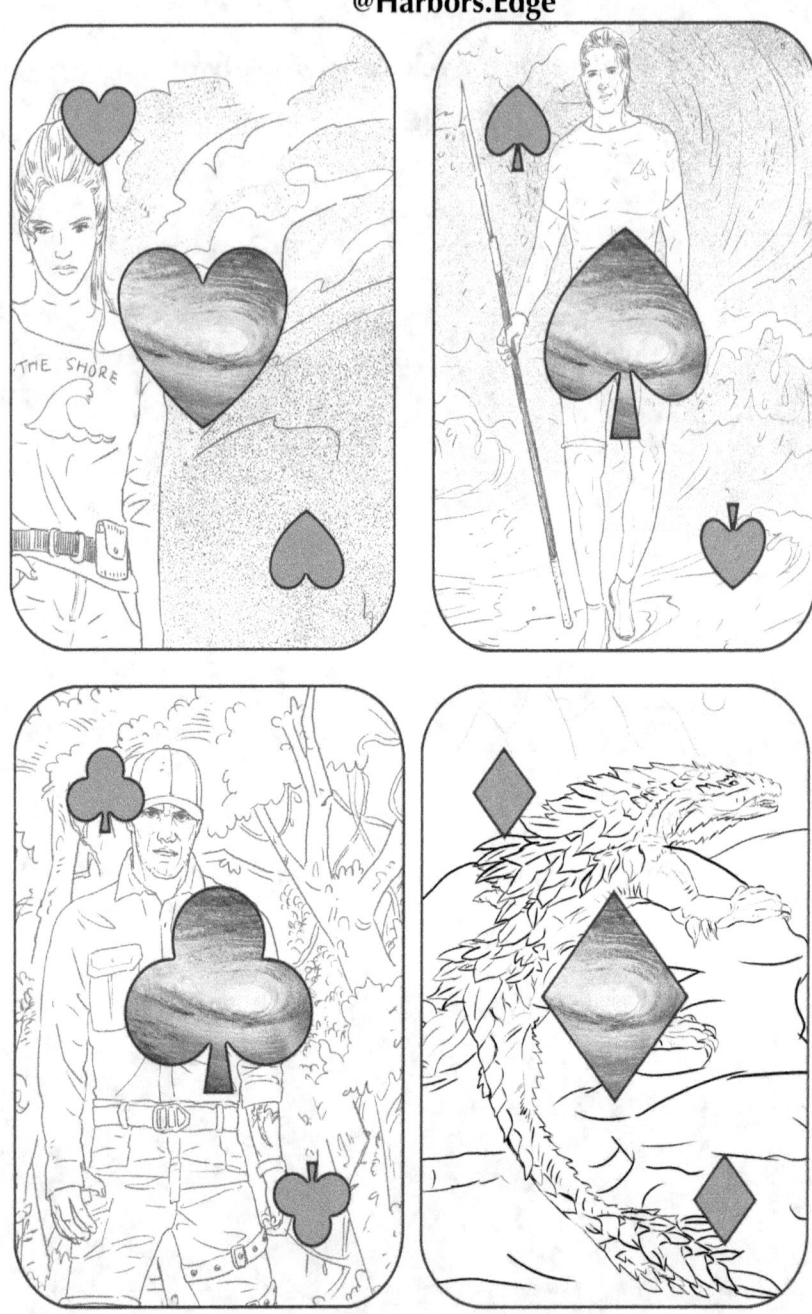

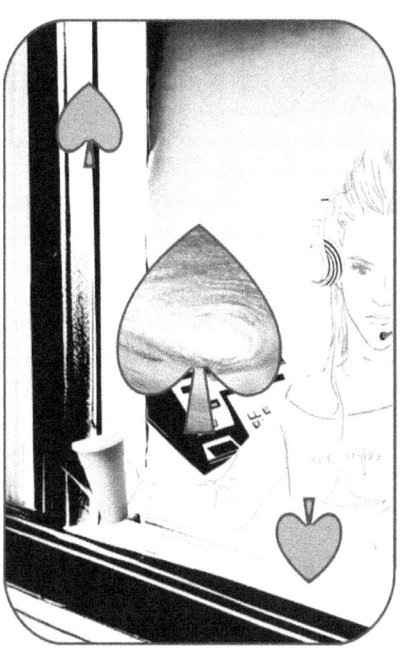

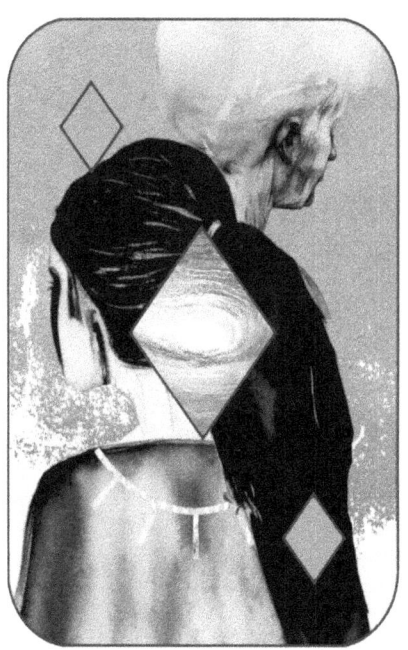

431

The Shore
Burgers & more!

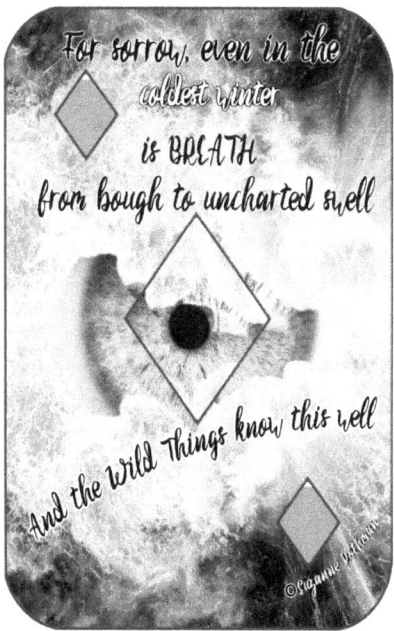

For sorrow, even in the
coldest winter
is BREATH
from bough to uncharted swell

And the wild things know this well

©suzanne victoria

433

Real monsters never hide under the bed
@Harbors.Edge